TIES THAT BIND

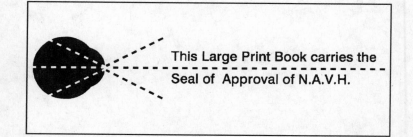

THE AMISH OF SUMMER GROVE, BOOK 1

TIES THAT BIND

CINDY WOODSMALL

THORNDIKE PRESS
A part of Gale, Cengage Learning

GALE
CENGAGE Learning·

Farmington Hills, Mich • San Francisco • New York • Waterville, Maine
Meriden, Conn • Mason, Ohio • Chicago

LIBRARY OF CONGRESS CATALOGING-IN-PUBLICATION DATA

Woodsmall, Cindy.
  Ties that bind / Cindy Woodsmall. — Large print edition.
    pages cm. — (The Amish of summer grove ; 1) (Thorndike Press large print Christian fiction)
    ISBN 978-1-4104-8233-4 (hardback) — ISBN 1-4104-8233-2 (hardcover)
    1. Large type books. I. Title.
  PS3623.O678T54 2015b
  813'.6—dc23   2015029207

Published in 2015 by arrangement with WaterBrook, an imprint of the Crown Publishing Group, a division of Penguin Random House LLC

Printed in the United States of America
1 2 3 4 5 6 7 19 18 17 16 15

To Erin and Shweta, my daughters-in-law. Despite my hopeful, expectant heart concerning your arrival in my sons' lives, I never imagined anyone as wonderful as you. Gifts beyond measure. I love and admire "my girls," and I cannot envision my life without you!

ONE

Summer Grove, Pennsylvania

Gnarled fingers of smoke seeped under the closed door of the old house. Fear threatened to steal Lovina's ability to obey her husband's departing words to stay put. She eyed a door in the bedroom that led outside. Could she get to it on her own?

Her husband and the midwife had left her about ten minutes ago. Isaac was trying to put out the kitchen fire, and Rachel was going to the phone shanty to call the fire department. Maybe Rachel never made it to the shanty. Perhaps she was down the hallway of the birthing center, delivering the other woman's baby.

Lovina's head swam from exhaustion and the muddled thoughts of a woman who'd taken something for pain — although she couldn't recall what. This was her sixth baby, and each birth had been easier than the one before . . . until this time. She didn't understand.

Another hard contraction engulfed her. She grabbed the rails of the birthing bed, panting and trembling as she squeezed the warm metal mercilessly. When the pain eased, she drew a breath. "Rachel?" Her usually strong voice came out as a mere whisper. Even the sharp ears of a midwife wouldn't have heard that, especially not over the commotion of a kitchen fire.

The last time Rachel had checked Lovina's progress, she'd barely dilated to five centimeters. But she had an overwhelming urge to start pushing. Could she walk to the hallway door in this state?

Like storm clouds gathering, dark thoughts of what might be ahead filled her mind. Were Isaac and Rachel so busy putting out the fire that she would give birth by herself? Had her husband and her friend been overcome with smoke? What had begun as a kitchen fire could easily spread throughout this old house, like setting a box of matches on fire, she imagined.

Squelching her sense of panic, she tried to scoot to the edge of the bed. Her round belly and aching body had no agility, and with the rails latched in place, she couldn't shift to get around them. Breathing hard, she lay back on her pillow, drenched in sweat.

The oppressive heat made trying to move even harder. It did little good to have the windows open when there wasn't even a slight breeze stirring the sticky air.

Smoke billowed under the door now, and a gray mass of it passed by the window like rolling fog. Her husband's horse was tethered to a hitching post not more than twenty feet away. While Lovina had been at the clinic last night, Isaac had stayed with their other children. Then he'd ridden here bareback. The horse stomped and reared, trying to break free, probably afraid of the swelling smoke.

As the seconds ticked by and the muscles throughout her torso worked together to force the child from her, nothing else seemed to exist. She pushed with all she had. "Rachel!" The groaning that often came with this phase of labor caused her voice to return, and she intended to use it. "Isaac! The baby's coming!"

She heard muffled voices as heavy footsteps grew louder. The door banged open, letting in a swirl of smoke. Rachel hurried inside, cradling in her arms a new-born swaddled in a pink blanket. Lovina's husband barreled in behind her, pushing a disheveled, sleepy woman in a wheelchair. "Lovina!" He slammed shut the door to the hallway with his foot and pointed to the door that led outside. *"Kumm! Mach's schnell!"*

Come, and make it quick? She could hardly move. *"Ich kannscht. Bobbeli iss glei do."*

He stopped short, eyes wide. "The baby's almost here?"

"Ya."

"I'll check her." Rachel rushed to the bassinet beside Lovina's bed and put the other woman's baby in it. "Take Brandi outside. Get her clear of the smoke, and carefully place her on a blanket. Be easy with her. She's lost a lot of blood. Then hurry back for her baby. A newborn doesn't need to breathe this smoke."

"Wait a minute, Rach!" He waved his arms with exasperation. These two, Lovina's husband and her closest friend, had experienced their share of disagreements over the years, but Isaac had never looked truly upset during any of their rounds. "You just saw how the fire jumped from a slow burn to engulf the front birthing rooms and half the hallway. I'm not leaving without my wife, if I have to carry her myself."

"Okay. You carry her." Rachel nodded.

10

"But Brandi is in no shape to hold her baby while I wheel her out. I'll have to take one and return for the other."

Lovina groaned, giving in to the need to push.

"For land's sake, Lovina, don't push!" Rachel said.

Lovina held her breath, trying to obey. "I . . . I can't stop!"

Rachel pulled Lovina's knees apart, and terror filled her eyes.

"What?" Lovina panted. *"Iss mei Bobbeli allrecht?"*

"Ya, I'm sure the baby's fine, but it isn't going to wait for us to get out of the house. Its head is crowning. If we move you now, we could paralyze the baby." Rachel turned to Isaac. He seemed unwilling to budge. Rachel put a hand on one hip and waved a finger in his face. "Isaac Brenneman, do as I said! Get Brandi out of here and hurry back with the wheelchair."

He nodded and sprinted toward the door. The *Englisch* woman's silky, white-blond hair dangled about, and Lovina thought it odd the little things a person noticed while in the middle of such chaos. As he opened the door, the wheelchair thudded against it.

Rachel looked up. "Be easy with the woman, Isaac. I packed her insides best I

11

could to stop the bleeding until the ambulance arrives, but she can't afford to be jostled."

Isaac nodded. "Sorry." He disappeared outside, leaving the door open.

Rachel drew a breath. "We're safe . . . for now. But let's get this child born and get out of here." Rachel put on gloves and wheeled a metal table next to the bed. The table had a sterile tray with several instruments and two folded blankets, a blue one and a pink one. During the long night of labor, Lovina had done some mending on her children's clothes. When those were done, she'd used white thread to embroider a tiny pair of baby feet on the corner of each blanket. Which color would Rachel wrap her newborn in this time?

Rachel wiped her forehead with the back of her wrist. "Could today be worse?"

"First fire and first Englisch woman to give birth here. Coincidence?" Lovina teased her weary friend.

Rachel chuckled. "Or did she bring bad luck?" she whispered, peering out the door as if the woman could hear her. "Why is she alone in an unfamiliar place?" Rachel ripped the sterile wrapping off the scissors and umbilical clamp. "I hope family arrives to support and help her once she's at the hospital." Rachel glanced into the bassinet. "She isn't doing great. She had all sorts of complications during delivery, and I doubt she'll be able to have another child, but her girl seems to be in perfect health."

Lovina's heart went out to the woman. It was telling enough that she was in a strange place by herself. It yanked at Lovina's soul to know she would likely be told she couldn't have any other children. "We need to remember to pray for . . ."

Rachel unfolded a towel, seeming lost in concentration as she studied the items on the tray. "Brandi Nash."

Lovina nodded, bracing as another wave of pain engulfed her. She knew they would talk about this night for years to come — wonder about Brandi Nash, laugh at their panic over the fire, cry with relief. But right now all Lovina could manage were moans while trying not to push until Rachel was in place to catch the baby.

Rachel moved into her spot. "Let's do this." Despite her friend's earlier efforts at idle chitchat, Lovina recognized the weariness and concern in Rachel's voice. "Kumm on little one." Rachel looked up. "Will you have an Ariana or an Abram?" She grinned. "Take a deep breath. That's right. Now push hard . . . two, three, four, five . . . push,

push, push."

Soon Lovina heard the wailing of her newborn. Relief washed over her, a joy unlike ever before. The child had arrived, and they could get out of here.

"You have a third daughter!" Rachel moved quickly, tying off and cutting the umbilical cord. "Welcome, little Ariana," Rachel cooed as she wiped off the baby. "Your two big sisters have been waiting for you." She wrapped her in a pink blanket.

"And her three older brothers will be bitterly disappointed," Lovina added.

Rachel chuckled. "Don't know why. They're bound to have a younger brother soon enough."

Isaac ran back inside, pushing the wheelchair. "Sorry, I didn't mean to take so long. I ran into numerous complications."

Rachel placed Ariana in her arms while looking at Isaac. "How's Brandi?"

"In and out of consciousness and pretty panicked when awake, but I heard sirens, so help will arrive soon."

Lovina clutched her daughter close. "Isaac, she's beautiful." She turned to her husband. "Look, isn't she a pretty little thing?"

Isaac barely glanced. "She sure is." He pushed the wheelchair to the bed. "Kumm."

He shook the railing, trying to lower it.

"She has all ten fingers and toes." Rachel pulled off her gloves. "Now let's get you and these babies out of here." She pushed a button and lowered the rail before taking the baby from Lovina. "I'll hold Ariana while Isaac helps you get in the wheelchair. It's best not to chance a very shaky *Mamm* dropping her newborn."

Isaac held out his hand to Lovina. "Kumm."

When Lovina put her legs over the side of the bed, a gush of fluid left her body. "Rachel, what just happened?"

Rachel glanced at the wet sheets, and she seemed to understand. She passed Ariana to Isaac and then pressed on Lovina's stomach from several angles. "There's another one."

"Twins?" Lovina hadn't been that large, had she?

Rachel pushed the bassinet toward Isaac. "Get the babies out of here."

"*Nee!* Rachel, look!" He pointed to the door that led to the hallway. "The shellac is bubbling and peeling from the heat on the opposite side. The fire could explode into this room." He put Ariana in the bassinet.

Rachel hesitated as she stared at the melted shellac running down the door. Was she frozen in place?

Isaac put one arm under Lovina's knees and one around her back, lifting her into the wheelchair. "Rachel! Get the bassinet and let's get out. Now!"

TWO

Twenty years later . . .

The mid-August air trilled with the sound of insects, and the clammy breeze played with the tattered beige sheers hanging from the lone window. Ariana glanced at the faded numbers on the clock that had hung on the bedroom wall as far back as she could remember. The clock and sheers matched most of what was inside her home — useful but having seen better days. Singing softly, she ran a comb through her hair and pinned it up anew.

Date night. For almost three years she'd been going out with various young men. It used to be little more than a pleasant distraction from thoughts of Quill, but lately dating held new feelings and hopes. The cause for that was Rudy Herschberger, a kind and handsome twenty-one-year-old who had moved to this area a year ago.

Maybe he could make her forget the

heartache . . . the confusion . . .

"Ariana?" Mamm tapped on the bedroom door.

"Kumm." Ariana put on her prayer *Kapp* and secured it with two white bobby pins.

"So" — Mamm closed the gap between them — "let me check on my handiwork." She ran her fingers across the shoulders of Ariana's pale-green dress. "I managed to hide the worst of the threadbare seams, but it gives you less room to move your shoulders."

"It's fine, Mamm." Ariana turned to face the dresser mirror. Streaks and spots of discoloration on the old glass made her face look as tattered and worn as her dress. "If Rudy's head is turned by a girl wearing better clothes, I need to know that now rather than later."

What money she earned was earmarked. All of it, because from her earliest memories, she'd had a strange, determined hope to get her and her family free from poverty. When she was sixteen, God had changed her dreams to a set plan to purchase a café. The place was as old as historic Summer Grove, and it sat on Main Street, sharing walls with the buildings on each side of it. She loved the two-hundred-year-old interior brick walls, maple hardwood floors, and huge staircase that led to an upstairs storage room with endearing character in every nook and cranny.

But she had only forty-seven more days to finish earning the needed money. With a lot of help from Abram, she had managed to save $16,257. All of that would go toward the mandatory down payment at closing. She needed $6,843 more.

To reach that goal, she and Abram would have to save nearly $1,000 a week between now and then. She barely made $200 a week. After Abram met his financial obligations, he had between $150 and $250 a week, depending on whether he could get any overtime. Their combined money was a far cry from the needed $1,000 per week. How were they going to make up the difference? There had to be a way. God simply hadn't revealed it yet.

Right, God?

Mamm adjusted the back of Ariana's black apron, redoing two of the straight pins. "After what the last ten days have been like for you with the responsibility of Berta and helping even more than usual with Salome's children, I hate to ask, but I need you to be home by ten tonight."

Disappointment pricked her heart. "Why?"

She'd worked really hard this week, doing extra cooking and laundry preparation so she could have a free evening, one that lasted until midnight or after.

Mamm peered around Ariana, looking at her in the mirror. "Salome is showing signs of early labor."

Ariana loved her siblings dearly, and her four sisters were her best friends. She couldn't imagine a day without any of them. Sometimes their lives were as interwoven as threads on a loom, and sometimes they competed with each other. But for the last year, Salome had consistently needed more than her sisters or Mamm were able to give. Because Berta was now in the hospital and Ariana had promised to be the one to tend to her horse twice each day until she returned home, it would give Ariana and Rudy even less time to while away their evening. Still . . . "I'll be home by ten."

Mamm repositioned herself and cupped Ariana's face. "You're a keeper."

Ariana lifted her chin, giving her best regal look as she smoothed her well-worn apron. "I know."

"And you're humble too." Mamm grinned, and they both chuckled.

A burst of humid wind zipped through the room, making the sheers dance wildly.

Was that the faint rumble of thunder?

"Hallo." Her *Daed*'s louder-than-usual greeting caught her attention. She went to the window and pulled back the beige sheer to see if Rudy had arrived.

Instead, Daed had two of his grandchildren in his arms, responding to their arrival as if he hadn't seen them just last night. It made her smile. The crowded yard echoed with the dull roar of her large family talking to one another. The Brenneman summer tradition continued in full swing even as August was halfway over. More than two dozen family members were busy talking and playing — her Daed, eight of her nine siblings, the married ones' spouses, and all her nieces and nephews.

Her family spent their summer evenings here. The Brenneman homestead wasn't much, but a nice breeze flowed almost constantly across the yard, and there was a large flat area where little ones could play. Long picnic tables and lawn chairs sat under the huge oaks, and that's where they ate dinner most summer evenings. Being indoors was way too hot this time of year, especially when the women canned during the day.

Watching the commotion, she was reminded of the family tradition that had

21

taken place each summer of her life. The adults talked and took turns looking after the little ones. Children played until bath time — tag, hide-and-seek, badminton, horseshoes, and various games with a beach-ball.

Rudy's carriage entered the driveway, and Ariana's heart jumped. "He's here." Ariana released the beige sheer. "I have to go."

Mamm gave that motherly I-love-you smile. "You really like this one, don't you?"

Ariana had been months past her seventeenth birthday when she went on her first date, but since then she'd dated a lot. Few young men had lasted more than two or three weeks before she simply didn't wish to go out with them again. Rudy was the exception.

Ariana wiggled her eyebrows. "Seems so, doesn't it?" Without pausing another second she bounded down the stairs and out the side door. Rudy stood near the carriage, talking with Salome's husband. After seven months of dating, Rudy knew the routine. He had to stay close to the carriage or they would never get away, which was fine sometimes, but they were both itching to talk uninterrupted.

Her Daed strode to her. "What's on the agenda for tonight?"

He was doing what he did best, using small talk to gauge how she was. He did that with all his children. "We'll ride to Summer Grove and waste a few hours, probably get some ice cream and browse the stores that stay open on Friday nights."

"You could stay here tonight." He shrugged. "Just to visit with your old Daed." His familiar, lazy smile indicated he already knew her answer, but he had to ask. The man loved having all his family around.

A beachball that was hurled from the pack of nieces and nephews bounced its way toward the road. Mark, Ariana's third oldest brother, chased it. Ariana put out her foot, stopping the ball. Then she grabbed it and tossed it back.

Mark waved. *"Denki."*

"I need to go, Daed. You and I will get some time later this weekend." She glanced at Salome, who was in a lawn chair, rubbing her protruding belly. "Maybe."

He chuckled. "Ya, maybe."

She hurried to the rig. "Rudy, you ready?"

He turned, his eyes reflecting the liveliness that drew her. "Absolutely." He excused himself from his conversation with Emanuel and opened her door to the carriage.

She climbed in and yelled a farewell to

anyone who was listening and received a chorus of good-byes.

Rudy took the reins in hand. "You look great, even on a sultry summer night. How do you manage that?"

"Maids, swimming pools, and a date with you."

His soft laughter filled the carriage. "Which means today you cleaned houses and swimming pools for the Englisch, and now we're going out."

"Apparently it makes me look great."

"Evidence does point in that direction." He clicked his tongue, tapping the reins against the horse as they began going up a hill. "All week I've been looking forward to tonight. Care for some ice cream?"

"Most definitely. So, tell me the weirdest thing that happened this week."

Rudy helped his uncle build backyard sheds, and they ran into some interesting people along the way.

"Hmm. The weirdest. . . ." His brows furrowed. "Wait. I got it . . ."

They started talking and barely paused, even while getting out of the rig or ordering ice cream. Thunder rumbled in the distance as they walked through town eating their ice cream and laughing at the smallest of things. They peered into the filthy window

of the abandoned café before finally returning to the carriage. Rudy let the horse amble
along the many roads around old town
Summer Grove. Before she knew it, the sun
had slipped into hiding, leaving a trail of
darkness.

"Hey." Rudy gripped the reins. "Let's go
to Little Falls."

"What?" She laughed. "That would take
at least an hour one direction."

Even through the darkness of a cloudy
summer night, his grin and wildly curly hair
were apparent. "The last time we made that
trip was with a group after a Sunday night
singing."

The word *singing* was Amish code for "ap-
proved method for spouse hunting." Like a
lot of Amish traditions, singings were fun.
She loved the Old Ways and found them
very fulfilling. She wished she didn't need
to go home early tonight.

"An answer . . ." — Rudy leaned in, his
adorable smile in place — "pretty please."
His whisper caused a tingle to run down
her spine. Was she more attracted to him
than she knew?

"I would love that . . ."

"Yes!" His raised voice caused the horse
to snort and wag his head in protest. Rudy
slowed the rig and turned on his left blinker.

"If we'd thought of it earlier, maybe we could have gone, but I've got to be home by ten, and we need to stop by Berta's place first." She held out her hands for the reins. "Give them up."

Disappointment showed on his face, but he gave them to her. "Are you in trouble or something? You've never had to be home this early."

She grasped the leather straps as her Daed had taught her. "Salome will go to the birthing clinic tonight, if she hasn't gone already. And two of her four little ones tend to get up during the night, so I need to be there to help."

"Okay. Sure. I didn't realize that."

She should've mentioned it earlier. Since Rudy was such an agreeable guy, it didn't dawn on her to forewarn him. His good nature about having a short date and his willingness to help tend to Berta's place made her want a kiss from him. What would it be like to kiss Rudy? She'd wondered about it before, and it seemed time to find out. The side road up ahead was the perfect place.

Rudy stretched his legs. "Have Salome and Emanuel always lived under the same roof as your parents?"

"No. She and Emanuel had their own

place from the time they married, about eleven years ago, until they sold it because of some sort of financial issues last year." She pulled off the main road and onto a homeless, dead-end street.

"Oh. I like Emanuel." He leaned back, looking totally relaxed. "Where are we going?"

She shrugged and guided the carriage to make the circular turn in the cul-de-sac. Before the economy tanked a few years back, a developer was going to build houses down this short block.

"I thought . . ." She brought the rig to a halt.

Rudy's brows knit. "Did you expect this road to go all the way through?"

"Nee. I know all the roads in Summer Grove." She looped the reins around the stob on the dashboard of the carriage and turned to face him. Rudy waited, studying her. She touched his face, and his eyes indicated he understood. He leaned in until his mouth met hers. The warmth of his lips on hers was more welcome than she'd expected. That was good. Moreover, his respectful, gentle moves made her feel beautiful and protected. She hadn't anticipated either of those.

"Wow." He backed away, staring into her

eyes. "That was worth waiting for."

With her face close to his, she gazed into his eyes. "For sure and certain."

He traced a finger down her cheek and kissed her again. "So . . . ," he whispered, "does this mean I can tell my parents I'm seeing someone?"

This was Rudy, no pretense that she could see. He wanted to mean more to her than any other guy she'd dated, and at times, like now, he didn't mind looking for signs of it. What was the saying — what you see is what you get? That's who Rudy was, and after the deception that turned her life upside down five years ago, she desperately needed that in anyone who wanted to get close.

"Absolutely."

He brushed his thumb over her lips. "Denki."

Knowing Rudy, she was confident he intended his thank-you to be all-inclusive — for the kiss and for saying she was committed to him. Her Mamm used to tell her she would never regret going slowly with a guy — not sharing too much or letting him kiss her or even hold her hand too soon. Based on the moment they'd just shared and the earnestness in Rudy's voice, Ariana knew that her Mamm had been right.

He leaned in, kissing her again. A gust of

wind shoved against the rig as lightning shot across the sky. It startled her, and she pulled away from him, leaned toward the windshield, and gazed up at the sky.

Rudy placed his hand on the middle of her back. "It's a good sign."

She glanced at him.

He chuckled. "We made the heavens rumble and the winds howl."

Was Rudy's heart pounding like hers from the kiss? Now they had to return to behaving like normal? Was that even possible? She removed the reins from the stob and clicked her tongue for the horse to start walking.

Rudy stretched his arm across the back of the seat behind her. Until now they had each stayed on their side of the carriage. It was silly not to. What kind of needy girl couldn't sit in her own space while going down the road?

He ran his thumb up and down her shoulder. "If my parents visit, would you come to my uncle's home and meet them?"

She nibbled on the inside of her lip, thinking. Was she *that* committed to this relationship? "Ya."

"Very cool." His deep, soft voice indicated pleasure.

A light rain began to patter against the windshield, and she turned on the battery-powered wiper blade. Rudy seemed different than anyone else, as if he understood her true value and respected it. It'd been a long, slow journey to get beyond the betrayal by her two closest friends, but Rudy had a real shot at stealing her heart.

Most of it anyway. Or at least enough of it.

"Who's Berta again?" Rudy asked. "I mean, you're in and out of her place, helping her regularly. And you said she's in the hospital for a few days because of dehydration from a bug of some sort. But doesn't she have children who can look after her horse?"

His question caused an unwelcome ache to pierce her heart. "None that remained Amish. Or live close."

Rain fell harder as she pulled onto Berta's driveway.

"None?"

She stared in the distance, wishing for the zillionth time she had a different answer. "None," she whispered.

"That's sad, but at least she has you."

The word *sad* didn't begin to explain it. Neither Berta nor Eli, her deceased husband, had family in the area. Ariana's Mamm said the couple moved here almost forty years ago, not long after they were married. They came here for an apprentice-ship, which turned into a secure position for Berta's husband, but Ariana had no idea why Berta hadn't returned to her childhood home rather than living here without any relatives.

"I'll grab the mail before we pull up to the barn." Rudy jumped out of the rig and hurried toward the mailbox.

Lightning flashed, and the perfect silhouette of a man appeared between the old homestead and the dilapidated barn. Her heart pounded. Were her eyes playing tricks?

Squinting, she stared out the window. Lightning streaked across the sky again, and the ghostlike figure now stood ten or so feet closer, staring right at her.

Rudy climbed back into the carriage, rain dripping off his straw hat. "I think it's only junk mail."

She couldn't take a breath for staring at the hatless man in what appeared to be jeans and a white T-shirt that was plastered to him. The strobe illuminations from the lightning ceased, and the man once again became a shadowy figure before he seem-ingly disappeared behind the house.

After all these years had Quill Schlabach returned to check on his Mamm? The idea made the hairs on the back of her neck rise, and the sensation slowly eased down her torso and arms until she was covered in goose bumps.

/ She hated feeling any kind of hope when it came to him and Frieda. Well . . . she hoped they were happy and safe, but she wanted her emotions rooted firmly in reality where Berta was concerned.

If Quill was here, Ariana couldn't imagine how to make herself speak to him. He put his Mamm and her in such an awful position. Was he worthy of tossing even a crumb of bread to? But she knew that was sheer anger, and God asked people to treat others as He would treat them. So how would He treat Quill in this situation? Seemed to her that God had the perfect chance to strike the man with lightning, but He hadn't.

"Rudy, would you tend to the horses? I . . . I need to check on the cat."

Rudy touched her shoulder. "You okay?"

She could hardly breathe for the anger stirring to life again. Rudy put his hand on her back, and the gentle query relaxed her. "Ya." She wiped the foggy windshield with her hand, trying to catch another glimpse of the figure. "Would you mind climbing into the haymow and tossing down enough hay to last a few days?" That should keep Rudy

32

busy for a few extra minutes.

If Quill was here, he wasn't likely to risk Rudy seeing him on his mother's property. It could cause more trouble for Berta, and regardless of Quill's lack of character, Ariana was positive he wouldn't do anything that might hurt his Mamm worse than he already had.

He was a dishonest, shady person who seemed to have limits on how low he would go.

"I don't mind a bit." Rudy pulled the rig up to the sidewalk that led to the side entry of the porch. "I didn't bring an umbrella."

"I won't melt."

"Once you hop out, I'll drive the rig into the barn to get the horse out of the rain for a bit."

"Okay." Did he notice that her voice sounded hollow and distant? Her mouth was dry as she forced herself to get a key out of her purse before leaving the carriage. Cold, prickly rain doused her. By the time she ran up the sidewalk and climbed the porch stairs, she was drenched.

She walked to the back of the wraparound porch. Wet footprints led to an open window in Quill's former bedroom. It wasn't a burglar. There hadn't been a break-in around these parts for as far back as she could remember. The so-called Amish Nightcrawler did the only thievery around here, and he took willing Amish folk like Quill and Frieda, not items found in a widow-woman's home.

Shaking all over, she returned to the side door and let herself in. After locating the matches on the old laminate countertop, she struck one, illuminating the kitchen as she held the flame to the wick of a candle. Goose bumps covered her again as she carried the old metal candlestick holder down the hallway toward the bedroom at the end, the one with the open window. "Quill?"

Eerie silence followed. She supposed it could be one of his four older brothers, but she was certain it wasn't.

"I know you're here." She could feel it. Hadn't she felt this same weird, pinprickly, hair-raising thing several times over the last five years?

If he'd come to check on his Mamm and she hadn't been here for a few days, he would be confused. "Your Mamm is fine." Would a man who'd broken his mother's heart and embarrassed her in front of everyone care enough to keep checking on her?

The cat meowed from inside Quill's room, but it didn't run to her as usual. She'd forgotten that it had been Quill's cat at one time.

Still seeing no one, she chose to press on — out of respect for the love Berta had for Quill more than anything else. Of Berta's five children, who had left the Amish at different times, Quill, her youngest, had given no forewarning. He hadn't argued with his Mamm about it or whispered to Ariana about it. When he'd taken off at twenty years old, he'd taken more than Ariana's heart. He'd taken with him a teen girl, the daughter of Berta's closest friend. The betrayal seemed unforgiveable to Ariana, but Berta still spoke of Quill as if he'd done nothing wrong.

Ariana stopped a few feet from his room. "Your Mamm was really sick with a virus of some sort, and she needed to spend a few days in the hospital." She spoke into the dark as if she could see him "That's all. She's expected to come home in a day or two." She felt silly talking like this, and with every second that passed, anger grew — anger at Quill, at herself, and at the fact that the grass outside the Amish community looked greener for far too many.

She'd told him plenty, perhaps more than he deserved, so she headed for the kitchen. When she reached the end of the hallway and had the front door in sight, she heard the floor creak behind her. After stopping short, she waited.

The home seemed to fill with their voices and laughter from years ago. She and Quill had been buds of sorts — she the tomboy little sister of Quill's friend, and Quill the daredevil who schemed to find new ways to endanger his life.

But the laughter had stopped when his Daed died unexpectedly. She'd been almost fourteen, and their games and hilarity ended like a match thrown into a sink of water. After that, she would sit with him in an empty hay wagon or on the porch steps or in the tree house or on a rock by the creek and listen as he shared memory after memory of his Daed and him — the good and the difficult. She'd thought she knew Quill.

Later she realized that because he was nearly five years older than she was, he'd had the upper hand. He knew her well, but she'd known only whatever he let her know. Then he'd used her feelings for him to get what he wanted — a way to hide that he and Frieda were planning to leave the Amish.

"You're good to her." His voice was deeper than it'd been when he'd left here at barely twenty, and his accent was closer to the Englisch. "Even better than I'd hoped."

Fresh chills ran over her skin, and her eyes pricked with tears. The memory of their last hour together flashed in her mind. She and Frieda had been camping out near the creek. Ariana used to love camping out, but she'd not been since that night. When she'd awakened the next morning, Frieda was gone. A note addressed to Ariana lay on Frieda's sleeping bag, saying she and Quill had left the Amish and she was sorry to hurt Ariana like this.

After reading it Ariana had barreled out of the tent in a panic. Quill was sitting on a nearby rock, waiting for her. His deep-blue eyes, the color of a cloudless summer sky, were filled with understanding and maybe remorse for what he was about to put her through.

He'd known she would panic, so he'd taken Frieda somewhere safe, a place where the Amish couldn't find her. Then he'd returned to calm and reassure Ariana that Frieda was indeed safe and that even though it was upsetting that he and Frieda were leaving, it was for the best. He'd handed her an envelope, saying it contained a letter from him, and that when she was calmer, it would help her understand a little better.

He'd been so gentle and kind during that time it'd taken Ariana weeks to realize he'd used her. They both had. The camping trip was nothing more than a deceitful ploy so Quill could take Frieda far away while all the adults thought the two girls were sleeping in a tent at their favorite spot by the creek.

Until that day she hadn't had a clue that he and seventeen-year-old Frieda were in love. Or that either wanted to leave the Amish. Ariana had thought Quill cared for *her* and that one day the wild, adventurous Quill would want to marry her.

He cleared his throat, dispersing her memories. "Ari, I . . . I appreciate what you do for my mother far more than you can imagine."

She turned. Quill was still hardly visible inside his room at the end of the hallway, but she could imagine his blue eyes staring into her soul. The thought angered her. "I don't do it for you." That was completely true, but should she feel bad about how mean it sounded? She didn't. What she wanted to do was tell him what she really thought.

"Still . . ." He moved out of the shadows. She couldn't see his face well, but his frame was apparent, and she realized he'd hardly been a man at all when he'd left here. Now he had broad, thick shoulders and stood a few inches taller. "I am indebted to you."

"That and several dollars would get me a cup of coffee, wouldn't it?"

He gave a solemn nod. "Anyway, I'm glad you saw me and came inside. I needed to tell you —"

The side door opened, and Rudy stepped inside. "Your chariot awaits, my lady."

The kitchen and walled hallway ran parallel to each other, so she was thankful he couldn't see down the hall. But what did Quill need to tell her? Was Frieda okay? Ariana clutched the candleholder with both hands, trying to stop it from shaking. "I'll be there in a minute."

"You need help with something?" Rudy started toward her.

"Nee!" She thrust her hand up. "Please."

He froze in place.

This secret wasn't like when she'd told him of her dream to buy the café. Quill was a bad secret. She needed to tell Rudy about him but not like this. "Rudy, would you wait for me in the carriage?"

He angled his head. "What's going on?"

"Trust me?"

He studied her, the seriousness in his eyes melting into tenderness. "Ya, with no reservations."

The warmth of his respect enveloped her. "Denki." She was able to take a full breath again. "I'm fine, and I'll be out shortly. Okay?"

He nodded, but it was apparent he didn't want to leave her there. When he walked out, he left the door open a few inches. He could hear her if she yelled for him, but the rain would drown out a normal tone. She turned to face Quill. There was only one question she wanted him to answer, one she'd ached to have answered every day for five years. "How's Frieda?"

"Good . . . better."

"Better?" What did that mean? Had she been sick?

He stood his ground, his broad shoulders straight, his feet planted firmly in place, and he didn't give so much as a shrug in response to her question. That was so typical of Quill. When he was in silent mode, a concrete wall had more give to it. She'd seen it a hundred times, maybe a thousand, but she'd never been on the receiving end of it, at least not in a way she'd recognized. Giving up on getting a satisfactory answer about Frieda, she asked, "What do you need to tell me?"

"That I'm truly sorry."

40

The day he'd left they'd talked. Actually she'd railed at him, pacing beside the creek and flailing her arms, and he'd talked softly for almost an hour before she broke into defeated sobs. He had held her, his first time to actually touch her other than poking her a few times on the shoulder or pulling the strings to her prayer Kapp. He'd apologized then, saying he was sorry she was caught in the mess and if there was any other way to get out with Frieda, he would.

She shooed away the embarrassing memory. Whenever she looked back, disgust at how vulnerable she'd been with him ate at her. She wasn't that wide-eyed, trusting young teen anymore. "You apologized clearly five years ago before you disappeared."

"Ari . . ." He took a step toward her and then came to a halt a few feet outside the doorway of his bedroom. "Remember when I said that we have to allow people to make their own decisions about what's right or wrong for them?"

She remembered. He'd whispered it to her as he held her while she cried. At the time, his words brought a warm, hopeful sensation, causing her to believe she might survive what he and Frieda were doing.

"When I left here, I promised myself I

wouldn't ever do anything that would hurt you again." His voice carried grief, as it had for more than a year after his Daed died. "But like you used to say, the threads of your life are woven into the fabric of mine, and I . . . I'm truly sorry."

She didn't understand. If she asked, would he answer? She doubted it. He seemed to enjoy tormenting her. As his words registered, they began to form into clues. For years there'd been rumors that a man returned at night to help Amish leave so that no one could hinder their exit. People called him the Amish Nightcrawler. Was that who'd helped Quill and Frieda leave? If so, then Quill knew the man — the traitor.

Wait!

Realization of what he was saying dawned, and her knees threatened to give way. Quill had apologized because he knew the Nightcrawler was going to take someone else she loved! Maybe Quill was in the area to help the Nightcrawler.

Thief! Liar! Names for him pummeled her, and tears welled. She choked them back. She'd fallen apart five years ago, begging Quill to change his mind . . . for all the good it did her. She would maintain control this time.

Wanting to hide from his prying eyes, she

blew out the candle. Faint coils of smoke floated upward and disappeared. Quill volunteered nothing else, and she couldn't speak for fighting with tears. They just stood there.

How appropriate — she and Quill at opposite ends of a passageway with nothing between them except darkness and unspoken words.

THREE

Abram stared out the window as the work van headed for his home. Roofing houses in August was difficult enough without doing it twelve hours a day, six days a week. But pounding nails on a Saturday had earned him extra money. It was cash he would use to pay bills, go on his first date tomorrow night, and give to Ariana for purchasing the café.

Not only did Ariana need help getting cash, but she needed extra encouragement right now. The moment his twin had walked into their home, drenched, at three minutes past ten last night, Abram knew something was troubling her. But she acted normally, keeping her tone even and her smile pleasant. After Salome and Emanuel went to the birthing center and everyone else had gone to bed, Abram set his hunting magazine aside, ready for her to tell him what was going on.

He listened, but he didn't possess the words to express to his sister what this news did to him. No one had the power to mess with Ariana's sense of peace the way Quill did. As hard as it was to believe that another Amish person or family wished to steal away like a thief in the night, it was even harder to believe that Quill had stepped out of the shadows to speak with Ariana. Hadn't he done enough damage already? And what did his cryptic message really mean?

"This is your stop." The driver's announcement startled Abram from his thoughts.

He grabbed his tool belt from the floor, realizing items from it were strewn. His back was stiff as he bent to gather the stuff.

The driver pulled onto the shoulder of the road beside Abram's house. "Well?"

Apparently Abram was moving too slowly. He figured Mr. Carver was worn-out and grumpy from a week of working in ninety-something-degree weather. Abram had plenty of aches and irritability himself, and he wasn't pushing sixty years old. The hammer and the handful of nails he'd collected slipped from his hand and scattered across the floorboard again.

Mr. Carver looked over his shoulder. "Sometime today would be nice."

Abram said nothing, and the other men chuckled. The words that fit Abram best were *quiet* and *socially awkward.* Ariana assured him he could will himself out of being so reclusive. Since he wanted to start dating, Ariana had spent a lot of time over the last few months trying to help him become more outspoken, but progress was slow — like trying to make an old, aloof cat behave like a friendly pup.

As he plucked the last few nails from the crevices of the rubber floor mats, thoughts of Barbie came to him again. He hoped his efforts with Ariana over the last few months would pay off while he was out with Barbie. He was making progress; otherwise, he wouldn't have managed to ask her out. She'd hardly left his mind for the past three months.

With everything back in his tool belt, he grabbed his lunchbox and got out of the vehicle. Heat bore down on him as he left the air-conditioned van. He meandered toward the house, hearing the many voices of his family floating on the air.

As he rounded the side of the house, he spotted Ariana. Despite her congenial demeanor as she served lemonade to their loved ones, he saw heaviness in her. The clear mark left by Quill. But she would

46

bounce back. She had before.

She spotted him and waved. "You're home."

A humorous retort came to mind, one that should make her smile, but he wouldn't broadcast it for all to hear. He kept most of his thoughts for Ariana. Talking to her was comfortable, like talking to himself, only with more thoughtful replies. But they'd had their share of arguments over the years. They were opposites, and at times they grated on each other's nerves. Still, they had that famed twin thing between them — an invisible bond that somehow strengthened both of them.

She passed a glass of lemonade to Salome, who'd given birth at 4:06 that morning. Then Ariana knelt in front of their niece Esther and tied her shoe. The scars on four-year-old Esther didn't seem to bother her, but Salome hadn't fared as well. Two and a half years ago Esther had fallen while playing near the firepit and had seriously burned her face. Salome continued to live in the nightmare that followed, and it pulled her into depression time and again.

Ariana had Esther in fits of laughter before she kissed her cheek and headed for Abram, but her usual smile was subdued.

Her white-blond hair reflected sunlight, as

if she had shards of crystal in it. She stopped directly in front of him. "You're late."

"So far you've stated that I'm here and I'm late. Should we change your name to Captain Obvious?" Abram fidgeted with the leather tool belt. "How you holding up?"

"We're not talking about it." She placed her index finger to her lips. "Today I'm enjoying that everyone is here and safe." She took his lunch pail. "Everyone else has eaten. I saved you plenty of grilled chicken legs, a large bowl of orange Jell-O, and five buttermilk biscuits."

When his sister set her will, it was best to abide by that without challenging her. He was sure she needed a day or so simply to think before she sprang into action. "If you left the food unmanned, it's gone by now."

"I hid it in the back of the fridge, and I put a threatening note on the plate, so if someone does find it, they've been warned what will happen if they eat it."

"What was the threat?"

"If the food came up missing, I would go on strike for two days."

"That would do it." He glanced into her eyes, challenging her. "But could you make yourself follow through?"

His sister was better at talking a mean game than playing one.

She shrugged. "Don't know, but if someone challenges me on it, I'll pass out from the shock of it." She motioned toward the picnic tables. "I'll get your plate from the fridge. Go, find a seat."

He glanced at the beehive of family members. His exhaustion made his reclusive side tug on him more than usual. He just wanted peace and quiet.

A knowing look flickered in Ariana's eyes. "You're fine. Eat with the family, survive their intrusiveness, and then you can disappear to your room."

She was right, and he sighed. "Fine, but I need a few minutes first." He reached into his pocket and felt the folded money. "I hate to reward bossiness, but . . ." He took the cash from his pocket, kept enough money to pay his bills and a twenty for his date tomorrow night — because hamburgers and fries would do just fine — and held out the rest to her. "For you."

Ariana's brow creased, a mixture of doubt and hope on her face. "The whole wad?"

"Ya."

"Denki." As she leafed through it, her eyes lit up. "Five hundred dollars. No way!" She tucked it into her apron pocket. "Overtime pay is quite profitable." She punched his arm. "Look at you!"

"Ouch! No beating me up over it." He laughed. "You'll get that café yet, Ari."

She nodded, but he saw uncertainty in her eyes. The window of time for her option to buy was closing. Even if they could get enough money to go to closing, she would need at least $4,000 to $5,000 more to get the café operational.

He decided to change the subject. "So what are you doing home on a Saturday night?"

"Seriously? Did you miss the announcement that we have a new niece?"

"Oh, I heard it loud and clear. Daed bellowed it to the household around four forty-five this morning — Katie Ann Glick. My response was to cover my head with a pillow while mumbling that babies should arrive only during the day."

"You're about as much fun to talk to about the new baby as Susie is."

"I'm not that bad." No one had mastered the art of being smart mouthed and difficult quite as well as their eighteen-year-old sister.

Ariana smacked him while laughing. "Abram, be nice."

He rubbed his arm, laughing. "You're the one who's hitting, and I'm not being nice?"

A rig pulled onto the semicircle driveway. He narrowed his eyes, trying to see who it was, and when he did, his thoughts scattered.

Barbie.

His heart raced at the sight of her. Unfortunately, he looked like a man who'd spent twelve hours doing manual labor. He and his clothes were filthy and disheveled, but it was really cool that she'd stopped by. Since his home had a fairly long driveway, he had a minute to gather himself before she would reach him and Ariana.

"Ah. A visitor." Ariana smiled as Barbie drove the rig toward them. "I'll let you two be alone, but don't hesitate to invite her in."

"What?" he whispered. "You're going to leave me here?"

"I don't have to, but . . ."

"Good. Stay."

"Why do I feel as if you should pat me on the head now?"

"Because you know that good sisters and dogs both deserve a pat every now and then?" he mumbled and nodded a hello at Barbie.

Barbie pulled on the reins and set the brake.

Ariana nudged Abram with her elbow, but he couldn't make himself speak. At least he'd smiled and nodded a hello.

"Hi, Barbie. This is a pleasant surprise." Ariana motioned for her to get down. "Would you like to sit under a shade tree for a spell?"

Barbie's face seemed taut and stressed. "Denki, Ariana. Maybe another time."

A wave of nervousness ran through Abram as he sensed this wasn't a friendly visit. For months he'd gone against his reclusive nature and attended every youth event — volleyball, softball, hayrides, potlucks, and singings — in order to get time around Barbie. Had all that effort been for nothing? "Ari . . ." He nodded toward the house, and his sister waved and hurried away. He turned to Barbie. "What's up?" He saw no reason to beat around the bush.

She clenched her lips, shaking her head. "I'm sorry, but I . . . I've changed my mind about Sunday night."

Disappointment seemed to flood him, quickly carrying him downstream, moving him rapidly from the shores of hope to the unknown. "Just Sunday night?"

She shook her head. "I shouldn't have agreed to go out, but I . . . I . . ."

The rest of that sentence was *felt sorry for you.* He wouldn't make her spell it out. "Okay, I get it." One thing about living in a small, rural community is that everyone knew he'd never gone out before . . . just as everyone would know Barbie broke off the date the day before he was to take her home from the singing.

He looked to the ground before shifting and taking in the house. He stifled a sigh while studying a scratch on her rig. He kept his eyes anywhere but directly focused on her. Maybe the saddest part was that he'd liked her for years. He'd made himself learn how to speak up so he could ask her out.

While standing there, he wasn't sure what he had feared so badly about asking her out, because this current situation was much worse. And since she'd said what she came to say, why was she studying him? His face had to have humiliation written all over it.

He looked at her, feeling the rush of hurt pulling him under. Just how old would he be before he went on a first date? Thirty? "It was good of you to come by, Barbie."

She nodded, released the brake, and slowly maneuvered the rig to complete the semicircle and then pulled onto the paved road.

FOUR

The mattress beneath Lovina felt wonderful as she snuggled against it. She'd longed all week for this between Sunday to arrive. No church and only necessary chores. As she drew a deep breath, she smelled bacon and coffee.

Really?

She opened one eye. It was daylight. Barely.

Did someone have to be somewhere, maybe visiting an Amish district that did have church today, and she'd forgotten? She eased out of bed, leaving her husband sound asleep. After grabbing her housecoat, she slipped out of the room and tiptoed down the wooden steps, hoping not to wake her grandchildren. Her own children slept until seven or eight on between Sundays, but when it was daylight, Salome's young brood woke easily.

Once on the last few steps, Lovina could

54

peer into the kitchen.

Ariana.

Ah, the joys of having a daughter who loved to bake. Sunday wasn't meant for earning money, but baking for the family was welcome. Despite being groggy Lovina felt a smile cross her lips. As she passed the twenty-foot beat-up table in the dining room, dozens of memories flitted through her mind. After a few more steps, she was in the kitchen and could see that Salome's newborn was cradled in the nook of Ariana's arm. That was par for Ariana. She was a helper at heart, and she'd taken the night shifts for the first month or two with each sibling's newborn. With fourteen nieces and nephews, Ariana had spent many a night cuddling newborns.

But Ariana's movements weren't her usual smooth, gentle ones. Her shoulders were stiff, and each action was choppy, as if anger or panic was smoldering just under the surface, not that anyone else would see what Lovina could — except Abram.

Perhaps Ariana was simply tired. Had she rested at all last night? The counters were covered in the familiar clues that fresh croissants were in the oven. Since Ariana hadn't even begun them by the time Lovina went to bed, they would've taken rounds of attention during the night to be ready to bake for breakfast. *"Guder Marye."*

Ariana glanced up, and Lovina saw distress in her gorgeous green-blue eyes. "Good morning." Ariana continued bustling around the kitchen, using one hand to scrub counters and set dirty cookware in the sink while holding the newest member of the family in the crook of her other arm.

Disquiet settled over Lovina. Ariana was no brooder. When she was upset for long, it was rooted in something serious. "I heard that Berta is coming home soon, right?"

"Ya." Ariana seemed completely distracted.

"I'm guessing once she's released, a driver will take you to the hospital to get her."

She nodded.

"And you'll stay with her during the day as much as you can until she's on her feet again?"

Ariana nodded again.

Lovina slid her hands into her housecoat pockets. "Something seems to be bothering you, and I gather it's not Berta's health. Ya?"

Ariana closed her eyes and gave a slight shrug. "Ya."

The heaviness in her daughter's voice sent chills down Lovina's back. "Since when?"

"Night before last." With the baby bundled warmly and tucked safely in her arm, Ariana opened the refrigerator and just stood there, staring inside.

Lovina grabbed the tongs and turned the bacon. "What's going on?"

Her daughter, who was less than three feet from her, didn't seem to have heard her, and Lovina's heart sank. Had she and Rudy broken up? It wasn't like Ariana to get out of sorts over a breakup, but Rudy was the first man Ariana had shown any real interest in.

The timer dinged, and Ariana must not have heard that either because she didn't budge. Lovina peered into each of the two ovens, seeing four large baking sheets covered in golden brown croissants. Why had her daughter made this many croissants? The ovens were old hand-me-downs that her husband constantly repaired, but with their large family, having two felt like a necessity. She took out the pans and placed them on the cooling racks Ariana had already set out. When she turned, Ariana was still staring into the refrigerator. Lovina moved in close and placed her hand on her daughter's back. "Ariana, honey, whatever you're looking for, you won't find it in there."

Ariana turned. Her usually sun-kissed skin was pale. She pressed her lips tight, as if she'd keep the trouble to herself — or more likely between her and Abram. Ariana started to speak. But then she glanced at the stairs, and Lovina knew that whatever was going on, Ariana didn't want to chance anyone overhearing.

Lovina shut the refrigerator door. "What's wrong?" she whispered.

"I . . . I think someone is planning on leaving the Amish."

Lovina's heart skipped a beat. "Someone among the Summer Grove community?"

Ariana nodded and wrapped both arms protectively around Katie Ann.

Lovina's head spun, and she willed her knees to remain strong. She pulled out a barstool from the island, gesturing for Ariana to sit. "What makes you think that?"

Ariana barely shook her head before she lowered her eyes. Her sense of lostness seemed to mix with the wonder of the newborn resting in her arms.

Lovina went to the cabinet, took out two mugs, and poured them each a cup of coffee. "You could be mistaken, right?" Lovina was ready to launch into an encouraging sermon. "I mean, there's no cause to borrow worry when —"

"I ran into Quill night before last."

Lovina's pep talk melted, and all hopeful words of wisdom vanished. "Where?"

Soft moos from their small herd of dairy cows drifted inside. They were milked a little later on between Sundays than any other day.

"I saw him in his home." Ariana raised her eyes. "He apologized to me."

Lovina's hackles rose at the mention of Quill. "And well he should, but that doesn't mean —"

"It was clear his apology wasn't for what he'd already done."

Terror crept into Lovina's heart.

This was the fear Amish parents lived with — every bridge being burned between them and their offspring. What an awful way to end such a beautiful beginning — welcoming newborns into the fold, watching over them with love and prayers for two decades, give or take, and then to see them across a great divide, standing in the world with the Amish on the other side. Did Englisch parents live with such fears for their children — the terror that the fires of hell would swallow their loved ones? "Did Quill give you cause to believe that the someone leaving is a part of our family?"

She shrugged, frustration and disgust

evident on her face. "I'm unclear what he meant, but late last night after everyone had gone home, I knew what I needed to do. So I called the married sibs, and without explaining why, I invited them to breakfast. They're all coming."

Now it made sense why Ariana had made so many croissants. "Ari, honey, this is awful news, and my insides are shaking, but you can't directly ask your siblings. That will sound accusatory. Besides, if someone is planning to sneak off, do you think that person would answer truthfully?" Her question sounded callous even though her heart threatened to break at the thought of losing someone. But she understood the issues with confronting someone who was on the verge of leaving, and Ariana didn't.

"What do you want me to do, Mamm?" Ariana's face flushed with anger. The whisper barely contained her desperation. "Maybe my plan won't work, but it's better than doing nothing, isn't it?"

And there it was — her daughter's unbearable guilt for doing nothing when Frieda disappeared into the world with Quill. Lovina supposed it was like survivor's guilt. There wasn't anything Ariana could have done to keep Frieda and Quill from leaving, but because she was with them when they disappeared, she carried guilt.

"Ariana, honey . . ." Lovina wished she knew what to say. Maybe she should wake Abram. Lovina rarely had the words that could reach inside her daughter's heart and make a difference.

Quill had once had that power, and his misuse of it caused Ariana to dissect every word spoken to her.

The stairs moaned and creaked, and Lovina stopped searching for the right words. A few moments later Mark stumbled into the kitchen, his shirt half buttoned and one suspender over his shoulder, keeping up his pants. "Coffee." He plunked onto the barstool next to his sister, clueless that he'd just entered a room filled with emotion. He rubbed his eyes, and Ariana scooted her mug to him.

He gazed into the dark brew. "Now that's good service." He patted Ariana's shoulder. "For once." He took several sips of the black liquid. "Live somewhere long enough and you'll finally get decent service."

"Think so?" Ariana raised both brows, staring at him, a forced humor for Mark's sake. "Because I've been here almost as long as you, and it's not happened yet."

He motioned toward Lovina. "Ya, Mamm, what's the deal with that?"

Lovina chuckled. "I think she meant you haven't given her any timely help."

He frowned. "Really?" He shook his head. "Nah, she can't mean that. After all" — he held up one arm and flexed a muscle — "it's me. All the girls think everything I do is perfect, right?"

Mark, Lovina's third son, was the jokester of the family. Lovina was fairly sure he had tenderness underneath all his swagger, but she had to take that on faith because he didn't let her actually see what was in his heart. At twenty-three he was losing his boyish looks and had the appearance of a man ready to find a wife. Did he wish to leave the Amish to do so?

Lovina's eyes met Ariana's, and she seemed to be wondering the same thing. Ariana got up and eased the sleeping baby into Lovina's arms before she went to the cooling racks. "Mark?" Ariana took a spatula to several croissants, moving them to a platter. "I heard someone in these parts is thinking of leaving the Amish." She paused her actions and turned to study her brother.

"Again?" He seemed completely surprised, and Lovina felt the same relief she saw on her daughter's face. "Well" — he stood and buttoned his shirt before slipping the other suspender over his shoulder

— "maybe it'll open up more work for me, something with better pay than a small dairy and more permanent than doing odd jobs." He gulped half the cup of coffee. "Take next Saturday for instance." He set the mug down and swiped the back of his hand across his mouth. "I heard about a job through the grapevine, and on Saturday I will help build a stage on the green space of some subdivision. What's an Amish man doing building a stage for a bunch of college actors and singers?" He grinned, clearly pleased with his humorous observations. The Amish often did whatever work came along, but they didn't believe in being in the spotlight, nor did they think higher education was helpful toward staying humble and rooted to home.

A cow bellowed. "But this morning I have cows to milk." Mark popped his suspenders. "I gotta go."

Ariana passed him a croissant. Lovina heard a soft rumble of noise from upstairs. More of her family would come down soon.

"Denki, Sis. You're the best." His faint smile spread into a mischievous grin. "The question is . . . the best at what?" He shrugged. "No one has yet to figure that out."

Ariana wagged a finger in his face, taunting him.

He swatted at it while backing away. "I hate when you do that."

"I've known that since I was ten." She moved forward, wagging her finger in his face and chuckling. He ate a bite of the croissant and grabbed his straw hat off a peg near the back door. Mark would milk the cows this morning. Someone would probably join him in a bit to help, but with such a small herd, one person could easily take care of it. "I would say I'll be back when you're less annoying, but then I'd have to spend my life in the barn." He laughed, and the back door slammed shut.

Ariana looked out the kitchen window, watching her brother disappear into the barn. She drew a deep breath. "At least we know he's not making arrangements to leave."

Was this Ariana's plan — to casually bring up the topic and read her siblings' faces?

The baby began to wriggle and fuss, probably waking to feed. Lovina swayed her newest granddaughter back and forth. "Should I take her to Salome?"

Ariana shook her head. "Her milk isn't in yet, and she thinks sleep is the best remedy. I doubt she will join us for breakfast, but Malinda put several bottles of breast milk in the fridge yesterday."

Salome's younger sister Malinda produced enough milk to feed her babies and half of the other Amish babies in these parts. Since Salome had always struggled to provide milk for her own babies, it was nice that her sister had more than enough and willingly shared.

Susie came down the steps with Esther on her hip. "Somebody wants her *Aenti* Ari." Susie rolled her eyes. "I don't mind that part, but why does she have to wake me up while she's looking for you?"

"Uh, because we share a bedroom?" Ariana lifted Esther from Susie's arms before going to the croissants and tossing one to Susie.

Susie grabbed it. "Okay, fine. This almost makes her waking me up worth it. But I need my rest at this age — for brain growth. Can't someone teach her that?"

"Even though you're a teen, you're an adult now, Susie," Lovina reminded her. "And you should be up helping your sister every morning."

"Great, Mamm. No more benefits than being seventeen and twice the responsibility. Don't become a salesman. We'd starve to death." She winked at Ariana.

Lovina couldn't help but laugh at her

daughter being her usual sassy self. Through the window Lovina saw two rigs pull onto the driveway, each belonging to one of her married children and carrying some of her fourteen grandchildren. Lovina's main concern of late was Salome's personal battle with God over Esther's physical scars. She prayed for Salome and doted on her, but today, as she caught a glimpse of life through Ariana's eyes, Lovina realized she had neglected to pray for her other children as fervently as she did for Salome.

Lovina should've spent years on her knees for each child, because she couldn't imagine who she would become if she lost any of her children to the world.

FIVE

Quill pulled into a parking spot at the hospital and left the engine running. His eyes burned from lack of sleep. At least Mingo was only a couple of hours from here, but typically his job as an electrician for Schlabach Home Builders had a lot more flexibility than it had yesterday. With the new homes crawling with inspectors and closing deadlines looming, Quill had been unable to get away to visit his mom.

His real trade, however, the one that mattered most, was to help the distressed and oppressed Amish work through their emotions and make the best decision for their lives. He'd helped more Amish see that they needed to stay than he'd helped to leave. But people didn't know that aspect. All they knew was that sometimes entire families, usually younger couples with only a child or two, disappeared during the night.

"You ready?"

Frieda reached into the console and grabbed Quill's leather-bound copy of William Bradford's *The Plymouth Settlement.* It had been a gift from his dad for his thirteenth birthday, and Quill went nowhere without it. For that same birthday his dad had taken him to Massachusetts to see the Pilgrim Monument. That's what his dad called it, and that had been its name at one time, but now it was called The National Monument to the Forefathers. Those few days of learning that history had changed how Quill saw life.

Frieda's hands trembled as she ran her fingers over the gold embossing on the leather cover. "No. Not at all." She handed him the book, offering him a way to pass some time while she calmed her nerves.

He opened it, hoping to find comfort. The book covered the time period of 1608 to 1650 and included the persecution of Puritans, their flight from England, and their settlement in Holland. It continued on, telling of the difficult voyage to America and the hardships endured once they arrived. He never tired of reading the day-to-day accounts of the new colony, but what held particular interest was the internal fighting among the believers.

Even though both the Puritans and

Separatists were so loyal to God that they would gladly die for Him, they argued over interpretations of specific verses. Puritans believed that persecution was from God and should be embraced, trusting that God would reward them in the afterlife. The Separatists believed that persecution was the tyranny of people and that the only way to stop it was to stand one's ground — to fight or flee but never go willingly to prison or execution.

Inside that overly simplistic definition was the heart of the trouble between Quill and the Old Ways. The Amish had too easily accepted what had happened to Frieda as God's will — as a type of godly persecution.

Since Quill's Mamm and Frieda's Mamm were close friends and distant cousins and fifteen-year-old Frieda needed to get away from her home in Ohio, she had moved in with the Schlabach family.

Frieda and thirteen-year-old Ariana had become good friends. But within two years of Frieda's arriving at Quill's home, it was clear that she needed what he had to offer far more than she needed a girlfriend.

"I hate this place." Frieda toyed with the colorful plastic beads on the fringe of her purse while staring at the hospital.

Quill closed the book. "I know you do. Me too."

The first year after they left the Amish, they had lived near here because Frieda had needed to spend as much time in this hospital as out of it. When the worst of her physical needs were met, she began seeing a psychiatrist who was on staff at the hospital as well as a psychologist.

The whole journey had been long and painful.

And lonely.

But tainted memories had little to do with why his nerves were on edge. He took several deep, slow breaths, hoping to find relief from the pent-up anxiety. After years of seeing Ariana come in and out of his Mamm's place with a smile on her lips and a lilt in her steps, hearing her sing of God's faithfulness with that gorgeous voice, he'd thought that by now she would have found peace with what had happened. So he'd expected that if they ever met again, it would be awkward at first but they'd end up with some understanding between them. He'd been wrong. She didn't understand what he'd done any better today than she had five years ago. She saw his actions as a betrayal to the faith, so how she felt about him made perfect sense. He got it. So why did his heart ache much as it had when his Daed died?

Still, he had made his choices, and he would have to live with the fallout of every decision. Perhaps much of what was eating at him was the knowledge of what lay ahead for her family.

Frieda's hands no longer trembled, and he turned off the car. "You ready?"

"I guess." Frieda opened her door.

They made a beeline across the crowded lot and headed toward the north entry of the hospital. They both knew the layout of this facility well. Too well. Once they were on the crosswalk, he stepped behind Frieda, making room for oncoming people. Clearly a Sunday morning was a busy time to visit.

Frieda stopped short, and Quill stumbled against her. Someone bumped into him, and he turned to those behind them. "Sorry." He smiled and nodded as people frowned and went around them. Quill placed his hand on the small of Frieda's back, nudging her toward the sidewalk.

She glanced back at him. Then she hurried out of the way and didn't stop until she was near a metal bench. She turned. "Sorry about that."

"If the worst thing that happens today to any of those people is we slowed them down for a bit, they're having a good day. Don't you think?"

"I doubt they see it that way, but yeah." She picked at the fringe on her purse. "Look, I thought I could do this, but I can't."

He was used to this kind of resistance, and he wouldn't insist she go in, but he would reframe the scenario so she would think about it clearly. She struggled on all fronts, and who could blame her? "So you had a driver bring you seven hours one way from Kentucky, and you spent most of yesterday in a car, and *now* you're going to back out?"

Frieda had needed a hired driver to bring her because Quill was working and staying in Mingo, two hours away. Schlabach Home Builders built spec homes for subdivisions, which could take months or even a couple of years, depending on the number of houses and how far the job site was from their home in Kentucky. So Quill and his brothers would rent a small house or trailer near the construction site, which they dubbed a *temp house.* No one liked staying there, so when possible, they headed home early on Friday afternoons for the weekend.

"Your mother doesn't want to see me."

"Of course she does." He'd told Frieda

that for years, but she'd yet to join him when he made one of his visits. She blamed herself for causing Quill to leave as he had. That wasn't true. *They* chose. Navigating guilt and remorse was a tricky thing, especially for former Amish. He should know. He lived in a community of them in Kentucky. Of all the issues people dealt with in life, he thought self-condemnation was the trickiest weight. Before last night he hadn't stoned himself over his mistakes. Actually, he'd felt pretty good all these years — until he saw himself through Ariana's eyes.

Regardless of why Frieda didn't come with him on visits home, it was just as well that she didn't. It was really hard sneaking around to see his Mamm in a way that didn't get her into trouble with the church leaders. But that was easy compared to experiencing the contentment of home and all they'd left behind and then to have to pull away hours before sunrise. The reality that anything could happen to his mother between his visits hung over him.

Frieda sat on the bench and looked up at him. "Even if she did want to see me, what if someone is visiting her and spots us?"

"It's a Sunday morning. Do you know any Amish who hire a driver on a Sunday morning? Besides, it's a public facility, and we're checking on her while she's in the hospital. If someone saw us — and that's a huge *if* — they couldn't hold Mamm accountable, so what else can they do?"

"Judge us."

"Oh, I'd say that horse went rogue long ago, wouldn't you?" He forced a smile, hoping she didn't see through it. Apparently even Ariana judged him now, but after talking to her, he figured her condemnation was probably the kindest emotion she felt toward him.

Frieda stared across the parking lot filled with vehicles. "And if we see Ariana?"

"We deal with it, just as I did Friday night."

"Yeah, we made our bed, and we have to lie in it, but what about her? I was her friend, and I knew how she felt about you."

He didn't want to talk about this again or even think about it for the rest of his life. When he lay in bed on long, quiet nights, listening to the crickets chirp, the truth he'd buried whispered to him. With a five-year age gap between them, for most of his life he'd thought of Ariana only as the little sister of his closest friend. But as she grew older, she became his friend — an odd little creature who somehow worked her way into his confidence. Not long after her fifteenth birthday, he began to see the young, vibrant woman in her, and he decided to wait for her. They could've begun dating when she was sixteen, but with their age gap he thought it best to wait until she was at least eighteen. Maybe twenty.

He turned his attention to Frieda. "It would do you good to force your way through the anxiety and visit Mamm with me." It was her decision, and normally he wouldn't push like this, but Frieda had come such a long way — physically by car and emotionally by hard work with counselors. If Quill couldn't get her to visit his Mamm today, he wasn't sure she ever would.

She put her hand in his and jiggled it. "I understand your need to answer the call to help Amish leave, even when it's Ariana's family, but can't we come up with something that would make life easier for her?"

He'd wondered that same thing for the first few years after they left. "Our hands are tied when it comes to her." He sat on the bench next to Frieda. This past week had been emotionally hard on both of them. First his mom was missing, and they had no way of finding out why. Then, after praying Ariana's sister would change her mind and choose to remain Amish, she sent a confirmation letter to his post-office box. When Ariana caught him at his mother's, he'd been rendered nearly speechless as she stood in that dark hallway holding a candle, looking so grown, as years of good memories pummeled him. "We knew the cost from the start."

"Did we?"

He'd been twenty and Frieda was seventeen. "We understood enough." He got up. "Do you want to undo it?"

Her eyes grew large and she shuddered. "No, never. But —"

"But nothing." Given the situation he and Frieda had been caught in, they had devised a reasonable plan and carried it out. If a person wanted to leave, the Amish — church leaders, all relatives, and every friend a person had ever known — would begin by gently tugging on the person to do as the *Ordnung,* the rules of the people, taught. If a gentle tug didn't work, they would send letters and visit daily, preaching judgment — hellfire and damnation — until the dissenter yielded his or her rights of freedom to them or the person left, having been mortally stabbed through the heart. It was an unbearable wound to have one's Mamm,

Daed, brothers, sisters, and friends assure you that you'd go to hell for your wicked ways. It broke something inside most people.

The faithful Amish were like cockleburs on a long-haired dog. They didn't hurt, but there were only two ways to get rid of them: pull them out one by one, taking some hair from the roots, or cut off the hair.

The only way for most to get free was to disappear. That's where he and his brothers came in. While growing up, Quill had no intention of leaving the Amish, let alone helping his brothers establish a haven for other Amish.

But then the reality of what put his father in the grave hit Quill so hard he couldn't stay. So now he helped families know how to prepare to leave. Not many wanted to leave, which was good, but when they did, he worked with them for a year or more while he and his brothers secured them jobs and a place to live. There were several rules, but the two most important were that the person or family had to spend at least a year praying before they gave a final decision about leaving, and they had to write a respectful, kind letter to leave behind. Had Ariana gleaned nothing from the letter he'd written to her? He had to stop thinking about this.

He glanced toward the entrance of the hospital. "You going? As I said, it'll be good for you."

"I fully agree, but I can't." She gestured down the sidewalk. "Go without me."

Quill stifled his internal reaction. Her doctors said she had to make her own decisions concerning each step. She'd come to Pennsylvania for the first time in years. Apparently that was as far as she would get . . . this time. "Okay."

"Thanks, and give your Mamm my love, will you?"

"Sure."

She stood. "I can't stay out here in the open."

Being back in this area had Frieda's fears running rampant, and he had to wonder if she would ever return again.

He looked for a less conspicuous spot for Frieda to wait for him until they could return to Mingo to meet her driver. He trusted no Amish would be here on a Sunday, but she didn't, and he had to respect that. He pointed to another bench a few hundred feet away. "That spot has a shade tree, and no one will recognize you from that distance."

Appreciation radiated from her eyes. "I'll

be right there when you get back."

"I could be a while."

"Not a problem." She pulled her tablet from her purse, and he knew she'd spend the time doing e-mail, text messages, and games.

He went inside, and a group of people got in the elevator with him. It never ceased to amaze him how many folks visited at this hospital. He moved to the back. "Five, please." The woman standing in front of the control panel pressed the number five.

The elevator stopped at his floor, and he made his way to the front and stepped off. The bell rang behind him as he strode down the corridor, looking for room 522. Once at the right room, he eased inside.

His mother's frail-looking body was limp against the bed. Her skin seemed translucent with dark veins looking like railroad tracks. An IV was attached to the back of one hand, and she had a nasal cannula giving her oxygen. Did she feel as poorly as she looked? Her salt-and-pepper hair had a lot more salt than he remembered. Then again, he was able to see her only late at night, and the light from a kerosene lamp wasn't much.

Sweat beaded across his forehead as he wrestled with the shock of seeing her so vulnerable. Would he ever find an end to the hundreds of life issues he hadn't considered before leaving?

He slipped into the chair beside her bed. "*Ach,* Mamm." He clasped his hands together, breathing words into them. "What have I . . . we done?" His mind spun with thoughts — not so much regret, because he'd do it all again, but with the magnitude of every decision.

His Mamm opened her eyes and smiled at him. "You figured out where I was."

"I did. You gave me quite a scare."

"I'm sure. It's not as if I can leave you a note."

She couldn't call him either. She'd had five sons leave the Amish, and she was forbidden to make it easier on them, so she wasn't supposed to have any contact with them. Even though she was willing to go around that edict in certain areas of life, he and his brothers couldn't chance calling her, because several families shared the phone shanty. Some of the young teens and children thought it was a game to call *69, reaching the last person called on that phone. And then there was always caller ID to contend with. So they wrote to her, leaving the return address blank, or they dropped in for a visit late at night.

She studied him for a moment, giving off that motherly vibe that said she loved him far more than herself. "You do know all this" — she shook her arm with the IV and touched the oxygen tube — "is about getting sympathy from my unsuspecting son, right?" She rested her arms at her sides.

"Then it's doing its job." He placed his hand over hers. "How are you doing, Mamm?"

"A lot better."

"That's good to hear."

"How's Frieda?"

"Good." He shrugged. "She's here, but she couldn't quite make it to your room for fear of seeing someone who would know her. And she can't make herself face you, as if you would hold her responsible. I'll keep talking with her, but right now I'm far more concerned for you."

"Ahhh." She waved her hand across the bed. "They're only keeping me here because I don't have someone who can stay round the clock."

Was that statement supposed to make him feel better?

She narrowed her eyes. "I've not seen that look of torment on your face in a lot of years."

He nodded. "I'm fine."

"What you are is *schtarkeppich.*"

"Yeah, but I learned *stubborn* from its inventor — you."

"True enough." She gave a reluctant slight nod. "So tell me what's got you out of sorts."

"I spoke to Ariana on Friday night."

"That's the hardest part of all this, isn't it?" She pursed her lips and nodded.

"Apparently so." He hadn't meant to use Ariana as a shield, but regardless of what the girl thought she knew, she was still clueless . . . and fiercely loyal to his Mamm. If Ari knew that his Mamm had supported Quill's decision to leave with Frieda, would she remain loyal to his mom? His Mamm hadn't known when or how Quill and Frieda would leave. That would have been taboo to discuss, but weeks beforehand she'd given them what money she had.

"I need you to listen to me, Quill. You were so young, and every miscalculation was mine, not yours." She pointed a shaky finger. "You wipe that guilt off your face and from your soul. We made a decision based on what had to be done. Hold on to that, and let everything else go."

"I'm trying." He'd done a decent job of it . . . until a couple of nights ago.

"You need to take some time off. Get

away, just you. Maybe to a beach or mountain. That always helps."

"Can't."

She narrowed her eyes, studying him, and she seemed to know there was another family to move, but they wouldn't talk about it. They never talked about it.

She pointed at his chest. "What's that?"

He looked down and realized his necklace was showing. She wasn't criticizing because the Amish didn't believe in jewelry. She was simply curious, or maybe she wanted to understand him better.

He tucked the necklace back under his pale-yellow T-shirt. "Nothing." But often he returned to a time when he could hear the pinging of metal coming from the barn as Ariana forged it. He hadn't known what she was doing at the time, but later, when she gave it to him, it had helped him find his way out of the seclusion and loneliness of losing his Daed. She had made life bearable.

Why had he agreed to help her sister leave the order?

Six

Eight of Ariana's nine siblings were at the kitchen table — Malinda, Abner, Ivan, Mark, Abram, Susie, Martha, and John — looking relaxed as they chatted. Only Salome, Emanuel, and their newborn were absent. Ariana's parents were at each head of the long oak table. Also here were the spouses of Ariana's siblings and all their offspring. Unlike the evening family gatherings, where everyone was tired and milled about the yard to play with children, her siblings were alert and remained in place.

Although Ariana had refilled the coffee mugs, all the plates were now empty and pushed toward the center of the table.

"So, Ariana," — Ivan set his mug on the table — "aside from you once again proving that no one can bake a better breakfast, why are we here?"

"Well, I was, uh, wondering . . ." She hadn't prepared herself for a direct question. "See, we never discuss how we feel about each other, our district, and our faith. So I was . . . wondering . . . you know . . . how each of you felt."

Abram crossed his arms, looking as if he felt sorry for her and how poorly she was handling this situation. She sounded nervous and scattered, making her appear to have something to hide. What had happened to her plan of being calm and cool while asking general questions?

Mark propped his elbows on the table. "I feel very full and in need of a nap."

Most of her sibs laughed.

"I'm grateful." Abram shrugged, clearly trying to bring the conversation back around to Ariana's agenda. "This family fits the saying — we may not have it all together, but together we have it all." He paused. "Don't we?"

Everyone nodded in agreement, mumbling niceties to one another about how blessed they felt. All except Susie.

Ariana watched her younger sister, and when their eyes met, Susie appeared frustrated and embarrassed before she looked away. Was it her younger sister closest in age who wished to leave? Ariana's heart moved to her throat, and she found it hard to breathe. She could easily imagine the world using someone pure of heart like Susie, leaving her wrecked and ruined for the duration of her days. But Susie wouldn't leave without good cause.

What had Quill dangled in front of Ariana's little sister that had her wanting to leave?

Malinda stood and began stacking plates. "Sometimes the Old Ways get wearisome, but so does every part of life that requires self-control over self-indulgence. I believe the harvest we'll reap, the harvest we'll offer to God because of it, is worth the sacrifices we make."

A chorus of agreement went up, and some clapped. Susie had a faint smile as she rose and helped clear the table. Ariana stood, and soon all the women were cleaning up the kitchen while the men dispersed to the yard to sit in chairs and talk as the children played.

Susie filled the sink with hot, sudsy water.

Ariana slid a handful of flatware into the water. "You seemed to disagree with Abram's statement about us having it all."

"Who me? Disagree with Abram? Can't be true." Susie's usual lightheartedness seemed covered with a heavy dose of grouchy. "But let's drop it."

"I don't want to drop it. Spill the beans.

'Be frank. Come on." She bumped her shoulder against Susie's. "Vent."

Susie scrubbed the tines of a fork. "Abram said that together we have it all. We don't. If he and the rest want to believe that love is all we need, I'm fine with that. But I won't join in the chorus. Love is only part of any answer."

"Okay, that's fair. So you're feeling discontent. List the top five changes you would make if you could."

She grinned. "To dream the impossible dream . . ."

All the Brenneman girls had learned a lot of songs while cleaning houses and caring for the sick or injured. The Englisch loved their noises — television, radio, iHomes, CD players, Internet radio. But Susie singing those few words caused a faded memory to step out of the fog, and the made-up words "to slave for the impossible employers" came to mind.

Ariana's heart skipped. "Is that what's bothering you, working for the Beshears?"

For the last two years, Susie had been the in-home caregiver for a crotchety old couple. The man was suffering from dementia, and he blamed Susie if he couldn't remember how to button his shirt. The woman was worse. She'd been wheelchair bound for nearly three years, and she was unbearably angry about it.

Plunging her hands into the water, Susie scoffed. "I have to find something with dignity to it before I forget how to dream altogether." She rolled her eyes, sighing. "No matter how hard I work or what I do for the Beshears, they write me up for some minor infraction and make me sign the paper. It seems the only purpose of that documentation, as they call it, is to wag it at me while complaining. Just last week I had to sign a paper because when Mrs. Beshears went into the bathroom Monday morning, there wasn't any toilet paper on the roll. I didn't work the day before, and they'd used it up themselves, but I'm responsible? I was docked five dollars for that."

Ariana's pulse ran hot with frustration . . . and excitement. She hadn't realized the Beshears had gotten that unreasonable. At the same time, if this was Susie's issue, surely the café was the answer. "So if you had a job you liked, you would feel differently?"

"It wouldn't hurt. That's for sure." She washed a plate and rinsed it. "The whole time we were growing up, I kept thinking I could be okay with our lives — you know, the lack, the hard work, the strictness of the rules — if I could have one thing that stirred excitement of some kind, and, trust me, the Beshears are not it."

"No, clearly not." Ariana took a cleansing breath.

Susie was the one Quill intended to help leave. The key was to make staying more appealing to Susie than leaving.

Would the answer be as easy . . . and as difficult . . . as buying the café and making Susie a partner?

A Saturday evening breeze played with Abram's straw hat as he pushed the reel mower across the lawn. The churning blades cut the grass, spewing tiny pieces in all directions at once. The action matched what was taking place inside his mind and heart.

Between Barbie refusing to go out with him and Quill returning to Summer Grove, Abram couldn't find a peaceful thought to hang on to. He tried not to, but sometimes he hated Quill Schlabach. The man knew exactly how to knock Ariana's feet out from under her. Was Susie really thinking of leaving?

Ariana had tried to set up an appointment with the real-estate agent for the café last week, but the woman had been on vacation. So Ariana would try to see her as early next week as possible. If Quill intended to take Susie, when? If the down payment for the café could be negotiated, how quickly could Ariana go to closing?

/"Abram!" Mark hung out the window of the driver's vehicle. "You won't believe it!" As soon as the vehicle stopped, Mark jumped out and hurried toward Abram.

Extroverts. Abram sighed, rubbing the back of his neck. Sometimes Mark was brash and way too loud. Of course Mark thought Abram was overly calm and way too quiet.

Abram stopped pushing the reel mower, and all the blades came to a halt. "Ya?"

"Where's Ariana?"

She hadn't wanted to go out tonight, but Abram had convinced her to take Rudy to the abandoned café and give him a tour of the place. She had a key, and Abram armed her with a good flashlight. "Out with Rudy."

"So what sister is here that would go with me — Malinda, Susie, or Martha?"

"Only Salome and Martha are here." Abram released the handle of the mower. "Salome won't go anywhere. She has too much to do, and Martha is helping with her children. What's up?"

"Rats!" He motioned to the waiting driver. "I wanted at least one sister to go with me

90

so I could show her something. No one's going to believe me unless they see it with their own eyes!"

"See what?"

Mark strode toward the house, but he turned, walking backward. "I'm going to get Mamm and Daed. They'll want to see this."

Abram shrugged and grabbed the rubber handles of the mower. Before he pushed it a foot, Mark returned to him. "I saw a college girl who looks so much like Salome you won't believe it."

Abram removed his straw hat and wiped his brow with the back of his hand. "Ya? Where'd you see her?" Abram didn't really care, but it seemed rude not to show some interest.

"On the stage I helped build today. She's one of the performers from some artsy community college, and the students were doing what they call a musical. You'll have to see this girl to believe it."

Abram shook his head, suppressing a sigh. "No thanks. You're all excited over nothing. Who cares?"

"Maybe Mamm and Daed."

"They aren't going to invite trouble from the bishop by going to a musical in order to satisfy your" — Abram motioned from the top of Mark's head to his feet — "whatever this is."

Mark looked at the house and then at Abram a few times before scowling. "I guess you're right."

"There's no guessing about it. If they went today, they'd get a visit from the bishop early next week."

Mark shoved his hands into his pockets. "You go with me. Looking at this girl is like looking at Salome a few years ago. I promise. They could be twins."

"I'm fine right here, getting some things done that will make Mamm's week easier. You should try it sometime."

"I wasn't out playing. I was doing a job. And I'll do the yard for a month if you'll come with me. Someone besides me has to see this. You know no one ever believes me."

"Maybe if you didn't exaggerate so much . . ."

"I'm not! Not this time. Kumm on. I can prove it."

Abram shrugged. "Fine. I'll need to change." He'd helped haul hay before this, and his clothes were soaked with sweat.

"There's not time. It's after seven now, and the performances are scheduled to end by eight." Mark pulled a crumpled flier out of his pocket. "See?" He opened it, pointing to the schedule.

The leaflet had four columns of names. Abram focused on the names. "Which one is she?"

"No idea. But you should see the commotion those Englisch create to have a silly performance. It's crazy." He motioned toward the car. "Let's see if we can put a name to the face."

Mamm came out the front door, carrying a clothesbasket dripping with water. She glanced up. "Hey, Mark, I'm glad you're home. I need you to —"

"I came to get Abram. The driver is waiting to take us to see a play."

Concern flickered across Mamm's face. "Just last Sunday you said that an Amish man has no place building a stage for a play. Now you're enlisting siblings to watch one?"

"There's a girl in it who is the spitting image of Salome."

"I've always heard that everyone has a twin. Maybe you found Salome's." Mamm dropped the basket on the ground. "Another kitchen pipe broke."

"Again?" Mark's face crinkled with exasperation. "The whole house has been falling apart for the last fifteen years."

"Be that as it may, I've turned off the water valve to the house, but you're the

93

plumber of the family, so you have to work on it immediately. We won't have any water to the house until it's repaired."

"Okay, I'll get to it just as soon as we get back. Abram's gotta see this girl."

Mamm picked up a towel from the basket and began wringing water out of it. "You're way too old to get carried away about something so trivial." She tossed the towel over one arm and grabbed another. "And it's a play. What are you thinking, talking a younger sibling into something like this?"

"I normally wouldn't, but this girl looks exactly like a younger Salome. I swear it."

"Hey." Mamm frowned in the motherly way that said she disapproved and was disappointed simultaneously. "Don't swear."

Mark plucked the flier from Abram's hand. "I give you my word. Somewhere in this list of girls is one who looks just like I said. Want to go with me to see?"

Mamm wrung the life out of the towel in her hand. "Nee." Despite her refusal she glanced at the open flier Mark waved in front of her. "How do they fit that many people on a stage you built this morning?" She dropped the wet towels into the basket and dried her hands on her black apron.

"Well, it doesn't take long to build a stage, and they don't all fit on it at the same time.

Even when the largest portion of them are performing, they're moving through the audience."

She took the flier from him and skimmed the front, middle, and back. "Pay your driver and dismiss him. Life becomes a monumental task when there's no water."

A moan of displeasure emerged from Mark's throat, but he went to the driver to do as she said.

"A play." She sighed and held the flier out to Abram. Her brows furrowed as if something on the program caught her eye. She pulled it back, studying it.

She inhaled sharply and pointed to a spot on the back of the flier. "What's the woman's name next to the words 'costume designer'?"

"Brandi Nash."

Mamm stared at the flier.

Abram peered over her shoulder. "You know her?"

Mamm didn't answer. After a full minute or two, he waved his hand in front of her eyes, but she didn't budge. Was she having a stroke? "Mamm, you okay?"

Finally she blinked. "Ya. Of course." But she shook her head as if disagreeing with herself. "God's world is filled with co-incidences. All the time. Every day." She took a breath, nodding. "And Mark exaggerates."

"That's true. All of it."

"Nash is a common last name, and the given name Brandi is bound to be even more so for the Englisch, right? Like John Smith or Jimmy Jones."

"I wouldn't know." He shrugged. "Is it important?"

She wadded up the flier until it disappeared inside her fist. "No."

But as Abram remained in place, watching her walk around the side of the house, he saw her open the flier and study it before she vanished around the far corner.

SEVEN

With everyone at work and Monday's laundry on the line, Lovina tiptoed up the attic steps. Salome was resting, and her little ones were at Malinda's. Berta had come home late yesterday, so Ariana would stay with her until bedtime.

Finally Lovina had some time to herself, and tears welled. One of her children wished to leave? If that wasn't enough to break a mother's heart, and it was, fears she'd tucked away long ago seemed to be shrieking ruthlessly as they came out of hiding. Steadying her frantic emotions, she closed her eyes and tried to soak in peaceful thoughts.

The attic smelled of old wood and generations of memories. She made her way to the back of the attic, and sweat poured down her neck as she dragged useless items out of her way — broken rockers and quilt stands, butter churns, and old toys. She crawled around dusty boxes of hand-me-down clothes and knelt in front of the locked chest. Her heart pounded in her ears as she pulled the skeleton key from her apron pocket. Her moist hands shook, and she couldn't make herself slide the key into the keyhole.

Life was so busy, and until two days ago she had successfully quieted the fears that tried to whisper to her. Feeding and clothing ten children was difficult. Ignoring irrational fears was easy . . . or had been until Mark brought home that flier. Now her anxiety was becoming unbearable, searing her conscience like a fire engulfing an old birthing center.

Her knees began to ache, and she finally unlocked the chest. She removed tattered quilts that had been sewn by her great-grandmother and grandmother. Tucked under them were the baby blankets the midwife had wrapped every one of Lovina's newborns in. She pulled out the stack and removed the thick plastic protective covering from each one. Ten blankets. Five blue. Five pink. Lovina had pinned a tag of information on each one — name of child, birth date, weight, and memories of the day or night surrounding the birth. She supposed it was as close to a photo album as she could get.

She opened the folded blue blanket that Abram had been wrapped in. The white embroidered baby feet had yellowed slightly. She ran her fingers across them before opening Ariana's blanket. She inspected it just as she'd done several times over the years. But today was the same as every other time. No matter how diligently she searched for the embroidered baby feet, she couldn't find them. Somehow Rachel had mixed up the blankets. It was no wonder. What a day of terror that had been.

Lovina pulled the downy fabric to her chest. "Dear God," she whispered, "please let it be that the blankets were mixed up that day." A sob escaped her. "Please."

Ariana jolted from a sound sleep, her eyes opening wide as she gulped in a lungful of air. Rudy! He was picking her up, and they had a meeting with the real-estate agent tonight. What time was it? Sunlight and shadows spilled across her bare feet and arms as a waning sun filtered through the dancing leaves of the old oak outside her window. A humid breeze flowed through the open windows, but sweltering heat hung in the air.

There was a tap at the door. "Ariana?"

Salome called softly. Was it her sister's voice that had jolted her awake moments ago?

"Kumm." Ariana sat up, brushing damp strands of hair from her face.

Her sister opened the door and slipped inside. She had her newborn in her arms and a gentle smile on her face. "I was surprised to hear that you're going out on a Tuesday night."

"I am." She glanced at the clock. "In about forty-five minutes."

"Why?"

She stretched. "Because I have someone lined up to stay with Berta this afternoon as well as tonight, and Rudy and I have made arrangements to meet the real-estate agent at the café. Hopefully I can renegotiate the agreement to pay down less or something so I can purchase the café sooner."

Salome moved closer to the bed. "I was hoping to snag a few uninterrupted minutes with my very busy, beautiful, and oh-so-popular sister." She looked around as if searching for something. "But Susie isn't in here, is she?"

Ariana broke into laughter. "So you woke me to be mean?"

"Is there a better reason?"

"I had thought so, but based on what you just said, the answer is no."

Salome must be feeling more like herself again since she was teasing. Maybe the birth of her new daughter would douse the fire of resentment that had burned in her since Esther was injured.

Ariana stretched. "If you hadn't awakened me, I think I could have slept straight through until my shift for the baby."

"I'm sure you could after helping Berta so much since she returned from the hospital, as well as all the sleep you've been missing during the night while keeping Katie Ann for me."

"Ya, what's with that baby of yours?" Ariana teased. "She sleeps great as long as someone is holding her."

Salome chuckled. "It's no great mystery to me. She's difficult and demanding . . . just like her Aenti Ariana."

"Ya." She dragged out the word while going to her closet. "That's it." She began looking through a dozen hand-me-down dresses, searching for one that wasn't as tattered as what she had on.

"So," Salome laughed, "you've finally matured enough to admit it."

This was the kind of nonsense chat she'd missed having with Salome since Esther's injury two and a half years ago — a silly conversation that was simple and amusing, where neither of them ever took offense. Only enjoyment and camaraderie.

Ariana pulled out a rose-colored dress.

Salome moved to the bed and sat. "I . . . I heard about the breakfast you had on Sunday before last where you invited all the sibs. Mamm explained why."

"I haven't mentioned it because I didn't really want you burdened right now. You've got enough to think about." She put the dress over her arm and went to her dresser. "Can we talk later? I need to jump in the shower before Rudy gets here."

"What made you think someone, anyone in Summer Grove is leaving the Amish?"

"Salome, I just asked if we could talk later."

If Mamm hadn't told Salome, a married adult who lived with them, about Quill being at his mother's place, then Mamm hadn't told anyone. That was good. It would be best if as few people as possible knew Quill visited his mother. The last thing Berta needed was a church leader questioning her.

"But how do you know someone is planning to leave?"

"That's not important, and it could be an uncle, aunt, or cousin, but I don't think so. Whoever it is, I have a bit of information this time, and that gives me the ability to plan. I won't be caught completely blind, and I'll put a stop to it before it happens."

"Ari . . . , honey, listen to yourself. I know this is far more distressing to you than most of us can under—"

"I can fix this. I know I can."

"See, that's what we need to talk about." Everything about her sister seemed as calm as the summer breeze floating through the open window, but her eyes held deep concern. "Could you maybe have a short date with Rudy, just go for an hour drive and come back home?"

Laughter one minute and having to stand her ground the next. Sisterhood was like having a vivid rainbow and a gloomy thunderstorm in the same room at the same time. "I'll be home to keep Katie Ann tonight. I need the help I'm giving to be enough right now, okay?" Quill was not stealing another person from her. Ever. "I have a plan, a reward for staying."

Salome looked grieved as she put the baby on the bed and moved to Ariana. "I need you to listen to me. You have a good heart, and I know you think you're doing the right thing here, but you're setting yourself up for heartbreak. No one can change people's minds on a matter this serious with some sort of bribery. A desire to stay has to come from deep within a person."

"Susie is hardly more than a child. If I can buy that café, I know I can change her mind."

Salome's brows wrinkled. "Wait." She gazed into Ariana's eyes, seemingly confused. "You think it's Susie?" Her sister's words were hardly more than a whisper.

"I was surprised too, but it makes sense." Ariana pulled a pair of scissors out of her nightstand. "She's got the backbone for it, and she's restless living inside the Old Ways." She put her clothes for tonight on the bed.

"Ariana?" Malinda tapped on the door.

"Kumm." Ariana snipped frayed threads off the dress, hoping to make it look less old. Was she going to get a chance to jump in the shower or not?

Malinda opened the door. "Hallo." She held out a glass of icy water to Ariana.

"Ach, denki."

"You're welcome. Sorry, Salome. I didn't realize you were in here. Besides, my hands were full."

"That's okay." Salome took the drink from Ariana and drank about half of it. "See? Not a problem." She passed it back to Ariana.

Ariana shook her head while chuckling. "At least she saved me half."

Malinda grinned and pulled a brown bag from behind her back. "Before you get excited, the gift isn't actually for you." Malinda passed it to her.

Ariana laid the scissors on her dress and slid the soft fleecy item from its paper container. She knew immediately who it was for. After Berta went into the hospital, Ariana realized she needed a housecoat. As good fortune would have it, she'd found some fleecy material for a dollar at an Englisch neighbor's yard sale later that same day. "You did make it for me." Ariana had worked on making Berta a new housecoat, but she never got past cutting it out. It didn't help that Ariana wasn't very good at sewing, so trying to create something unusual like a housecoat, with a collar that was part of the length of the garment itself, took her a really long time. Ariana ran her hands over the downy material. "And it's the perfect gift for me. Denki."

"How's Berta?"

"Still a bit weak but nothing like she was when she went into the hospital."

"That's good. You and Rudy going by there tonight?"

"No. We're going into the historic district."

Susie was at work right now, but she would meet Rudy and Ariana at the café.

Ariana was ready to divulge her secret hope about the café. It wasn't as if she had been overly secretive about the café. Susie knew Ariana had spent years saving up to buy an old shop in town, but the dream never had much luster to Susie, so they hadn't talked about it in a long time. Ariana prayed she could get Susie excited about it too. Surely she would then stop thinking she had to leave the Amish to have a fulfilled life.

Ariana glanced at the dress she'd chosen for tonight. She was fairly sure magenta was Rudy's favorite color. "I could take the housecoat by Berta's first, but the Esh girls are with her until bedtime, and she's staying the night by herself." Did Quill come by after everyone was gone, or had he returned to hiding now that he knew what was going on with his mother? "The Esh girls will fix her dinner and tend to —"

"Ariana, sweetie?" Mamm called.

Salome giggled. "Sweetie?"

"Maybe if you baked lots of carbs for her, she would call you that too," Ariana teased.

Despite Mamm's calm demeanor she hadn't been herself in days. Was she more worried about losing a child to the world than she'd let on?

Carrying the housecoat, Ariana went into the hallway. "Ya?"

"I need a favor, please." Mamm's hoarse voice came from the foot of the steps.

Ariana moved to the landing and peered down at her. "Sure. What's up?"

"The water pressure is low again, which means there must be another leak somewhere. I hate to ask this of you, but would you mind getting a fresh barrel from the old cooperage shop? Your oldest brother borrowed the other one you brought home, and whatever he used it for, it no longer holds water."

Berta's husband had been a barrel maker before his death. Quill had followed in his footsteps, but since he'd left the Amish, the shop sat idle. Berta didn't allow anyone in the shop except Ariana, and even she hadn't gone inside it more than maybe three times in the last five years. In Berta's heart it was like a memorial to her husband. Maybe to her sons too, since all of them learned the trade before leaving the Amish.

If her mother could think of another way to meet the need, she wouldn't have asked Ariana to do this.

"I don't mind." Ariana held up the housecoat. "Malinda brought a gift for Berta. Look."

"Very nice."

"I'll take it to her, and I'll search for

another good barrel. But I have plans I can't be late for, so I'll set it somewhere — at the back of her property or beside her house — for someone else to swing by and grab."

"I understand. Just move the barrel from the cooperage to the end of her driveway."

"Okay. Rather than me trying to get back here before Rudy arrives, would you send him to Berta's to get me? He won't mind, but tell him to wait for me in his rig. That'll keep us from getting caught in a conversation with the Esh girls."

"I'll do it."

This was how things constantly went in their home — lots of little but specific plans to meet all needs in as inexpensive and timely a manner as possible. The house was held together by love and baling wire, and she hoped to purchase a café ahead of schedule? Doubt and a feeling of foolishness prickled her skin for a moment, but she could make this work . . . She just didn't yet know how. *Surely You have a plan, right, God?*

Ariana came back to herself and realized that her Mamm was still in place, staring up at her. Were those tears in her eyes? "You're my girl. Just you remember that."

What a strange thing to say. "Okay, I'm

your girl, but don't tell Rudy. He thinks I'm his."

Her Mamm should've liked those words. Ariana hadn't considered herself anyone's girl before Rudy, but only a faint smile crossed her Mamm's face before she lowered her eyes to the steps, seemingly lost in thought.

Mamm had to be worried about one of her children planning to disappear during the night. Fresh anger and determination seized Ariana.

She would win Susie's heart in this, and she would figure out how to get the café — even if she had to beg, borrow, or marry.

EIGHT

On the pallet in his cramped loft, Quill read a favorite passage from the leather-bound account of the Plymouth Colony: "All great and honorable actions are accompanied with great difficulties . . ."

The words lacked the hope he was looking for as he realized that dishonorable actions were also accompanied with great difficulties. Hardship wasn't an indicator of being right or wrong. It was a sign of being alive.

Although that phrase wasn't complex, some of Bradford's wording took time to comprehend, which was understandable since the book had been written during the same time as the King James Version of the Bible. Sometimes Quill's brothers teased him that he didn't speak like a normal guy. There was some truth to that.

He closed the book and peered down from the loft of the cooperage. He had loved this place as a child. His Daed had what the Englisch called an open-door policy. Whether Quill had wanted to play under his Daed's feet or begin learning the trade, his father had been welcoming and patient to a fault. Even now he could see his dad's huge hands and broad shoulders as he worked with the barrels. Quill could smell the fires that helped season and prepare the barrels for liquid. He could hear the scraping of oak staves as his father put the pieces into place — one wide, one medium, one thin, round and round each stave was placed.

But now the floors were covered with a layer of gray dust, showing only faint footprints of a few visitors over the years. Most of the tools were neatly hanging from the pegboard. Some were just as they'd been the day his dad died.

Would his dad be proud of him? of the choices he'd made?

The door handle rattled, and then he heard the rusty hinges creak. It wasn't possible his mother felt well enough to walk all the way out here, was it?

He waited in place, quiet and watchful.

Ariana.

Even from this odd view, he recognized

that white-blond hair through her prayer Kapp.

He swallowed hard as half a dozen emotions assaulted him — frustration, grief, loneliness, admiration, and homesickness being the strongest. Yet he'd do it all again. Bury his feelings for her and leave just as he had. Could a methodical, literal believer in the Ordnung understand someone like him?

Holding something in one arm, she eased into the room as if going to an altar. Her fingers trailed through the dust on the workbench. Was she also going down memory lane? They used to play in this workshop when they were young. When he got old enough to apprentice, she was his helper, handing him and his Daed tools while they worked.

But that was a lifetime ago, and it would be best for all involved if they didn't have another face-to-face encounter. If he moved farther back in the loft, she would hear him. The floor under him was made of planks, like a hayloft. His best chance of not being spotted was to remain completely still and hope she didn't look up.

Shafts of light came through the dirty windows, hanging on the dusty air as if it were fog, and the glow surrounded her, making her look like one of his dreams of returning home. How could a man disagree so fully with the Ordnung and at the same time miss living here?

She turned from the bench and went to the A-frame stack of barrels. Some had been made the week he left. One guideline about leaving the community without causing an uproar was to continue working until the last minute.

Ariana set the folded brown bag on a bench and moved so close to the loft area that he couldn't see her. The ladder to the loft creaked. Was she climbing it? His heart picked up its pace, and he realized that even after all these years, when it came to Ariana, he had opposing desires — to avoid her at all costs and to see her eye to eye. Until last week he'd gone with the first of those two desires.

The barrels began to shake, and he leaned forward, hoping to remain unseen while he figured out what she was doing. She had climbed partway up the ladder and then stepped onto the second row of barrels. The balls of her feet were on the edge of a barrel while she reached up to the third row, trying to shove one free.

What an absurd plan!

The stack began swaying. Didn't she know this could cause the whole pyramid to tumble, taking her down with it! They were made of solid oak, and each one weighed at least eighty pounds.

It could kill her.

The barrels moaned as some began to tilt. "Ariana, no! Stop moving. Now!" He scurried halfway down the ladder. Holding on with one foot and one hand, he swung out to steady the barrels. Despite the awkward, painful strain, he quickly secured the barrels. He glanced up into wide, beautiful eyes. So many thoughts and questions were reflected in them. To have such things shared with him would be a good day, but days where he really connected with someone were rare.

"What are you doing here?" She sounded offended at his presence.

"Currently I'm trying to save you from serious injury." He panted his answer as he focused on her feet and motioned with his hand. "Come."

She hesitated.

"Hate me later. Right now, do as I say." Would his command anger her and only make things worse?

Recognition flitted across her face. On her fifteenth birthday, after talking her into exploring an abandoned home with a caved-in roof, he'd had to yell the same thing at her.

He motioned, and she began to inch his way. "That's it. Slow and steady. Step on the central edge of each barrel."

While she worked her way to him, he recalled that outing on her fifteenth birthday. They had gone horseback riding, and when they'd stumbled onto an old house, Quill wanted to check it out. She didn't like the idea, but she agreed because she trusted him. Going through it had been fun until they went upstairs and he realized the floor was spongy, a sign it could give way. He was in the middle of saying "We need to go . . ." when her body jolted, and she screamed as a section of the floor gave way under her, trapping her foot. He'd sprawled spread eagle on the floor to distribute his weight, and he'd freed her foot. But rather than crawling to the stairway, as he told her to do, she remained in place, furious and shaken, until he screamed those words at her. In the hours that followed the incident, as they rode their horses back toward home, he realized that he had let his sense of adventure put Ariana in harm's way, and he knew he would never do so again.

Her eyes met his, and his memories fled. "You're doing great. Just a little farther."

When she was close enough, he used his free arm to snatch her off the barrels. Still holding on to the ladder to the loft, he pulled her close. "That was very dangerous." He shifted, and she put her feet on the ladder while grasping the rungs with her hands. She'd been in his arms the day he left here, and the familiar feeling of not wanting to let go of her coursed through him. "You okay?"

She nodded, taking in a ragged breath. "Ya. I . . . I've got my footing. You can let go now."

Against all that he held in his heart for her, he released her and waited as she descended the ladder. He hopped down. "You're way too smart to do something that stupid. What were you thinking?" Why was he griping at her? And then he knew . . . He couldn't be here to protect or care for her or his Mamm, and it frustrated him.

"*You* are correcting *my* behavior?" Her voice was eerily calm. "At least mine wasn't planned and plotted. It was simply a mistake."

Beneath her civil tone and behavior, she was seething with anger toward him, and he wished he knew how to free her of it. Despite all his planning, he'd overlooked dozens of important life connections that, once broken, he couldn't get back. His shortsightedness was far worse than hers. "I'm sorry. I shouldn't have —"

"Shouldn't have . . .," she hissed, sounding like water boiling over the edge of a pot. "If you're going to begin a list of all you shouldn't have done, we'll be here for months."

"Maybe. And I apologize for every part that has hurt you . . . or will hurt you."

"But saying that fixes nothing. They're empty words spoken by a man I once thought only said what he meant."

It seemed as if nothing between them could be fixed, not even for a few moments of resentment-free conversation. He'd seen her and the fruit of her hands over the last five years. He knew her well. She didn't have that same advantage. Would she like him any better if she knew more about him? Did it matter? He had chosen the path of his life, and she stood in opposition to it.

He grabbed a barrel and took it to the door. Then he backed away, waiting for her to take the cue and leave. He didn't want to argue. "I think it would be best if you go now."

She grabbed the brown bag she'd entered with. "This is for your Mamm. Please see that she gets it." She thrust it at him.

"You're not winning, not this time, Quill."

He took it. "Winning?"

"I don't know what all you have dangled in front of my sister, what promises you've made of rainbows or pots of gold, but I will not let you win."

So she knew who intended to leave. Relief coursed through him.

She narrowed her eyes. "You should be ashamed to do this kind of thing to your own people."

Did she understand nothing? He didn't do it *to* them. He did it *for* them. "I'm sorry you feel that way."

"Aren't you tired of saying those words? I'm sick of hearing them."

Yes, he was weary of apologizing, but he didn't know anything else to say. "Just go, Ari."

"You can tell the Nightcrawler that I have a plan, and he can forget taking my sister."

"A plan?"

"Ya, you know, the kind of thing you create and carry out while others sleep."

That's what he had done to her. Didn't she know that painful surgeries were best done while the patient slept? Regardless of what she did or didn't understand, he prayed her plan concerning her sister would work. "Good. I mean that sincerely. If you

118

think I want to help anyone leave, especially someone in your family, you're wrong."

"Who are you?" Her piercing eyes captured him. "You say one thing and do another, and I . . . I can't seem to get a handle on what to make of you."

"You have no idea at all?" Did the letter he wrote and placed in her hand before leaving explain nothing? It was scant on certain information, but for her sake he had shared as much as he dared, and it should've helped her understand a few things.

"I guess it would save us a lot of trouble if you just assumed I'm too stupid to put anything together."

"You're not stupid. Far from it. A little blind maybe . . ."

"Blind? And your eyes are open?"

"To some things, yeah." His strong suit was holding his tongue, so why wasn't he doing that? "Look, I get that you don't like what I do, but people have the right to choose."

"Yeah? What choice did you leave me that day when you took Frieda and left? Oh, I remember. I had the choice of telling the community all I knew or keeping it a secret while they searched frantically for a seventeen-year-old girl!"

"I explained what I could in the letter."

Anger drained from her face, and he saw a glimpse of a young woman still confused by what had taken place. "What did the letter say?"

How could she not know? The letter was in her hand when he pulled away from a final embrace and left.

She shook her head. "Never mind. I don't want to know. It was probably filled with your rationalizations."

"What happened to the letter, Ariana?"

Her cheeks flushed pink and she shrugged.

He could see in her eyes that his presence had opened more than the lid to her anger. Old wounds were being cut fresh again, but he couldn't prevent that. "What happened, Ari?"

She crossed her arms, giving another shrug. "I had it in my hand when I ran home to tell Daed what had happened. I . . . I guess I should've stopped to read it, but I was so confused that it seemed only my Daed could make sense of everything. When I got home, the deacon was at our table having breakfast. It was just a happenstance visit, and I must've looked as upset as I felt, because the adults pressed me to tell them what was going on. When I explained, the deacon insisted I give him the letter."

"He didn't let you read it?"

"I was afraid to give it to him, afraid it said things that could make the situation worse for your Mamm . . . and you and Frieda. So I ripped it up while hurrying to the sink, and then I held the pieces under a running faucet."

Quill couldn't respond, could hardly breathe. Even the day she thought he'd run off with Frieda, she continued to treat him and Frieda as true friends. If the church ministers had read the letter, it would've made a lot of things harder on his mother, Frieda, and him.

Ariana's face was chiseled with anger again. "I wish you'd never given me the letter. It only made me look like I was a part of your betrayal." She nibbled her bottom lip. "But that's not important, not anymore. The only thing that matters is you are not taking my sister with you."

"Nothing would make me happier."

"Who could possibly know if you mean it? Certainly not me."

"Yeah, I understand." He motioned to the stack of barrels. "I'll unstack them before I leave. It'll fill up the floor, but you'll be able to safely get whatever you need for years to come."

She looked from the barrels to him, and her guard seemed to lower for a moment.

"How do you manage to sound so sincere? You comforted me five years ago as if you actually cared. You stand here saying you hope my sister chooses not to go with you, but it's all just words for you, isn't it?"

"What can I say, Ariana? You're not going to believe anything that sounds contrary to what you already believe." And even if she did believe what he said, there were many aspects of what had taken place that he wasn't free to tell her. Some of the information would do her more harm than good, so he would keep that to himself. The parts that could be helpful were private info. Confidentiality was a harsh overseer.

She went to the barrel and pushed open the tattered screen door with her foot. "I can't trust you for good reason, Quill, and you know it." She struggled to scoot the barrel inch by inch through the door.

He set the bag on the bench and grabbed an old hand truck from the wall, hoping the wheels were still good. "Wait." He pushed the dolly to the barrel, and with a bit of effort, he slid the flat ledge under the base. He tilted it back, making her task easier.

"Denki." Her tone was cold with only a hint of politeness. She balanced the dolly, straining a bit to do so. Before pushing it forward, her eyes met his. "Is there something I can do to prevent us from meeting again?"

Her calm, collected words were like a knife sliding into his gut. He wanted to say that he was leaving for home soon, and when he did return for visits, he would do as he had been doing for years — all he could to avoid an encounter.

But when he opened his mouth, his heart overrode his will. "We should talk for a while first. You know, hash out a few things. I think it would help both of us." There were a few bits of information he could share that might defuse her anger, weren't there?

She blinked, staring at him in disbelief. Since all she wanted to do was get away from him, he was asking a lot, but from the moment he'd looked into her eyes last week, the longing to establish a little peace between them had been building inside him.

They could never be close again. He accepted that. He would never get the chance to date her or marry her or raise children with her inside this community as he'd once dreamed. In many ways they were both children when he had wanted that. Now they were adults, seeing the world in the harsh light of reality. But couldn't he at least remove a bit of tarnish from her good memories of them?

She shook her head. "No thanks." But then she stopped abruptly as if an idea had come to her. "But . . . would you answer one question?"

"If I can't, I'll tell you so straight up."

"How long do I have to change my sister's mind?"

"Three, maybe four weeks. What's your plan?"

"Seriously?" Her eyes widened. "Why would I give you a chance to undermine it?"

"I can't break confidences, but if I knew what you were thinking, I might be able to guide you in which plans could help with your goal."

"Didn't we just agree that whatever you said, I wouldn't be able to believe you anyway?"

"Yeah, but then you trusted me enough to ask about your sister." He shifted.

"I asked out of desperation, hoping your eyes and body language would tell me more than any words you spoke. That isn't trust."

People's points of view were tricky in any relationship. That was especially true in their case. He had a helicopter view of the events in broad daylight. Her view was from a small plot of ground in the dead of night. She wasn't to blame for seeing him from the only vantage point available to her.

"Look, I know I've not told you everything in the past. But I couldn't, not without asking you to keep secrets for me. What I did tell you was truthful."

"I need to go." She pushed the dolly with her foot to get the wheels moving.

"An hour at your favorite spot by the creek. That's all I ask. Then I'll disappear, never to bother you again."

"I don't meet married men for private conversations."

He knew she believed that he and Frieda were married. He had wanted her to think that for several reasons. He and Frieda needed the community to believe they were going to marry. Plenty of people would try to find a single teenage girl so they could talk her into returning to the fold, but few would spend much time trying to track down a married woman. To the Amish a married woman belonged with her husband. Period. "I'm not married."

She released the dolly, and the bottom of the barrel thudded against the ground as she stared at him as if he'd grown a second head. "You ran off with my friend, and then you didn't even marry her?"

"For her sake, so no one makes an effort to find her and talk her into returning here, it would be best if you keep what I'm about to tell you between us. See, it wasn't like that, not for her or me."

She stared at him in disbelief, unmoving for several moments. "And yet you dare say you've never lied to me?" Shock at his marital status faded, and something dull filled her eyes — maybe resignation. Or disgust.

"I did mislead you on that. I know I did, and it's part of what I've apologized for. We had no choice." He could see on her face that he was making things worse between them.

"Whatever." She shrugged. "I also avoid any relationship with single Amish men who dabble in the Englisch world, so there's no possibility I'll have another conversation with you."

Did she realize what a snob she'd become? She needed someone to challenge her closed-minded thinking. "You think you're so much better than Englisch people? I guess that thinking helps you gladly accept the segregation the Amish are so comfortable with."

"We separate from the world — in it but not of it, as the Word says. But I'm not surprised you find fault with that."

"Isn't that the same world Christ died to

save and sent all people into in order to make disciples?"

"Is that what you do, Quill? Make disciples?"

"Well . . . no, but —"

"But you know how to talk the talk, to convince hurting families and teenage girls to come into the world with you, right?"

"That's not what I do."

"You've also said you've never lied to me, which just begs the question — what constitutes a lie in your mind? Seems to me, you're the kind of man that your wife would have to ask you specifically, did you cheat on me this month? Otherwise, if you cheated and she never directly asked about it, you're not a liar."

He considered himself slow to anger, but she'd pushed him about as far as he could take. Still, his guilt over the past curbed his tongue.

An old car horn, like those often used on Amish rigs by younger folk, sounded. *Ahooga.*

"Rudy's here, and I need to go." She tried to get the barrel tilted back on the dolly again.

Rudy. Clearly a man who'd never crossed into the Englisch world to experience it beyond what was necessary for survival or business. "See me however you like, Ari, but open your eyes and see yourself. For hundreds of years, sweet, obedient Amish girls such as yourself have been used by family and church leaders as Amish nectar, giving men the energy and drive to stay under the Ordnung."

Her face flushed red, and he stiffened as the palm of her hand swung toward him. But she stopped before slapping him. Trembling, she lowered her hand, tears glistening.

His jaded attitude had managed to insult and hurt her simultaneously.

She drew several ragged breaths, gaining control once again. Soon the tears in her eyes disappeared, and she touched the back of her prayer Kapp, making sure her hair and cap were still in place. "Without end you are a disappointment."

A physical slap would have been less painful. He was clear on the main reasons he'd never reached out to her after leaving, but maybe hidden somewhere deep inside him, he'd known she would be unable to accept any of the truths he saw, the ones that highlighted the less-than-noble aspects of the Old Ways. Even knowing all he did, he still believed this way of life was one of the better ones available. But some serious changes needed to be made, the kind that would have spared his Daed's life and made ways to protect its innocent people from the bad apples.

He slid the barrel in place and tilted it back for her. "I'm sorry. I shouldn't have said that." He considered it true, but it was rude and maybe spiteful to voice it.

She clasped the handles.

He knew they were done.

Completely finished.

He'd been naive to hope they could clear the air and sustain a friendship, frail as it might be.

"Bye, Ariana. I pray you'll have a good and fulfilling life."

NINE

Lovina watched at the doorway of the barn, making sure none of her children came near as she tried to talk to her husband once again about a topic he didn't wish to discuss. He continued to pick the horse's hoofs as if that animal's comfort was more important than hers.

Her desire to remain respectful grew thin as she fidgeted with the flier from the play. "Isaac, please." Her whisper echoed in her ears, but he didn't flinch. "We may have raised a child who is planning to leave. And this thing with the flier and Ariana has me terrified. I can't deal with these things in silence. I need you to talk to me."

"Don't borrow trouble, Lovina." Isaac spoke without pausing or looking up. "Other than a cryptic message from Quill, we have no hint that one of our own is planning to leave. Ariana needs to work through her fears her way, and I understand that, but I will not believe a report that the sky is falling."

Lovina's anxiety eased concerning the possibility that one of her children might leave the Order. "That's a good answer, Husband. Denki." But a much harder topic for them to discuss was the events surrounding Ariana's birth. They hadn't broached the subject often. "But what about the flier and Ariana?"

After wrestling with her fears on her own, she'd shared them with him late last night as they crawled into bed. First she reminded him of the pink blanket without the embroidered feet, but he dismissed that just as he had years ago, saying that in the panicked shuffle to get everyone outside during the fire, the blankets had fallen off the girls, but the babies' identities were handled carefully. When she explained what Mark had seen and the name Brandi being in the flier, he froze. But then he told her it was nothing to consider, just her imagination running wild. He blew out the candle and rolled over to face the wall, unwilling to discuss the possibility.

She wiped sweat from her brow. "Could you please stop for one minute and look at me?"

Without raising his head, he moved to a

different leg of the horse. "This is nonsense. Ariana is ours. God gave her to us, and I won't question it."

"Won't question it? Isaac, you have to talk to me. I feel as if I'm going crazy. My heart has beaten so fast since Mark brought home that flier that I can hardly breathe, and I've never been so nauseated in all my life."

He stood upright and slipped the hoof pick into his pocket. "You won't like what I think."

"I've got to know." As desperate as her voice sounded, it didn't begin to express how she felt.

He blew out a long, steady breath. "I've not forgotten the chaos that took place the night the twins were born. The incident with the blankets has bothered me over the years, and I know your fear about the two girls being swapped is certainly feasible. But . . ."

Her heart seemed to pause, unable to beat until he finished his thoughts. "Go on."

He pursed his lips, a frown creasing his face. "If God deemed this incident to happen, seems to me that we would be wrong to intervene."

"What?" she whispered, chills covering her as if she were standing naked in the barn in midwinter.

He said nothing else.

"Isaac." Was it her ingrained beliefs of how to speak to a husband or the pounding at her temples that kept her voice so soft? "You can't mean that."

"I do. Leave it be, *Frau.*"

He only called her *wife* when he needed her to remember that her place was not to be the leader. "Just drop it?" She grabbed his arm. "You can't have thought this through."

"Since she was little, sometimes I look at her and see a girl who is unlike our other daughters. Not so much physically, but . . . something is different about her. So for years I've thought about what you're saying. It doesn't change my stance."

Did he need a mother's heart to understand how she felt? "Is it that simple for you?"

"Is that what you think of your husband, that because a decision is hard, he must be a hard man?" His voice shook, the first hint of emotion he'd shown. "It's eating me up inside! I can't sleep. I can hardly speak our girl's name without fear and anxiety choking me." He looked through the barn door and toward their run-down farmhouse. "I don't even understand what I'm so terrified of. But it's in my gut like nothing I've ever experienced before, and I know we must leave this alone. That's what my gut tells me."

"Which gut feeling? The mankind one that longs to avoid every scary situation? Or the gut feeling that is between you and the Creator?" She stepped closer. "Isn't it possible that God has opened our eyes to this possibility because He needs us to act?"

He froze, staring at her for what seemed like forever. He then walked the horse to its stall and put her away. "Until just then I was holding on to the thought that He doesn't need our help." He closed the gate behind the horse and remained there. His hands trembled as he removed his straw hat. "But He uses people every day to help others, to keep others safe from harm. When He gave us children, He made it our responsibility to watch after them. But . . ."

How self-centered was she, doubting that her husband cared. His emotional upheaval equaled hers. It simply revealed itself differently. He wanted to deny their responsibility, hoping it was God's will to leave the situation alone. "Husband, what if we have a daughter out there who needs us? Will we stay so focused on the blessings God's given us that we won't inconvenience our lives to seek truth?"

He rubbed his forehead with the back of

his wrist. "What will it do to Ariana?"

"Our love for her cannot be dampened by this any more than it would if we welcomed another baby into the fold."

"This is different, Lovina. You're not seeing it for what it is. If she's not ours," — he gestured at their home — "she's not related to anyone of this household." Tears sprang from his eyes. "What would that do to a girl like our Ariana?"

Shame dripped its hot wax onto her aching heart. She hadn't thought of it in those terms. All she knew for sure is her heart screamed out for the child she may have given birth to — the one raised in an Englisch world by a stranger. "Ariana's faith is strong. Her character is strong. Whatever the truth is, she will not be undone by it. I know she won't."

"Ya, she has a lot of inner strength." Isaac went to the doorway and stared at their home. "A thought came to me earlier today. Perhaps it is from God."

Lovina moved to his side. "What is it?"

"If parents could give their children all they needed, if we could prevent all pain, lack, or confusion, none would need God."

Lovina mulled over his words, struck by the powerful truth, but its meaning and timing terrified her.

His shoulders slumped. "I guess I need to trust that regardless of what the truth is, it will only draw Ariana closer to God."

Lovina placed her arm on Isaac's, and he took his cue, engulfing her in a reassuring hug. How many times in their years of marriage had his broad shoulders and strong arms felt like all she needed to get through any storm?

"Daed?" Their youngest called out, and Isaac turned toward his voice. "Water is going everywhere again!"

Isaac released her and cupped his hands around his mouth. "Turn it off at the main, and I'll be inside in five."

John waved and nodded.

"Where do we begin?" Lovina didn't like pushing Isaac to talk, but she had to know the truth.

"With the midwife." He rested his hands on her shoulders.

That did make sense. "Rachel may remember something so specific it will put our minds at ease."

"Ya."

"Today, then?"

"Nee." Her husband's hands slowly moved to her neck and he held her face with his thumbs. "If we take off tonight, it'll raise questions, and we'd have to come up with excuses. We can't let our actions alert anyone." He pulled her closer and kissed her forehead. "Besides, there are pipes to fix and children to feed."

"Isaac, I need to talk to Rachel soon."

"I know, but let's be cautious." He put his forehead on hers. "Maybe when we do talk to Rachel, we'll find out that our fears are nothing."

"Ya. Maybe so."

But he didn't believe that. She could see it in his eyes and feel it in the trembling of his hands, and it made her insides churn with a sickening nervousness.

Standing on the sidewalk, holding on to the brass key, Ariana peered through the streaked window of the abandoned café. After Abram's weeks of overtime, she needed only $6,270 more.

Only?

Reality tried to grab her ankle and pull her under the choppy waters of discouragement, but she broke free. She wasn't giving up, even though they had just thirty-six days left to get it. Maybe the real-estate agent could give her an extension for the closing. Her breathing tightened with thoughts of how much more money she would need to make a go of this diner, funds that she didn't know how to obtain. This place no longer felt like a dream. It was a necessity. Hearts were at stake, and she could spare her loved ones so much pain if she could keep Susie from leaving.

"Ariana?" Standing next to her, Rudy tapped on the grimy window. "Hello?" Confusion shone in his dark-brown eyes. "What's going on? You haven't been yourself at all since I picked you up at Berta's house."

She ran her fingernail along the jagged edges of the key. Sliding a key into a lock could open anyone's life to new experiences — even if one was going home to family after a day at work. She longed for Susie to let this door be unlocked for her, not the door to living in the Englisch world.

Rudy placed his warm hands over hers. "Talk to me. Please."

She noted how well his hands covered hers, so strong and protective. Her ability to carefully choose what she shared with him evaporated. "How much do you want to know?"

"From ninety-something percent of the people in my life, as little as possible. From you, I want to know anything you're willing to share."

"I'll try to make sense, but our time before

the agent arrives is so limited."

"Then I will tell her we need to reschedule."

The fact that anything Ariana had to say came ahead of keeping the appointment with the real-estate agent told her a lot. He cared more about her than about how breaking the appointment would look to the agent. Rudy seemed like a perfect mixture of strength and kindness. Looking at him in contrast to Quill, she realized how very likable her beau was. Steady and caring.

What was wrong with Quill anyway? First he left, taking Frieda, and now he intended to take her sister — all the while acting as if Ariana's feelings and well-being mattered. How had she ever been so foolish as to care for him?

Not married. Quill would never know how disgusted she was to learn he was single. It was evidence of just how deep his deceit went. He'd never said directly that he intended to marry Frieda, but it was implied. If Ariana had known the two hadn't married, she probably would've helped the leaders try to find her.

Rudy squeezed her hands gently. "Are you . . . tired of seeing me?"

"What?" She blinked, coming back to herself. "No. Just the opposite."

139

"*Gut.* I like your shocked response and absolute firmness about it." He clutched his chest, sighing relief. "*Denki.*" He meant his thank-you to be humorous, but nothing was the least bit funny right now.

He took her hands again, waiting on her to say something. When she had said she didn't want to talk about what took place that rainy night at Berta's, he'd accepted it. When he picked her up earlier today and she was seething with anger, he left her alone while she smoldered in silence. Was he as perfect for her as he seemed?

He motioned to the curb, and they sat down.

She wrapped her arms around her bent legs, thinking back on dozens of memories. Her first memory of Quill was when she was five or six, and he had been kind and patient with her, treating her like a real person rather than the pesky little sister of his friend Mark. When she struggled to learn to write, Quill was encouraging, and he injected humor, making her realize it wasn't the end of the world to be unable to hold a pencil correctly. She had frightened easily in those days, and he seemed able to stare down a rattlesnake . . . and make *it* crawl off. But despite his deceitful nature, she was sure he'd benefited from their relationship too. He used to get balled up inside himself with thoughts and feelings, and she was able to help him sort out how he felt and why.

When she was twelve, she'd told her Mamm that she intended to marry Quill Schlabach, and she never wavered in that thinking until the day he disappeared with Frieda.

No wonder she didn't want to tell Rudy. It was embarrassing how foolish she'd been when it came to Quill. Sometimes in the still of the night when she woke, she recalled her feelings for him so clearly it seemed as if some part of them still existed. But they didn't.

"Remember once asking me who my first crush was?"

"Ya."

"Well . . ." She began sharing, telling as little as she knew how and yet enough for the journey to make sense.

Rudy intertwined his fingers with hers. "He's returned for your sister?"

The way he asked made Quill sound like a monster from the deep.

"Ya."

"You should use the church leaders more. It's what they are here to do — protect us from those who want to cause division and strife. You can't continue to protect him."

"I'm not trying to protect *him*. Berta needs me to keep everything quiet. If the church leaders realize he's been visiting all these years, she'll be held accountable. All I have to do is find a way to change Susie's mind about leaving, and nothing Quill has done so far matters."

"I get what you want to do, but I see a lot of caution flags. You're taking on responsibilities that aren't yours. Why do you feel it's your place to protect and take care of Berta? Why are you trying to build a life Susie is willing to stay in?"

"Would you have done any less?"

"Everyone has to do less than you aim to, Ari. It's not good to run around trying to make everything okay for everyone else."

"But . . . God asks us to carry one another's burdens. Like with Berta and Susie."

He didn't look convinced, but he nodded. "Even if by some miracle you get this restaurant and Susie agrees to stay because of it, how long before she regrets giving her word? Jobs get old quickly. What if you go into debt up to your ears trying to open this restaurant before you're financially ready, and then she decides in a few months that she still wants to leave? Are you aware that restaurants are the number-one small business to go under?"

Maybe she was too wrung out from her earlier encounter with Quill, but instead of finding words to share how she felt, she leaned her head on his shoulder. "I have to try. Please tell me you understand that I have to try."

He put his arm around her shoulders and sighed. "Sure, I understand. I don't necessarily agree, but it takes someone like you to care this much about a little sister. Wherever and whenever you need help, I want to be at your side. I wish I could help financially, and maybe I can later on, but right now my money is tied up in the family business back home."

Even after growing up poor, she was just now beginning to understand how hard money was to come by. "I just appreciate that you understand my position."

"I get it." He squeezed her shoulder. "Any idea how you'll come up with enough money to go to closing?"

"Marry someone with money?"

He chuckled and rubbed her shoulder. "I can see why the idea might momentarily sound appealing."

She sighed. "You mean the money would be attached to a real person?"

"Afraid so."

They shared a laugh, and she remained snuggled under his arm. "Is begging door to door an option?"

He smiled down at her. "Maybe we should give it a little more thought. Any siblings besides Abram who might be willing to help?"

"Mark and Susie are the only others who earn money and don't have children, but they pooled their money to buy a horse and carriage for Mamm and Daed a year ago."

Rudy whistled. "That set them back."

"Ya, I imagine they don't have a thousand dollars between them."

"There will be a Labor Day event here in town. If we set up a booth, you could make some money over that long weekend."

"Ya. Maybe so. I would need to check into the specifics of permits and such."

The real-estate agent pulled her shiny red car into a parking space near them and got out. The thirty-something woman wore a navy-blue dress that molded to her pregnant body. She carried a folder of papers. "So, Ariana, do you have some good news for me today?"

Ariana swallowed hard while standing up. "I was hoping you could renegotiate exactly what it will take for me to open this shop. Maybe I could rent it for a while before needing the full twenty percent to go to closing. See, if I can use the money I've saved to get it operational, I can make money. Then I can buy the place."

"I don't think we're seeing this in the same light." She ran her manicured hands over her belly. "Mrs. McCormick, the owner, gave you a verbal agreement, one that I didn't think was advisable. She wants you to have this place, and if it were solely up to her, she'd be more flexible. But her children are pushing me to find a serious buyer with the money to go to closing. And there are some interested parties. You and Mrs. McCormick have a special bond since you cleaned her house and cooked for her for years before she moved into the retirement home. She would give you the moon if she could, but I think you should release her from the verbal agreement."

The *clippety-clop* of a horse caught Ariana's attention. Susie waved as she pulled the rig across several parking spaces to find enough room for it.

Ariana's mouth was dry. This wasn't the meeting she'd been hoping for. Rudy knew business. Couldn't he think of an alternative to buy Ariana some time? She studied him, waiting for him to rescue her with some sort of plan, but he shrugged.

Ariana held the key firmly in the palm of her hand. "I'm sorry it's inconvenient for Lila's children, but she said she would give me until October first."

The agent nodded, looking more perturbed than disappointed. "If that's how you feel, I'll let the family know. But I can assure you that you won't be given one day more." She headed for her car.

"Hey." Susie hopped down. "Why such hush-hush stuff about meeting you here?"

While Rudy tethered Susie's horse, Ariana motioned for her sister to come with her. "I think it's time you see my dream. You may fall in love with it." Ariana unlocked the door and showed her through the old building. Dust hung in the air, making the room look like fog bathed in sunlight. Strange and yet beautiful. She prayed for the right words. "We could make it a success, Susie, and the rest of the family could work here as money from the café and their schedules allow. Just think, the two of us as the owners of a thriving café in town." Would Susie like this old building? Or would she find fault where Ariana saw beauty in the jagged brick walls, slanted wood floors, and filth. "It needs elbow grease."

"Oh, you poor, delusional thing." Susie laughed. "That doesn't begin to cover all it

146

needs." She looked skeptical, but her interest seemed piqued. After years of taking care of difficult employers, Susie had to be a little intrigued with the idea of owning a café. In addition, being the poorest family around was embarrassing, and this place could change that for the whole family. But her little sister was a smart cookie, and she would know that this plan would be really labor intensive. Would its potential be enough to keep her from leaving?

Susie pointed to the wide stairs with a beautiful banister. "So where do the steps lead?"

"To sort of a storage-room loft."

Susie's eyes lit up. "As in . . . could it be a place for me to sleep? You know, a girl's own bedroom without the need to share it with her older and younger sisters?" She grabbed Ariana's hand and ran up the stairs.

The space was filled with old boxes, and Ariana had calculated it was the only place to store nonrefrigerated supplies for the café. Still . . .

"I don't have all the financing lined up, but if I can buy the café and if you want this space as your room, it's yours."

"You mean you wouldn't claim this as your own?"

"Not if you were willing to stay . . .

Amish." Ariana wouldn't add any other stipulation, like the need to work in the café or keep the loft decently straight. She wanted only one promise from her sister.

Susie nibbled on her bottom lip, looking thoughtful. "Stay Amish . . ." She rolled the words slowly off her tongue before weaving between the boxes and walking to the railing that overlooked the café. "The way the loft is built, no one has a view from below, but it still doesn't offer a lot of privacy."

"If I get the place, I intend to open around seven. But we'll close at two in the afternoon. After we prep for the next day, the whole building will be as private as you like."

Susie waggled her brows in unison, almost fluttering them. "Now this is worth talking about. You're a good big sister and all, but, oh, what I would do for a room of my own. Do you think Daed would let me live here?"

Having a little independence from the family was much more important to Susie than Ariana had realized. How had they shared a room all these years without discussing something this critical to her little sister?

Ariana's insides were quivering. "I think we could talk Daed into it if you agreed to things like a curfew and no boys without supervision, and you still attending church meetings."

"A place of my own and a café." She grinned. "The Brenneman Brew."

Ariana laughed, and tears of hope tried to break free. "Well, I'm not quite sure about that name. I know you mean coffee, but there's a beer-brewing place a few blocks from here."

"Are you sure I meant coffee?" Susie staggered as if she'd been drinking.

"Susie," Ariana corrected, suddenly sounding like their mother. No wonder her feisty sister was desperate for a room away from Ariana.

"Okay, fine. I'm sure the idea of brewing one's own beer is overrated anyway. Hmm. What about Brennemans' Perks?"

"Not bad." Ariana dragged her fingers across the top of a filthy box. "So . . . what do you think?"

Susie looked around, contemplating the question.

Ariana was offering a plan she might not be able to follow through on, but there had to be a solution concerning the money. God had planted the desire to save for this café in Ariana and Abram years ago. Then He let Ariana know that Susie was making plans to leave, giving Ariana an opportunity to change her mind. If Susie agreed to stay, surely God would show Ariana how to earn the money.

Susie thrust out her hand. "We have a deal!"

Ariana ran toward her sister, tripping over a box before she engulfed Susie in a hug. "Perfect!"

"Ari," her sister rasped, "Susie can't breathe."

Ariana released her. "Oh, sorry." Ariana wrapped her arm around Susie's shoulders, and they went down the steps.

Now all Ariana had ahead was the simple trick of pulling thousands of dollars out of a hat.

Ten

The faint smell of exhaust permeated the inside of the work van as Abram looked out the window on the way home from work. The miles of pastureland and narrow two-lane roads seemed to go on forever. Dozing in the van was as impossible as sleeping at night had been lately. There was too much weirdness happening inside his home. He understood Ariana's anxiety concerning Quill's hint that he would take one of their siblings, but other things were bothering him. Whispers between his parents. Tears his Mamm brushed away, thinking no one noticed. Mamm hadn't been much of a crier until recently.

In his twenty years of life, he'd never been confused by the happenings in his household. He'd often been overwhelmed by the activity and the vast amount of energy and emotions coming from his parents and nine siblings, but he'd never been perplexed.

Added to those things, it was the third of September. Ariana now had twenty-seven days to earn about $5,500. Time was slipping through their hands, and Abram was taking as much overtime as he could get. Ariana could hardly manage her regular housecleaning jobs because of Salome's constant neediness. It irked Abram, but he knew better than to get between sisters.

The van passed a woman standing in a moving cart attached to a horse. He couldn't see who it was. She was bent over, reaching as far as she could toward the horse, and Abram immediately knew she was having trouble with the rig. A small cart like that was as springy as a frightened rabbit. And standing as she was, if she hit one small rock or tiny bump in the road, she would sail through the air and land with a thud. He knew of a man some ten years ago who was in a similar situation and had broken his back because of it. If the horse and cart were threatening to separate, she should bring the rig to a halt before trying to address the issue. But if a stave had worked its way free, she might be having difficulty getting stopped.

Abram tapped Mr. Carver on the shoulder. "Stop the van."

Mr. Carver looked in his rearview mirror. "Are you sure it's necessary? She looks to have it under control."

The two other Amish men in the van sat upright, paying attention for the first time in many miles. "What's up?"

"We're needed . . . now." Abram pointed, and while he grabbed an apple out of his lunchbox, his two Amish coworkers looked through the back window of the van. Pretty sure the issue was with breeching and the buckles on the trace lines, Abram grabbed his tool belt.

"Abram's right. Let us out."

Mr. Carver pressed the brakes without another question, and they began to slow. The woman and rig were already several hundred feet behind them but were coming their way at a quick pace.

Mr. Carver brought the vehicle to a complete stop. "I'll give you guys a few minutes, but I'm not waiting for long. I'm tired, and I'm hungry."

Abram scurried out of the van. J. B. and Benny were right behind him. While heading for the far side of the road, Abram strapped on his tool belt and tucked the apple inside it, freeing his hands so he could catch the horse if he broke from his constraints.

"What's the plan?" Benny asked, taking long strides with his short legs. The man carried an extra hundred pounds, and he wouldn't be much help catching up with the rig.

"J. B., you try to get in the cart with her. If things go awry, help her get out. Benny, watch for oncoming vehicles. Slow them and warn us. I'll aim to stop the horse."

"Hey." J. B. trotted after Abram. "Is that Cilla and Barbie?"

Abram hoped it wasn't Barbie, but another look said it was.

Great. Just what he needed to add more confusion to his life — a woman he didn't understand. So what were Barbie and her younger sister Cilla doing out here anyway? They were in the boonies, and Cilla's health was too fragile to chance her getting caught in a situation like this.

He held up the apple, hoping the horse would catch a whiff and want to stop. Now that the horse was closer, Abram thought he could see several issues and why Barbie was standing to address the problem. Although the horse was approaching at a speedy trot, it appeared a tug had broken and a stave had flopped free. With the lightweight cart bouncing all over the place, if Barbie stopped in the wrong way, the horse could end up impaled on the stave.

"Easy, boy."

For the first time Barbie looked up from her efforts with the trace lines. Relief eased the tension on her face, and the sweet, welcoming smile he'd come to know over the last few months, the one that had encouraged him to ask her out, graced her lips.

Women. There was simply no way for someone like Abram to understand them, even though he had a twin sister. One might think that would give him an edge, and maybe it would someday, but evidently it wouldn't do so with the one woman who counted most.

Not wanting to startle the horse by speaking loud enough for Barbie to hear him, he motioned toward J. B., who was still running toward the cart. Abram showed the apple to Barbie before he motioned to the horse. She nodded and pointed to the trace line. He could only assume a trace line had broken, but what about the harness? Her family, like his, struggled financially, which meant things like harnesses weren't replaced or repaired as often as needed.

The horse must've noticed the apple because he planted his two front hoofs firm for a moment, trying to come to a halt. He then whinnied as if in pain and continued onward. Abram's best guess was the stave had jabbed him as he tried to stop, so Abram grabbed the dangling stave and held on to it with all he had, knowing what was about to happen.

Barbie pulled back on the lines. "Whoa!"

Abram bore the brunt of the pressure on the stave as the horse came to a halt. Abram's heart pounded mercilessly, and he'd broken out in a sweat, but as easy as that, the dangerous situation was resolved. He panted while patting the horse and regaining his breath. It was odd how a situation could be dangerous one moment and only a minor inconvenience the next.

Unfortunately, now came the really tricky part — facing Barbie. Maybe he was feeling a bit dramatic because his adrenaline was running pretty high, but after preventing the horse from being speared by the stave, Abram felt as if a sharp object might impale him. He'd admired her from afar for a couple of years, and it had been bad enough that she had come to his home to end the relationship before the first date.

Cilla stood, a bright grin on her face as she leaned out to see him. "Denki, Abram."

"*Gern gschehne,* Cilla."

Benny hurried over to them, and while he

and J. B. checked on Barbie and Cilla, Abram walked from the side of the horse to its front, patting its neck reassuringly before using his pocketknife to slice the apple and feed the fruit to the horse.

"Denki." Barbie was out of breath. "I didn't know what I was going to do."

"You can thank Abram. We didn't even see you," Benny said.

Abram kept his focus on the horse, but he could see that Barbie was looking at him.

"Denki, Abram."

Abram gave the worn-out harness a once-over. "Not a problem." But this rigging should've been retired years ago.

"Hey!" Mr. Carver hung his arm out the window. "How much longer?"

J. B. moved toward Abram. "Can you fix this on your own and get her to her place? It's not more than a one-man job, and if it's all the same to you, I think we'll go on home."

Abram agreed that it required only one of them, but did it have to be him?

On second thought he knew the other three men had wives and children waiting for them. With Ariana busy trying to earn money so she could afford the café, Abram was sure no one would mind or feel unsettled because he wasn't home on time.

"Sure." He checked a pocket of his tool belt to verify he had his leather hole punch. Clearly the harness would need repairs. "I need some leather strips from the van, and then you can go."

"Sure thing." J. B. turned to Benny. "Abram can handle this."

While J. B. and Benny spoke to Barbie, Abram went to the van and grabbed the only leather strap left in the scrap box. He hoped this would be enough if he needed to add an extender or replace a segment to mend the harness. The Amish men he knew were as prepared to deal with faulty harnesses and issues with horses as any Englisch mechanic was to work on a car.

The men got in the van and waved as they pulled off. Having just gotten the strip of leather from the van, Abram was on the side of the road where the van had been. Once they were gone, he couldn't have been more uncomfortable if he had been wearing only a towel after getting out of a shower.

Barbie watched him. Cilla too, but she didn't rattle him. He drew a deep breath before crossing the road. He could do this. It was certainly easier than the awkward misery of trying to strike up a conversation after a singing. Once the singing was over and the separation between the boys and girls ended, the young people would mingle. The chaperones, which meant family, neighbors, and church leaders — a few of whom were waiting for something embarrassing to happen so they would have stories to talk about — watched like hawks as the young people ate from the spread of treats they'd provided. If being shy and uncomfortable around girls wasn't difficult enough, having an audience of onlooking parents added to the misery.

Eighteen-year-old Cilla started to step out of the cart, but Barbie grabbed her arm and shook her head. Cilla frowned but took a seat beside her older sister. Both remained in the cart, sitting on the bench and observing Abram as he went to the harness to assess what needed to be done first and how. The air around them was stifling with thoughts no one voiced. The only one seemingly at ease and content to be there was the horse, which continued to chomp on the apple.

"Well, there's good news." Abram noted that the breeching, the part that went around the horse's rump, needed repairing before the tug, and then he would have to add an extender to the trace lines. What a jumbled mess of tattered leather. "It's a good thing this didn't happen to you at night or while it was raining."

"True." Barbie's singular word sounded forced.

He didn't look at her. It would only make it harder not to be lured into longing for a real and deep relationship with her. *Just be yourself and stick to the job.* Sounded easy enough, so why was his heart racing like mad? "I'll have it fixed within the hour, but it would be best if you didn't use this harness again."

"It was my fault," Cilla said. "When I hitched the horse, I wasn't paying attention. I was in a hurry, and now I've just made things worse."

Abram got the leather hole punch out of his tool belt and added fresh holes to the leather patch. "Since you're in a hurry, if you give me your word you won't use this harness again, I'll rig it together and get you two on your way as soon as possible."

"If I give you my word," Barbie said, "would you trust it? I mean, after, you know . . ."

"I'm sure you had good reasons to call off our date."

He heard the two sisters whispering, and Cilla had a scolding tone, but that's all he could tell.

"I . . . I think I did." Her voice wavered.

It had to be from the stress of what had just happened.

He wanted to look her in the eye and ask what the reason was, but his desire to understand wasn't even close to the most important thing going on in his life. "You're safe, Barbie. Just take a few moments to relax and let that sink in." Using a metal brad from his tool belt, he connected the old leather of the breeching to a piece of the new leather.

"Ya, we are. Thanks to you," Cilla said.

He couldn't keep from looking up. Cilla was relaxed against the bench seat, all smiles. Barbie had her forehead buried in her hand, hiding the rest of her face. Surely there was something he could say to make her feel better. "Knock, knock."

Cilla laughed, and Barbie looked up, bewildered.

He chuckled and shrugged before trying again. "Knock, knock."

"Who's there?" Barbie sounded as if she was afraid those weren't the right words.

"Beets."

"Are you serious?" She stared wide eyed, but his goal was to get her mind off the stress and danger, and he wasn't giving up.

With the breeching patched, he moved to the tug and began working with another small piece of leather. He couldn't see her from this spot. "You want to start from the beginning? Or pick it up from when I said 'beets'?"

There was a long pause, and the girls whispered to each other again before he heard her faint voice. "Beets who?"

"Beets me."

He heard one girl laugh — obviously Cilla, so he decided to try again. "Knock, knock."

Barbie must've moved to the far side of the bench, because she was peering around the horse to see him. "Who's there?"

"Yacht."

"Yacht who?"

"Yacht a know me by now."

Cilla stifled a giggle.

"Abram?" Barbie sounded better, a little calmer.

He cut a thin piece of leather from the tug. "Ya?"

Barbie climbed down. "You're different tonight."

"Am I?" He thought about it for a moment.

"Ya."

She patted the horse's back, her hand trembling. "I'm not sure what would've

162

happened if you hadn't come by when you did."

"My part was a coincidence, so God gets the credit for the timing."

"Seems odd, but" — Cilla got out of the wagon — "after all these years of knowing you, I'm still caught off guard by your kindness." She looked at Barbie and shook her head, as if annoyed with her.

Barbie shrugged.

Rather than get caught between two feuding sisters, Abram decided to change the subject. "So what has you two in a hurry and in the boondocks?"

Neither girl responded, but Abram saw Cilla nudge Barbie with her elbow. When Barbie didn't speak up, Cilla did. "Our brother Eli needs a medicine that wasn't available at the closest pharmacy. We're returning home with it."

That explained everything. Two of the Yoder siblings dealt with illness — Cilla and Eli. Sometimes, like today, Cilla seemed as strong as any other young woman, and then she'd be sick and unable to leave the house for a month or more. She had cystic fibrosis. Eli had asthma.

But it had taken him entirely too long to get this vital piece of information. If either girl had said something when they finally stopped the horse, Mr. Carver could've taken them home. Abram began removing the rigging from the horse. "Get the medicine out of the cart, and you can both ride home bareback."

Barbie stroked the horse again. "We can't leave the cart. Someone could take it or damage it, and Daed needs it to make a living."

Their Daed worked at a local market, and he made deliveries to Englisch shut-ins. This rig was lightweight and fast, so it was vital to her Daed's job. "I'll stay with the cart. Send your brother Matt back for it. I'll have the harness repaired by then."

Barbie didn't move. "Cilla can't ride bareback. It's physically exhausting and can trigger issues with her breathing."

Cilla's cheeks turned pink, but she looked more angry than embarrassed by what Barbie had said. "Sorry."

"You have nothing to apologize for. Barbie should go ahead, though." He motioned toward the cart. "Go on, Barbie. Get the medicine." While she did as he said, he rushed to get the unnecessary harness off, leaving the bridle and reins. She returned with the small white bag, and he intertwined his fingers and offered her a boost onto the horse.

She paused, seeming as if she had hundreds of words on the tip of her tongue. But she simply smiled and gave a nod of gratitude before she put her booted foot in his hands.

Was this incident more than just Abram being the closest person to lend a hand? Had God allowed him to be a part of it for a reason that might draw Barbie to him after all?

ELEVEN

Lovina tapped on the screen door of Rachel's home. The lack of horses at the hitching post could mean there weren't any women here today to deliver babies. She hoped so, because what had to be said needed privacy, and Lovina didn't think she could stand waiting one more day.

Isaac shifted. "Do you usually knock?"

"Nee. But since you are with me, I thought I would." Lovina found that every word took effort. Shortness of breath had been a regular thing since Mark had brought home the flier.

"Kumm." Rachel came into sight, carrying a basket of laundry. She smiled and motioned for them.

Isaac opened the door, and Lovina went in first.

Rachel set the laundry basket on the kitchen table. "What has you two coming by here? I know you're not with child again . . . right?"

Since Lovina was fifty-five years old, her days of having babies were long gone. It didn't make her sad exactly, but it did make her feel old. Some days it seemed as if the future, with its chaos and energy and special joys, belonged to the young people.

"Nee. Nothing like that." Lovina reached into the bib of her apron and touched the well-worn flier. The more she considered the possibility that she had a daughter out in the world, the more she kept this flier close to her heart. Still, she prayed fervently, even when she was awakened in the middle of the night, that her imagination had come up with this nonsense. What would she do if she had a daughter out there somewhere? "Are there any expectant moms here today?"

"Nee. The place is quiet and empty." Rachel went to the cabinet and grabbed two glasses. "Do you have time for some ice water or lemonade?" She set them on the counter and reached for a third.

"Not today." Isaac folded his arms. "What do you remember —"

Lovina elbowed him. What? No lead-in? No softening of the subject so Rachel wouldn't feel they were questioning her integrity as a midwife?

Rachel turned, glass in hand. "You sure?"

"I'm sure." Isaac glanced at Lovina, his expression reminding her that he was here for only one purpose — the truth.

"Rach." Lovina's mouth was dry. Was it from the discomfort of putting her friend on the spot or fear of what they might find out? She glanced around. "Do you still like this new birthing center better than the other one?"

"Ya, sure. What's not to like?" Rachel moved to the sink and filled the glass with water. "You're here about the rumors of the out-of-wedlock pregnancy, aren't you?"

This was the first Lovina had heard of this rumor.

Isaac's face flushed, obviously offended by the question. "If we were in doubt about such a thing, we wouldn't come to you. We would talk to our sons and daughters."

"Well, I can assure you it's not one of your girls, and the girl didn't mention your sons." She took a sip of water.

Isaac looked more perturbed by the minute. These two, Rachel and Isaac, simply rubbed each other the wrong way.

Lovina inched forward, hoping her husband would take the hint and let her do the talking. "Rach," — Lovina swallowed hard — "we've talked many times about the day you delivered our twins, recounting the fire and the craziness."

"That we have." She lifted the glass to her lips but then lowered it before taking a drink. "But why bring this up now?" Was that fear in her friend's eyes?

"Well," — Lovina removed the flier from the bib of her apron — "what else do you remember about that day? Anything that we've never talked about?"

"I . . . I don't know what you mean. You were there. What's to tell that we haven't discussed?" She took a long drink, appearing to Lovina as if she was trying to hide behind the glass of water.

"True. But I was wondering if there was any possibility . . ." Lovina couldn't finish the question. It was too close to accusing Rachel of being negligent.

Isaac pressed his fingers against the table in front of him. "Is there any chance, any at all, that maybe the two girls were switched?"

Rachel choked on the water, not a normal cough that she'd get over easily. She put the glass on the counter, fighting for air, and lifted her hands above her head and paced the floor. Lovina glanced at Isaac, seeing as much accusation in his eyes as there must have been fear in hers.

Isaac paused for a few moments, probably

giving Rachel time to catch her breath. Then he took the flier from Lovina's hand and strode toward Rachel. "We've learned there's a girl who looks remarkably like Salome. The girl is connected to this flier, and there is a woman in this flier named Brandi Nash."

Rachel lowered her arms, still coughing and clearing her throat. "Ariana is yours. I'm sure of it."

"How sure, Rach?" Lovina's voice trembled.

"Abram wouldn't hush crying until I put her in the bassinet with him. I know they shared the same womb."

Lovina's world began to tilt. "Are you saying you were uncertain which girl was ours, and Abram hushing at the right time was the test?"

"No. I . . . I'm absolutely positive each girl went home with the right family, the family God intended."

Isaac turned to Lovina. "Is it just me, or is she wording things on purpose so we can't be sure what she means?"

Lovina eyed her old friend, and upon reflection she realized what Isaac had heard. "I don't think it's you."

He left the room and returned a few seconds later with a Bible in hand. He held it out. "Put your hand on the Bible, Rachel."

"What? Why?"

Isaac thrust the Bible toward her. "Put your hand on it, and before God tell us that, to your knowledge, you're confident Ariana is the daughter Lovina gave birth to."

Rachel stared at him for several long moments. She buried her head in both hands and sat in the closest chair. "I . . . I can't," she whispered.

Lovina's emotions ran in every direction. Anger. Terror. Fear. Grief. What was she supposed to do with this information? It was too much. She had a hundred questions. A thousand shards of rage.

"How likely is it that they were switched?" Isaac asked.

Rachel didn't raise her head, but Lovina heard raspy breathing, as if she had been running. And maybe she had . . . for two decades. "I . . . I'm not sure." She raised her head, looking at Isaac. "While you took the woman outside, I put her baby girl in the bassinet beside Lovina as she gave birth to a daughter. We had the girls separated, but then Lovina's water broke for a second time, and I realized there was another baby coming. We had to get out of the house because of the fire, and we put the girls in the same bassinet."

"I don't recall the girls being put in the same crib." Lovina's heart pounded as she grasped what Rachel was admitting to, and something Lovina had never felt before took hold of her — rage. "How could you go all these years and never tell me that part?" Lovina screeched, not recognizing her own voice. Whose emotions were these? "When I realized I had the wrong pink blanket, before Ariana was a year old, I came to you, and you promised me that I had nothing to worry about!" Lovina flew across the kitchen and smacked Rachel on the side of the head before her husband wrapped his arm around her waist and pulled her back. Lovina struggled to get free. "We knew Brandi Nash's life was probably a train wreck! We talked about it!" Lovina swung her arms at Rachel, wanting to make contact. "What kind of disaster did you let my daughter grow up in?"

Her world went red.

The next thing Lovina noticed was the familiar *clippety-clop* of the horse's hoofs against the wooden boards of the covered bridge. How did they get here?

Isaac had one hand on the reins and one around her shoulders. She gulped in air. "What happened?"

172

"You don't remember?"

She shook her head.

"I think you blacked out from the rage."

Lovina snuggled against her husband and broke into sobs. "How can this be happening? Why didn't we follow through on our fears . . ."

Isaac rubbed her arm sympathetically. "I don't know, but those aren't the right questions. We have to focus on the right ones." His voice cracked, and when she looked up, there were tears in his eyes.

She sat upright, wiping her face. "Like what?"

"What does God want us to do from here? What do we tell Ariana? What do we tell our other children?"

Lovina didn't recall ever being angry or disappointed with God before. "He knew this situation the whole time, and He's allowed us to know it now. So I think the next decisions are up to us."

Isaac nodded. "Seems reasonable."

Lovina needed answers, but she didn't feel like praying. Still she longed to. How did anyone operate without prayer? How was she to talk to God when she felt betrayed by Him?

Isaac turned onto a narrow dirt road they hadn't been on in twenty years. He was meandering the back roads, giving them time and privacy. "We shouldn't say anything to Ariana, and we have to be sure no rumors get started."

"What about Rachel?"

Isaac's jaw clenched. "I warned her not to speak of this to anyone, and she agreed. I don't think a woman who kept the possibility of this a secret all these years will begin talking about it now."

How could Rachel have deceived her like this? The possibility that the girls had been switched had nagged both her and Isaac a few times over the years. Why hadn't they pursued it?

Lush branches swayed on a familiar huge oak on the creek bank, bringing back sweet memories. She and Isaac used to picnic under that tree. When courting, they would come here to talk without fear of being heard. A tiny fragment of thankfulness tugged at her heart. At least she had Isaac as she went through this, the one person who had been at her side since she was younger than Ariana, and apparently he loved her even when she blacked out with rage.

She put her arm through his. "Ya, without question we must keep this quiet, but I have to see her." Beyond all the confusion and hurt, Lovina's gut told her she would know the next step once she saw her. "How would we locate the girl?" Using the word *girl* made her feel dirty somehow. If she was their daughter, she deserved a better term than *girl*.

Isaac shook his head. "I'm not sure."

"Does Rachel have records? A name, an old address, something?"

"All Rachel had was lost in the fire, and probably from the full panic of the night, Rachel's been unable to recall more than the woman's name."

"Brandi Nash." Even Lovina knew that much. Since that night at the birthing clinic, Lovina had prayed for her and her daughter . . . maybe *their* daughter. But Lovina hadn't been extremely consistent with her prayers. If she'd known the girl might be hers, she would've been much more faithful to pray.

Isaac grabbed the brim of his hat, adjusting it. "Because she was sent to the hospital, Rachel didn't have to file a birth certificate. The hospital did that."

"Then we can go to the courthouse and search for babies born on that day, right?"

"Maybe. Is that what we're going to do? Two Amish people at the courthouse searching through birth records that match the day our twins were born?"

He was right, of course. It felt as if their hands were tied. No one would stick out as much as Amish people combing through government records. It just wasn't their way. But there had to be a solution.

Lovina gasped, grabbing her husband's arm as a name came to her. She shuddered. Surely not. She hated the idea, but the longer she thought about it, the more she knew it would work. "Quill Schlabach."

"We need someone we can trust, and you think Quill is the answer?" He sounded baffled and angry.

"Apparently he's been able to sneak in and take a few single people and a whole family away without the slightest rumor giving forewarning. He knows how to plan and execute with no one being the wiser. We need that skill."

"Quill has betrayed the Amish more than once, and if we use him for our benefit, we are guilty of betrayal too."

"He knows our ways and the Englisch ways. He must be very savvy."

"*Deceptive* is the word."

"He apparently is quite familiar with the world's system, and we need that skill too. He has a car that could take us wherever we need to go to see this young woman."

"True. If we get a lead, we can't hire an Englisch driver, or that could become the source of rumors. I guess we have no choice."

"But how do Amish people even reach Quill?" She'd wondered that many times over the years, but she still didn't have a clue.

"I don't know, but right now, since his Mamm has been sick, my guess is she knows how to reach him."

Everything about this felt dishonest. Good Amish people didn't pry into the comings or goings of ex-Amish. They didn't use a sick mom to reach her wayward son in order to get help. But if Lovina knew anything at all, she knew Berta would get the message to her son if she could, and she wouldn't say anything to anyone.

Isaac tugged on the reins, stopping the rig before pulling onto the paved road. If he turned right, it would lead back to their home, and if he turned left, it would take them by Berta's. "If we choose to pursue this, there is no going back."

Lovina's whole body ached from the pain inside her heart. "I can't live without closure. I just can't."

He nodded. "Can we trust Quill enough to make ourselves reach out to him?"

"I would never reach out to him just as a person, but in this, ya. I can't live in this miserable state of not knowing."

Besides, what option did they have other than to trust Quill?

TWELVE

Bellflower Creek, Pennsylvania

Skylar Nash chewed on her thumbnail as she drove down the campus road toward the theater. Of all the days to run late . . .

Her boyfriend unwrapped a piece of gum. "Want one?"

"No." If she walked into the theater with gum in her mouth, Patrick would have her removing gum from under the campus café tables for hours. Another round of jitters ran through her. Patrick Merrow was a great drama teacher, but he was a hard man to figure. He had endless patience when helping students improve their performances but no mercy for their being more than a few minutes late to class. He allowed some leeway for students coming from classes on the far side of the campus, but she didn't have that excuse. Surely he wouldn't give Brittany the part Skylar had worked so hard to earn just because she was late on the day he intended to make the announcements.

Cody leaned across her, looking at the gauges on the dashboard. "You're out of gas, and I'm out of money."

With one hand on the wheel, she dug into the pocket of her jeans shorts. Where was the cash her mom had given her this morning? She felt the edge of the paper money and wriggled it out of the tight fit. "This won't get much, but it's all I have for now."

Cody glanced at the fifteen dollars. "Thanks." He tucked it into his shirt pocket. "I get paid tomorrow, and I'll make this up to you then."

"Don't worry about it. We both use the car, and we both put gas in it." Her mom wasn't a fan of Skylar lending her car, but her dad had given her the used car, and she was free to do with it what she wanted. One of the perks of parents not living together is that each allowed things the other didn't. And she usually knew how to play that game to her advantage. Actually, she should be better at it than she was since her experience pretty much covered her life span.

"What time are you done today?" Cody asked.

"Hard to tell. Last class is over at two, and we don't have a performance tonight since it's Labor Day weekend, but we have to hit the pavement and sell tickets for the last performances next weekend. No matter where Patrick sends us to sell tickets, we'll be done by nine."

"It still seems weird that you call the drama teacher by his first name."

"Everyone does. It's what he wants."

Cody played with the empty gum wrapper. "Can you hitch a ride with someone?"

"Of course." She had gone to high school with several of the people now attending this community college. Friends who would give her a lift were easy to come by, and she had bought lunch for others lots of times, so someone would buy her one today, since she'd just given away all her cash.

He rolled his eyes. "My bad. I forget what it's like for the local star."

She reached across the console and pinched his cheek mockingly. "Better get used to it." She laughed at her joke, but they both knew she had plans.

This community college was a stepping-stone. She'd been a part of the theater here since she was a sophomore in high school with dual enrollment. Her goal was to be accepted to the Carnegie Mellon University, School of Drama — specifically to study acting and musical theater. If she could just get in, she would be able to fulfill her every dream. The reason she had yet to apply irked her.

After studying music and acting since she was young, in hopes of going to CMU, she'd been caught breaking one of her parents' arbitrary rules when she was a senior in high school. If they'd known all she'd done, they would have had her handcuffed to a chaperon. Because of what they had discovered, her dad refused to pay for her to go away to college, insisting she live at home to attend school until they were confident she was mature enough to handle moving out.

That was bull. If she lived at home throughout all of college, she was never going to see things as her dad wanted her to.

One would think a man as into the arts as he was — teaching voice and music on the college level — would be a little more relaxed about popping an occasional pill or smoking some pot. He probably had been at one point. Since she didn't really know him, she could only guess at such things.

Unfortunately, when it came to substance use, her mother fully agreed with her dad. Her mom had even leveled a look at her and said, *"We are free to choose, but we are not free from the consequences of our choices."*

Some parents were chill. Hers were not.

Shaking free of her meandering thoughts, she drove toward the drama building. The parking lot at the side entrance of the theater was full, a clear reminder of how late she was. She hoped Patrick was too busy dealing with the sound system, lights, or costumes to notice.

It wasn't her fault that just as she stepped out her door with plenty of time to get here, Cody called, saying his car had broken down. He couldn't afford to miss another day of work, even if he did detest his job as stock boy at a clothing store in the local mall.

She put the car in Park and opened her door. "I gotta go before Patrick cuts my solo during the last performances next weekend."

Cody held up her backpack and wagged it back and forth. "Want this?"

"Yeah." She grabbed it, but he didn't let go.

He grinned, a sort of cynical smile that also hinted of mischief. "I'm holding out for a kiss."

"Uh, not this morning, you aren't." She tugged hard, snatching it free from his hands. "There's no time." Once his lips were on hers, she would linger too long. She raised her eyebrows in quick succession. "Rain check." She hopped out of the car and ran toward the theater building.

Cody whistled, one long, shrill sound that equaled calling her name. When she turned, he was out of the car, going to the driver's side. She didn't have any time to lose. Hadn't she given him enough of her morning already?

He pulled the tip of a sandwich baggie out of his jeans pocket with one hand and held up fingers to his mouth as if smoking the joint. "Should I save this until we're together tonight?"

She shook her head. She mouthed the word *no* and extended her hand in the air as if to say, *What are you thinking?* How many times did she need to tell him this?

Cody nodded. He was looking for permission to smoke it at will, and she'd given it to him. Since being caught with pot at seventeen, she had to pee in a cup for drug testing at the whim of her mom and dad. Drug testing. Skylar hated it, but she had no choice — not if she wanted her dad to pay for tuition to Carnegie.

When her mom had found the stash three years ago, she'd threatened to call the police. Skylar talked her out of it by agreeing to give up her current boyfriend, who had given her the drugs and paraphernalia, and to take a drug test at any point after that. With the amount of pot and paraphernalia her mom found, Skylar would've been charged with intent to distribute. As a first-time offender, she probably would have been given probation, but it would've blown all chances of getting into CMU.

Skylar still didn't understand why her mom considered it such a big deal. Recreational use was legalized in some states, and Skylar was sure the Pennsylvania laws would catch up with reality in a few years. In the meantime she wouldn't let any archaic laws ruin her chance at a future.

Besides, when she wanted to get high, pot was not what she looked for. As to other drugs, well, she was glad her parents hadn't required a drug test in nearly a year. They simply asked her if she'd smoked any pot, and she was able to answer honestly — absolutely not. None. They never asked about any other substance.

She hurried into the building, but she didn't hear the usual clamoring voices. That could only mean one thing — class had already started — and it set her nerves on edge. How many nights' sleep had she missed because she longed for the lead in the next play?

A big show was planned for the fall, commemorating the college's fiftieth anniversary. Patrick was staging *Oklahoma,* using alumni from productions over the last few decades as well as the current drama students. If Skylar played Laurey, her name would appear in all the publicity and alumni write-ups, which would add some weight to her application to CMU. She'd heard that the alumni cast included a CEO and a nonprofit board member or two. If she could work with them on the musical, she could probably get a letter of recommendation for CMU. This role was her best shot at garnering serious attention.

Easing open the door to the auditorium, she peered inside. Sure enough, everyone was in the theater seats watching the stage as Patrick talked with his roster in hand. Only the first few rows of chairs had students, and that's where she needed to get without being noticed. She tiptoed down the side and slipped into a chair, hoping to remain unseen.

Patrick didn't glance her way as he continued talking, and after a minute she released a breath, relaxing.

"So" — Patrick held up the iPad in his hand — "we've had one venue cancellation due to the scheduling mix-up, so next Saturday night's performance will be the last for the summertime drama team."

The room vibrated with loud applause, whistles, and shouting.

Patrick gave them a minute to settle. "I appreciate everyone's patience and loyalty as the weeks dragged on just a tiny bit" — he held his thumb and index finger an inch apart — "past the usual cutoff date."

Some of her friends groaned in protest, and others laughed at his joke. The fall semester had begun two weeks ago, and yet they were still performing the summer venues. The summer troupe traveled from place to place to perform, and everything got fouled up when the scheduler had double-booked them. In order to perform at each place as promised, they'd had to reschedule the dates and then continue performing past the start-up of the fall semester.

"All right." Patrick sighed, sounding unusually down and tired. "Let's get this practice under way."

"Hey, Patrick?" Brittany held up her hand, and Skylar slunk back in her cushioned chair, waiting for the girl to say something useless. It was part of her trademark.

"Yes?"

"It's Thursday, the first week in September, right?"

Some of the kids laughed.

Brittany knew what day it was. Not only had she and Skylar been waiting since last spring to learn which of them would be the lead in the next musical, but everyone in this room wanted to know what part they'd earned.

Brad held up his cell phone, showing her the time of day in bold numbers. "You need us to let you know if it's morning or night, too?" he asked.

Brittany wanted to play Laurey every bit as much as Skylar, and the girl was really good. An airhead but a talented one.

Brittany didn't blink at the heckling. She stood. "Well." Her short brown hair bounced as she moved with great animation. She reminded Skylar of Elle Woods from *Legally Blonde,* and similar to Elle she performed every sentence with the wide-eyed enthusiasm of an excited cheerleader. "If Patrick isn't finished yet, we shouldn't rush him, right?"

Did she think her tactics fooled anyone? The scarecrow in Oz came to mind. *"If I only had a brain."* Patrick looked confused by Brittany's question, which was odd, because the man usually gave an answer before the question was asked.

Brad propped his foot on the seat in front of him. "She wants you to say who got what part for the next musical."

"Oh." Patrick glanced at Skylar, and she realized if he knew where she was sitting, he'd known when she came in. "Uh, yeah, well, my plan is to put a list on the corkboard outside my room later today."

That's not how he'd done it in the past. He'd made the announcements from the stage. And why had he looked at Skylar when Brittany asked that question? Brittany wasn't as good an actor, and sometimes her voice got pitchy. On the other hand, Skylar had been late to a few practices, and she'd missed her singing cue twice during the summer.

Patrick lowered the iPad. "If there isn't anything else, let's get started."

Everyone meandered in different directions until they were scattered. The lighting and sound people went to their spots. The stage managers and stagehands began shifting props. Skylar put the strap of her backpack on her shoulder and fell in behind the other actors, heading for the stairs that led backstage.

Patrick waited at the top of the steps, speaking to people as they passed. He caught Skylar's eye and motioned for her. "Could I speak to you for a moment?"

Her heart picked up its pace. "Yeah, sure." She broke rank with the others and followed him out of the theater. "I'm sorry I was late."

"Let's talk in my office." They stepped into his tiny space, and he closed the door. "This isn't about being late, although maybe I should add that to the list."

The list? There was a list? Had she done stuff she was unaware of? She put her backpack on the floor at her feet and sat in the uncomfortable chair across from him. Despite trying not to fidget, she bounced one leg up and down in quick succession. Outside of the theater it wasn't like her to get nervous. Her mode of operation was cavalier, which was a huge part of what got her in trouble. Deadlines for projects and studying didn't matter until it was too late to do anything about them.

He pulled a folder out of a small desk drawer and laid it on the desk. "You know I believe in your talent. You've been a part of this team since you were in high school, and you're seriously one of the best I've worked with. Because of that and because of all your mom does to help out, I've cut you too much slack."

"No you haven't." Without even a pause her mind raced with rationalizations and possible angles for changing his mind. "I work hard, and I have some flaws that need to be ironed out. That's why you cut me some slack. I'll work even harder. I promise."

He rapped his fingers on the folder, and she stared at it. Whatever it held, she wished she could run it through the paper shredder.

"You weren't honest with me, Skylar." Patrick tapped the folder with his index finger.

Had she lied to him? She didn't recall doing so, although in her get-out-of-trouble mode, she tended to say whatever it took to convince the person. "I don't understand."

"At the end of the spring semester, you told me you were going to take summer classes that would fix the issue with your GPA."

"That wasn't a lie. I have proof that I attended school all summer." The last time she'd checked her grades, which was online two weeks ago, right after her summer finals were posted, her grades looked good. "I passed my two summer classes with a high B in each." And it hadn't been easy, especially considering how grueling the summer theater program was this year. "That pulled my GPA above requirements to stay in theater." She had hoped to do better than a B in those classes, but unlike a full semester, she'd had to cover a ton of information packed into just a few weeks of class time.

She pulled her phone out of her pocket, ready to show him how well she had done.

"Put it away, Skylar. I have the same information in this folder. Of the two classes you took, you did well. The problem is you failed psychology last spring."

"But I told you that at the end of the semester."

"Yes, you did. And it was my understanding that you were retaking it over the summer."

"I tried, but psychology isn't offered in the summer. I began it two weeks ago with the fall courses, and I've already made an A on the first test. I can pass the course this time. I know I can."

Why had she chosen to go on a weekend trip last spring when she'd needed that time to study for the final? She'd known she was on the cusp of pass or fail, but she'd followed Peter, her then boyfriend, to the beach with a group of his friends. Then after she failed the class, she learned he'd been cheating on her for months. "I made a silly mistake, and it cost me a passing grade. It won't happen again."

"I wish that were good enough." He played with the edge of the file. "I hate to have to tell you this, but —"

"Nooo. Please, Patrick." She knew she was whining, but she didn't care. "If you don't want to say it, then don't. I can make this right."

"I believe you. But there are two protocols to being allowed to participate in extracurricular activities at this school. Your summer classes pulled up your GPA, but that's only one of the criteria. No one can have a failing grade in any mandatory class and continue performing in sports or the arts."

"Oh, come on, Patrick."

"Sorry, Sky. You're on academic probation, and the only reason you weren't told that months ago is because your counselor had her baby prematurely, and some grades slipped through the cracks." He opened his desk drawer. "The rules are what they are. When you finish the psychology course, the two grades — the failing one and this semester's — will be averaged, and if that gives you a passing grade for psychology, you will be allowed to rejoin tryouts for the following performance. While on academic probation, you could be a stagehand."

"You want me to make sure Brittany's spotlight, sound equipment, and costumes are in good order? No thanks."

"Then you'll need to drop theater for this semester. Maybe a break will do you some good." He put the file in the drawer and locked it. "I did what I could, but it seems we're both in some trouble here. Even though the front office was unaware you'd failed a mandatory class, I wasn't, and I shouldn't have let you continue in the summer program. The bit of good news is that because of that A you've already made on your first psychology test, I managed to get permission for you to finish the last performances of the current musical, but that's all I could do."

"I've put effort into doing everything you've wanted for four years."

"I know, and you're a huge part of the reason our ticket sales have increased over the last couple of years."

"But the theater's fiftieth-anniversary performance would be my best chance to stand out in a sea of applicants to CMU."

"I don't want to discourage you, and I know you believe in the dream, but I doubt you can pull up your GPA enough to satisfy CMU. Maybe you should rethink that plan."

Was that true? She grabbed her backpack, slung it at the closed door, and cursed.

Patrick didn't flinch. "Pick up your bag and watch your language, Sky."

She snatched her bag off the floor. But the hardness of his soft-spoken words was unbearable. Had she been living in a fantasy world to hold on to her dream of CMU? Skylar put the strap of her bag on her shoulder. "So if this hadn't happened?"

He stood. "Yeah, you were going to be the lead."

She leaned against the door and thudded the back of her head against it numerous times. Why had she let anyone, especially cheater Peter, talk her into going away that weekend? After gaining some control, she stood upright and wrapped both hands around the strap of her backpack. "I'd like to cut practice today."

"I understand. You know your part well."

"Thanks. Any chance you could hold off posting the information until after my last performance next weekend?" That would keep her from having to face the entire troupe once they realized she didn't even get a bit part in the next play.

"I'm not sure, but I'll see what I can do."

"I appreciate it, and thanks for fighting for me."

"I would say *anytime,* but I need this job." He didn't look as much like a teacher right now as a middle-aged man who'd been backed into a corner by his boss.

She left his office, and anger warred within her as she walked toward the exit.

Brittany looked at her as she passed. She turned away quickly, but not before she saw the smirk on Brittany's face.

Wasn't there something she could do to reverse this decision? There had to be. Ideas began pounding her brain. Oh, so many ideas.

But just how far was she willing to go to get back on stage before the semester was over?

THIRTEEN

From behind a booth on the green space of old town Summer Grove, Ariana paused to take in the view. The town buzzed with people for Labor Day weekend. A band was on a stage, playing patriotic music. Booths were set up here and there, some of them selling foods but most selling crafts.

For the first time since they began selling foods at nine that morning, they had no one at their booth. Using a hand towel, she wiped sweat from her face. They could use a roof over their booth to give them some reprieve from the sun.

She pulled a wristwatch out of her apron pocket. Eight minutes past three. What a wonderfully busy day it'd been. At last count they had made nearly $400 today. She still needed thousands more to go to closing, but what a testimony to the idea of owning the café. Four hundred dollars in profits in a day? Her head was spinning. Of course, this type of town event was rare, but if the café made a fourth of that six days a week, that would be nearly $30,000 a year before taxes. If they could make $200 a day, lack for her parents and siblings would become a memory. Oh, how she longed for that.

She removed the last tray of sandwiches from the cooler. She'd baked the croissants as the sun rose and then loaded the bread with thinly sliced deli meats and wrapped them individually. This was the kind of item she wanted to sell at the café. Simple and tasty.

She turned to Susie. "Where are the other trays of sandwiches?"

Scrubbing mustard stains off the booth's countertops, Susie grinned. "Everything is selling like hot cakes. Isn't it great?"

Ariana had soaked in every passing minute since Susie had agreed not to leave the Amish, and her sister was wildly enthusiastic about their endeavors, even when they stayed up baking half the night. So Ariana didn't wish to dampen her sister's fun, but she held up the now-empty tray, silently asking about it.

"Ya," Susie said, "that's the last of what we brought. I thought Rudy let you know."

Rudy entered the booth, carrying a

grocery bag. They had needed more coffee, sugar, and cream, so he had run to the closest store for them. "Did I hear my name?"

Ariana pursed her lips, half smirking at Susie. "What you heard was my little sister throwing you under the buggy."

"Well," — Rudy winked at Ariana — "as long as you are with me, I won't mind." He set the items on the counter. "So what's the problem?"

"We are going to be out of sandwiches soon, and I didn't realize that." Ariana wondered how quickly she and Susie could run home, put more together, and return.

Susie opened the grocery bag and pulled out the coffee. "So here's the good news: apparently opening a café that sells sandwiches, scones, and other simple lunch items is going to be quite hot." She licked her index finger and pressed it against Ariana's shoulder and made a sizzling noise. "Yes, folks. Hot like my big sister."

Ariana suppressed the desire to correct her sister's risqué remarks. It seemed to her it would be best not to nitpick. "Be that as it may," — Ariana pulled the sugar and cream out of the bag — "you and I need to go home and make more sandwiches. I hope Mamm put the rest of the croissants in to bake after we left."

"You're going to leave Rudy here by himself?"

"He doesn't mind. The two of us will make short work of it."

"Oh, face it, Ariana." Susie put both hands on her hips, a mischievous smile on her lips. "You just want to make your little sister a clone of yourself."

Rudy's eyes met Ari's, and he seemed to be thinking the same thing she was — sometimes it was difficult to know how to take Susie's cheekiness.

His smile replaced the hint of uncertainty. "It would be okay with me if you become a clone of Ariana. You could do the work while I take your sister out. I like that plan, actually."

"We're leaving now." Susie grabbed Ariana's hand and tugged her out of the booth. "And I hope you are overrun with throngs of people wanting sandwiches you do not happen to have."

Rudy held up a couple of sandwiches. "But I have some and plenty of coffee," he teased.

Ariana waved at Rudy, and then she decided to do something she had not done to any adult — she blew him a kiss. His dimpled grin greeted the action. Then she picked up the pace, pulling Susie along while hurrying away.

They wasted no time hopping into the rig. Ariana reached for the reins, but Susie grabbed them. "I'll take those. Denki."

"Fine by me. Just be careful of pedestrians. It will only slow us down if you run over someone and we have to stop to deal with it."

Susie burst into laughter. "All right! My sarcastic ways are finally beginning to rub off on my big sister."

After winding their way through the busyness of town, they were able to pick up speed and make up for a little lost time. Ariana leaned back, tired but really happy.

Where was Quill about now? Susie had surely told him that she didn't intend to leave the Amish. Had he gone home, back to wherever he lived?

As they passed his mother's home, she saw a car at the foot of the porch stairs with the passenger door open. The screen door banged open, and Quill walked out, carrying his mother.

What was Quill up to now? Ariana took the reins from Susie. "I need to check on this."

Was Berta sick again? Did Quill think he could run off with her as he'd done with Frieda? Ariana's thoughts made little sense, and all she knew for sure was she didn't trust Quill Schlabach — not concerning his Mamm's health or his respect for her wishes.

"Who is that carrying Berta?"

Apparently Susie didn't recognize Quill with his baseball cap on and in jeans and a T-shirt. Susie's main contact with him had probably been during the cover of night. Or maybe they'd made all plans through phone calls and letters.

"Just stay put, okay?" Ariana barely stopped the rig before she tossed the reins at Susie and jumped out. "What's going on?" She hurried up the steps.

"She passed out cold, and since rousing a bit, she's been addled. I'm taking her to the hospital."

Is that what Berta needed, to be rushed to the ER? Unless medical help was absolutely necessary, it wasn't worth how draining it would be on Berta emotionally. Probably financially too — at least that's what Ariana had assumed before she realized Quill was a part of her life. "Put her down and let me think for a second, okay?"

Quill paused, looking unsure whether to trust Ariana in such matters. "But —"

"I . . . I'm okay." His Mamm's eyes fluttered open, and she looked more asleep than awake. She lifted her hand to his cheek. "Do as she says."

He awkwardly eased her onto the top step. Ariana knelt beside her. Quill got on the other side.

She pressed her fingers against Berta's wrist. "How are you feeling?" Her pulse seemed shallow, and Ariana wished she knew more about such matters.

"Dizzy, but better," Berta whispered.

What little Ariana knew about the pulse, fainting, and blood pressure, she'd learned from the nurses and doctors during Berta's most recent illness. "She began blood-pressure medicine a few weeks ago. The doctor said that while her body was adjusting to the medication, fainting could be a side effect."

Quill seemed relieved. "Does that mean there's no real danger?"

Ariana studied Berta, disliking the gray tint to her skin. "I think so."

"If you're not sure, I'm taking her in to be seen."

Ariana finished checking Berta's pulse before she looked up. The desire to point a finger at Quill and do all within her power to make him see how wrong he'd been all these years was overwhelming. When had she stepped into those hideous shoes, the ones that belonged to some bitter, self-righteous minister's wife? "Just give me a few minutes!" After snapping, she wrestled her inner grudge holder into submission and forced the next word to the surface. "Pl . . . please?"

"It can't hurt to take her in." Quill's steely blue eyes bore into her. "What's the issue? Are you afraid I'm going to kidnap her?"

Ariana's cheeks tingled, and she hoped they weren't turning red.

He scoffed, releasing a burst of laughter that mixed with sharp disbelief. "You're kidding. Seriously, Ari?"

"She hates hospitals, and they're expensive, but . . ." Should she admit how little she trusted him? She released a slow breath of air, hoping to take the edge off her uptight emotions. "Ya, the . . . the kidnapping thought did sort of cross my mind."

"Even you should know I wouldn't do anything against someone's will."

"Even me? Just what does that mean?" As soon as she asked, she held up her hand, shushing him before he could respond. "I don't want to know." They had to call a truce, a real one where they came to an understanding that they would never agree about anything of real value, but right now their focus needed to be on Berta.

"Friede dezwische du Zwee," Berta whispered breathlessly.

"So denk ich aa." Ariana nodded, assuring Berta that she wanted peace between them too. She was weary of falling just short of hating Quill . . . if she fell short of it.

Berta seemed unable to catch a full breath. "None of what happened was within Quill's power to stop." She turned to her son. "Tell her."

Quill gently sandwiched his Mamm's hand between his. "Sh. Mamm, *es iss all-recht.*"

His assurance that it would be all right and his tenderness with his Mamm warred with the strange words Berta had spoken. Except for the loss of his Daed, Quill had never seemed to have a powerless moment in his life. He took control, even of his own fears and grief.

Berta grasped Ariana's wrist and placed her palm on the back of Quill's hand and then sandwiched their hands between hers. "Peace."

Ariana's heart felt as if it would explode from the opposing emotions swelling within it — the need for peace and the desire to unleash years of bitter disappointment in Quill. She prayed for help while fighting against her righteous indignation.

Taking a breath — and a step of faith — she wrapped her fingers over his and squeezed. Unlike her, he didn't hesitate in his response. He returned the gesture. Moments ago it had seemed obvious that she and Quill needed to find some measure of goodwill between them, but maybe it was just she who needed to find it.

She pulled her hand free and checked Berta's pulse again. "What was going on right before she fainted?"

"She was on the couch, reading, when I went in to say good-bye. She seemed fine until she stood. The next thing I knew she was swaying, and by the time I grabbed her, she was out cold."

"Ya, standing up too fast with this new med in her was probably the cause." She checked the pulse points in her feet as the doctor had showed her, making sure her circulation was normal. "Remember, Berta, we talked about how slowly you need to get up if you want to stay by yourself at night?"

Berta's eyes barely opened, but she nodded.

Susie came up the steps. "Is there anything I can do?"

Ariana pressed her fingers against Berta's

206

forehead. She felt a little clammy but not bad.

"Quill Schlabach?" Susie sounded confused, as if she was surprised he was still in the area. "What are you doing here?"

Ariana didn't want these two talking or spending even a minute together. "Susie, we've got this. You need to go on to the house and make the sandwiches and take them to Rudy. Tell Rudy and Mamm what's going on with Berta's health and that I need to stay with her tonight."

Susie remained in place, eyeing Quill.

"Please do as I asked." Ariana checked Berta's pulse again. It was stronger this time.

Quill walked down the steps with Susie and stayed by the carriage, talking to her.

"Quill?" Ariana called him.

He said bye to Susie and then turned. "Ya?"

"I need her blood-pressure cuff. Do you know where she keeps it?"

"Nee."

"It's in the nightstand on the right side of her bed, second drawer from the top. Bring that and a glass of water, please." Her use of the word *please,* which almost choked her, had less to do with politeness and more to do with begging him to get away from her sister.

Ariana would call the doctor after she gathered a bit more information.

"Berta, how are you feeling?" Ariana patted her hand, trying to get her to rouse more.

"Dizzy and weak."

Quill returned with both items in hand. Ariana took the glass of water and helped Berta take several sips. She put the blood-pressure cuff on Berta's arm as Dr. Sidman had taught her to do. "While I check this, you need to hide your car for your Mamm's sake."

Without a word Quill did as she'd said. It didn't take him long to drive it behind the barn. She was sure he put it in the old shed that remained locked. No wonder she'd never seen a key to that building. After checking Berta's blood pressure, Ariana left the cuff on and helped Berta take several more sips of water.

Quill strode back into sight, wasting no time approaching the porch. He gestured toward the gauge. "I know nothing about blood pressure."

"I didn't either until recently. Ideally her readings would be one hundred twenty over eighty. Currently she's at eighty-five over fifty-five. It's low but not dangerously so."

Ariana removed the cuff. "Is it possible you took one too many blood-pressure pills today?"

Berta shrugged. "Not that I know of. I certainly hope not."

Taking medication of any kind was new for Berta, and Ariana regretted she hadn't made sure she or whoever was staying with Berta doled out the meds. Ariana should be able to tell if Berta had taken two pills today by checking the number in the bottle against the date it was filled.

Ariana helped Berta with another sip of water, and as she drank, it seemed to wake her and clear her mind. "I think we need to move her inside, out of this heat. I want to check a few more things. Then I'll call the doctor."

Quill moved to help her. "Do you need to be carried?"

"Nee." Berta shooed him away.

Quill didn't back up. "Then take my arm and let me help you."

Berta nodded, and Quill helped her shuffle into the house.

Quill led his Mamm to the couch, and Ariana went to the medicine cabinet. She took the container to the kitchen table and, after carefully pouring the contents of the bottle onto the table, counted the pills.

Quill returned to the kitchen, watching intently as Ariana finished counting.

"I think I have good news." Ariana slid the pills into her hand and then into the bottle. "Your Mamm took two blood-pressure pills today. I'll call the doctor, but my guess is all she needs is lots of fluids and monitoring until the extra dose wears off."

Quill seemed to melt into the chair next to her, relieved at the news.

She put the lid on the bottle and set it to the side. "I'll make the call and stay the night. Since you were telling her good-bye when this happened, you could finish that while I'm at the community phone waiting to hear back from the doctor. When I return, you can go."

Quill didn't so much as flinch as she politely requested he hit the trail as soon as possible. He picked up the pill container, studying the label. "Remember the time we solved the incident of my grandmother's missing medications?"

"Ya. It took your *Grossmammi* about a month to convince family and friends that she wasn't misplacing them or accidently throwing them out."

"Yeah, but after you and I believed her, it took us two long days and several flashlight batteries to solve the mystery."

"Stupid cat." Aiming to sow peace, Ariana repeated a phrase she used to say to him when teasing. The trouble began when his grandmother started setting the bottles in a different place, and the family cat must have thought the bottle was a new toy. She'd knocked each bottle to the ground and batted it until it rolled through the oversized gap under the threshold of the door to an old unused cellar.

Quill chortled. "Smart cat."

Something besides distrust and anger began to stir in her, and the smile lifting the corners of her mouth while in Quill's presence felt odd. "Cat lover."

Memories of solving the mystery flooded her. She had been nine and Quill fourteen. He was bored because he'd recently broken his arm, a bad break, and he was supposed to stay indoors the first couple of days; otherwise, he never would have helped a scrawny kid solve the case of the missing medicine. Then again, until the day he left, she couldn't recall a time he hadn't helped when she asked.

"You hissin' at me?" A rare hint of a smile embraced his handsome face.

For a moment he didn't feel like an enemy. He also didn't feel like a friend.

He set the bottle on the table. "I would like to stay until I'm sure she's fine . . . if you don't mind."

It was his Mamm, so he didn't need Ariana's permission to stay. Maybe this was his way of acknowledging she had earned certain rights. But had he just buttered her up with that walk down memory lane and then asked? Regardless, she couldn't fault him for not wanting to leave yet. "Okay." She picked up the medicine bottle and tucked it in her apron. She would dole out the medications until she had a weekly medicine organizer for Berta. "What did your Mamm mean on the porch about you being powerless in what happened?"

He stared at the table. "Nothing." He closed his eyes and sighed. "Nothing at all."

She should've known better than to ask. Besides, she had other matters to tend to. "Are you fine while I call the doctor?"

"Sure." He angled his head, looking up at her with a trace of cautious amusement. "I won't kidnap her or anything."

Now that she was calmer — and maybe a little less bitter — she could see how humorous it was to think he might snatch his Mamm, and she couldn't resist a chuckle. "I appreciate that."

The community phone was only a brisk,

five-minute walk from Berta's place, and she hurried down the road. After talking to the doctor on call, she was armed with good information, so she ran back to Berta's. Once inside, she saw Quill encouraging his mother to drink more water. The poor woman would be getting up half the night to go to the rest room, but according to the doctor, rest and fluids were the best remedy.

Watching Quill with Berta made Ariana wish she could make sense of who he was. Was he the kind, caring daredevil she'd once known him to be, or was he the manipulating liar he'd appeared to be for the last five years? Was it possible to be both?

He looked up, and his eyes glued to hers. Did he know what she was thinking? He had always seemed able to read her mind.

She pushed away the eerie thought. "The doctor says she won't need to be seen as long as she doesn't get worse. But if her blood pressure isn't normal by morning, she needs to go to the ER."

"That's good, but did he say what we need to do?"

"The things we're already doing, plus check her blood pressure once an hour until it returns to normal."

Berta closed her eyes. "Could you two stop fussing around me, please?" She gestured toward the kitchen. "If you can't return to your usual lives, at least take it in the other room."

That was Berta. She had more starch than a Sunday shirt. Ariana went into the kitchen.

Quill followed her and sat at the table. "She's still so young. Early sixties. How is she going to make it on her own for the rest of her life?"

Ariana couldn't possibly think of an answer to that right now. She had questions about Quill going through her head. Where did he live? If he hadn't left because he wanted to, why had he left? "You hungry?" She went to the sink.

He slid the glass salt and pepper shakers back and forth on the table, tapping the bottoms together as he did. It was as if he hadn't heard her. "I imagine Mamm here alone, things happening like her passing out and no one being here, and I wonder if I made the right decision."

She needed no clarification concerning what decision, and she was glad she was at the sink with her back to him. Cool water ran across the bar of soap, creating bubbles as it slid over Ariana's palms. Her impulse to confront him about what he'd done fizzled before the emotion could form words. He was sharing as one person who cared about Berta to another, and Ariana tried to dig past her prejudices against him and find something in her that could relate to making tough decisions. He was unsure of what he'd done, and yet Berta had said it wasn't within his power to do anything but leave. What could Ariana say to him? Every decision she'd made in life seemed pretty cut-and-dried — whether or not to save for the café, who to date, how best to help her family.

She turned off the water and grabbed a dishtowel. As she searched her mind, a memory came to her — Quill endangering his life to set a poor creature free. "Maybe some things are like freeing a trapped bobcat. There's no right way, only a wrong way." He used to say that the only wrong way to do something was to do nothing at all.

While he seemed deep in thought, she pulled out a chair across from him and sat, recalling the bobcat incident. She'd been ten when she'd overheard the adults talking after church about a poacher who'd caught a bobcat in a steel trap, and he was keeping it in his backyard. They were discussing whether to turn him in, but there was concern about retribution. Rumors said the man was mean and violent. Upset about the bobcat, she had told Quill. Right then he started making plans to free it. She'd wanted him to tell the authorities, but he thought Wildlife Management was likely to send it to the local game ranch. Quill never could tolerate the idea of something being caged — legal or illegal. Rescuing it had taken planning and guts, and it had involved a chain, a pulley, a wagon, and nerves of steel. But Quill pulled it off. He drove a wagon twenty miles into the mountains and set the animal free.

"True. Very true." His smile almost returned, and he slid the shakers back to their spot. "So what were you and Susie up to today?"

"We — Susie, Rudy, and me — were selling sandwiches, baked goods, and coffee at the Labor Day weekend festivities because I'm trying to raise money to buy a tiny box of a restaurant."

"Wait." He frowned as if thinking hard. "Could it possibly be the old café in Summer Grove?"

"How did you . . ."

He laughed. "Because you swooned over that place when it was open and cried when it closed."

"I did not swoon."

Blank-faced, he folded his arms across his

216

chest and waited.

"Fine, I swooned. But for good reason!"

"For girlish reasons."

"Did you always gig me like this?"

"Pretty much, yeah. You found it charming and fun."

"And how did you find it?"

"Entertaining."

"Of course you did." She pursed her lips, mocking exasperation. "Still, looking back, it seems you stopped your teasing at some point."

"Ah, so you do possess the power of observation."

"What I'd like to possess is the power to make you be nice. Maybe a shock collar could prove useful in retraining what you say."

He clutched his throat, looking pained. "Ouch."

Was it her imagination, or had some of the persistent sorrow in his eyes faded as they talked? She had a thousand questions. Why did he hate the Amish so much? Or maybe he didn't. Was her perception of that like a lot of things between them — confused and twisted?

"Why did you stop teasing me mercilessly?"

"You got older, and by the time a girl is

nearing sixteen, she cries about such things. I stayed in enough trouble without your telling Mamm I made you cry."

She stifled her laugh, shaking her head. "You still make up stuff left and right, don't you?"

"It's called being fast on my feet."

"It's called lying."

"Tomato, to-mah-to." He shrugged, a spark of fun in his eyes.

She chortled, covering her mouth with the dishcloth to muffle the noise. Why was that so funny? Quill grinned, remaining silent of course. She'd forgotten how boisterous she was in comparison to him.

He interlaced his fingers. "Speaking of food, tell me how the money raising is going."

"What was it you used to call me when it came to money? Oh, ya, a debt magnet."

"That's because you lost every coin your parents gave you. More time was spent looking for the money than riding to town to buy anything."

"That only happened twice."

"And yet it gave me a lifetime of gigging-you rights. What are the odds?"

"Anyway, my point is that I'm no longer a debt magnet. I'm proud of the headway Abram and I have made, but I don't know that I'll have the down payment by October first."

"But you've qualified for the loan?"

"Ya. The owner —"

"Lila McCormick."

"Ya, that's right." Ariana was surprised he remembered. "She's willing to do owner financing. It all has to go through her lawyers, but before that can happen, I must have twenty percent of the loan by October first, or someone else will buy it. Her children are pushing about the time line and down payment, so there's no give in it."

"Ah, my forte." He cracked his knuckles.

"What's a forte?"

"Something a person is particularly good at, and lucky for you, I'm amazing at devising plans that make good money."

She didn't like his use of the word *lucky,* but for the sake of their truce, she chose not to share her thoughts . . . or judge his ways. How had they managed to have so much fun when he lived to push the limits of every line and it frightened her to do so?

He shooed her away. "Go get paper and pen."

Was he serious?

"Well, go on." He nodded his head in the right direction. "You know where Mamm keeps paper and pens, right?"

"Ya, sure." She headed for the desk in the living room.

"And do note," Quill hollered after her, "that I said *pen* and not *pencil.*"

He was harassing her over her old lead-breaking habits? It would be enough if they could get through the next few hours without anger or resentment. But was it possible that the man who'd caused her so much turmoil and heartache would be able to devise a plan to earn the down payment for the café?

FOURTEEN

The alarm on Quill's cell phone vibrated, waking him from a deep sleep. He shifted against the old recliner, causing it to moan as he reached into his pocket to turn off the alarm.

As consciousness began to flow to him, he could sense the good feelings last night had stirred. Usually the weight of reality began settling over him as soon as he awoke. How long had it been since he'd enjoyed a few hours like that? Instilling a little hope in Ariana as well as jesting and sharing a few laughs made the unspoken depravities of life bearable for a while.

Unlike him, Ariana didn't know about moral corruption or families having to survive the unthinkable. She knew only loyalty and love, and he'd go to his grave before he'd put on her the knowledge that was a part of him. No one could unknow something, so the key was to stop Ariana from learning it.

It was odd how light his shoulders felt this morning. Opening his eyes, he saw a silver glow of moonlight streaming inside. The outline of his mother's body under the white sheet moved at a slow, rhythmic pace. She was sleeping peacefully. The last few blood-pressure readings indicated normalcy had returned.

The sounds of crickets and night creatures chirping loudly floated through the open window. Maybe it would be a good day. Last night he and Ari had made a list of things she could do to earn money, but he hoped she would follow through on one specific plan he'd shared. The Amish held benefits when one of their own or an Englisch family needed help. Benefits were reserved for needy families who'd hit really bad times, ones who would lose their home or be unable to get medical help. But he wanted Ariana to pursue having one for the purpose of earning the down payment. She'd been reluctant to take his advice about this, and for good reasons. She would meet with some opposition, but if she would follow through on that plan, she would be able to buy the café. He knew that without any doubt, because if she did as he said, he would be able to give the needed money anonymously — if he had to sell everything he owned and live in his car to do it.

He eased the lever of the recliner forward, lowering the footrest as quietly as possible. In thirty minutes he had a meeting, and it wouldn't be daylight for another hour. Only the Amish would ask to meet at such a time. He dreaded this meeting as much as the one when Ariana's sister had reached out to him.

He didn't mind helping those who wished to leave, but sometimes it hit too close to home. Still, he couldn't refuse to assist people from his hometown. He slipped out of his mother's bedroom and went to the hallway bathroom. After brushing his teeth and washing his face, he moved through the dark house gathering his few belongings.

It was past time for him to leave Summer Grove, so he grabbed paper and pen to tell Ariana good-bye. It might be another five years before they saw each other again. He placed the pen against the paper several times, but he couldn't make himself write a note. Instead, he jotted down his cell number. Folding it, he walked into the living room.

The sight of her asleep on the couch made him smile, but for every ounce of pleasure he felt, he sensed the weight of the world returning. He had to go. There was no choice.

He sat on the coffee table next to her. "Ari."

She stretched and shifted but didn't wake.

He touched her arm. "Ariana."

She took in a sharp breath. "Quill?" Without opening her eyes she eased her hand over his. *"Bischt du allrecht?"*

Was he all right? Her instinctive reaction was to care about his well-being. Would she feel any of that if she were wide awake? The moment crashed over him, reminding him of all he'd left behind, all he would never have. "Yeah, but I need to go."

With her eyes still closed, she pulled the sheet to her chest, cuddling the wad while looking relaxed and peaceful. Did he ever have that kind of rest? Certainly not since learning the news that had killed his Daed.

"Now?" She rubbed her eyes and then finally opened them for a few seconds.

"Yeah. I just wanted to say bye. You can go back to sleep." He put the folded paper in her hand. "If you need to reach me for anything, you call." He'd had this cell number since leaving the Amish, but he'd shared it with only four others. She would be the fifth.

"Denki," she mumbled. A moment later

224

she was breathing deeply again, and he hoped she would remember that he woke her. It would take him months to shake all she had stirred in him since that rainy evening three weeks ago when she had stood at one end of the hallway and he at the other.

Had he been right to allow their friendship to be destroyed in order to protect her from all he knew?

The calm of night greeted him when he stepped outside, and he sensed God's peace assuring him he'd done the right thing. He took a deep breath and tried to shake off what Ariana did to his spirit. White stars glistened against the black sky. The beauty was enough to make the world seem like a hopeful place, with pockets of faith and love. He hoped for Ariana's sake and her future children that would be enough. He unlocked the shed, opened the double-wide doors, backed out his car, and headed to the meeting place.

Of all the odd messages he'd received, the one that came through his mother from Isaac Brenneman took the cake. Was this going to be an intervention of some sort? Did he have the church leaders with him? Quill might not agree with people's decisions, but he believed in their right to

225

choose, and he would pay the price to help his fellow Amish. They had a right to leave without months of virtual emotional and spiritual beatings. Since their education and their connections outside the Amish world were limited and their jobs were anchored in the Amish community, they needed the kind of help he provided to start fresh.

Maybe he shouldn't have hinted to Ariana about her sister wanting to leave, but apparently it had worked. When Ariana shared that her sister intended to remain Amish, it'd taken willpower to keep from whooping a victory yell for her. That was probably why some of the usual weight had been lifted from him.

He slowed, looking for the dirt road his mother assured him he could find. Funny, he'd forgotten there was a narrow dirt road near here. What else had he forgotten? He put his lights on bright and saw several deer feeding in the pasture. He spotted the entrance to an unmarked dirt road and turned onto it. This must belong to someone rather than being a state or county road. When he saw red reflectors gleaming out of nowhere, he turned off his headlights and pressed the brakes until he was going less than five miles an hour. He pulled in behind the carriage and turned off his car.

As he got out, he saw the silhouettes of a man and a woman walking toward him from across the field, coming from the creek bank. Was that Isaac and Lovina? It had to be. He'd expected to see Isaac with a group of church leaders, not his wife. Whatever was going on, this was no setup.

Quill leaned against his car and folded his arms, waiting for them. Sometimes in the busyness of life, he forgot how much he liked good Amish people such as the Brennemans. Standing here under the starry sky, he realized that the chaos surrounding his inevitable leaving had erased more than his future. It'd also erased some of the wonderful memories of his upbringing.

"Quill," — Isaac nodded, speaking to him as he helped Lovina navigate the small embankment from the pasture to the dirt road — "we appreciate you coming out to meet us."

His voice was restrained and gentle, a trait few Englisch showed during meetings like this.

"Isaac, what can I do for you?"

Isaac said nothing else until he and his wife were standing on the dirt road. "We don't want to be here, and we don't want to need your help."

They needed help? His help? Was this

about Quill agreeing to assist a member of their family in leaving? He couldn't ask.

"What do you need?"

Lovina wouldn't even look his way as she stood by her husband's side, holding his hand. Neither of Ariana's parents said a word for the next few minutes. Quill tried not to rush people because they often needed time to form their thoughts, to allow their brains to catch up with their hearts.

Lovina touched the top of his car, running her fingers across it. "We learned . . ." She looked heavenward, and the silvery glow of moonlight was enough to reveal the desperation and fear on her face.

Perhaps it was time he made this a little easier on them. "Can you tell me the subject you need my help with?"

Using the layer of dew that had fallen, Lovina made squiggles on the top of his car. "Ariana." She spoke barely above a whisper.

"Ari?" Had he heard her right? The mention of her name, especially under this circumstance, had his heart pounding with concern.

"We're here because we need absolute confidentiality," Isaac said. "Can you promise us that?"

"Yeah, absolutely. What's going on?"

"Remember the story about the birthing center burning down the night Ariana and Abram were born?" Isaac asked.

"All of Summer Grove knows that story better than the events surrounding their own births."

Lovina pressed her damp fingers into the palm of her dry hand and rubbed them together. "None of us knew the story quite as well as we thought."

The weight that had eased settled over him anew. "What do you mean?"

There was another long silence, a sure sign the information was dreadfully heavy.

Isaac sighed. "We have reason to believe the two girls born that night, the Amish baby and the Englisch one, were switched."

What? The news was too much. Quill jerked open the car door and plopped onto the seat. Even with his backside planted firmly and his feet on the gravel road, he felt as if he were spiraling round and round. While he took deep breaths, waiting for the shock to wear off, Isaac and Lovina took turns sharing information they had clearly not come to grips with.

As surely as there was a God in heaven, there was no truth to this outrageous fear. Ariana loved her family and the Amish with all of who she was. It would rend her in two if this chaos was true.

"I . . . I thought you were here to convince me not to help any . . . family leave."

"No."

Quill rested his head in his hands. "That would be easier than this."

"Almost anything would be easier," Isaac snapped. "We can hardly maintain control of our emotions enough to be at home with the others. How are we supposed to act normal so our children don't ask questions?"

"Maybe we need to get away for a few days here and there, husband, especially on the weekend when everyone is there expecting us to be our usual selves or explain why we're not." Lovina's voice was a mere whisper.

"It might help." Isaac nodded.

"Let's not forget that we have some good news, Isaac. Ariana is sure she has Susie convinced to stay."

Susie? Had Quill heard Lovina right? Ariana thought he was here to help Susie leave? This meeting was getting worse by the moment.

Isaac passed him a piece of paper. "This is the flier . . . for what it's worth."

It had more value than Isaac realized. Quill could use the information on the flier as a beginning point. It wouldn't take him long to piece together enough to have a few facts, and that information would let Isaac and Lovina know whether their fears had any validity.

Isaac slid his hands into his pants pockets. "The flier lists three girls with the last name Nash."

Quill's heart palpitated and his head spun. He had to get a grip. "I don't think I can help you. If you're right, Ariana's world will be torn apart." He had done that to her once, and he would not be a part of doing it again.

"I thought you were all about seeking those things," Isaac said. "The truth at all costs. Freedom, regardless of what it takes to attain it. Isn't that what the rumors say about you?"

"Ya, but this is different. Way different. When I left, my goal, despite how poorly I've carried it out, was to protect Ariana and all the innocent Amish like her." There were plenty of men and women like her, faithful Amish souls who embraced the Old Ways from a young age just as fully as they embraced God's Word. "And what you're talking about has nothing to do with giving her freedom or protecting her. If this is true, I can't be a part of it."

"What about the girl who may be our daughter?" Lovina crouched in front of him. "What if she's never been told about God or the life and death of Jesus? Would you withhold protection from her in order to guard one who's had every good thing we could give her throughout her life?"

Quill's head roared with voices and fears. He remembered experiencing much the same reaction when he learned of the awful things that led to his Daed's heart attack.

As he stewed in his determination not to be a part of this, a question hit him — who would they turn to if he refused them?

They could get someone who would come to the wrong conclusion or someone who would make the situation worse for Ariana. Perhaps someone who would sell the story to the newspapers. But if he helped, he could keep all of it private, and he would make sure to triple-check all facts, eliminating any bungling that would make the situation harder for Ari.

"Okay." He lifted his head, looking up at them. "Go home and say nothing to anyone."

FIFTEEN

Under the glow of the street lamps, Skylar drove through her subdivision. She pulled into her driveway and parked in her designated spot. The dread of owning up to her mom pounded inside her chest. How had a whole week passed already? It'd taken days to admit the finality of defeat to herself. Wasn't there some way around having to tell her mom?

She turned off the engine and grabbed her backpack. After opening the car door, she stared at the beige brick home, trying to muster the courage to go inside and disappoint her mom . . . again. A life on center stage was in Skylar's blood, much as it had been in her grandfather's and great-grandfather's. And her mother was the one who had made the necessary sacrifices over the years, doing all she could so Skylar at least had a chance to make it.

She drew a deep breath and got out of her

car. Each step across the brick sidewalk and into the house echoed with the sounds of her mom's disappointment. The familiar hum of the sewing machine told Skylar where to find her mom. When Mom went to the college tomorrow for the play, she would see Patrick. It would then take her about three seconds to pick up on the man's demeanor. If Skylar didn't wish for him to spill the beans, she had to come clean.

Voices from the television grabbed her attention, and she walked down the long hall, passing several rooms before she entered the living room. Her stepdad and stepsister were laughing at *America's Funniest Home Videos.* It was their favorite show, and they had a ton of them recorded on the DVR.

Until three years ago, when Skylar was seventeen, she and her stepsister got along. Then Cameron posted information about Skylar on Facebook, telling the world that she had pot stashed in her car. That's how Skylar's mom learned that bit of unpleasant news about her only child.

Skylar came unglued at Cameron over it. Cameron lied, saying it'd been an accident to post that on Facebook. They had barely spoken since. Maybe the stash of pot in Skylar's car was something Cameron needed to talk about, but she shouldn't have ratted her out, especially not on Facebook. That was the act of someone who hated her. Up to that point, she had thought Cameron liked her.

Neither of her parents seemed to care that the pot and paraphernalia belonged to her boyfriend. Maybe they instinctually knew she was heading down a path that led to far worse things — at least worse according to them and US laws.

Gabe looked her way. "Hey, Sky Blue. What's shaking?" As nice as her stepdad's welcomes were, their relationship went no deeper than warm hellos and good-byes, and it made loneliness curl up inside her like a living, breathing thing. Evidently the romanticized portrayal of family life often seen in movies and commercials didn't exist any more than the fairy tales played out on school stages.

"Not much." She shrugged.

Gabe had been divorced with sole custody of Cameron for three years when he met Skylar's mom. They began dating when Skylar was nine and Cameron was four. They married a year later. Life got a lot easier for Mom after that. Gabe said that's when his life got easier too, but Skylar didn't really understand that part. It seemed to her as if he had it made whether he stayed single or got married. But there was a lot about the tangled web of family life and human needs that Skylar didn't get. All she knew for sure was that life was an ugly mess at best.

Gabe didn't move his eyes from hers, and she saw a hint of concern. She hoped he stayed inside the unspoken boundaries and didn't ask any probing questions. There were a lot of things worse than the ball of loneliness inside her, and number one on the list was being vulnerable . . . with anyone.

Cameron punched his arm. "You missed it, Dad. Back it up and pay attention."

He hit Pause. "Care to join us?"

Her stepsister turned her head, looking squarely at Skylar with indifference. There were five years between them, and apparently Cameron felt no love for her. But Gabe was pretty cool. He was about fifteen years younger than Skylar's dad and around a lot more.

Then again, in her dad's defense, he never wanted Skylar to be born in the first place. That wasn't a surprise to her. She'd figured that out by the time she was ten. What she hadn't known was that he was married when her mom became pregnant with her.

She learned that on her sixteenth birthday when her dad took her out to dinner. After he had several drinks, he started talking. She would never forget sitting in a public place learning those things.

A taxi driver had taken Skylar home that night, and she was in tears as she asked her mom about the stuff her dad had said. That's when her mom confirmed that she'd had an affair with Skylar's dad while he was married. Her mom was nineteen when the affair began and twenty when Skylar was born. Her mom had thought he was in a failed marriage and was going to divorce his wife. Apparently that wasn't the case.

The next day after the birthday dinner, her dad came to the house and apologized. He backtracked, saying that Skylar was the best thing to ever happen to him and that even though the timing of her birth wasn't ideal, he was grateful she'd been born. But it was too late. He'd told the truth the night before while drunk, and they both knew it. The hurt of what she'd learned had run deep for months, almost paralyzing her. At the same time, it had explained a lot of things about her life. Her dad's first marriage had eventually failed, probably due to the affair with her mom. He was now married to a woman named Lynn, and he had two stepsons through her. Whatever. Gabe was a lot nicer than her own dad anyway, but Cameron was the easy child, and Skylar was the black sheep.

Gabe patted the seat next to him.

"Nah. I'm going up to see Mom."

Cameron looked pleased with that answer and settled against the couch with her bowl of popcorn. Gabe pushed buttons on the control, backing up the screen so he could see what Cameron said he'd missed. They were laughing as Skylar made her way to the kitchen.

Butterflies filled her stomach and chest much as they did just before she stepped on stage, only this time there would be no applause at the end. She opened the drawer on the stainless-steel french-door fridge and grabbed two wine coolers before heading up the carpeted stairs and into the sewing room. Dropping her backpack on the floor, she sank into her favorite chair.

"Hey, sweet thing." Mom released the pedal of her machine, making it stop. "I didn't hear you come in. I saved dinner for you."

"Thanks. We had pizza during practice, so I'm not hungry."

Mom pressed the pedal and began threading material under the presser foot. "Let me get to a stopping place, and we'll chat, okay?"

A kitchen scrubby seemed to run across Skylar's skin as her nerves did a tap dance. She nodded and opened one of the wine coolers. As she took a long sip, dozens of memories of her mom's faithfulness flooded her. One defining moment stood out. She'd been a third grader, sobbing into her pillow as her mom tried to console her. Skylar had lost the only solo in the school play to a girl who sang every note off key. After asking Skylar questions that seemed unimportant, her mom said the loss was her fault because the girl who'd won had two parents who were helping the teacher. The girl's mom was making costumes, and the dad was building props. Skylar's mother apologized to her, saying teachers needed help, and they tended to favor students whose parents lent a hand. That's when her mom made a promise. If Skylar would dedicate herself to voice lessons and acting classes, Mom would sew costumes and make props for the school as well as the community theater group.

Skylar had met her mother's promise with skepticism. Mom didn't own a machine, nor did she know how to sew. Besides, as a single parent, she barely had time to cook a meal or sleep. But the following weekend her mom had a yard sale, selling important pieces of furniture, including her bed, as well as almost everything in her closet. With that money she purchased a sewing machine. Skylar had sold some old toys and clothes that no longer fit.

How long would Skylar keep being this person — the one who sacrificed very little while her mom gave her all? After that yard sale, her mom slept on the sofa. When she wasn't at work, she was in front of a sewing machine, determined to learn how to create specific outfits from flat pieces of fabric.

By the time Skylar turned ten, she was the lead child actor in the local theater company.

The motor of the sewing machine quieted, and Mom took her pincushion to a table that had a new pattern lying over denim cloth. "So what's new?"

If her mom really had time for that answer, she wouldn't have moved from the noisier machine to work on something quieter so they could chat. She would have come to the couch and tried to snuggle with her, which Skylar could use about now, but she always protested such overt shows of affection.

"Not much."

All types of fabrics from organdy and tulle to burlap and tweed were on bolts stacked in every corner. Her mom sewed for the college and the local theater. Yards of a silky gold material lay across the thick beige carpet. Costumes of all kinds were in various stages of completion and were hanging on hooks and clothes racks. Her mom was making outfits for the community Christmas play, a musical rendition of *A Christmas Carol.* Skylar wasn't in it. Those practices would have conflicted with the practices for the college play, so she hadn't tried out.

Man, she did not want to tell her mom about her grades. Her mother trusted her to take care of that. Skylar took another long swallow.

Her mom eyed the drink, probably thinking the same thing she'd said on numerous occasions — Skylar wasn't of drinking age. "So you're in for the night, huh?"

"Yeah." That was the rule. If Skylar chose to drink, even a few sips, she couldn't leave the house. At least her mom gave her some breathing room about a little alcohol. Her mother not abiding by an arbitrary law about the drinking age had actually helped Skylar not to be as drawn to prescription drugs.

Mom put two pins in her mouth and used one to attach the pattern to the fabric. "Something seems to be nagging you. Care to enlighten your old mom?"

Her mom wasn't old, not even close, and she looked a decade younger than she was, which meant the boys at college thought she was Skylar's older, gorgeous sister. When Skylar didn't answer, her mom studied her.

"Those bangles look nice with the bling in your shirt, Sky."

Skylar glanced down. "Thanks. I bought both a few weeks ago using your card."

"You made good choices," Mom said around the straight pin clenched between her teeth.

Skylar held out the unopened wine cooler, but her mom shook her head. "I'm good. Thanks."

"You won't be." Skylar pushed it toward her again. "Just take a drink and a deep breath and remember that you love me."

Her mom took the pin from her mouth and jabbed it into a pincushion, and then she moved to the armless love seat and sat next to Skylar. "Speeding ticket?"

She shook her head. "You wish."

Her mother nudged her shoulder against Skylar's. "You seem sad, so my next guess is you're having trouble with that boyfriend of yours."

"Again, you wish."

Her mother nodded. "That's because I can see what you can't."

"Mom!" Skylar got up, ready to end the conversation immediately. No amount of guilt was going to make her listen to her mom put down Cody. He smoked a little pot and drank some, but he wasn't a loser. He was kind to her and he didn't cheat. What else did her mom expect of a twenty-one-year-old guy?

"I'm sorry." She grabbed the back pocket on Skylar's jeans and tugged her onto the chair. "My bad." She raised her fists in the air like an excited cheerleader. "Go, Cody." She smiled and put her arms around Skylar. "So before I get in trouble again, tell me what you did wrong." Her mother raised an eyebrow. "You didn't get your tickets sold for the play, did you? Is that what this is about? You need me to take off from work to sell tickets?"

"No. I haven't sold my batch, but I will." She'd known for a week she couldn't ask her mom that favor, so she had made plans with some of her friends. "A group of us are going out tomorrow after classes to hit the hot spots."

"So?"

Skylar fought to say the words.

Her mom pulled her close. "Guess what I

picked up today? The new fabric for the fiftieth-anniversary play. Next semester will be here before we know it. Your skin color will be gorgeous with the new bronze-colored fabric. Has Patrick made the announcements yet?"

"Yeah, about that . . ."

"You didn't get it?" She released Skylar, looking at her in disbelief. "Patrick wouldn't make such a stupid decision as to put a lesser-skilled girl in your stead when his reputation is riding on —"

"Mom, just stop talking and let me tell you what's going on."

Her mother froze, clearly waiting for some scrap of hopeful news.

Skylar had known this would be hard. She guzzled the rest of her wine cooler, wishing she'd chosen to fix herself a rum and Coke instead. "I won the part, but it went to someone else because of my grades."

"What?" Mom stared, disbelief and disappointment deepening by the moment. "Skylar Louise Nash, you tell me right this instant that you didn't mess up this chance we've been working toward for years!" Her mother's face flushed red. "Does this go back to that stupid Peter?"

Skylar shrugged. It made no sense to try to lie about it. She'd talked to her about all of that several months ago, so Mom knew the answer to her question.

Mom stomped to her machine and sat, jerking the chair with every movement. "I told you not to get involved with him in the first place." She pressed the pedal, making the machine hum. "Why can't you trust me about boys? I know a thing or two about them. I learned the hard way, and you won't trust my opinion about any of it."

Gabe came to the doorway. "Anyone up for trading in screaming for some ice cream? Get it?" He focused on the toe of his shoe as he thumbed toward the stairway. "We have chocolate with chocolate chips."

Her mother ignored Gabe, or maybe she was too angry to hear him. "If you weren't capable of making good grades, that would be one thing!" Her voice rose above the machine, even as she sewed faster by the moment. "But every mess since you entered high school boils down to you following some idiotic guy who can't find his way out of a paper bag!" She released the pedal, and the machine instantly hushed. "I can't take this anymore, Skylar!"

Skylar longed to scream back at her, *At least I didn't mess up like you did, coming up pregnant at nineteen by a married man!*

But Skylar had only one person who actually cared. Her mom.

Cody cared too, but she knew something would come between them within a year . . . if they lasted that long. Skylar knew how life worked. Relationships were transient. Fleeting. Fragile.

Way too often they were fake. But regardless of whether she and her mom were huddled together against storms or angry with each other, they were real.

Gabe shot a sympathetic look at Skylar, and it seemed as if he was going to say something on her behalf, but then Cameron came up beside him. He turned toward his daughter and put a hand on her shoulder. "Don't you have some homework?"

When married couples with children ended their relationship, one parent stayed. For Cameron, Gabe was that parent. Because of it, he and his daughter were as tied at the hip as Skylar and her mom. Always the obedient one, Cameron nodded and disappeared. Skylar was confident the girl had done her homework hours ago.

Gabe turned back toward his wife and stepdaughter, and Skylar could see by his face that he'd lost the courage to speak up. It wasn't as if her mom turned into an angry woman often . . . or easily, and Gabe didn't mind arguing with her on his own behalf, but as a stepparent who hadn't met Skylar until she was nine, he tried to stay out of their scuffles.

Skylar picked up her backpack. "You know, Mom . . ." Tears blurred her vision. "I expected you to be disappointed and angry, and that's okay, because you've worked hard and I've let you down. But I never expected you to throw the past in my face." She put the backpack strap on her shoulder.

She stormed to the doorway, and Gabe moved out of her way. Should she just leave? She hadn't popped an illegal pill in a while now, but she was going to need a hit of something to dull the unbearable pain. Maybe she should find Cody. He might not be in her life for long, but he was hers for now, and talking to him was warm and comforting.

"Skylar, wait."

She longed to ignore her mom, but it would only make things worse, so she turned around.

Her mom's long blond hair swayed as her willowy body hurried toward her. "I'm sorry. I shouldn't have said what I did. Okay?"

The ache inside Skylar seemed to open up like an abyss, and she knew the pain wouldn't subside anytime soon. Why did it hurt so much? What secret agony had they accidentally unearthed? "It's okay, Mom."

Her mother embraced her. "Forgive me?"

"Yeah. Sure." She hugged her and then let go. "I'm pretty wiped out, so I'm just gonna slip off to my room for the night, okay?" Her calm and gentle demeanor was a lie. She could feel herself reeling off the edge.

Sixteen

The old carriage creaked along with Abram gripping the reins, the leather biting into his palms as he drove toward a strip of Amish stores that sat outside of town.

Ariana had pencil and paper in hand, trying to whittle the grocery list down to affordable and still get what was needed. When she wasn't scratching items off, she was staring out the open window, deep in thought.

"Why aren't you out with Rudy on a Friday night?"

"Hmm?" She turned, the distant look in her eyes fading. "Oh. I think he must've gotten behind at work. His aunt dropped by the house this morning to say he had things he needed to do this weekend." Ariana tapped the pencil on the paper. "Quill's fund-raising suggestion?"

She had asked Abram a few times to share his thoughts, but he really didn't want to. In contrast to her being a helium balloon and an optimist, he was a weight and a realist. And to an optimist, a dose of reality only sounded like pessimism.

"Kumm on, Abram. Speak up."

He shrugged. "You're not going to like it, and I could be wrong."

"Still, if you don't tell me, I won't be forewarned, right?"

"The last thing I want to do is be discouraging."

"Then call it being honest."

He drew a deep breath. "Okay. I have some serious concerns. We both know that buying a business as a single woman is stepping outside the traditional roles upheld in the Old Ways." If she were married and her husband supported the plan, the ministers and community would view the situation differently, perhaps even as heroic. "We also know that regardless of who is offended or who frowns on you for purchasing a restaurant, you have the right to do it."

"And you're helping me buy it, so I'm not just a single woman. It's us, as a team."

"No one is going to believe it's my plan to buy a restaurant, nor would anyone believe I have an interest in or the skills for running it. For years I've turned over to you part of my pay from construction to support your dream. Any mention of me doing more than that will be seen for what it is — a cover-up of the truth. If you had the money without doing a benefit, it wouldn't matter who frowned on it. But to ask people to support your cause by participating in a benefit may be similar to smacking a beehive with a stick."

Ariana sighed, looking deflated. He should be mature enough that it didn't hurt his feelings whenever she was disappointed, but it didn't work that way. He slowed the horse as they approached a red light.

"So is that all of your concerns?"

He hesitated.

She closed her eyes, shaking her head, which, for his sister, was equal to rolling her eyes. "Finish, please."

After bringing the rig to a stop, he kept his eyes on the light. "Organizing a benefit will cost a lot in money and time."

"You think Quill is giving bad advice on purpose?"

Abram hadn't considered that. "Do you?"

"I constantly waver when it comes to Quill. Since he left years ago, everything about him messes with my mind."

When the light turned green, he tapped the reins against the horse and clicked his tongue. "Look, Quill is grateful you're a faithful friend to his mother, so it doesn't make sense for him to lead you wrong on purpose. He's shared what he thinks will work. I've shared my concerns about his plan. But the fact is, time is not on your side. You need to decide what to do."

"He gave me all the barrels in the cooperage to make various items to sell, and that's really generous, but I can't see how we could possibly have enough money to go to closing unless we have a benefit."

"If you do a benefit, the worst that can happen is you appear to be self-centered, and because of that, few in the community, if any, participate. Best-case scenario is the community backs you, and in the end you have enough money to purchase the café."

"And then I would feel as if I owe Quill something."

"Ah. I didn't realize that was part of what is troubling you."

"Me either until just now."

"You have to be tired of thinking about Quill. I know I'm tired of yakking about him."

"Sorry." Ariana doodled on the paper for several moments. "Okay. Change of subject. Tell me more about your chance encounter with Barbie on the road last week."

Abram easily recalled the details. Within

forty minutes of sending Barbie home with the medicine, her brother Matt returned with a fresh horse to hitch to the wagon. Matt and Cilla then drove Abram home. "I can't figure it out, but I wasn't all thumbs and silence around Barbie that time."

"You've been practicing how to be more outspoken for months, and you're doing a hundred percent better this year than last. Maybe it just all kicked in right then."

"Maybe. But it had a different feel to it, like socializing was easy and fun."

"Interesting." Ariana marked out another item on her list and made a note, probably listing a less expensive item that would do almost as well. "Any idea why she didn't go out with you?"

"Not really, except what I already told you — that when I was getting out of the wagon, Matt said, 'It's not you; it's her.' I asked what he meant, and he said, 'She likes you well enough.' "

"Sounds to me as if you need to ask Barbie why she didn't go out with you after agreeing to."

"That seems pushy."

"It would've been better to ask the night she stopped by the house. But when plans are changed, I expect an answer, and I would have to give one if I were in a similar situation and broke the date."

"It would help to know. Then I could let this go . . . eventually." Abram scanned the carriages in the parking lot of the dry goods store. Even though all the buggies were basically the same, each one had something telling about it — dents, touch-up paint, different side mirrors or lights. When he saw Barbie's family carriage, he pulled in.

"Why are we stopping here?"

"You're going inside to buy a spool of thread, and while you're in there, find out if Barbie is in there or if it's someone else from her family." He set the brake.

Ariana opened the door. "Sure. You got a plan if she is here?"

"Not a clue."

Ariana grinned. "But you stopped anyway." She gave a thumbs-up and hopped out. She reached through the window of the rig and dropped the pencil and paper onto the seat. "Be right back."

She was still at the side of the carriage when the bell on the fabric-store door clanged, and Cilla walked out. She appeared to be having a really good spell right now despite her cystic fibrosis. Abram couldn't recall her being out this often or looking this healthy in several years. She spotted Ariana and hurried toward her, smiling.

"Hey, Ari."

"Hi, Cilla."

"It's good to see you." Cilla peered into the carriage. "Abram, hi. I thought you might be in this buggy."

"Hello. Is your sis—"

"Knock, knock." Cilla rapped on the closed door to the carriage.

Abram recalled the knock-knock jokes he'd told when their rig broke down. He squelched his desire to know if Barbie was here. "Who's there?"

"Adore."

"Adore who?"

"Adore is between us. Open up!"

He chuckled. "Good one. Is your sister here?"

"Ya." Cilla nodded. "She's making a purchase, so she'll be out shortly. Abram, you won't believe what I saw the other . . ."

Cilla continued talking, but the words garbled in his head when the bell on the door clanged again. An Amish man Abram didn't recognize opened the door for Barbie. She had two colors of neatly folded fabric tied with string in one arm as she talked and smiled at the man beside her.

Before Abram could think clearly, he jumped out of the buggy and strode toward Barbie. Apparently disappointment and frustration overrode shyness. "Barbie."

She came to an abrupt halt, eyes wide as her smile faded. "Hi, Abram."

He ignored the man and focused on her. But words failed him. "How's your brother?" Couldn't he have asked Cilla that?

"Better. Denki."

Abram glanced at the stranger and held out his hand. "Abram."

The man neither offered to shake Abram's hand nor said his name, but there was no trace of offense on his face. He simply looked distracted, studying something behind Abram. Then he pointed. "Your girl?"

Abram turned. Cilla was no longer by his carriage. She was in hers. Ariana had gotten back in the buggy. Is that what had his attention? "My sister."

The man's lips curved down, but he was nodding.

Whoever he was, he obviously wasn't seeing Barbie. He passed a small brown bag to her. "Spoken for?"

"Nathaniel." Barbie sighed. "You're being rude, and, yes, she's dating someone."

Hadn't Barbie mentioned the name Nathaniel to Abram a few times over the years? If this was the same one, he was a cousin from Indiana, one Barbie liked as much as she disliked. Abram was beginning to see why.

"Dating someone could be a roadblock." Nathaniel grinned. "Then again" — he took one long stride forward before leaning back toward Barbie — "that's up to her, ain't it?"

"Nathaniel, no." Barbie shook her head in short, harsh movements.

But Abram wasn't going to object. He wanted a few minutes with Barbie, and it would take more than an overly confident Amish man to cause Ariana any stress. Nathaniel winked at Barbie and made a beeline for the carriage.

Barbie shifted, lowering her eyes to the pavement.

Abram tried to think of something to say. He'd been so sure he could hold up his end of a conversation that he'd jumped out of the buggy, and now his insides felt like ice. "Need a hand?"

"Nee. I'm fine. It's just a bit of fabric. Cilla and I got a job sewing dresses for Mervin's girls for the wedding."

"That's nice."

He knew the rest. Mervin Lapp and his wife had six little girls, and his sister was getting married soon, so they all needed new clothes before the wedding.

Abram removed his hat. "I . . . I need to

know . . ."

Her cheeks deepened with color. "I came to your home a month ago to break off our date, and you accepted it without question. I don't know why it's coming up again, but I'd appreciate it a lot if you'd just drop it."

"I tried. I did."

"And I'm grateful you cared enough to ponder on me." Finally she quit staring at the pavement and peered up at him. "But please, Abram. It's not proper to make a girl give a reason." She stepped around him and went to her carriage.

He followed her. "Tell me one thing. Just one. Did you break the date because you wanted to?"

She turned to face him, but she wouldn't look him in the eye. "You have a lot of good qualities. Otherwise I wouldn't have agreed for us to go out. But there's something about you I can't get past."

He wanted to know what the *something* was, but he had pressed her enough. This was as far from the ending he'd hoped for as a man could get. "Okay, I hear you. Bye, Barbie."

Ariana remained inside the carriage, talking to Nathaniel through the window. "So how long have you been writing poetry?" Had she asked a reasonable question? Nathaniel was on the hunt for a girl, and she didn't want him to think she was interested, but she was trying to give Abram as much time as possible to talk with Barbie. She wished Cilla hadn't gone to her carriage so quickly, but maybe she needed to get out of the sun and to sit for a spell.

Out of Ariana's peripheral vision, she saw an Amish man toting boards and plastic bags out of the hardware store.

Rudy.

When had he arrived? Had he seen her talking to Nathaniel? What must he think? Rudy shoved the two-by-fours into the wagon and tossed the bags on top. He glanced her way, paused a moment, and then pulled a red flag from his pocket and began tying it to the end of the wood.

She tried to open the door to the carriage, but Nathaniel was in the way. "Could you back up? I need to get out of the carriage, please."

"Sure, little lady. Anything you'd like." He opened the door for her.

She scrambled out. "Rudy!" She hurried across the parking lot, but he didn't look up. Was he so angry with her that he wasn't even going to respond?

This caring about what a guy thought was

new, and she couldn't say it was particularly appealing. Nonetheless she ran, waving her arms and willingly looking desperate. "Rudy!"

He paused, frowning. A moment later his beautiful smile lightened her heart. "Well, look who's here."

He hadn't seen her before now? Relief that he wasn't angry caused her to keep running until she was in his arms. Public displays of affection were frowned on, but at this moment she didn't care. What he did to her heart was just short of amazing, and she didn't want to lose it. He picked her up and twirled her around once, laughing, and then set her feet on the ground. His smile said it all. He was very pleased to see her. "What are you doing here?" He looked past her and saw Nathaniel beside the door of her carriage.

"He's a cousin of Barbie's, visiting from Indiana, and I was keeping him busy talking so Abram could get a moment alone with Barbie. What are you doing here?"

"Right now," Rudy chuckled, "I'm enjoying that you're intent on making sure the record is straight about Barbie's cousin."

Her heart pounded. "That obvious, huh?"

"Don't let it rattle you." He held her hand and kissed her cheek. "I'm here because I care about you. Yesterday I had an idea about some items I could make that should fetch a good price at a yard sale or something, and we can use the money to go toward the café."

"You're doing that for me?"

He squeezed her hand. "That's why we aren't going out tonight."

"Denki."

"Strange to be thanked for *not* taking you on a date, but just as strange to say you're welcome and mean it."

Chuckling, they squeezed each other's hand before letting go.

"Rudy . . ." Her nerves jiggled a bit, anticipating how he might respond. "I've been thinking of having a benefit to raise money to buy the café."

"To acquire a private business? For a girl? I think you're inviting the bishop to come to your home to correct you."

Had Quill realized that? It seemed to her that he didn't like any kind of boundaries and tried to zip past them as if they didn't exist. She preferred to figure out where the lines were so she could avoid going anywhere near them. "Yeah, Abram had those same thoughts."

Rudy leaned against the wagon, a mischievous smile beaming down at her.

"But that getting-in-trouble thing isn't an altogether detestable plan since it could benefit me." He grinned, looking sheepish, and she assumed it was embarrassment over his selfish proclamation.

"How?"

"If you need a place to escape to while the anger dies down, you could go to my parents' home in Indiana. You know, to get a reprieve from the fallout, and my family could get to know you and you them. See, win-win . . . for me."

"You're assuming they'd like me."

"Not true. I'm assuming they would love you."

"You're very sweet, and I appreciate that about you." She pointed a finger at him. "Now stop the nonsense and focus. Are you saying you wouldn't be against it if I decided to do a benefit?"

"For better or worse, I'm on board with whatever you think you need to do to get the café."

She wrapped her hands around his suspenders and tugged. "I couldn't have a better boyfriend."

"Remember that when we argue."

They hadn't argued over anything yet, but they would. "Deal." She released his suspenders and took a step back.

He straightened his shirt. "So, are we having a yard sale or a benefit?"

She owned hardly anything that could be sold. If something in the Brenneman household was serviceable, including secondhand and third-hand clothing, furniture, or cookware, she and her family were using it. How could she possibly pull off a successful yard sale if she didn't have anything to sell? Usually part of having a benefit was that skilled Amish men and women made items and donated them to be sold. Would anyone donate items to help her close on the café? Would Amish people even come to the benefit — other than the bishop to correct her?

"I don't know . . . yet."

SEVENTEEN

Sitting in his car at the back of a college campus parking lot, Quill turned up the music filtering through his earbuds attached to his cell phone. He chose an upbeat playlist, but it wasn't helping in his battle against feeling down. Watching the theater doors, he couldn't keep his mind off Ariana.

Her life would be traumatized if the girl who supposedly looked like Salome was actually a Brenneman. He fiddled with the flier. If the babies had been mixed up, that event wouldn't do any justice to the Nash girl either.

He felt so powerless, an experience he'd had too many times in his life before leaving the Amish. He had been so sure that if he took Frieda and left, he would never have to go through this kind of helplessness again.

What do you want from me, God? I'm trying here. Where am I missing it?

There was nothing as isolating as doing what he believed was right in God's eyes and then having almost everyone he respected or cared about consider him a traitor.

Four of the faded-red double doors swung open with a bang, and people tumbled out — loud, boisterous young men and women who appeared to have no weight on their shoulders at all. But he knew better. Anyone who understood life knew better.

Although he was tempted to use his binoculars, he left them in his backpack. He removed his earbuds and leaned forward, searching for a girl who looked like Salome.

The group talked loudly across the lot about selling tickets and when to meet back here. People waved, some hugged, and the jumbled masses of energy soon dispersed to their cars. He scanned every girl, seeing no one who fit the description. Most of the crowd left. Had he missed her? The remainder of the people formed small groups around a few vehicles.

The number of people thinned even more as they moved to different spots around three cars that were next to each other.

Wait. Was that her?

A girl opened her car door and tossed a backpack and purse inside. While staring at her back and hoping he could get a good look at her face, his heart moved to his throat, and he couldn't catch his breath.

She closed the car door and stood upright, almost facing him directly. A cold chill ran through him. It was her. If she and Salome were the same age and an onlooker went by just their faces, the two could have been twins.

She leaned back against her vehicle, facing him directly. Two guys and a girl joined her as they talked to others who were by the two remaining cars. Several of them lit cigarettes, but the girl who favored Salome didn't.

He had prayed that Mark had exaggerated how similar Salome and this girl looked. He couldn't have dropped his investigation based on outward appearance alone, but it would've given his nerves a bit of relief. Getting a clear view of her only intensified his anxiety, and it felt as if God had once again ignored his fervent pleas.

Then a new thought came to him, the kind that carried hints of peace with its insight. If the girls had been switched at birth, what were his prayers supposed to accomplish? Was God going to miraculously undo what had begun two decades ago? Faith was one thing. Dreamy prayers, as if

God were a star to wish upon, were totally another. He apologized to God for being shallow and quick to feel abandoned by Him. It just felt as if so much of Ariana's happiness and well-being was riding on the outcome of the true identity of this stranger.

Aside from her face, nothing else about her favored the Brennemans. She wore a sleeveless knit shirt that clung to her body as if she'd outgrown it before puberty. Her boots were silver and black with a metallic-looking heel. Her jeans were tattered with gaping holes, and he wondered how much she'd paid for them to look that way. She wore an abundance of jewelry everywhere — fingers, wrists, neck, ears, and ankles. Maybe her nose too, but he was too far away to see that. She had the same shade of dirty-blond hair as Salome, except for two streaks of dyed hair — one black and one purple.

The remaining youth were leaning against three different cars, bantering loudly amid their laughter. He could overhear bits and pieces of the conversation, most of it silly and useless as they exaggerated tales of mishaps during rehearsals and poked fun of one another and talked about how much they hated certain subjects.

The girl seemed quieter than the others, sadder somehow, despite the smile that peeked out. If she had been born to Lovina and Isaac and had been raised with them, would she and Quill have been close friends growing up, as he and Ariana had been? Ariana had helped him keep his sanity when his dad died. Without her help in navigating his anger and depression, he shuddered to think where he'd be. In jail. Maimed. Dead. All were viable possibilities for him at that time. Because of that, he couldn't imagine anyone taking her place during those years. She'd understood and strengthened him in ways no one else came close to.

The guy nearest the Salome-lookalike pulled out another cigarette and lit it. No wonder these cars were parked so close to the back of the lot. This was a smoke-free campus.

Quill took no joy in behaving like a stalker, but he continued to watch and listen. He needed to speak with this girl. A casual but inquisitive conversation would let him know if she'd been born in an Amish birthing center. If she hadn't been, he could leave her alone forever. But there were too many other people around right now for him to approach her. He wanted to avoid drawing questions from her or her friends. She took the half-smoked cigarette from one of the guys and inhaled deeply. Her eyes closed, and she held the smoke inside her before passing the cigarette back to the guy. Her eyes didn't open until she released the smoke from her lungs. He knew that look, that desperation. He would bet she was hooked and was trying to quit or cut way down.

She pushed away from the car and stood. "I'm going to Ankara Mall." She went to the driver's side of the car and opened the door. "Anyone who wants to come, hop in, or I'll see you there. I'll be by the food court doors, and I better not see any of you losers selling tickets to my peeps."

There was an uproar of laughter, and he guessed that some part of what she'd said was an inside joke. Several of her friends made comments that Quill couldn't distinguish, but he caught the words *mall cops* and *trouble*.

The flier listed three girls with the surname Nash, so he didn't have confirmation of her first name yet, but he could recognize her anywhere now, and he had a plan. While he waited for the cars to leave the lot, he searched for Ankara Mall on his phone's GPS.

He eased from the lot, taking what the GPS said would be the quickest route and hoping to get to the mall before they did.

Minutes later he found the outside entrance to the food court, but he didn't spot the car she was driving. He parked and went inside, his mind swirling with various plans. He had to create an opportunity to speak with her, and during those few minutes he needed to find out a lot without her having any clue what he was doing.

While waiting, he bought a drink and took a seat just inside the row of double-wide glass doors. It wasn't long before he saw her driving across the parking lot, but the people who'd left with her were gone. She parked and walked toward the mall, a purse strap on her shoulder and tickets in her hand.

If she didn't ask him if he wanted to buy a ticket, he would come up with some sort of icebreaker as he passed, maybe remarking about the boatload of tickets in her hand. And she would ask if he wanted to buy one.

Even in his efforts to help Amish leave, had he ever needed to be this calculating toward innocents? Ariana would say yes, but she was the exception, and he'd done it for her own good. Besides, he'd never baited someone for information, and he didn't like it.

Once she was on the sidewalk, he left the

mall, catching her eye to give a friendly nod.

She smiled and said "Hi" as she approached him. "I'm Skylar, a drama student at the community college. Remember loving Dr. Seuss as a kid?"

He actually did. "One fish. Two fish. Red fish. Blue fish."

She nodded, looking sincere and pleased. "And how about 'A person's a person, no matter how small'? It's from *Horton Hears a Who.*"

"Neat saying. I remember the title of the book but not that line."

"Maybe you need a refresher course. We're putting on a great show for adults and children. It's a musical called *Seussical.*"

"And like the phrase 'musical *Seussical,*' the songs will be filled with rhymes, right?"

"Exactly. But there's even more than the musical. Our troupe has skilled dancers and singers, all of whom will surprise you by their ability to act, and the event is filled with superb costumes, thanks to my mom."

It appeared that drawing her into a friendly conversation would be pretty easy, but his gut knotted tighter than ever. She enjoyed being part of the troupe, but if she were Amish, her family wouldn't be able to embrace that part of her. Nor could they share in her enthusiasm about her mother being a costume designer. His mouth was dry and his palms sweaty as he tried to push those thoughts aside. He had a goal to accomplish — confirmation of where she'd been born or her birth date. Learning either of those could answer a lot of his questions. "How much?"

"Fifteen dollars apiece."

He tried to whistle, but his mouth was too dry. He took a sip of his drink. "That's pricey, isn't it?" But his remark had more to do with keeping the conversation going than with money.

"You ever gone to a college play?"

He shook his head. The only plays he'd attended were in a one-room schoolhouse at Christmastime.

She pulled a flier from her purse. "A lot goes into making one. Buy some tickets and come watch. You'll see what I mean."

He took the flier. It was the same one Lovina had given him. "I guess I could use a ticket or two." He put his mouth on the straw and took another sip of Coke, trying to look casual. He flipped open the flier. "You in the play?"

"I am."

He separated three tens from the rest of his cash. With that in one hand, he maintained eye contact as he slyly got out three one-dollar bills and hid them in the palm of his other hand. "The cast has to sell tickets?" He put the bills between his index and middle finger.

"Yeah." She took the money, slid it into her jeans pocket, and passed him two tickets. Her black nail polish stood out as if screaming at him. The Amish frowned on clear nail polish. All of it was considered vanity.

He'd successfully executed the sleight of hand. In a few minutes he'd bring it to her attention, and if she thought it was funny, he would use the levity to steer them into a different conversation, maybe one that would answer all his questions. But right now he studied the list of names. "So which character are you?"

"I'm the cat in *The Cat in the Hat,* and as fun as that part is, it's not my favorite for the evening. After the play is over, we do an olio, which is a medley of popular songs that we've paid the rights to use."

He spotted the words "Cat in the Hat" and with his finger followed the line that went to the person's real name: Skylar Nash.

He hated the number of clues stacking up, and he longed to scream at God, *No, please, no!* She strongly favored Salome, and she had the same surname as Brandi. "You have the same last name as a couple of people in this flier, including someone named Brandi."

"It's a playbill, actually, and, yeah, I share a last name with people I'm unrelated to, except Brandi. She's my mom, and she makes most of the costumes."

He struggled to temper his mounting disappointment as he aimed to stay on task. "According to the list of solo performances, you'll sing."

"During the olio, yeah."

Had she explained what that was? The noise inside his head and the panic rushing adrenaline through his body had him as spacey as he'd ever been. He willed himself to think. If Lovina and Isaac wanted to see her without her seeing them, they would both need tickets. "I . . . I have friends who've never seen a college play either, and I think they would be very interested in coming to this one." Could he call Lovina and Isaac friends? Would they want anyone besides the three of them attending, like maybe Abram?

If Lovina and Isaac saw her on stage performing, perhaps it would convince them to leave well enough alone in both girls' lives. On the other hand, that would be morally wrong, wouldn't it? Adults have a right to know the truth about who they are and to choose whether to get to know their real parents. But every part of him wanted to avoid Ariana getting hurt. "So these tickets are for this weekend, but can I buy tickets for next weekend?"

"Sorry. This play closes tomorrow night, and there won't be another one for sixteen weeks."

"Sixteen weeks?"

"They — the cast — have to learn their lines, and costumes and props have to be made."

"So if *they* need to learn their lines, does that mean you have your lines down pat?" He hated this role, measuring his words carefully while digging for answers that were none of his business.

"I won't be in any plays for a while." She shrugged, but he thought he saw raw hurt in her hazelnut eyes. Then she held up the remaining tickets. "But I have plenty of tickets for tonight's and tomorrow night's performances."

"I can see that, but I'm not sure you want to sell me more tickets."

"Why?"

He forced lightheartedness onto his face. "Did you count the money I gave you?"

"I saw you give me thirty dollars."

"Did you?" He smiled. "Are you positive?"

She narrowed her eyes while pulling the cash out of her pocket. "Three ones?" She broke into laughter. "What happened to the tens, and how did you manage the switch?"

He took the three dollars from her and pulled three tens from the pocket of his pants. Showing her the tens, he then folded them, slid them between his index and middle finger, and held the tip of them toward her.

She took them, but when she unfolded them, she laughed. "These are the ones again. How are you doing that?"

He retrieved the tens from their hiding place and held them out. "It's magic, and magicians do not reveal their secrets."

She cautiously eased the cash from his hand and then held each bill up to the sky, inspecting them. "I gotta know how you did that."

"I'm not sure you're old enough for me to teach you that."

"What's age got to do with it?" Her cell phone sounded as if she'd received a text, but she ignored it.

"A guy you don't know is going to teach you tricks that involve hiding money in your jeans' pocket. That sounds like a recipe that could land me in jail. Are you even eighteen?" He had to guess wrong, but his hope was that she would volunteer her real age.

"Twenty." Her cell phone went off again, numerous times in a row, as if several people were texting her, but as long as she was ignoring it, he would do the same.

"Twenty?" He raised his brows as if surprised, and then he nodded before he straightened the ones and quickly showed her how to fold them so they fit inside his palm unseen. "You got a license to prove that?" If he could catch a glimpse of her license, he wouldn't need to ask her anything else. If she and Ariana shared the same birth date, he would know plenty . . . and it would start the journey toward the girls getting a DNA test.

"Sure."

Before she could get her billfold from her purse, yellow lights flashed, grabbing their attention. A mall security vehicle pulled up to the curb near them. The car looked like an enclosed golf cart with lights on top.

Skylar cursed under her breath and tried to jam the cash and the rest of the tickets that were in her hand into her purse. Instead of hiding the items, cash and tickets scattered across the sidewalk. She bent to gather them.

Quill turned his back to the vehicle and crouched, helping her gather tickets. "What's the big deal?"

"Soliciting isn't allowed." She glanced up, looking around Quill at the man coming toward them. "It's not my first time to get caught by this guy. But rules are for breaking, right?"

He chuckled. "Sometimes I resemble that remark."

"He said the next time I was caught he would confiscate the tickets and I would be banned from coming here for a year. If he takes the tickets, I'll get in trouble for —"

"Excuse me, miss." A burly man in a uniform stood on the sidewalk about twenty feet from Quill and Skylar. They both had tickets in hand, and there was no hiding that from the man at this point. He ambled toward them.

They rose from their crouched positions and turned toward him.

Recognition entered the man's eyes. "Oh, it's you." He held out his hand, palm up. "I've said it before, soliciting isn't allowed."

As Skylar passed him the tickets, her cell phone sounded again.

"Actually," — Quill stepped forward — "I came here to buy tickets from her."

The man looked doubtful. "You're saying

278

you know her." His comment was more a statement of disbelief than a question.

"Yeah, this is Skylar Nash, and I was showing her some tricks with money while we were discussing how many tickets I needed." He turned to Skylar. "We were about to get a bite to eat, weren't we?"

Skylar looked amused . . . and relieved not to be in trouble with mall security. "Yeah, sure."

The security cop propped one hand on the two-way radio attached to his belt while studying the tickets. "Less than ten minutes ago I caught several others about your age selling tickets. I confiscated them, and these look the same to me."

A dozen scenarios ran through Quill's mind, and he selected one he thought would work. "You took tickets from young people who were selling them for a musical at a local college?"

"Soliciting is not allow—"

Quill held up his hand. "I got that much. It's wrong, and you want to make them pay for going against mall policy. But the local college keeps this mall in business." He wasn't positive that was the case here, but it was often true in similar situations. "So wouldn't it be better to give them back the tickets and tell them they need to leave? I mean, if you don't and the college paper reports it, couldn't that news make shoppers, many of whom are family and friends of these students, boycott this place?"

As Quill's words sank in, the man's countenance changed. He lingered, unmoving for a bit. "Those students would have to agree not to solicit for a year."

"I'm sure they would agree to that." Quill wasn't as sure they would keep their agreement.

Skylar shrugged. "I won't come here to sell anything for a year."

The man gave her back the tickets. "Let your friends know if they'll meet me at the mall office, I'll return their tickets." He got into his vehicle and left.

"Wow." Skylar breathed giggles of relief. "You're really sharp, aren't you?" She took her phone out of her purse. "Ha. Look." She held up her phone, and the screen was filled with texts warning her about the mall cop. She began texting while talking to Quill. "You weren't nervous or angry while you dismantled his self-righteous attitude."

His Daed had taught him how to remain calm while trying to reason with a person. "I'm glad I was here to help."

"No kidding. Me too." She lowered her phone. "That would've been a mess. I swear if I get into any more trouble right now, my mom won't stop at figuratively cutting out my heart."

Despite her jesting tone Quill saw pain on her face as she spoke about her mom. Whatever had happened had been recent and had cut deep. Is that what Ariana had to look forward to if this nightmare turned real?

Skylar's phone vibrated, and she looked at the screen and chuckled. "My friends are stoked about getting their tickets back."

"It'll probably take them a few minutes to get it sorted out. Food court is right there. Care for a bite to eat?"

She fidgeted with the tickets in her hand. "Sure. Why not?" She turned and headed for the doors. "But I pay for my own. Chick-fil-A sound good?"

He held the door for her. "Very."

"I don't even know your name."

"Quill."

"You're kidding." She slowed once inside, waiting on him to release the door and walk next to her. "That has to be your last name or a nickname."

"It's my given name. It's Amish."

"Like the people who drive a horse and buggy?"

"Yep."

"So you're named after someone Amish, or you were raised as one?"

"Born and raised Amish in Summer Grove." He detected in her no sense of connection on this topic. If the name of the town meant anything to her or if she'd been born in an Amish birthing clinic, she would've mentioned it by now. That gave him a bit of hope, until ten seconds later when it dawned on him that she might not know her place of birth.

"And I thought my upbringing was strange."

They continued past tables and toward Chick-fil-A, but he wouldn't use that time to ask what she meant. It was too personal. "Know anything about the Amish?"

"Only what little I've seen while passing a horse and buggy on the road. I know they dress differently and travel differently. I heard they don't use electricity or watch television or movies. But the main thing I know is they need to get that slow-moving, horse-drawn contraption off the road, especially when I'm running late." She made a face. "Sorry. I guess that's rude, considering who you are and how much you helped me today."

"Forgiven. And we know that's how the Englisch feel."

"So I'm English?"

"Yeah, among other things . . . as best I can tell since meeting you."

She grinned. "You've seen the movie *Guardians of the Galaxy,* right?"

They got in line behind the three people already waiting.

"No, should I?"

"You're midtwenties?"

"Yeah, although I've yet to see your license to prove your age." He hoped she'd show it to him, but she simply shrugged.

"You must be the only guy your age who hasn't seen that movie. You at least know the hero's name is Quill, right? Well, it's his last name, but it ends up being what everyone calls him."

"Had no clue until just now." How could he smoothly turn this conversation so he could find out her birth date?"

"You need to see the movie." She fiddled with something inside her purse and then swiped a finger across her lips, leaving them glossy.

"Is it that good?"

"I liked it, but then again, I love movies." She rubbed her fingertips across her palm, wiping off the gloss. "There's this amazing power in them to make you feel and think, either through relating to it or because it's totally outside yourself. You do see movies now that you're not Amish?"

"Some. Not much." He'd really liked a few of them. His favorite was *The Village.* As ex-Amish he could identify with many of the fears and beliefs of those in the town.

"I think I'd go crazy if I couldn't watch new movies several times a month. My great-grandfather was in vaudeville. When that ended for him, he bought the first movie theater in the county. It's on Main Street in downtown Bellflower Creek. My uncle still owns it, mostly because no developer is willing to buy it. According to old newspaper clippings from my great-granddad's days, the theater was really something in its heyday, but my mom says that by the time she came along, it was tattered and musty. It hasn't been torn down, but the old screen hasn't seen a movie in twenty years or more. Sometimes I sneak in there to sit and stare at the shabby velvet curtains that partially cover the old screen."

"That helps?"

"Well, you know, if one can't get high for whatever reason . . ." A hardened, sarcastic look overshadowed her natural beauty, making her appear fed up with the world at twenty years old.

Her statement caused concern to ripple

through Quill, and he focused on her pupils. Was it normal for her to have such large pupils?

The man just ahead of them went to the ordering line, so they stepped forward, remaining behind the "Wait here" sign.

She shrugged. "Anyway, somehow or other going there helps. Maybe because of the sense of nostalgia, thinking of all those people who used to enter the grand place, what they saw, and how it might have inspired and changed them. Or maybe going there helps because I want to be a part of the movie industry. I hope to begin by acting, but my biggest dream is to direct."

The young man behind the counter motioned for them, smiling. "What can I get for you today?"

Quill waited while Skylar ordered. After she paid, he placed his order and paid. They moved away from the counter to wait.

If this young woman was Lovina's daughter, would the family accept her? Could she accept them? Would each side only aim to change the other? But those weren't the hardest questions. The ones that made him sick to think about were, could Ariana accept that Abram wasn't her twin and that her beloved family wasn't related to her? As much as she loved all things

Amish, what would it do to her if her DNA and family history came from a *very* non-Plain bloodline?

"Here I am talking up a storm. Your turn. You got a girl?"

He shrugged. "Define the word *got*."

"Ouch. I had a boyfriend last year who cheated. Stinks big time."

"I didn't mean . . ."

She crossed her arms, looking relaxed. "What did you mean?"

"I should've just said, no, I don't have a girlfriend."

"Yeah, but that's not what you said, and there's a reason. You don't have to tell me, of course."

The young man behind the counter held up a bag, reading off the side. "Skylar." He grabbed another and held it up. "Quill."

They took the bags and went to a table. It seemed fair that he would share something honest with her since he was mining for gold in her life. "Truth?"

"No." She plunked the bag on the table. "Lie to me." She sat. "Of course I want the truth."

He took a seat and got out his sandwich and fries. "I've cared about the same girl my whole life. It began with me just thinking she wasn't so bad. Then I favored her, as if she was a favorite cousin or something. By the time she was eleven or so, I considered her a friend, and that kept growing until at some point when I wasn't looking it turned into love."

"Oh, you were looking. That much I know. I'd say that love part happened about the time she went from being a flat-chested girl to a curvy woman."

That was probably more true than he wanted to admit. "She changed from being a half-grown kid to a whole person."

"Sure. I get that." Skylar took a sip of her water. "So how did she feel about you?"

"For lots of reasons we never discussed it, but I know she cared about me too . . . for a while."

"What happened?" She opened her container of fresh fruit.

"It's complicated. I had to do certain things to protect someone, and she thinks I committed sins to do what I did. I wanted her to think that for a while in order to protect her, and —"

"Geez, Quill." Ignoring the plastic fork, she used her fingers to pick up a piece of pineapple. "Who died and left you protector of the universe?"

"What do you mean?"

"Crap happens. You can't stop it or keep

people from being hit with it."

Considering what might be facing Ariana soon, Skylar had a valid point, but he had spared Ariana the one thing that could have destroyed her outlook, her sense of security, and her natural buoyant hope in a troubled world.

Skylar ate a section of a mandarin orange before licking her fingers. "And it's just wrong to assume she's too weak to cope. You survived it, didn't you?"

He wasn't so sure he had, but that would be too much to explain. "Anyway, sometimes I think I'll die still in love with her."

"What?" Skylar wiped the white pith and yellow juice onto a napkin. "No way. You're just a really good liar, right? There are no men in the history of the world who loved anyone that much, except maybe their mothers."

So why was he telling her all this? "I don't believe how I feel either. I've spent years wanting to get her out from under my skin, and if I could figure a way, I would." It had been hard enough to shake that desire before he'd returned to Summer Grove.

"So convince her you didn't do what she thinks you did."

"Even if I managed that, we have a

hundred other obstacles in line behind that, and they are as unmovable as this mall. But I actually knew all of that five years ago."

"Five years . . ." Her whisper was haunting as her brown eyes bore into him. "Man, that whole story gives me shivers. I hope the guy I'm dating lasts one year, and you . . . wow."

"If you think he won't last, why put yourself through a year of waiting to find out?"

"You know how almost every kid goes through a phase of fearing monsters are lurking under the bed or in their closet at night?"

"Yeah."

"I think children are intuitive, and the word *monster* is the only way they can express what they know to be true — that parents leave and there is a monster in the empty spaces. It screeches out from under the bed, threatening to swallow us, and if you ask, you'll learn its name — loneliness. When I got older, I figured out how to keep it at bay. All I need is someone special in my heart who is waiting to hear from me each day when I wake up. Like the others before him, he won't be here next year, but all I need is someone for tomorrow."

On one hand Quill could relate to the

sense of loneliness she expressed, but how she dealt with it was sad and unhealthy. "But —"

"Sky Blue!" Several voices chanted at once.

Smiling, she looked around and then pointed to the second-story walkway that overlooked the food court. They were waving tickets. "They've got them back." She waved. The group disappeared, and he was sure they would be at their table soon.

"I like your nickname." Quill thought it seemed fitting because she seemed to sail high and hopeful, like a child's balloon that'd been set free, and yet she seemed quite blue deep within.

"My stepdad made it up years ago."

"Your stepdad did?" Where was her . . . or Ariana's . . . biological dad?

"Yeah. Mostly he uses it and a few nutty friends who were at my house one time and overheard him." She rose, leaving her drink and a nearly empty bowl of fruit on the table. "I need to go. If you come to the play, stay afterward, and the cast will come out and mingle. I can't afford a detour of intros right now, but after I tell my friends what you did today, they'll want to meet you."

"I need to buy two more tickets."

"Sure." She slid two tickets across the table.

He handed her thirty dollars. "Before I would consider meeting your friends after the play, I would need a glimpse of your driver's license. You know, to prove your age."

"You've earned your request." She dug her billfold out of her purse. "But I'm in college. How many underage girls attend college? Although I participated in college drama while in high school, so I'll cut you some slack." She held up her license.

Skylar's birth date was the same as Ariana's. The information hit like a thief in the night, one that had the power to strip everything from Ariana.

"Satisfied?" She tucked her license into her billfold and jammed it into her purse.

"Yeah. Thanks."

"I gotta go." Skylar waved at him and hurried toward her oncoming friends.

A lot of contradictions seemed to describe her. He'd looked into her eyes, and despite her outward confidence she held herself together by nothing more than ragged bailing twine.

What would this kind of news do to her?

EIGHTEEN

Ariana thrust the bottom ridge of her palm into a huge wad of dough over and over again. Time was running out, and rather than making a decision, she continued to wallow in uncertainty. A week ago today she'd thought that all her decisions in life were cut-and-dried. Then as she and Quill tended to his Mamm, he had shared a list of ways to earn the money to go to closing.

A week ago, Ariana!

Yet she continued to waver, letting fear grip her as if the world might end if she did something that looked self-serving to her community. She hadn't realized this scaredy-cat trait was a part of who she was. At least she'd cleaned houses a lot of this past week and had earned some money. Not nearly enough, but some. Susie staying Amish depended on her getting the café, but organizing a benefit would be costly. What if she lost more than she made?

What should I do, God?

She worked the bread dough, unable to connect with any of the conversations going on around her. The whole day had been sucked into a vortex of uncertainty and indecision. Now as the sun began to set, she was in the same room she'd been in since before sunrise — the kitchen. Three of her four sisters were with her, along with Salome's daughters. The menfolk had eaten dinner and dispersed to do evening chores.

The built-in bookshelves lining the dining room walls held no books. She used the shelves to hold baked goods, and currently they were filled with rolls, croissants, and an array of breakfast breads. Right now the strongest aroma filling the home was that of raspberry, white-chocolate scones.

What was she going to do with all this food? Money was tight, and here she was baking as if she had a plan to earn money. If it were any time of the week except Saturday evening, she could package it to sell at the local dry-goods store. She'd done that before when she'd baked too much while working through an issue. But she'd been too busy all day trying to decide about the benefit to consider what to do with all the food she was making. The store would close soon, and everything would be stale by the time it reopened Monday.

Her well-established method of decision making hadn't worked — not today and not all week.

It would help if her Mamm were here to talk to, but her parents had been gone more than they were home the last two weekends. When Mamm was here, she was . . . different. Distracted and distant. Clearly, Ariana wasn't the only one with things on her mind.

"Would you look at this?" Fifteen-year-old Martha stood in front of an ironing board, moving a hot pressing iron over a prayer Kapp. She set the iron upright and removed the prayer Kapp from the board, frowning. "Never mind. I almost have the hang of tending to these." She put the Kapp on the board again, pressing the iron against it.

Prayer Kapps were easy to rip, hard to keep clean, and difficult to iron correctly.

"I think it looks great," Ariana said. "I would wear it to church."

"Really?" Martha seemed unsure and hopeful at the same time.

All the sisters nodded while making encouraging comments.

Martha grinned. "If you say so . . ." She took it upstairs, and Ariana was sure she'd put it away until time to dress for a meeting.

"Aenti Ari." Esther clutched her little fingers around the spindles of a kitchen chair and started shoving it toward the island. The sweet innocence of her spirit was easily seen in her eyes, but the angry scar on her face was her most prominent feature. *"Kann Ich helfe?"*

Her niece wanted to help, and once again today Ariana would let her. Even if anxiety had her heart shriveled and quaking, she wouldn't turn down Esther. With the exception of a short nap, Esther had been Ariana's shadow since sunrise almost twelve hours ago. But Salome had been up to tending to the baby during most of the day. *"Ya. Ich lieb sell."* It was honest. Ariana loved for Esther to help, but it made hiding her mood a tougher job. She pinched off a small handful of dough and placed it on the counter in front of Esther.

Esther grinned. *"Lieb du."*

Ariana kissed the top of her bare head. "I love you too." Even though she was too distracted to feel much warm and fuzzy love for anyone right now, love's virtue remained intact, with its thriving desire to be kind, encouraging, and protective. Moods changed as drastically as the seasons —

summertime sunshine on good days and bitter cold winds on bad days. Thankfully, virtue held its ground no matter what.

Martha bounded down the stairs. "I finally got tending to a prayer Kapp right, and Mamm isn't even here to see it. Doesn't it feel odd for her and Daed to be gone so much lately? What are they up to?"

Susie rinsed another dinner dish and set it on the drying rack. "Mamm said they needed uninterrupted time to talk, days of it. Since that's the case, we should be glad they're going off by themselves to do it and not dragging us into the boring stuff."

"I think it's about time they got away by themselves some," Salome said.

"Ya, I guess you're right." Martha picked up a wrinkled white shirt belonging to one of their brothers and put it on the pressing board. "They've had thirty-something years of young children. Now we are all finally in double digits."

Susie put a hand on her hip. "Some are more of an idjit than others."

"Huh?" Martha asked.

As Susie explained her quip exchanging the word *idjit* for *digit,* Salome poured a glass of lemonade while holding Katie Ann in one arm.

She walked over to Ariana and leaned her

backside against the counter. "You and Rudy aren't going out tonight?"

Ariana shook her head. Rudy was busy building things for her to sell at either a yard sale or a benefit. A very profitable yard sale might clear a thousand dollars, maybe two. A successful benefit, even one thrown together quickly, should be closer to four or five thousand — unless the Amish boycotted it.

"You okay?" Salome set the drink on the counter.

"Ya." Ariana wasn't willing to tell anyone else about the decision she needed to make. She had enough opinions already. Now it was between her and God. She hoped she would hear Him clearly on the matter *before* October first. Was she waiting on God, as the Word said, or was she simply wavering in indecision? "A better question is, how are you?"

Salome studied Esther's scar. "I'm fine."

But she wasn't. Ariana saw grief and lostness in Salome's eyes. Resentment had been shored up in her sister's heart, and Ariana had no idea how to help her release it. Time and again Ariana had tried to find the right words, but none had penetrated Salome's anger and hurt.

When the accident happened, the church

leaders and community had pressured Salome to stick to the Old Ways of using a tried-and-true home remedy specifically for burns on Esther. Emanuel had sided with the community, and Salome had considered disobeying her husband and doing as the Englisch doctors wanted. They had recommended skin grafts for the sake of faster, less painful healing and minimal scarring. Part of Salome had wanted to take Esther to the hospital and follow the Englisch ways. But she had tempered her mother's intuition, obeyed her husband's wishes, and followed the Old Ways.

Ariana gestured toward Esther. "Don't let her get too close to the edge of the chair, please."

Salome moved into Ariana's spot while she went to the oven and removed the lightly browned scones and then put a second batch into the oven.

Ariana returned to her dough, and Salome moved to the side. She had been assured that Esther would heal by using the poultices, but her daughter's suffering had been unbearable, and the scarring was much worse than expected. Now, more than two years later, Salome had yet to forgive herself or those in the community who'd pressured her. She had confided in Ariana that Emanuel had asked for her forgiveness for siding with the community. It had taken months of effort, but Salome had forgiven him.

When the rest of the Amish sided with the church leaders in not doing skin grafts, Ariana had made herself stay neutral, aiming to encourage Salome in whatever her final decision was. Now Salome was working her way through anger and depression, and all Ariana knew to do was be a good sister.

The way Salome hovered, looking hesitant but needy, Ariana was sure something was bothering her. "What's on your mind?" Ariana got a clean bowl out of the cabinet beneath her.

Salome shifted the newborn. "I hate to ask, but would you be willing to baby-sit for me and Emanuel tomorrow?"

She set the bowl on the counter. "Sure."

"You would miss the singing tomorrow night."

"Okay." Ariana knew Rudy wouldn't mind. He would be fine spending an evening here even if it meant playing with her nieces and nephews more than visiting with her.

Salome took another sip of her drink. "We had one of Emanuel's sisters lined up to watch them, but that fell through. We'll take

Katie Ann with us, because there's a possibility we'll stay overnight. You know, maybe get a quiet visit with his aunt and uncle in Lancaster."

"Sounds like a good plan." How would she feel if she didn't at least try to hold a benefit? There was no way to earn enough money without it, and then Susie would leave. At least if she tried to have one, she would know she did her absolute best. Maybe that would be more consoling than any efforts she made to keep the community from getting its feathers ruffled.

Salome nudged her shoulder. "You're agreeing to things, and I'm not the least bit sure you've heard anything I've said." With eyebrows raised at Ariana, Salome took a sip of her lemonade.

"I heard." She flipped the dough over and pounded it. "Would you trust a suggestion made by Quill?"

Salome choked on the lemonade. "What? Why would you ask that?"

Ariana quickly filled in her sister about crossing paths with Quill again last Saturday and his opinions on how to earn the closing money.

"Oh." Relief was evident in her voice.

"Surely you know better than to fear I would leave."

Salome played with the condensation on the glass. "Ya, I know how you feel. You have more judgment than grace for those who leave . . . and I fear we will both live to regret that."

The words stung. "Do I?"

Salome's facial expression held an apology as she barely nodded. "Anyway, my alarm was only because I thought Quill might have confided things he shouldn't have. Rumors have it that he's always cared about you."

Ariana paused. "He and Frieda ran off together, so why would anyone say he cared for me?" It was easy to believe that people had whispered for years about how much Ariana had cared for Quill, but she'd never imagined anyone thinking he had feelings for her.

"Because" — Salome put the baby on her shoulder and patted her back — "when he meets with those who are thinking about leaving the Amish, he asks about you."

"How would you know that?"

Salome's eyes widened. "I . . . I . . . heard that's what he —"

"Look." Susie pointed out the kitchen window. "Maybe you and Rudy have a date and you just don't know it."

"He's here?" Ariana's heart immediately

felt lighter, and she looked through the window. "It is him."

"You think I could be wrong?" Susie laughed. "What's the matter with you, girl?"

Ariana removed the kitchen towel from her shoulder and looped it around the back of Susie's neck. "Watch the scones and don't let them burn. Can you manage it?"

Susie clutched her shoulders, a wry smile making her faint dimple show itself. "No."

Ariana tugged on each end of the towel. "Do it anyway." She hurried out the door and ran toward the hitching post near the barn. Out of breath, she rounded the carriage to the driver's side and ran into Rudy.

He caught her, laughing. "Whoa." He backed up, glancing at the house before he slid his hands around her waist and tugged her to the blind spot behind the rig. "Hey." His soft, gentle voice was welcoming.

Despite her desire to be cautious, they were getting bolder with their feelings and their flirting. "What are you doing here?"

"I *had* to see you."

"Did you?" Her heart raced, and a ton of pent-up anxieties began to melt. This was an unexpected perk to their relationship.

Their happenstance meeting yesterday afternoon in the parking lot of the fabric store had increased her feelings for him exponentially. His kindness about her desire to purchase the café wasn't enough to do this to her heart. Her feelings came from who he was and who they were when together and apart.

He pulled her closer. "I would ask if you mind, but I think we've moved past that."

"Definitely."

His hands were strong and secure against her back, and she stopped resisting. He put his lips over hers, and she felt as if she could conquer her foe and win every battle. If this was what it meant to fall in love, she better understood the longing inside her to find a good man and build a big, beautiful family. The kiss grew deeper and more passionate by the moment.

She put her hands on his chest and pressed. He took his cue and put some distance between them.

There was a lot to be thankful for when it came to Rudy. He wasn't like Barbie and Cilla's cousin Nathaniel, and she was grateful he wasn't like the one and only Quill. He wasn't like any of the others she had dated, who were either cocky or closed off or temperamental or uninteresting.

Rudy leaned against the carriage. "I think we should get out of here for a bit." He took her hand into his, playing with it as if distracted. "Thoughts?" The fire in his eyes was undeniable.

Feeling much the same way, she realized that Rudy had become like a drug or a strong drink as she'd heard them described — chasing away the cares that weighed on her and making her feel strong and capable. But getting away by themselves sounded dangerous. "As much as I like the idea, I think I'd better stay here and work. But if you would like to get out for a bit on your own, I'll understand."

He shook his head, eyes closed, as if he couldn't believe how daft she was. "Suggesting that I go by myself is missing my point, ya?"

She leaned in and gazed into his eyes. "I didn't miss anything, Rudy . . . except, perhaps, the opportunity to cross a line."

He released her hand. "I won't pretend I'm confused about what you're saying." He folded his arms. "It's only going to get more difficult, isn't it?"

Since Rudy could easily cause her disquiet to flee, it was going to be tougher than she'd ever imagined. The chemistry between them, the feelings that showed up out of nowhere, elated her as much as they scared her. "Ya."

"I have a solution."

"Ariana!" Susie called.

Rudy ran his thumb across her lips. "You should marry me."

Marry him? She'd been so focused on the various dramas in her life — Berta getting sick, closing on the café, Susie wanting to leave the Amish, and Quill reentering her life — that she hadn't been waiting on or expecting him to ask such a question anytime soon. But she wasn't against the idea. "Think so?"

"I know so, not one doubt."

She did like the idea. "I promised Susie I'd get the café up and running."

"We will. Getting married doesn't have to change any of that."

His use of the word *we* worked its way deep into her heart, and fresh relief washed over her. "You are entirely too charming for my good."

He laughed. "Me, charming?"

Susie's footsteps grew louder against the gravel, and Rudy put space between him and Ariana. Susie came around the boxy gray rig, looking toward the barn. "Ariana?"

Rudy chuckled. "With observant folks like Susie around, we don't need a blind spot in which to hide," he whispered.

Ariana stepped away from the carriage. "Here."

Susie turned, wide eyed. "What are you doing there?" Susie held up her hand. "Wait, I got it! Apparently your life isn't a 'perfect graveyard of buried hopes.'"

It was a line from a book they used to read as children. Fresh memories washed over Ariana, ones of boisterous giggles between sisters as they hid under the sheets with a flashlight to read past bedtime. Salome was the one who had started the tradition. As the eldest sister, she set the precedent by tucking them in bed, waiting for their parents to go to sleep, and then reading to them by flashlight when they were supposed to be asleep.

What fun they'd had as sisters growing up, all five of them, and Ariana was so grateful Susie was going to stay Amish. Ariana looped one arm through Rudy's arm and one through Susie's. "Have I told you how happy I am that you're staying Amish?"

"Sort of, ya." Susie patted Ariana's arm. "But sometimes you say it as if I was making plans to steal away or something."

Ariana stopped cold, pulling Rudy and Susie backward. "You didn't have plans with Quill to leave?"

"Quill?" Susie seemed confused. "Until last Saturday I hadn't seen or spoken to him since he left years ago."

"But he walked you to your rig. It looked like you were picking up on a recent conversation."

"That wasn't what was happening, Ari. I was scared and confused. He saw that and calmed me down. When he did, I was able to do as you'd told me."

That was Quill's mode of operation — read a person and know just what needed to be said. She'd come to detest that about him.

If Susie wasn't the one planning to leave, who was it?

"When he meets with those who are thinking about leaving the Amish, he asks about you." Salome's soft voice rang an alarm in Ariana's heart.

But Salome couldn't be the sister leaving. She needed her family far more than most young women. Ariana's mind spun. Dozens of conversations she'd had with each sibling over the last few weeks hung in front of her like a word collage. Only Salome's words stood out.

"You have more judgment than grace for those who leave . . . and I fear we will both live to regret that."

Ariana's heart clenched, and she ran toward the house.

Nineteen

Sitting in the back corner of a half-empty restaurant, Lovina fought against queasiness as smells of various foods assaulted her. How long had they been in this booth as Quill gave his updates and tried to prepare them for the next step? She sipped icy water, hoping to deter the nausea.

Quill's eyes were kind and his gestures slow and gentle as he eased into explaining a little more about Skylar. They'd ordered only drinks, and the coffee in his mug had surely grown cold. But more than an hour ago he'd handed the server a good tip and assured her she didn't need to stop by the table again. Was he as sick to his stomach over this mess as Lovina was?

He fidgeted with the cup. "I need you to brace yourself for how Skylar will look. She's very non-Amish."

Isaac continued to open and close the blade of his pocketknife. "Meaning?"

"She likes jeans, jewelry, black nail polish, and different hair coloring. That's completely normal for how she's been raised."

"Normal," Lovina muttered. It certainly wasn't normal for one of her daughters. She dipped her fingertips into the cool water and dabbed it across her forehead. If she was theirs, could they undo enough of the worldliness that she could hear God's truth?

Quill held her gaze. "However stressful you find her outward appearance, especially when she's on stage, remember that you can't see the most important thing — her heart. And I . . . I believe she has a tender and good heart."

It was his second reference to her heart, and he'd stumbled each time. Why? Lovina couldn't make herself ask, but worry had her feeling faint. "You've evaded my question several times, and I'll ask again. Do you think she's ours?"

No matter how unglued she or Isaac became, Quill's responses remained as smooth and calm as water in a rain barrel on a clear day. "What I think is that we need to take one step at a time. Right now, based on your decision, that next step is attending the play."

Lovina reached across the table and

grabbed his hands. "Please, Quill, answer me."

He put his hands over hers. "Lovina, anything I say would be speculation. Your faith is strong, and you believe that everything is in God's hands and happens for a purpose. Lean on that and don't put your trust in anything I think."

Warmth wrapped around her, and she felt as if she could breathe again. "Okay."

"You can do this, all of it, wherever the path leads." He squeezed her hands. "Right?"

She studied him, wondering how she could gain such solace from one who'd rebelled against the Amish. As if reading her thoughts, he offered an understanding smile before he released her hands. She turned to her husband. "Ya," — she nodded — "we can do this."

"I know you can." Quill looked at his watch. "The play starts in an hour, and we're about fifteen minutes away from the college. I brought you each a change of clothes." He set two brown grocery bags on the table. "I know you won't like the idea of changing, but I feel it's really important you not stick out. Added to that, it's possible Brandi will be there, and we don't want to raise any red flags."

Lovina returned to rubbing the inside of her left palm with her thumb, peeling off layers of skin and making the blister worse on her thumb. Somehow the pain from the nervous gesture distracted her from the intensity of the hurt she carried inside. "I'm not changing clothes. I won't pretend to be someone I'm not. It's been twenty years. If I see Brandi, I doubt either one of us could recognize the other."

"You may be right, but you would give her a huge advantage in triggering memories if she sees you at her daughter's school wearing the same type of clothes she saw the night her daughter was born."

Isaac closed the knife. "I had more contact with her, and I would recognize her, but I agree with Lovina. We will not compromise the honesty of who we are during any of this."

Staring at the table, Quill took a deep breath. "I need to make sure you understand that my role here is to help and to guide, so the decisions are yours, but I strongly disagree with you attending a college play dressed in Amish clothes."

"It's who we are. You want us to pretend otherwise?" Heat burned Lovina's skin as hatred for the whole mess surged through her. "I won't wear Englisch clothes while seeing a girl who may be our daughter."

Quill interlaced his fingers. "We will be on Brandi and Skylar's turf, and entering their world wearing Englisch clothes would offer them the same discretion among their peers as you've given your children. It won't cause a buzz of whispers and questions. You'll look like any other couple going to a play, and if Brandi happens to see and recognize you, it will be her information to keep as quiet as she wants . . . for now."

Lovina snatched the bag closest to her. "You say the decision is ours, and then you use your gift of persuasion to convince us to do things your way." She clutched the bag against her. "I suppose I should be grateful you didn't use that smoothness on Ariana when she was fifteen." She looked inside the bag, seeing what appeared to be a navy-blue dress folded on top of a heavy sweater. "Fine." Passing the other bag to Isaac, she slid out of the booth.

Lovina's heart beat so fast she had to will herself to stay upright. She barely recalled changing clothes, leaving the restaurant, or riding to the college.

Quill drove past numerous buildings of various sizes, all made from the same red brick. He pulled into a parking spot and turned off the car. Isaac opened her door, saying something she couldn't make out. He moved, and Quill crouched beside her. "Release all the air in your lungs."

She did as he said.

"Close your mouth and take a slow, deep breath. Now pause. Good. Now exhale."

As she followed his instructions time after time, the numbness in her hands and arms eased a bit. He continued coaching her, and she lost track of time. "Good, Lovina. Every time you feel that tightness in your chest, you breathe just as we've been doing." He stood and held on to the door until she got out.

The parking lot was filled with cars, and the numerous windows in the building were bright with lights. They went through the double-wide doors, and just inside were three people sitting at a long table, taking money in exchange for tickets. Quill continued right past them, and Lovina and Isaac followed him. He gave the tickets to someone at the door, and then they went inside a room filled with rows of cushioned chairs. Had he come to the play last night? How else would he know this building so well?

Quill motioned for them, and they sat on the last row. Was she dreaming? Nothing felt real.

Quill leaned in. "Practice breathing. The first act will have a lot of cast members dance across the stage, but in less than a minute, she'll be center stage with only one other actor."

Center stage?

The lights around them went out. Music began and beams of moving light hit the curtains. Young people skipped onto the stage, talking to one another. Most of them had on bright yellow outfits. Some wore feathers and dresses with entirely too little material. Was she supposed to be able to make out what was being said? Quill handed both her and Isaac a pair of what he called theater glasses. She wasn't sure she needed a closer view, and she certainly didn't want Isaac getting a better look. Why did some of the girls have on dresses that barely covered their backsides?

Ignoring her knee-jerk reactions, Lovina put the glasses to her eyes and turned the focusing knob. A little boy came on the stage carrying a striped hat. He set the hat in the center of the stage and began talking. A minute later the curtains moved, and a girl poked out her head. She spoke, and then separated the curtains and stepped onto center stage. She pranced about in a black leotard with black tights, a white vest, red scarf, and a black jacket. A long tail followed behind her. Lovina tried to focus the glasses on the girl's face, but she couldn't manage to zoom the lens properly as the girl sashayed from one spot to another, singing, "Oh the thinks you can think . . ."

Then the girl stood still, facing the audience while singing, and . . .

"Nooo." Lovina was powerless to hold in the guttural sound. "It can't be. It just can't." She'd been warned how much Skylar favored Salome, but being told something and witnessing it were apparently completely different.

Several people in the row ahead of them turned and frowned.

"Sorry." Quill leaned toward the onlookers, smiling. "We completely surprised her with who's on stage."

The onlookers grinned and nodded before turning back around in their seats.

Lovina wanted to keep her eyes focused through the glasses, but tears blurred her vision.

Isaac wrapped an arm around her, pulling her close and whispering in her ear, "All things work for the good. All things work for the good." He breathed deeply, and she knew he was fighting tears also.

The song continued, and the girl faced

315

the curtains while spreading her arms wide. The curtains opened, and people in all sorts of strange outfits began singing. The words to the song made little sense, but Lovina was missing more of the words than she was catching. As others in the audience watched, seemingly mesmerized, Lovina was sure she was caught in some kind of nightmare. What were they going to do? Maybe they should keep their family intact and tell no one what they suspected. What good would it do to upset the applecart? Would they change who Skylar was or only change Ariana's life for the worse?

Why would Lovina give Brandi a chance to mess up both girls?

She no longer questioned whether Skylar was hers, but the confusion over what to do was overwhelming. Lovina seemed to lift from the seat and float above the crowd, hovering in darkness for no apparent reason. She knew she was in her seat, holding on to Isaac, but she felt as if she were detached from herself. From the life she'd known. From the love of God.

God . . . she'd forgotten about Him for a moment.

Dear God, what are we to do? Isaac and me . . . about our daughter? What are we to do?

The question churned and churned. Skylar disappeared from the stage for long periods, leaving Lovina breathless . . . and afraid. When Skylar did return, she sang by herself as the beam of light followed her.

Quill leaned in. "This next song is the ending to the play."

The ending? Hadn't it just begun? How much had she missed while begging God for an answer to what to do? The audience gave a standing ovation, but Lovina couldn't budge. Her legs would surely give way. A man in regular clothes came onto the stage, and people clapped harder. "Thank you. By popular demand we have an olio performance before the close of the evening. A grand finale to the finale of *Seussical.*"

The audience clapped and sat down. The lights went out, and they sat in pitch black for a few minutes.

Quill leaned in again. "The next song is 'Mad World.' Brace yourself for it to be a little disturbing. It's only a song. No more."

A lone white light focused on a girl's face. Skylar's. She had no expression whatsoever. It was the first time during the performance the girl hadn't been animated while talking, dancing, or singing. Where was the rest of her? Nothing showed but her face. That had to be a trick of some sort, but how did they do it?

Music filled the space. Skylar began singing, but her face remained expressionless as words slowly poured from her barely moving lips.

Lovina tried to focus on the words as Skylar sang something about it being a mad world and how alone she was.

There wasn't any way that her words were merely part of a song. Lovina could sense how lost Skylar felt.

Skylar turned, facing Lovina directly now. Could she see into the darkness? Lovina doubted it, but Skylar seemed to look right at her . . . at her Mamm.

". . . the dreams in which I'm dying are the best I've ever had . . ."

Chills ran wild over Lovina as tears filled her eyes. The song ended, and a different song began, one that was lively and had the audience clapping to the beat, but Lovina couldn't focus. When the lights came on, she couldn't budge as God Himself seemed to be whispering to her soul exactly what she needed to do next.

TWENTY

Abram paced the driveway, looking for signs
of Ariana. Where was she this late at night?
He heard a rustling from the pasture behind
him and turned. How many times over the
last hour had he thought he heard someone
walking toward him only to discover it was
a deer, a raccoon, or some other nocturnal
creature?

He'd already gone to the places he could
think of to look for her — the café, the
swimming hole at the creek, and the room
above the carriage house. All were sanctuar-
ies where he could find his twin. She didn't
use those places often, because her real
sanctuary was the kitchen, where she could
bake and talk to loved ones as she fed them.
Strange girl, really.

A cow mooed softly, making the evening
seem as if it should have its usual rhythm
and peace. The front door of the house
opened. Emanuel stepped outside, fully

clothed, including his straw hat. Salome followed behind, carrying a fussy Katie Ann. Emanuel headed to the barn, and since it was after eleven at night, Abram was sure his brother-in-law intended to hitch a carriage to a horse to search for Ariana.

Salome came toward Abram. "Still no sign of her?"

Abram shook his head. It was a rather annoying question. Obviously there was no sign of her or he wouldn't be standing here on the lookout. "What did you two talk about on that carriage ride?"

Salome shrugged. "Silly sister stuff."

Just how stupid did Salome think he was? "So what you would like me to believe is that, soon after Rudy arrived, she left him here to help Susie keep your children while she took you and the baby for a long buggy ride and she did so in order to discuss nothing more than silly sister stuff?"

"It doesn't matter what we talked about."

"Of course not."

He'd made good overtime money today, but right now he wished he'd gotten home sooner, at least early enough to know what was going on.

Salome swayed Katie Ann, patting her back. "Sometimes Ariana gets too upset over things that aren't her business."

"That's part of how we know she cares so much. And since when are you none of her business?"

Ariana didn't argue over silly things. She tried to let people do as they thought best unless she feared they were entering a situation they couldn't turn back from.

"Of course you disagree with me." Salome jiggled the baby. "You two have been thick as thieves since the day you were born."

Salome had been thirteen when they were born, so her recollections of their first months and years were pretty clear.

"So she drove you and Katie Ann back home, put the horse and carriage away, and took off on foot?"

"I guess. Once I got out of the rig, I didn't hang around to see what she did."

"And you didn't ask."

"Heavens, Abram, she's twenty years old. Most Amish girls her age are engaged or married by now. I didn't think I needed to baby-sit her. She was miffed and went for a walk. She's gone for long walks for a decade. What's the big deal?"

"It's late and she's alone. When we don't go together, she always leaves me a note."

"Always?"

He nodded.

"I didn't know that."

He could fill a library with all Salome didn't know about Ariana. But he wouldn't say that out loud. Salome's selfishness had his temper boiling. He had little doubt that whatever the argument was about, Salome was at fault.

Emanuel drove the courting buggy out of the barn and toward them. Without the usual sides and top of an everyday carriage, it would be easy to see out.

Maybe Abram needed to go with them and search for her again along the roads. Emanuel hopped out and helped Salome climb in with the baby in her arms and then turned to him. "I think you should stay here and wait for her. We will drive the roads, looking for her while getting Katie Ann to sleep." Emanuel nodded at him and then got in as if his words settled the matter.

Abram felt too antsy to stay put, but Emanuel's plan had a bit of wisdom. Ariana was more likely to return home on her own, coming through a back field, than to be found walking down the road. If Abram was here when she arrived, he could finally get some straight answers.

Driving the last few miles of the three-hour trip from the college, Quill's body ached from the stress. It was a type of weariness he hadn't experienced before.

He took a deep breath. "We're only ten minutes from where we stored your horse and carriage." The statement was actually a question. Were they up to changing clothes and getting into their carriage, or did they need him to drive more while the three of them talked? An hour ago he had pulled into a place where they could have changed into their Amish clothes, but between her sobs Lovina had assured him she was in no shape to get out of the car. Isaac had spoken up, saying they would wait and change right before getting into the buggy.

Quill looked in his rearview mirror. Isaac caught his eye and gave a nod while trying to comfort Lovina. The tension and grief inside the car were miserable, and he could use a break. But even if he hadn't witnessed firsthand Lovina and Isaac's emotional upheaval, he wouldn't be free of his own inner turmoil involving this nightmare.

Fear over Ariana's future wouldn't retreat for even a moment. He knew her — how she thought, how she felt — and losing all DNA connection to the people she'd grown up with could undo her.

When he looked in her eyes now, compared to five years ago, he no longer saw childhood tagging along behind her, nipping at her heels. He saw full-fledged adulthood. And she had an untapped strength buried inside her, didn't she?

Dear God, let that be true.

He'd dealt with a lot of situations over the last seven years. The pressure began when he was only eighteen and took on the fight his Daed began, but that paled in comparison to what was happening now. He was unprepared in every way, and he didn't know how to comfort or guide Lovina or Isaac. What could he say?

Lovina's sobs had quieted now, and Isaac held her, his voice wavering as he spoke words of comfort that he clearly didn't fully believe.

Now what? Since Quill had made the decision to leave with Frieda, he'd always known what to do. His decisions weren't easy, nor were they always right in everyone's eyes, including his own, but he'd known what had to be done. Each step. Every time.

Quill readjusted the rearview mirror so he could see them better. "I think you should let this situation with Ariana sit for now. She has seventeen days to finish earning the money for the café. If she can have that victory first, it'll help her cope with the news." But the news would still unravel her world. All Quill could do was help her attain one dream before she walked into a living nightmare . . . and hope that made her capable of keeping her feet under her.

Isaac reached across the back of the seat and patted Quill's shoulder. "Denki." His voice was raspy. "I agree, but how can she possibly earn that kind of money between now and then?"

It seemed that Isaac no longer viewed Quill as a traitor, which would help, because they needed to work together.

"She needs to have a benefit."

"A benefit?" Isaac repeated. "Between now and the first of October?"

Isaac's questions and his tone seemed to indicate that Ariana hadn't talked to her parents about the idea, but he didn't sound as if he was against it.

Quill squeezed the steering wheel. "I've put a lot of things into motion behind the scenes — things that can't be connected to me, for her sake. All of it will fall into place if she'll simply get the ball rolling to have a benefit." He glanced in the rearview mirror.

Isaac's smile said it all — he was truly grateful. "I don't know what to say."

"You're okay with the plan?"

Isaac had to know it could ruffle feathers. The Amish had three categories for their people's behavior: acceptable, frowned upon, and forbidden. Anything frowned upon could easily cause people to put up obstacles.

"We are if Ariana is." Isaac lifted Lovina's chin. "Right?"

Lovina wiped at her tears and nodded. "It would mean a lot to her if she could buy it."

"Good." Quill nodded. "Then, aside from Ariana, the only potential problem is how the people and ministers react to the idea. She doesn't have time to get bogged down in church politics and moral disapproval."

Isaac stared into the rearview mirror, his eyes locked on Quill's. "I . . . might be able to intervene on her behalf."

That was a pretty bold statement for Isaac. Quill only knew him as someone who supported the ministers, never as a man who asked them to reconsider their stand. "You're willing to try?" He glanced away from the rearview mirror, checking the road.

"Ya. But winning against hundreds of years of tradition isn't easy."

"True." Quill ran his fingers along the steering wheel, his mind churning. The ministers weren't bad people. They simply tended to think in the negative first, especially when the topic was a young woman establishing a new business. They worried over how inappropriate or selfish something might look or what model they were allowing. Quill needed to offer Isaac ways to present the positive sides and benefits.

While pondering that, he topped a hill and noticed a yellow glow in the distance. Focusing on it, he realized the light was coming from the windows of the community phone shanty. At nearly midnight? Was someone inside, or had a lamp accidentally been left burning?

He jolted when the phone that almost never received incoming calls began to vibrate. He pulled it from his pocket. The screen showed the community phone number, and a half-dozen possible scenarios crossed his mind.

His first goal was to protect Lovina and Isaac's privacy, so rather than pull up to the phone shanty, he immediately veered to the side of the road and parked under a huge oak. He turned off the engine, hoping to get out of the car and take the call before it disconnected. "I need to answer this." He opened the door to the car. "I'll be right back."

"No rush." Isaac sounded grateful. He and Lovina probably needed time to talk openly without him there and without any chance of family overhearing them.

Quill hopped out and closed the door. "Hello."

"Why, Quill?" Ariana's whisper was haunting. "I . . . I don't understand."

Her voice quavered, and emotions from deep within him rushed to the surface, threatening to take control of him. She was the length of a football field away with no idea he was nearby. Should he walk to her? He stared into the starless night, searching the vast blackness for answers as he prayed for wisdom. "What's going on, Ariana?"

"I thought we were building a bridge between your life on the outside and mine, one we could cross as needed for your Mamm's sake. But that's not at all what's been happening, so please just go away and leave my family alone."

Just politely end the call and get her parents out of here. Despite what he should do, he walked toward the phone shanty. With neither long strides nor timid ones, he headed for her like a fish being reeled in.

Had she learned what was going on with her parents? He kept his cards close to his vest and gave no information that might tip his hand, which meant she had to be the one to talk. "Take a breath and tell me what you are talking about."

"Salome. How could you let me think I was on the right track?"

"I thought you knew. You said she changed her mind about leaving."

"I was talking about Susie! You knew that!"

"Actually, I didn't. You only referred to her as your sister, and I thought you meant Salome."

"It's constant secrecy with you. Why couldn't you just tell me it was Salome?"

He stopped outside the open door. "I'm bound by confidentiality."

She wheeled around, her eyes filled with raw anger and maybe hope that he would find a solution. How was he going to help Salome, Emanuel, and their five children — Ariana's nieces and nephews — leave in the middle of what Lovina and Isaac needed to reveal to her? Maybe she was their biological daughter, but before DNA testing was done, they would have to tell her what might have happened the night she was born.

"Bound by secrecy?" She dropped the phone into its cradle. "The rest of us are bound by love, and you chain your life to secrecy? Why would you do that to yourself?"

If he opened up to her even a little, he feared he wouldn't be able to stop himself from saying too much. "I'm sorry, Ariana. I really am." He slid his phone into his pocket and stepped into the shanty. "I don't know what else to say to you." He went around her to the phone. He pushed an arrow, making the last number dialed — his number — come up on the screen, and then he deleted it.

She stared up at him, wide eyed and innocent in her anger. The cape dress didn't hide her curves any more than the reserve of the Old Ways could hide the intensity that was pent up inside her. Underneath all the gentle restraint, she was a fighter of causes. How many times had that high-spirited determination pulled him from his darkest days following his Daed's death? The light from the kerosene lamp danced against the soft skin of her cheeks.

Her brow furrowed, and she reached for the braided cord around his neck, tugging at it until it was free of his T-shirt. It was his most cherished possession. Disbelief etched across her face. She ran her fingers down the three-strand cord until she was cradling the silver medallion. She had cut three long strands of rawhide and braided them. Each one had a meaning — one cord represented God, one her, and one Quill. And she'd intertwined them because, as the book of

Ecclesiastes said, "a threefold cord is not quickly broken." The medallion had been forged from a silver spoon, and she'd drilled a hole in the center and carved angled braid marks across the round surface. He wasn't sure how she'd managed some of the intricacies, and he doubted she could replicate it if given years to do so.

Holding the silver piece, she shook her head. "I . . . I don't understand you."

How could she? He had shared everything with her until he learned the secret that shattered their future. Then he focused on what had to be done next, shutting her out of his plans. "You don't have to understand me to trust that no matter what's happening, I'm on your side."

He could see the battle inside her — to believe him or herself. Despite all her strength and determination, she still had a fragile innocence that needed protecting.

She traced the faux braiding on the silver piece before looking up again. "I don't think you understand what it means to be on someone's side. You're too busy marching to the beat of your own drummer and getting others to march with you." She released the necklace and walked out.

He drew a breath and tried to clear his head. There seemed to be no right words when it came to Ariana, and even the ones that would tell the complete truth wouldn't give her the answers she wanted.

Was she unknowingly heading straight for the car? He rushed ahead of her, turned around to face her, and caught her arm. "The only drum-beat I march to is my belief that every person has the right to serve God without any manmade rules dictating the believers' actions — just people and God communicating through prayer and scripture. There should be no interference by the Ordnung unless the believer trusts that's God's will for them."

"With the freedoms you champion, are you free? Has your liberty filled you with more peace than the Old Ways?"

"Life isn't that simple, Ari. Giving people the ability to follow their consciences is the right thing to do, and its success can't be measured by whether I feel free or have peace."

"Maybe that works for someone like you, but Salome is in no state of mind to make this kind of decision. Emanuel would do anything to help her. Surely you can see that."

"I see, but perhaps she needs to get away from the community that pressured her against her will, against her mother's intuition."

"Perhaps? You intend for her to sever all ties between her and her family based on *perhaps*?"

"I can't judge what Salome does or doesn't need. Neither can you. The decision is between her, Emanuel, and God."

Ariana pressed her fingertips against her forehead, shaking with clear exasperation and growling. "You're infuriating."

He was sure of that, especially from her very limited perspective of what he did and why. "My best advice is that you not approach Salome. If you make waves, if you make her feel more pressure, she could choose to leave tomorrow."

"Great." She thrust out both arms, fingers splayed. "Then I did exactly all the wrong things, didn't I?"

What had she done? Could he undo it? He'd spent the better part of two years trying to help Salome and Emanuel navigate the bitterness while giving them hope that they could escape when the time was right.

They'd sold their house and moved back home. When she found out she was expecting, Quill was able to slow their plans to leave. Now they'd had the baby, and Salome was bouncing back quicker than he'd planned. Quill had only so much power to delay a departure.

"Go home, Ariana. Apologize to Salome. Tell her that you'll love her no matter what her decision is. And don't bring up the subject again."

"You want me to give her a guilt-free pass to leave? I won't do it."

"Everyone has the right to choose."

"They have chosen! They joined the faith more than a decade ago. They promised to uphold the Old Ways. Have you forgotten?"

"They were nineteen, and they'd spent their entire lives being convinced it was necessary to do so to be saved."

"That's not what the preachers teach."

"It's part of it, and it's what Salome and many others heard. You've sat under the teachings. How many believe that joining the Amish faith is the only straight and narrow way?"

"For good reason. Have you seen what it's like out there, the loose morals?"

He had, but whatever existed out there also existed among the Amish. Ariana just didn't know much about that. "Salome and Emanuel's desire to leave has nothing to do with embracing loose morals. Look, I want Salome and Emanuel to do what's best for them and their family. We're not far apart on this topic."

334

"Except you're holding the door wide open for them."

"That's not an accurate depiction. It's where we differ, Ariana. I don't think I know what's best for others."

"Sure you do. You simply go about exercising your beliefs in a different way than the Amish."

She had some reasonable points, but they couldn't have a true debate on this topic unless she knew information that he would never divulge, so it was time to stop the circular argument. "Regardless of how differently we view things, I promise I'm on your side concerning Emanuel and Salome *and* the café. We can't control what anyone chooses to do. So focus on what you can control — your future business. Have the benefit. Draw Salome into helping you. Maybe that will make a difference for her."

"You think so?" There it was again — hope that he could help her.

"I know that working to buy the café won't harm Salome's desire to stay, and I know you need that place as much as it needs you."

She stared into his eyes, looking for truth.

"So" — he moved his hand to her forearm and wrist, holding it tightly — "we find ourselves needing to call another truce."

"It's more like we need to cross a shaky bridge of unknowns together."

She used to have nightmares about crossing bridges as they collapsed, so he understood what she meant. "Okay, we have a bridge to cross. Can you find it in yourself to trust me so we can work together?" How ironic that he had to ask that question as he blocked her view of his car and her parents.

Thoughts of her parents in his car made him hate how much he had to keep from her. When would they tell her what happened the day she was born? Tomorrow? Next week? He didn't know, but it wasn't his place to reveal such news.

His heart raced as she stared at his hand, wavering about whether to trust him. "Despite the apparent outward betrayal of what I've done, Ari, what does your gut tell you is true?"

Her eyes bore into his, and he couldn't help but smile. They were together and talking, working through the train wreck he'd caused. And yet, if Ariana knew the truth, she would understand that he'd been an innocent bystander who had tried to be a good Samaritan.

He wanted to pull her close and demand that she trust him and open her eyes. But of all the lessons he'd learned thus far, the one carved the deepest was that he could not will a person to do anything. He could only present what he knew to be true.

A whispery sound of acceptance, perhaps a short laugh at the absurdity of where they found themselves, fell from Ari's lips. "Okay," she breathed, clasping her hand around his arm in the same manner.

The moment washed over him, one he'd never imagined could happen. "Good."

But her trust in him was probably as easily broken as a twig underfoot.

Twenty-One

From the backseat of Quill's car, Lovina stared as the two shadows in the distance parted ways. The girl hurried across the field. Quill returned to the phone shanty. A moment later the light went out, and then he strode toward the car.

Isaac shifted, craning his neck. "You think that was Ariana?"

That's what Lovina had said ten minutes earlier. "What other woman would Quill allow to wag a finger at him? Who else would he then stand toe-to-toe with, talking for any length of time?"

"Why would she be out here?"

"To fight with him about helping the Amish leave." If anyone could get Quill to change his ways, it was Ariana.

"You think he told her about the night she was born?" Isaac asked.

"Nee. He wouldn't." Did her husband know Quill at all?

338

From the time Quill was young, he was quiet and willful. When he spoke, it was clear he'd first thought carefully. He seemed to have a level of intelligence that she'd never seen in anyone else, and it unnerved her. Other traits came to mind too, like integrity. Still, she didn't like him . . . or maybe she just didn't like what he did. But observing him now, she couldn't see him as someone who'd broken her daughter's heart while running off with another girl. She saw a man committed to leaving her young daughter's life intact.

He opened the car door, and without a word they were soon on their way again.

Wasn't he going to say anything about why they'd stopped? Should they ask him about it?

Lovina had been shocked when he ran off with Frieda. The girl was sweet, but her health was poor, and sickness chipped away at her emotional stability until her only strength seemed to be what Quill could do for her. The more Lovina saw of him and tried to piece together what she knew firsthand with what the rumors said surrounding his Daed's death, the less she understood what had happened to make him leave as he did. Whatever had happened, she had watched as the rumors and his actions mutilated his reputation.

The car hit a bump, pulling her from the rambling thoughts. Quill stopped the vehicle in front of the oversized, dilapidated shed on the far side of his Mamm's property. He jumped out, leaving the vehicle running as he unlocked and opened the shed doors. He returned to the car and drove it inside next to their carriage. Their horse was in a small stall with feed and water, and Lovina wondered how many Amish people had met Quill here over the years. People's ability to disappear during the night made more sense now. How much did his Mamm know of what went on?

"Kumm." Isaac motioned for her.

Lovina grabbed the sack with her clothes and got out of the car. Her mind was every bit as weary as her body. She felt as if her heart were walking through a thick fog, dragging her mind and body with it. The horse lifted its head, looking at them inquisitively. Sadly, she didn't have much more insight into what was going on than the animal did.

The inside of the building was lined with black roofing paper. When Quill lit the kerosene lantern, no light escaped to the outside. The faithful Amish weren't likely to think that a run-down shed would be used as a meeting or communication place.

Isaac glanced at Lovina, and she knew what was on his mind. They would need Quill's help again when they were ready to contact Brandi, have DNA testing done, and whatever else would become a part of this awful journey. What little she knew about DNA came from a lifetime of hearing about genetic disorders among the Amish. The Amish had their own Plain clinic for children with genetic issues, but they wouldn't need that service.

With keys in hand, Quill gestured toward the open shed door. "I'll step outside, and you two can change. Once you leave in your carriage, I'll lock the shed."

Their world was falling apart, and he continued to speak matter-of-factly as if none of what was happening affected him. She supposed it didn't. Quill remained in place, perhaps waiting for one of them to ask another question or nod, saying it was okay for him to leave. They did neither.

Isaac stepped forward. "Was that Ariana you were talking to?"

Quill looked at the toe of his boot as he used it to tamp down some dirt. "It will be very difficult to keep what's going on to yourselves, but it's best to say as little as possible to as few people as possible. The last thing Ariana needs is to overhear gossip about this. You want to be the ones to tell her at the right time."

Isaac blinked several times, looking a bit baffled, but she wasn't surprised that Quill didn't even acknowledge her husband's question.

Quill fidgeted with the keys, rattling them in the palm of his hand. "Isaac, when you talk to the ministers about Ariana and the benefit, be aware that if they catch wind of the situation with Skylar, they could try to remove from your hands what little control you have in this situation."

Lovina hadn't thought that far ahead, but he was right. If the ministers learned about any of the compromises she and Isaac had made tonight, they would be held accountable. Riding with someone who had left the community as Quill had was forbidden. A baptized member dressing like the Englisch was forbidden. What would be allowed concerning Skylar and Ariana? It wasn't as if anyone Amish had ever encountered a similar scenario.

Quill pushed the car keys into his jeans pocket. "When you talk to them, say that buying the café is about what your family needs, and God has given Ariana the dream and skill for it. Do you feel that's a true statement?"

"Ya." Lovina nodded. "The café would mean a lot to all of us."

"Good." Quill looked pleased. "Both of you have been very faithful to help every cause the ministers have brought to you over the years. Remind them of specific incidents, and explain how this is similar. Assure them you now need their help. They're good men, and if you tug on their heartstrings before anyone gets a chance to stir up strife against Ariana having a benefit, you'll win the battle."

Isaac fidgeted with his Englisch shirt, apparently ready to get out of it. "What you've said is gut. Denki."

Quill nodded and walked out, closing the double-wide doors behind him. Lovina set the bag of clothes on the trunk of his car. She had pulled her hair back in a ponytail of sorts and brushed her hair in a way that removed the part down the middle. She and Isaac would get home around one in the morning. Did her hair need to be fixed in order to walk through her home and to her bedroom? She supposed that depended on whether they would bump into one of their children along the way. At least Quill had briefed them on how to answer honestly and yet tell them nothing. He suggested saying things like "we were out . . . together." And then he said to smile as if it had been a wonderful evening. He called it the no-lie, no-facts zone.

No sharing honestly with her family? What an awful position to be in.

She heard the muted sound of a man's voice outside the shed. Was Quill talking to someone?

She and Isaac froze. Had whoever was out there already heard them moving around inside the shed?

"You know the agreement." Quill's tone was calm and firm. "You shouldn't be here right now. I need you to say not a word, not one. Just return home immediately. We'll talk tomorrow."

"We have to talk!" Sobs escaped a raspy voice.

Isaac's eyes met Lovina's, and he mouthed the words *Is that Salome?* Lovina's heart began thudding in her ears. If it was Salome . . .

Lovina's knees threatened to give way. If it was Salome, Isaac had been wrong. He had been so sure and had even convinced Lovina that any rumors about a child of theirs leaving the Amish were just that — rumors. Pain shot through her chest, and she knew she couldn't take much more.

"Ariana knows!" the voice said.

Isaac's eyes grew wide, and Lovina supposed he was realizing the same things she was.

"I'm aware," Quill answered softly.

Isaac went to the doors and pushed them open, apparently willing to reveal their presence. As he and Lovina walked outside, they saw Quill clearly directing Salome and Emanuel away from the shed, and they were about to get into the carriage.

"Salome?" Isaac's voice held complete disbelief. "What's going on?"

Salome turned, looking completely baffled. "Daed, Mamm, why are you dressed like that, and what are you doing here?"

Steely exasperation flashed through Quill's eyes before he motioned for all of them to go into the shed. He then closed the doors behind them, appearing for a moment as if he would like to lecture all four of them. But Lovina couldn't tolerate the questions pounding her.

What did Ariana know? Why were Salome and Emanuel here? How did they know to meet Quill here? It was too much to have two daughters under her roof whose lives were shrouded in secrets.

Quill leaned against the trunk of his car. "Before anyone speaks, think. You cannot un-tell something."

Lovina knew there was only one reason for Salome and Emanuel to have this kind of contact with Quill Schlabach. "You're planning to leave, aren't you?"

"What?" Isaac's eyes widened as he looked from his wife to his oldest daughter. "That's not possible. They're only here because . . . because . . . Why are you here?"

Salome's face showed desperation and embarrassment.

Emanuel put his arm around her shoulders. "We didn't want you to find out this way."

"You can't." Isaac moved in front of his daughter, facing her. "Please."

Guilt shrouded Salome's face. "This isn't a frivolous decision, and we will stick to our plan."

Isaac paced the floor. "If nothing else, at least tell us you won't leave soon, for your Mamm's sake and Ariana's. There's too much happening for us to bear one more heartache." His voice cracked.

Salome held her newborn close, looking completely baffled. "Does that mean you know where Ariana is?"

Isaac turned to Quill, desperation in his eyes. "Have you seen her?"

Quill nodded. "She's on her way home."

Salome breathed a sigh of relief. "It's my fault she sought out Quill. She discovered our intentions earlier today, and we argued over it."

Isaac's face turned red. "I can't believe you'd plan to steal away during the night. Why, Salome?"

"Daed, we're suffocating under the rules. My daughter's face is scarred for life because the church frowned on skin grafts. It wasn't their decision to make!"

"They didn't make that decision. You had a choice. Medical decisions are left up to the family."

"You say that now, but there wasn't any support for what I thought was best. Everyone quoted the Ordnung and scolded us about not trusting God's will. The constant pressure to do things according to the Old Ways came from everyone — except Ariana."

Isaac grabbed his forehead. "Maybe we did do that, and maybe we were wrong. We need to talk and —"

"No." Salome held up a hand. "I won't listen to one more word about how I need to submit to what everyone else thinks I ought to do or not do."

Isaac rubbed his forehead. "You can't leave now. We need you. Ariana needs you."

"What are you talking about?" Salome asked.

Isaac nodded, and then he gestured from Quill to Salome. Explaining the events was just too difficult right now, so they listened as Quill laid out what might have happened the night Ariana and Skylar were born.

Salome reacted with shock and tears as she engulfed Lovina, and it brought a welcomed sense of camaraderie between mother and daughter. Lovina prayed that somehow, through all that lay ahead, Salome and Emanuel would decide that family was more important than any reasons they had for leaving.

Twenty-Two

Hot water sluiced down Ariana, from the top of her head and over her back as she rinsed shampoo from her hair. The warmth eased the tightness across her shoulders, but it did little for the knot in her stomach.

She'd yet to see Salome, and she had an awkward apology to get through when she did see her. By the time Ariana had arrived home after talking with Quill, it was past midnight. Abram had been standing watch, looking for her. His worry was evident, and she'd felt bad for not leaving him a note. Despite the hour they'd moved to the porch steps and talked. She'd told him everything before leaning her head against his shoulder and falling asleep. He'd nudged her and sent her to bed. It was just as well. She'd been too sleepy to wait any longer for Salome to come home.

Ariana turned off the water and grabbed a towel. It didn't take long to comb her hair and to dress. Taking bobby pins and a prayer Kapp with her, she left her hair free to dry while she went downstairs and into the kitchen.

Salome was nearly elbow deep in sudsy water, doing the never-ending job of washing dishes.

Ariana's skin prickled with heat as she fought with her pride while needing to apologize. As she set the pins and Kapp on the table, the floor beneath her feet creaked, and Salome pulled her attention from staring at the waning suds. When she looked at Ariana, she seemed different somehow. Her eyes were puffy, as if she'd been crying. Regret twisted through Ariana, making her sorry for all the indignation she'd unleashed on her sister. How was it possible to love someone so much and yet rail at that person with unbridled anger?

Salome's weak smile quivered, but she seemed frozen.

Ariana lowered her eyes before grabbing a dry towel from the drawer. "I'm sorry." She went to the dish drainer. "I shouldn't have come at you the way I did."

Salome pulled her soapy hands from the water and put them around Ariana, embracing her tightly. "You have nothing to be sorry for. Anyone who cared would be just as upset to learn such news. I see that now. I should have seen it before."

Ariana wondered if that meant she would stay. "I need you to know that I will love you no matter what, and that is the truth, regardless of how intense I come across."

Salome took the dishtowel from Ariana and wiped soapy bubbles off her shaky hands. "I don't know what the future holds for any of us . . ." She sobbed before licking her lips and gulping in air. "But for now we're staying and rethinking our plans."

Why did Salome appear to be on the verge of a meltdown? Had Ariana done that to her?

Salome gestured to the bookshelves-turned-baking-shelves. "Susie finished wrapping up everything last night for you. What are you going to do with all these baked goods?"

"Not sure."

Salome got a mug out of the cupboard. "When I heard someone getting a shower upstairs, I prepared a fresh pot of coffee."

"Denki." Ariana took the mug and filled it. Her lungs begged for air. Their words were nice enough and their sentiments sincere, but she imagined it would be easier to trudge through several feet of mud than to move normally in this room. Had their argument sucked out all the normalcy between them?

The screen door thumped, and Abram walked inside. "Well, it's about time, Sister. A brother could starve to death waiting on you to get up and cook breakfast." He had bits of hay on his shirt, and she imagined he'd been tending the cows.

Salome put her hands on her hips. "Hey. I fixed you something to eat."

"True." He removed his straw hat and hung it on a spindle on the ladder-back chair. "Don't know what it was, but you prepared it."

Salome seemed to waver between hurt feelings and taking it in stride. She raised a finger and wagged it as a weak smile graced her face. Chuckling, Abram ducked while moving away from her.

"So what time are Mamm and Daed coming home?" Ariana set her mug on the table.

"They're home." Abram sat. "I guess they're sleeping in even later than you. Good thing it's a between Sunday." He looked behind him, toward the stairs. "I want to talk to Quill." He spoke his last words softly.

Ariana twisted her damp hair into a bun, pinned it in place, and secured her prayer Kapp. "Why?"

"I want to look him in the eye and ask about his plans to help you get the café."

"Oh, good." She picked up her cup of coffee.

Salome dug a spoon into the sugar bowl and slid it to Ariana. "He's different than you think. If he says his goal is to help, it is."

Abram shrugged. "Not sure your opinion is unbiased."

Salome glanced at Ariana, and Ariana knew what she was thinking. She was surprised, maybe disappointed, that Ariana had told him of Salome and Emanuel's plans.

Ariana stirred sugar into her coffee and took a sip, weighing her words. "He's quiet and trustworthy."

Salome's face seemed etched with pain, and tears welled.

Ariana had traversed many a mountaintop and valley to stay by Salome's side, but she seemed unusually emotional today. "Did I say something wrong?"

Salome shook her head. "I . . . I just . . . forget sometimes how close you two are."

Abram raised a brow and mumbled about being twins. Salome drew a ragged breath, looking as if she was ready to bolt from the room. Was she just now realizing all the ties between the siblings, the ties she had been all too ready to sever?

"Knock, knock." Rudy's voice rumbled through the kitchen.

Ariana jolted, and a nervous current went through her as she realized she'd agreed to do as Quill thought best without even considering talking to Rudy first. "Hallo." She hurried toward the door. "Kumm."

He stepped inside. "Morning." He smiled at her before he looked to Salome and Abram. "Hi." He gave them a nod and a brief smile before returning his attention to her. He took her hand into his. "I just wanted to check on you."

She turned to Abram and Salome and then motioned toward the door. "We're going for a walk."

Abram nodded, and Ariana tugged on Rudy's hand. They didn't say anything else until they were on the long walking trail between her house and Quill's. How many times over the years had she trod this old path? It went through pastureland and some patches of woods. The trees overhead rustled with the autumn breeze. The lush greenness was beginning to yield to hints of fall's gold and red colors. Rudy picked up a stick as they walked. Ariana went to a log and sat, and Rudy propped a foot on it.

He poked the stick against the ground. "I hated to leave last night, but when you didn't return, I didn't have a choice. What's going on?"

Ariana explained everything as best she could, and when she heard the words coming out of her mouth, she realized how absurd her actions sounded.

Rudy gripped the stick with each hand and broke it in half. "You did what?"

"I agreed to trust Quill's guidance concerning the benefit for the café."

"No." Anger flashed across his face. "Absolutely not."

"I understand how you feel. I thought the same thing, but —"

"Ya, I'm sure you did until you let persuasion-guy talk you into trusting him. Come on, Ariana. You of all people know what he is like. I don't want to see you get hurt or humiliated in front of the community by following his advice."

"Your points are valid, but . . . I agreed and, more than that, I think I was right to do so."

He pushed his foot away from the log and turned, facing the sky and yelling at the canopy of trees overhead. "This is unbelievable! Who does this?"

She'd not seen this side to him although

he'd told her that he could get quite loud when he was riled. He gave her lots of room for emotion, and she wanted to do the same for him. "I do." She kept her voice soft, hoping to defuse his anger, but as he stomped around, crunching dead leaves under his boots, she wasn't sure he'd heard her.

He raised his arms, exasperated. "Why would you open your life and put your name at risk for a disreputable man?"

His anger was disconcerting, which was making it harder for her to think. "I . . . I'm not sure I can explain it. I looked him in the eye, and I think he's trustworthy about this one thing."

"No one is trustworthy on just one thing. No one. Either he has inner character that guides him on a regular basis, or he doesn't. You're willing to put your reputation into the hands of an ex-Amish? I can't believe you'd do that."

"He wants me to get the café."

"Why?"

"Maybe as a thank-you for helping his Mamm."

"He's ex-Amish. You're entrusting your reputation to a guy who can't even show his face in this community. He's trouble for you, which makes him trouble for me. I tried to talk to you about marrying me, and you avoided the discussion, but you're willing to accept a business proposal from Quill!"

Ariana tried to decipher what he was feeling and put it into words. What she heard was that he was upset about two things, and it seemed best to address each one separately. "You're right that I might get hurt. He could submarine me, but that's a chance I'm willing to take. I won't break. I promise you that."

"He's done it to you before — broken you. How do you know that's not his goal this time?"

"I . . . don't think that's who he is."

"That's it?" He made a fist and pounded it into his other hand. "We're talking true damage to your heart and your reputation, and that's all you have to say?"

Ariana stood. "I need you to calm down."

"And I need you to get a clue!" He flailed his arms at her.

She wasn't sure what to think of this display of anger, but she wasn't afraid of him. He would never physically lash out at her or anyone. She moved in closer, standing her ground while she looked into his eyes. "Calm down." Her two words were as firm and soothing as she was capable of.

He stared into her eyes, and she could see

him returning to himself. "Sorry." He put his hands on her shoulders and released a breath.

"Why such anger?"

He dropped his hands to his sides. "I don't know."

"I have some suspicions, and the first one begins with the misunderstanding about the talk of marriage. I didn't take what you said about marrying as a proposal that needed a response but as the opening of a discussion on the topic, much like when I was dating someone else and you thought I should stop. Your exact words were 'I think you should date me.' "

He pursed his lips, twisting them to one side. "And then months later I said, 'I think you should marry me.' "

"Yep, and the dating thing worked out pretty well, don't you think?" She lifted a brow, flirting with him.

"I guess that depends on whether we're still dating after that outburst."

"Rudy Herschberger," — she put her hands on her hips — "if I have no more grace than that, no willingness to put up with loudness while aiming to hear your heart, *you* should be the one to walk away." Did he not realize how often he went out of his way to help and to understand her? Was it a one-way street? A woman could cry and yell and give her all to open a café, and a man couldn't raise his voice without being counted as unworthy?

He went to the log and sat, intertwining his fingers in his lap. "Look, even if Quill's help is exactly what you need to obtain the café, I don't want you involved with him at all — not even letters or phone calls, let alone anything else. I hate the idea of him being around you."

She rolled her eyes. "Baby clothes."

"What?"

"You heard me. I said 'baby clothes.' That's what Quill Schlabach is."

He laughed. "You know, I thought I had come up with every possible name to call that man. Apparently I was wrong. Care to clarify?"

"Sometimes my sisters and I go to the attic and open old boxes of clothing to try to find something that will fit one of my nieces or nephews. I'll look at some of my old baby clothes, and a sense of nostalgia and wonder will wrap around me. Some of those feelings take me back to a time that has precious memories, but I *never* want to return to that time. None of the innocence or enjoyment of that time outweighs the here and now. Do you honestly believe any memories of

Quill have more power than what exists between us? Or that I could possibly be drawn to a man who stands in rebellion against all I hold dear?"

"You cared for him before."

"Oh, I have so many responses to that. I was in love with who I thought he was. Besides that, he's not Amish anymore, so I'm not attracted to him anymore. For the most part it's really hard work to be nice to him."

"I have to say it again: he tricked you once. Who's to say he's not going to do that again?"

"It's a gamble I'm willing to take. I need that café. I know it's the answer to the lack and years of disappointment my family struggles with. Quill knows things, and I need his expertise."

Rudy sighed, looking resigned. "Okay. But if he hurts you, I will find where he lives, and I won't respond like a man who's been raised to forgive."

Ariana wasn't sure Rudy was exaggerating. "I'll make bread like bricks, and you can throw them at him. I can already hear the bishop defending you: 'What real harm could Rudy have meant to do? He beaned him with a loaf of bread!' "

Rudy grinned. "There's no love lost

between the church leaders and Quill, that's for sure and certain." His brows furrowed, and he looked up again as if pondering a new idea. "You have a recipe for brick bread?" He held out his hand for hers.

She moved in front of where he sat and intertwined her fingers with his. "No, but since I have no idea what I'll do with the goods I made yesterday, I can remove them from the wrap and let them sit in the open. I'm sure they will become rock-solid ammunition soon enough." An idea came to her that she was sure Rudy would approve of. "Later this afternoon, during between-Sunday visiting time, you and I could take the goods to as many families as there's time for."

His eyes widened, and the surprise melted into pleasure. "I'd like that."

Couples didn't necessarily tell even their family who they were seeing, and when the family learned of it, they weren't supposed to tell others. She appreciated the tradition that had allowed her to date without the community putting expectations on the relationship. If she and Rudy went visiting as a couple, no one would utter a word to them about the matter, but it would be a declaration, reserved for those who were

serious about each other.
She was ready for that.

TWENTY-THREE

Staring at the pill in her hand, Skylar couldn't quite remember how many of these she'd taken in the last twelve hours. Would this be the fourth or the fifth?

The walls of her bedroom seemed to move like an ocean wave gently rolling across the choppy water, and the window seat under her seemed to jiggle like a bed of gelatin. She took a deep breath and tossed the pill into her mouth. No water needed. Closing her eyes, she saw the same image that startled her awake at night — herself bogged in a swamp, sinking into the mire, and any effort to get out only making her sink deeper. Her sense of loneliness and failure loomed large inside her, and no amount of pills could make those feelings go away, but it did dull the pain.

For Pete's sake, concentrate!

She glanced at the open psychology book in her lap before closing it and staring out the window. Why did she continue to fight a system that was so unwelcoming of who she was? More performers had dropped out of college than had finished. Acting and singing were art forms, and she was tired of trying to get into the business by doing things her parents' way. Maybe she needed to pack her bags and head to New York.

"Skylar?" her mom called as she tapped on the door.

Skylar opened the psychology book and picked up her pencil. "Come in."

Her mother's smile looked forced, and she started to speak a couple of times.

Skylar tapped the eraser against the open page. "I'm fine, Mom." She wasn't, but her mom needed to believe that she was, and sometimes a parent needed to hear the lies.

Actually . . . most of what her mother knew about her of late was a lie — she was at the library studying, she was hanging out with the "clean" drama friends, and things were fine between her and Cody. Well, that one was sort of true, except Cody had become her supplier for prescription meds.

Her mom walked into the room and sat at the far end of the window seat. She ran her hand across the cushion. "It's about time we replaced this fabric."

"Maybe so." Skylar had become a pill-popping failure, but, sure, why not change something that made no difference at all?

"How goes the studying?" Her mom scratched at the dried blueberry yogurt on the lace.

"Fine." The only reason she was the least bit mobile was Ritalin. Without it, all she wanted to do was hide under the covers. With it, she was functional, even if she was jittery and her heart raced night and day as if she were running a long, hard race. The not-so-fun side effects were worth the high.

"I was thinking . . ." Mom fidgeted with her thumbs. "Maybe now that you don't have to practice in the evenings or perform on the weekends, you and I should get out some. You know, just us getting away, doing something different."

Her mom's eyes revealed concern. Maybe how much Skylar was struggling right now wasn't as hidden as she thought. Whether it was or wasn't, her mom was anxious, and Skylar had the power to ease her worry. "Sure, I guess. Where?"

"I've been thinking about that. When I was your age and I needed a break, I would go driving in Amish country. I'd ramble through quilt shops and dry goods stores. Oh, and the Amish have the best restaurants. Have you ever eaten at one?"

Skylar leaned her head back against the casing of the window seat. "No. The closest I've ever come to anything Amish is passing the rigs on the road, except for some guy I talked to last week."

"Was he Amish?"

"Former Amish. Nice guy. Sinfully handsome. If he's what Amish men are like, maybe I shouldn't have been looking down on them."

"Do you look down on them?"

"They're weird, Mom. As backwoods as people get in this country."

"*Backwoods* is derogatory, Sky. They choose to live a simple, unrefined life. They have faith in God and His Word, and they're willing to sacrifice for what they believe in."

Skylar couldn't recall her mom talking about God like this before. "If I repent for thinking poorly of them, will you ax the religious talk?"

She expected her mom to scoff and say something politely sarcastic and totally agree, but instead she looked remorseful. "It's my fault you're so disrespectful of faith, and I'm sorry I didn't handle things better. My mom was involved in church all the time while I was growing up. I practically lived there, and the things I saw and heard among church folk made me sick. I never wanted you to have to see that kind of nonsense and hypocrisy, but I'm not sure avoiding church altogether has been good for you either."

Skylar rolled her eyes. "God sounds like every other man I've known — you can't live with him, and you can't live without him."

Her mom shrugged and sighed. "Anyway, changing the subject back to Amish men, what little bit of contact I've had with them, they seem very different from the average American guy."

This was a much better topic, and Skylar relaxed against the frame of the window seat. "I know what you mean. I spent about thirty minutes with that guy, and not one crude word or innuendo came out of his mouth. Can you believe that?"

"I don't think guys were so crude when I was your age. It's become a game to make fun of the body and be as obscene as possible. Writers make millions of dollars putting that stuff on television, but my mother would have washed out their mouths with soap."

Skylar laughed. "Would she really?"

"Oh, yeah. And she would've used Lava soap."

"What's Lava soap?"

"Pretty much the opposite of Ivory soap."

"So you think that guy's parents washed his mouth out with soap?" She giggled. "That could explain why he was so nice *and* why he left the Amish life behind."

"Yeah, it could." Mom laughed. "I don't know how strict they are inside their homes. But they are known for being a very gentle people, so I sort of doubt that mistreatment was part of his training. I just know they were very good to me."

Was the Ritalin playing tricks on her, or did her mom misspeak? "Amish were good to you?"

Her mother's mouth opened for a moment, and Skylar knew her mom hadn't meant to let that piece of information slip. Skylar had too much Ritalin in her to gently pry for answers. "Mom! Come on!"

Her mom grimaced, but she nodded. "You were actually born in an Amish birthing clinic."

Skylar jumped to her feet. *This* was worth hearing. "I was?" Her melancholy feelings seemed to scamper away like performers running off stage to get ready for the next scene.

Her mom nodded.

"Well" — Skylar gestured with both hands as if hurrying her mother across the finish line — "tell me the story."

Mom drew a deep breath. "You weren't due for two weeks, and your dad and I had a huge argument the day before, so to clear my head, I took one of my long drives into Amish country. When I started the day, I had energy to burn, but as the hours passed, I kept having lower back pain that came and went. Of course now I know that while I was driving to different Amish towns, stopping to look at quilt shops and such, I was in labor the whole time. I got out at a yard sale an Amish woman was having, and while I was in her yard, my water broke. I didn't know where the closest hospital was or how long it would take to get back to the main road, but the woman told me there was an Amish birthing clinic about two miles up the road." Mom smiled. "She said the midwife would take good care of me until an ambulance arrived . . . if I wanted to get to a hospital. But the idea of having you in a peaceful home environment sounded perfect to me. I also didn't want to have to tell my mom or your dad that I was in labor. My mom was so unhappy with me for being pregnant, and your dad was still living with his wife. It had sounded like the ideal way for you and me to begin our journey — just a midwife in a simple home, delivering you into my arms."

Skylar sat next to her mom, facing her. "You were a romantic."

Mom brushed wisps of hair from Skylar's face. "I was young, very naive, and without any inner direction. But I found my road map that day, and it was you." She smiled, cupping Skylar's chin in her hand. "By the time I arrived at the birthing center, I was pretty far along in labor. But something was wrong. I was bleeding badly, and the midwife called for an ambulance. Not long after you were born, I was taken by ambulance to the hospital, but, yes, you were born there. Your dad still doesn't know that."

"Why?"

Mom drew a deep breath. "He's always been so against religion of any kind, against repression of desire and freedom of expression. I knew he'd never understand why I'd chosen to do such a thing."

Skylar rolled her eyes. "He would've said it was an immature thing to do, as if him being fifteen years older than you made him a model of mature thinking."

"Anyway" — Mom shrugged — "I was afraid he would go after the Amish midwife, as if it was her fault I was in ICU, so I didn't tell him. If anything, she saved both our lives."

"That's ridiculous. Dad was married. He had no right to voice his opinion about your decisions."

"Sky, honey, you see him wrong. *We* had the affair. I was just as much to blame as he was."

"You were nineteen when it began and barely twenty when I was born. He was thirty-five. Come on, Mom, stop defending him!"

"He loves you, Sky. You were a complication we hadn't prepared for, but you are the absolute best thing to happen to either of us. Could you at least try to believe me on that?" Her mom radiated sincerity.

Was it possible Skylar looked at the situation with too much cynicism? "Mom, he didn't give me his surname of Jenkins even after his divorce."

"If that was important to you, I'm sorry we haven't talked about it before now." A hint of defiance seemed to cross her face. "You and I have always gone by my maiden name, and at no point did I want to change that for either of us — not even after I married Gabe." She brushed invisible lint off the covering of the window seat. "I think your dad's guilt over his many failures concerning you keeps him from being able to show you how he feels, but he does love you, and he's very proud of you."

"Yeah, and our neighbors' German shepherd that mauled their teen only wanted to play."

Her mom opened her mouth, and Skylar clasped her hands over her mouth, miming *speak no evil.* It was their way of changing subjects. "But the people at the Amish clinic were nice, like you said?"

"Yeah, they were. It was a crazy day, though. The clinic caught on fire while I was in labor, and there was another woman giving birth at the same time. So I can't say I got a real feel for them. But the other woman's husband was gentle and encouraging as he took me to safety."

"Oh, my gosh!" Skylar laughed. "I wish I had known this when I talked to that guy Quill. He was so inquisitive, and he would've loved this story."

"Well, if you're going to Amish country with me, maybe we'll spot him." Her mom's smile was filled with mischief as she tried to coax Skylar into agreeing to go. They both knew they had zero chance of running into that guy. Skylar didn't know what area of Pennsylvania he was from, and a person could go a year without seeing their next-door neighbor. What were the odds of them spotting Quill?

"I wish I'd asked to see his driver's license the way he asked me. Then I'd know where he lives."

Her mother had that "you know better than to talk to strangers" look on her face. "So should I expect him to show up at our door?"

"Doubt it, but it would be fun if he did. I could tell him that story."

"So why did he ask to see your license?"

"He had some deep need to see my birth date."

"Your birth date?" Mom laughed.

"He said he wanted proof I wasn't so young it would get him arrested if he taught me some card tricks."

"I'm not liking this story, Sky."

"He was harmless. I could see it in his eyes. Speaking of eyes, you should've seen his when I showed him my license. Maybe my birth date has bad memories for him or something. The rest of his body language, including his face, gave away nothing, but his eyes said that date was bad news."

The upbeat smile drained from her mother's face.

"Don't go parental on me. He was cool. So just devise some other weird mom-fear to worry over."

Her mom didn't look convinced. "You need to be more careful."

"Yeah, I hear you." Skylar's phone buzzed, and she pulled it from her shorts pocket. She read the text from Cody. He had more pills and wondered about them getting together tonight. How was he scoring this much stuff without needing her to pay for it? "This weekend could we try to find that birthing clinic?"

"It burned down the day you were born."

"Completely?" She responded to the text with a *yes*. There was no sense in trying to study. She needed a distraction . . . and more pills.

"I'm sure whatever was left had to be demolished."

"Another one could've been built in its place." She slid her phone back into her pocket.

"Maybe." Her mom shrugged, suddenly looking as if she regretted this conversation. "I'll do some checking."

Skylar never saw much joy in pondering any part of her conception, birth, or first few years of life. This news about the Amish clinic was the bright spot in an otherwise dismal account, and now her mom seemed weird about it.

Wouldn't it be fun to see with her own eyes the one cool thing about her birth? "Mom, you can't finally tell me this news and then drop the idea of driving there. We need to go one weekend soon. End of discussion."

The matter was settled. If Skylar had one skill, it was talking her mom into things — at least, simple things.

TWENTY-FOUR

Quill left the bank with a cashier's check. His next stop would be Lila McCormick's home, current owner of the café. He'd already talked to her, and she'd agreed to rent the café to Ariana until after the benefit.

He was done skulking around so the Amish wouldn't catch a glimpse of him when he was in town. This was public property, and he had a right to be here. Added to that, it was time he reconsidered his methods of helping people leave. When Ariana asked him why he had bound himself to such secrecy, she had caused him to reassess the value, or rather lack of it, he'd placed on his life. Helping others establish a life outside the Old Ways was a part of who he was, but he would no longer do it at the expense of having to lurk in the shadows to ensure his every step was *that* covert. He would still have to be cautious about visiting his Mamm and about helping Ariana, but other than that, if he was spotted in town, he was.

He folded the cashier's check and slid it into his pocket. His goals for the benefit were more than just making it a success so she could go to closing with the needed funds. Potential regular customers, especially the base of non-Amish ones, needed to connect the café with Ariana's baked goods and the selling of various items on the green space. That meant the café needed to be open during the auction.

He believed she was really on to something with the café. This part of Summer Grove was busy and pleasant. An Amish café should do really well.

As he headed for his car, he heard a dog barking. Was that his dog? He turned and saw his golden retriever running toward him. She pranced about in a childlike bunny hop. He laughed and knelt. "What are you doing here?" He scratched her neck as she licked his face, her whole body wriggling with excitement. Quill saw his brother lumbering his way.

Dan smiled. "While we were on the phone yesterday, you said you were going to the bank first thing today."

Quill stood, barely getting upright before his brother clutched his shoulder and shook it, grinning. That was a bold move for Dan. He was a talker but didn't like shows of affection.

"Lexi missed you."

Quill continued rubbing the dog's head. "So you drove hours out of your way because a dog missed me." He knew better.

Dan crossed his arms and leaned against Quill's car. "You said all the right words on the phone yesterday. I'm relieved Salome and Emanuel have decided to stay, at least for now. But something in your tone reminded me of the months before and after you left with Frieda."

Quill had to admit that patting Lexi and talking to his brother helped somehow. Dreading what it was going to do to Ariana to learn that she wasn't a Brenneman and, worse, that she was part of what sounded like a dysfunctional family ate at him like nothing else.

Dan propped his foot on the curb. "You've been down a tough road once before where you were on your own coping with nightmares. I don't want that to happen to you again."

Quill rubbed Lexi's ears. "I appreciate it." And he did, but that didn't mean he was free to talk about what was going on.

"Regina said I would leave here not knowing much more than when I arrived." Dan scratched his close-shaven cheek with his left hand, and his gold wedding ring gleamed under the bright sun. "But while telling me that, she was packing food for me to bring to you and throwing some clean clothes in a bag in case I needed to stay for a few days."

Of his four brothers and sisters-in-law, Dan and Regina came the closest to understanding him. "Is any of that food left, or did you eat it all on the way here?"

"I'm not here to talk about food."

Quill felt the hardness of stress give way to a little humor. "Won't talk about what no longer exists?"

"It's a long ride, okay?"

They laughed, and Quill was sure Dan had saved at least half of the food Regina had packed.

Dan pulled sunglasses out of his pocket and put them on. "You gave no reason on the phone for needing to stay here this week, despite me asking."

"I'll be able to get to the job site in Mingo by Wednesday and finish wiring a few homes before I need to return here. That'll be the pattern for a while, but I can juggle work as needed."

"I know that." Dan sighed. "Whatever's

changed your plans and caused you to stay, how bad is it?"

When Lexi lay on the ground, feet skyward, Quill knelt and rubbed her belly. He didn't want to admit to himself, let alone anyone else, the answer Dan was looking for. "Bad."

"Subject?"

"Ariana."

Dan's cheeks puffed out as he released a long stream of air. "That explains a lot. But if Salome and Emanuel are staying, she should be good, right? Maybe she's angry with you but other than that she's fine."

"Something unrelated has come up." Quill stood. He hated not being able to tell her the truth, and yet he dreaded the day when she would learn it. The other day he'd snapped a picture with his phone, and she didn't have a clue. When it was time to approach Skylar's family, he might need a picture of Ariana to show them. The whole situation, and his part in it, made him sick.

"Is she okay?"

Quill moved beside his brother and leaned against the car. It was nice not having to hide for fear some Amish might see him. "As it stands, she's clueless. When the news hits . . . it could be worse than the fallout with Frieda."

"Unlike with Frieda, Daed didn't leave her as your responsibility."

Quill pulled the keys out of his pocket and stood. "I need to go. I'll do everything I can to get the jobs done on time, but Ariana comes first." He opened the car door, and Lexi pushed past him and jumped in. "Lexi, no. Come on, girl. Out. You can't go with me."

She stood on the seat, angling her head as if confused.

"I'm sorry." Dan put his hand on Quill's shoulder. "That was out of line."

Quill turned. "I'll be back at work on Wednesday."

"Look, I'm not here because of the stupid job list. And for you, in one way or another, Ariana has come first since the dawn of time, and I'm okay with that. But you gotta think about yourself too. You do all you can for Mom, Frieda, and the Amish who ask for your help. But I'm not sure you ever pause to ask yourself what you need."

"I need to help Ariana." He shrugged. "It's that simple and that complicated."

"It sounds as if you've been talking to her this time."

Quill nodded. "Yeah. We've had some healthy arguments and made a few necessary agreements."

"That's great. Hard to believe but very welcome news. Any chance of getting closure? Because you have to let go of this life."

"Yeah? Like you've let go, Dan? Because you and I both know there is no letting go of our childhood, of the people who loved us and we loved and left behind. We would do it again, but there's no freedom from the remorse or pain of it. All any of us can do is learn to live with it."

"The rest of us have learned to live with it while building a real life and a future. You haven't."

Quill stared at his oldest brother. There was a huge difference. His brothers left because they chose to. Quill left because circumstances forced him to. He and Frieda didn't connect with his brothers until two years after leaving Summer Grove. Mostly he worked days and stayed by Frieda's hospital bed at night. She healed physically before she gained any emotional strength. When she was finally strong enough to face people again, Quill moved her to an apartment in Kentucky, and he moved in with Dan until he could afford to rent a small home. When his brothers had left Summer Grove, each one took his girl with him or found a wife once he was living among the

Englisch. Quill had left his girl behind, and now she needed him.

"I have to go." But he couldn't get in the car until Lexi got out, and she stood there watching him, wagging her tail while her brown eyes begged to stay.

"Believe it or not, Quill, I didn't come to complain. It's hard pulling away like we have. It yanks out every thread in this stupid patchwork quilt of our childhood. Some of us have had an easier time adjusting than others, but you . . . you make it so much harder by coming back and trying to fix what can't be fixed. It doesn't matter how many people you help. At the end of the day, you only open fresh wounds in yourself."

"It matters to the people who are being helped. If I make it harder on me, that's my problem."

Dan went around to the passenger side and climbed into the car. Quill got behind the wheel and closed the door. The dog sat between them, looking happy and perking her ears.

"Wrong. It's our problem — you, me, and our brothers. Erastus, Leon, and Elam are on the construction site in Mingo, hoping I don't botch this visit. My plan in coming here was to listen and to encourage."

"Don't give up your day job."

"Yeah, I hear you. According to Regina, I can be rather dense about such matters, but she loves me anyway — just like I love you. So tell me, what can I do to help?"

"Ariana needs at least five thousand dollars to buy the old café here in town. In reality, to get the business operational and to cover overhead for a few months, she needs closer to ten thousand. The plan is for her to have a benefit."

"We're a little tapped out from all the prep work for Salome and Emanuel leaving, but we can at least pull together five thousand."

A three-bedroom, two-bath house had been rented for them with the first and last months' rent paid. Deposits had been paid so that electricity, gas, water, and phones were already operational. A vehicle had been purchased and insured, and Quill had been paying months of health insurance for the family. All were things people needed in the modern world. Emanuel would pay it all back . . . after he got his feet under him in the outside world. Of course at this point, he might not leave. Should they cancel everything? Which would be more expensive, paying for everything or letting it go and having to start fresh if they decided to leave in a few months?

The *we* Dan referred to was Quill's four brothers and sisters-in-law.

"I appreciate it, but it's about more than cash. She needs to feel supported by the community and powerful within herself." He turned the key and pushed a button to lower both windows.

"So what's the plan?"

"A benefit here in Summer Grove, Saturday after next."

Dan whistled. "In less than two weeks?"

"No wiggle room in the schedule."

"I'll put ads in the paper about the benefit, and I'll call home and get everyone busy making items to auction off."

One thing about being former Amish, his Kentucky family knew what needed to be done to hold an Amish benefit. "Now you're talking. If you still have connections inside city hall, we're going to need permits for the café and fast."

"I'll jump on that this morning."

"Thanks. The job site being only a couple of hours from here has been helpful since Mamm went into the hospital."

"Very true, but the only one who doesn't mind staying in the Mingo temp house throughout the workweek is your dog."

"Speaking of Mingo, how many houses have the framing inspection done and are ready for wiring?"

"Two. Could be three by Wednesday. I'll line up a crew to help you."

"I appreciate it, Dan."

"Of course you do." His brother grinned. "But this Brenneman family is costly."

"All family is costly. Haven't you figured that out yet?"

"I have, but most of us get a few perks for our sacrifices."

"Wimps need rewards."

Dan laughed. "Your owner made a joke." He rubbed Lexi's head. "Can you believe it?"

Quill's phone buzzed, and he pulled it from his pocket. The community number again.

Dan peered around Lexi. "What time —"

Quill held up his index finger to his brother while he answered the phone. "Hello."

"Hi. It's Ariana. Is it an okay time to talk?"

He much preferred this tone to the one she had used Saturday night. "Sure. Can you hold on for just a few minutes?"

"Ya."

He pushed the Mute button. "Take Lexi with you."

"What I just heard was, don't let the door hit you on your way out, Brother."

"Pretty much. You want to meet up for lunch?"

"No, I need to get moving on the permits, and then I'm going to sneak in and spend some time with Mamm."

Once Dan got his car into hiding without being seen, he couldn't necessarily get out at a set time. He was likely to have to wait until most people's bedtime. He and Mamm would share a meal in her bedroom with the curtains closed or maybe in the attic.

"She'll be really glad to see you. Did you bring pictures?"

"Regina packed a ton of them." He opened the door. "Call me later."

"Sure."

Dan started to close the door.

"Hey," Quill called, "you're forgetting to take Lexi."

"I didn't forget." Dan smiled and slammed the door, leaving Lexi in the car. How was Quill supposed to find a hotel that accepted dogs?

He took the phone off Mute. "You there?"

"Ya. Sorry to disrupt."

"No, I needed to talk to you today. I just hadn't figured out how yet." They needed a long conversation about the benefit, including how he could easily reach her during the next two weeks. "What's up?"

"Abram needs to talk to you."

"Sure. How about today at one?"

"You didn't even ask what he wants."

"I can imagine, and I'm fine with it. But for your sake, you need to be careful who knows that I'm helping you."

"Ya, I figured. Right now only some family members know. I've talked to each one, making sure they keep this discreet. Oh, and Rudy knows and wants to meet you too."

Rudy. That should be a thrill. "Sure. I understand that. Let's meet at the café."

"The café?"

"I'll have written permission by this afternoon for you to use it at will between now and October first."

"How? And why?"

Behind her brief questions were a dozen doubts. Unlike working with Amish who contacted him because they trusted him, Ariana was going to question him every step of the way. He would have to get used to answering and being open with her again.

"I rented the building. I think it's important that your name and product are connected to an actual place, more for the opening of the café than for the value it adds to the benefit."

"Makes sense."

He heard hesitancy. "I'll see you at one?"

The line was silent again.

"You're awfully quiet for a talkative girl."

"It's really nice having you working for me rather than against me."

Quill understood. But the stiltedness of this conversation had to stop. "I have my dog with me." He was reaching into their childhood in hopes of them both relaxing a bit.

"Finally got a dog, huh?"

"Yeah, about four years ago."

"Is it a female golden retriever?"

"Yep."

"Good for you. Is she . . . good for you?"

"She is the most obedient dog I've ever had."

"She's the only dog you've ever had."

"I rest my case."

Ariana laughed. It wasn't the warm, open laughter he overheard when she was at his mother's and didn't know he was there. But it was a start.

"I'll see you and your dog at one? Oh, and I know how to erase your number from this machine, so don't worry about that."

"Thanks. See you then."

As he ended the call, he realized he was hoping for a perk for helping her. A reward, as Dan called it. He wanted her to be happy and for them to become friends of sorts.

But more than that, he hoped at some point she wouldn't be disappointed in him. He couldn't help wondering, if she knew the truth about why he'd left as he did, would her disrespect melt like butter in a skillet?

Ultimately, it didn't matter. They could never be together. They lived in separate worlds, and neither wished to cross over.

TWENTY-FIVE

Sunlight stretched across the floor of the café, and Ariana paused to look at her handiwork — their handiwork. The dark wood had been scrubbed and polished, removing years of grime and filth. She'd put the fear of God into the floors, lunch counter, tables, and even the stairs and banister. Every part of the kitchen had been scoured with steel wool and soap, and it had passed inspection with flying colors. The old windows were pristine, displaying the hand-painted lettering that carried the name of the old café.

What a difference four days of hard work had made. She couldn't describe what being inside this building did to her. It felt as if she belonged here. Was her dream really coming true?

Keys jangled, and the back door to the kitchen opened. Quill walked in, but Lexi wasn't with him this time. "Hi." His smile, a mixture of tempered joy with definite undertones of sadness, greeted her. This was the smile she had grown used to after his dad died, but shouldn't it have returned to its normal brightness by now?

"You're here."

He chuckled. "Abram is right about your powers of observation."

If she had a witty comeback, she would use it. "I thought you weren't returning until Monday."

"Me too. But the inspector said if I could get this place rewired this weekend, he has time in his schedule to inspect it on Monday. If I don't get it done, he won't have another opening until after the benefit." Quill dropped his overnight bag on the floor. "So ta-da. Here I am."

The three of them — Abram, Quill, and Ariana — had worked really well together this week, accomplishing far more than they had put on the lists. Susie helped as time allowed, but she couldn't abandon the Beshears. She had dared to turn in her notice to them, and they were trying to hire someone new. Rudy continued to build items for them to sell at the benefit, and he had met with Quill on Monday, but his work schedule did not allow him much time to help with the café.

"Hungry?" She had a bit of a handle on what to expect from Quill. He had probably gotten up really early to meet the deadlines for Schlabach Home Builders, which currently meant he was working a couple of hours away in Pennsylvania. As soon as he was done with that job, he had headed this way without taking time to eat. Since Lexi wasn't with him, she knew his brother Dan had taken the dog from the temp house in Mingo back home to Kentucky.

"Very." He went to the sink and washed his hands. "I'm making pancakes, and we have a long night of work ahead of us. Would you care for some?" He knew this kitchen as well as she did, and he was comfortable making himself at home, which made sense because he, and sometimes Lexi, slept in the room upstairs when he was in the area, and he hated eating out.

"Sure. Abram will be here soon, so he may want some too." She grabbed a clean hand towel out of the bin and tossed it to him. "But you're going to turn into a pancake."

"I'll turn into a Snickers bar first." He pulled his phone from his pocket, and a moment later his thumbs were flying over the screen. "It's a text from Dan. He asked if we could get away with giving Mamm a new wringer washer for her birthday. I said 'doubtful.' Thoughts?"

Heat flushed Ariana's body. "He's in contact with Berta too?"

He looked up, taking her in as if she were a stranger. "Sorry, I shouldn't have sprung that on you. I wasn't thinking. He wasn't for a lot of years. None of my brothers were — each one trying to avoid being a bad influence on the younger brothers. But after Daed died, they needed to see Mamm, and she needed to see them."

"How did I never know that?"

"We didn't mean it as trickery or disrespect."

"I'm sure. I . . . I'm just sorry you didn't feel you could trust me."

"Trust was never the issue. It wouldn't have been right to ask you to bear a secret about that kind of disobedience to the Old Ways."

Needing a drink, she got a glass from a cabinet and filled it with tap water. Wasn't there some way she could help the brothers give gifts to their Mamm without the new items raising a red flag with those in the community who came in and out of Berta's home? "So when you left here, you joined your brothers?"

"No." Quill finished his message and slid the phone into his pocket. He got a bowl off the shelf. "How have you done on your list over the last couple of days?"

She'd asked one too many questions. It made her feel a bit eerie to realize more people than Quill had to circumvent her comings and goings so she didn't see them, but for Berta's sake she was grateful the brothers made the effort to sneak in to see her. Maybe one day Quill would answer a couple of questions about Frieda. "I'm done. And" — she spread her arms out wide and made a complete circle — "did you look around at all?"

He paused, shrugged, and got eggs and milk out of the refrigerator. "It looks exactly as I thought it would."

"Denki, I think. But I need you to ooh and aah over all this."

He chuckled. "Gotta appreciate a woman who is so direct about what she needs." He put the egg and milk on the counter and strolled through the café, looking from ceiling to floor. "It really looks amazing, Ariana." Without any other fanfare he returned to the kitchen and pulled the pancake mix from the pantry.

She followed him. "All my dreams didn't compare to what this feels like, and even if next Saturday doesn't go as we hope, I want you to know how completely grateful I am that you helped me get the best possible shot at it."

"You'll get the money to go to closing. I have no doubts."

"I'm glad you feel that way, but" — she pulled up a barstool to the waist-high pass-through counter — "you didn't hear me."

He paused and studied her. They had covered a lot of ground over the last week, starting with his coming to the phone shanty. Their conversations were woven between hard work and periods of rest, and they rarely strayed off the path of serious topics. Had they forgotten how to laugh together? It seemed as if they should've shared a few giggles either in person or on the phone as they discussed to-do lists while he was on a job site a couple of hours away.

She'd become comfortable with Quill again. Abram believed that Quill simply needed to make up for the damage he'd done to her life when he left.

He turned on the gas burner under the grill before he dumped some mix into the bowl. "My answer didn't match your statement?"

"I wasn't looking for encouragement."

His brows furrowed as he added ingredients to the bowl and stirred with a whisk. "Oh." Understanding lifted his face.

He came to the counter in front of her. "You are more than welcome, and I'm grateful you've allowed me to help."

Why was there such hesitancy in his eyes? Did he know something she needed to know, some aspect about the loan she was hoping to get?

"But?"

He put the hand towel on his shoulder and returned to the grill. "No buts."

"I know what I saw, and . . ." The rest of her words caught in her throat. She didn't believe him, but why push for answers he didn't wish to give? They would never see eye to eye, and there was nothing wrong with that. "Okay." She stood. "I should get back to work. Just leave the dishes in the sink, and I'll tend to them later."

Boxes of glass diner plates that had been in the storage room above needed to be unloaded. She pulled a box cutter from her apron pocket and knelt before ripping open a box.

Quill came into the dining room and crouched near her, looking calm as ever. "I am who I am, and because of it, my life has become a flytrap for secrets."

"I know, and I've chosen to be okay with that, but the hesitation I saw in your eyes scares me." What was burning? She looked toward the kitchen and saw plumes of black smoke rising from the grill. "Your pancakes!"

They ran into the kitchen. While she yanked the burned cakes off the grill and tossed them into the sink, he opened the back door.

He peered over her shoulder as she ran water onto the smoldering black circles. "Those are yours."

She scoffed. "Looks like the remains of our friendship after you left."

"Ya, and what my life tasted like for years."

She hadn't realized that, and questions she knew he wouldn't answer pounded her. She turned, and he stayed put, leaving only inches between them. "Would you let me fix you a real meal? I can have it ready, char free, within twenty minutes."

He eyed the burned pancake. "Sure."

The eggs were still on the counter, but she went to the fridge and got out the bacon. Once the bacon was on to cook, she got a clean bowl from the shelf.

Quill fished the burned pancake remnants out of the sink and tossed them into the trash. "Part of the problem is you're getting where you can read me, and that's not helpful."

"Stop hiding stuff." She cracked an egg

into a bowl and tossed the shell in the trash. "Problem solved."

He used the towel on his shoulder to dry his hands. "I'm working toward that goal. I really am, but there's nothing I can do right now about some of the confidential stuff."

It meant a lot to know he wanted to stop all secrecy, but it was time they changed the subject and injected a little playfulness. "A dance might help."

"What?"

"A dance." She made a circular motion with her hand. "You know the kind. Go on."

When he and her brother Mark were young and one of them lost at a game, the other one had to do a ballet dance — not that either of them knew much about what such a dance should look like.

"Fine," he teased. "I'll do one like you've never seen." He twirled the towel while making ballet-type moves. She could hardly believe he was doing it, and she laughed. Grinning playfully, he went from one end of the café to the other while humming.

He made his way back to the sink, where she was, stopped, and bowed.

She clapped heartily. "Those were the best moves I've ever seen by a former Amish man."

Breathless, he stood before her. "The only

ones you've ever seen — admit it."

"True." She gazed into his eyes while he stood so close, and she saw the truth. Whatever he said to her, he meant. "But if I'd seen dozens of others, yours would be my favorite — for now and always."

"Are we good?"

"We are, but then again, we were before you danced."

"Now you're just being mean, which is kind of refreshing. I didn't know you had it in you."

"I hate to burst your bubble when you're feeling refreshed due to my unkindness, but I have a thought about Dan's question and your Mamm's birthday."

He mocked a frustrated sigh. "Go ahead. What kindness are you up to this time?"

"Once I'm making decent money, if you or your brothers wish to purchase nice things for your Mamm, people will naturally think I did it for her. I can give you that." That would free them to buy anything or send cash to their Mamm whenever they wanted. Of course his Mamm would know the truth of who the gift was from.

Quill angled his head. "Let me make sure I've got this straight. If we buy gifts for Mamm, you're willing to take the credit."

"Yep." She squelched her desire to smile.

"That's a really nice offer. It's hard not being able to give Mamm much of anything."

Ariana could hardly believe she was willing to be a bridge between the sons who had left and their Amish Mamm, but she no longer saw their departure as a betrayal that deserved punishment. She only saw a family divided, and she could make the separation a little less painful for everyone. Was that wrong of her, a betrayal of the Old Ways?

Twenty-Six

Lovina's insides quaked, and she feared she would have to use the sickness bag that Quill had brought her.

How could this be happening? Every part of her kept screaming, *Nooooo!*

And yet here she sat. Quill's car was in Park, idling quietly and blowing cold air on her face as he crossed the road and went up the walkway to Brandi's home.

She watched as he knocked on the door. Quill assured her that Skylar was at school right now and no one would be home except Brandi. Isaac hadn't come. Ariana had needed his help repairing the front stoop at the café. The benefit was four days away, and as the time drew closer to tell Ariana the truth, Lovina found it almost impossible to breathe. Or sleep. Or eat.

Why had she pushed to dive quickly into the truth? She knew why. Fear for Skylar. She'd seemed so sad while singing that her dreams of dying were the best ones she'd ever had.

Quill stood on the porch, waiting for Brandi to open the door. He would talk with her by himself first, explaining the basics. If Brandi wanted to see Lovina, then Lovina would oblige her. But they were hoping not to overwhelm the poor mom. The news was enough to send anyone over the edge.

The door finally opened, and after a couple of minutes of the two talking, Quill went inside. Lovina rocked back and forth, cradling her aching stomach while willing herself not to throw up. Maybe she should have gone with Quill. Would that have been better or worse for Brandi? Who knew what was best in a crazy situation like this?

Minutes passed. About the time Lovina thought she couldn't stand much more, the front door of the home opened again. Quill stepped out and gestured toward his car. Brandi stood there, her feet bare, wearing jeans and a baggy sweater. The woman didn't look nearly as old as she had to be. Wasn't she at least forty by now?

Brandi said something, and Quill paused, talking with her. She looked angry rather than shocked or scared. The two headed toward the vehicle. Should Lovina get out? Quill motioned for her to lower the window, but no matter what button she pushed, the window didn't move. He opened the door, lowered the window, and eased the door almost shut again.

"Lovina, this is Brandi Nash. Brandi, this is Lovina Brenneman."

Lovina couldn't think of a thing to say, and maybe Brandi couldn't either because she just kept looking at her.

Quill propped his hand on the door. "Brandi is having some difficulty believing that this might be true. I told her that there is an auction this Saturday and that it might help her to see Ariana as much as it helped you to see Skylar."

"You're not taking my daughter." Brandi wrapped her open sweater around her as if holding on for dear life. "But Skylar and I had discussed driving to Amish country, so maybe we'll —"

"No." Lovina gasped, her heart racing. "Sorry. I mean, that's not a good idea. You could come, you and . . . anyone else. But I've seen Skylar, and she's a mirror image of my oldest daughter. She will stand out, and we haven't told Ariana yet."

"Look, you seem upset at the wacky idea you've conjured up about this baby swap twenty years ago, and I was just trying to be nice about it." She tilted her head back, jaw set and looking offended. "It doesn't matter who my daughter favors. She *is* mine, not yours! Are we clear on that?"

Lovina understood now why Quill had closed the door after he lowered the window. He wanted a barrier between this woman's anger and Lovina. But she didn't care if Brandi hit her. She had to get out of this vehicle and face her eye to eye. Lovina pushed against the door, giving Quill a look that said he needed to move. Quill released the door.

Her legs wobbled as she got her feet under her. "If the thought of the two babies being switched has never crossed your mind, I can't imagine how crazy it sounds. While in labor I . . . I embroidered a pair of baby feet on the bottom of a pink blanket that the midwife wrapped my daughter in."

Brandi's rage seemed to slough off her face. "I . . . I have that blanket." She looked from Quill to Lovina. "The blankets got mixed up. That's all."

"Maybe. But I no longer think so. If you saw how much my eldest daughter favors Skylar, you would have doubts too."

"No!" Brandi jerked her head downward once, as if that settled the matter. "I will not listen to this crap!"

Quill rubbed the back of his neck. "A

simple DNA test will settle the matter."

"Are you people deaf? I won't be a part of this. Skylar is my life!"

"My Ariana has white-blond hair like yours and beautiful green-blue eyes similar to yours — only more like polished emeralds."

Brandi's anger seemed to pause for a moment. Quill pulled out his cell phone, touched a few places on it, and held it up to Brandi.

Brandi stared at it, unmoving, and then she snatched the phone and held it closer to her face. "I'm . . . looking . . . at . . ." She glanced up, terror on her face. "She favors . . . my . . ." Brandi shoved the phone back at Quill. "How could something like this happen? How are you people so ill equipped that something like this could happen?" Her rant echoed off the nearby houses.

"I asked the midwife the same question, and I'm sure I sounded just as upset when I did. I'm furious and scared, and I wish I knew for sure what was the right thing to do." Tears rolled down Lovina's face.

"It's not the same for you. Skylar is everything to me. I . . . I have only one child!"

"Now that we know what may be true,

what choice do we have? To lie to our daughters for the rest of their lives?"

"I intend to protect my girl and keep her from people like you!"

When Lovina had first faced this possibility, she'd had some of the same thoughts and feelings, except she trusted that Ariana was strong enough to deal with the truth. "What about the young woman who is your child? I won't lie to her for the rest of my days. I can't do it. If you need time to adjust, we'll give you more time."

"What do you hope to gain by doing this?"

Lovina thought it best to keep those thoughts to herself. If Skylar had been raised in a manner that gave Lovina a sense of peace, would she be interested in uncovering the truth? She didn't know. That scenario hadn't been presented to her, and she hadn't thought about it. But the truth being revealed could backfire on her whole family and the Nash family. "I'm not sure anyone gains, but God's hand is in it, and He has revealed it for a reason. I believe that."

"You dare blame God. I hate when people do that." Brandi tightened her folded arms. "This is human error, hopefully yours, not the midwife's."

"I hope that too. But nothing short of

DNA testing will confirm it."

Brandi crossed her arms, staring at Lovina. "I'll think about it."

"But —"

"That's fine for now," Quill assured her. "Lovina, she needs time to think, just as you and Isaac did." He pulled a piece of paper from his pocket. "This is my phone number. You can call me at any time. Lovina and Isaac plan to tell Ariana the truth next week, probably Monday or Tuesday. That gives you a week to adjust, but if that's moving too fast and you feel you need another week or perhaps a little more, let us know."

Brandi looked at the paper. "Is that what you said your name was?"

"Quill Schlabach. Yes, that's what I said when I introduced myself at the door."

"You're the former Amish guy who asked to see my daughter's driver's license."

"Yes, I explained that in the house. I'm sure you're able to take in only so much information right now, but you can call me at any time. I needed to know her birth date as a way of verifying if our suspicions had any real foundation. After Ariana knows the truth, she and her mom will go in for DNA testing."

"She could refuse, you know."

"She could?" Lovina turned to Quill.

He half shrugged and half nodded. "As an adult, she has that right, but Ariana won't go against what you and Isaac ask of her." He angled his head, catching Brandi's eye. "What about Skylar?"

"There is no way I'm upsetting her with this nonsense! I'll simply have some blood work done during her routine pee-in-a-cup drug testing. I've done that before to check on her iron levels, so she won't think a thing about it. That way when this all turns out to be fear-mongering lies, she'll be left unscathed."

"Drug testing?" Lovina couldn't imagine why a beautiful young woman would need to be tested for drugs. Was she on medication of some type? Some of those required routine tests?

Brandi wagged her finger at Lovina. "Don't you dare stand in front of my house with your backwoods religion, glaring in my face while you judge me!"

Lovina's eyes burned with tears. The woman's body language was so much like Ariana's — little things, like the way she angled her head and bit one side of her lower lip when thinking and held her hand just so while pointing. Did that indicate genetic characteristics? Was that even possible? Or was her mind playing tricks on her because Ariana and Brandi favored each other?

Quill stepped between them. "If you have the right to receive those kinds of reports on your daughter, I can see how that plan would work for your family. And I think it's a good one."

It wouldn't work for Ariana. She hadn't been to the doctor in years. Besides that, Lovina wouldn't trick her.

Brandi pointed at Quill. "You stay away from my daughter. I'll have her tested tomorrow, and I'll have the results back within a week or two. Then all this business will be cleared up, and after that if you ever come close to my Sky Blue again, you'll be lucky if all I do is call the police or get a lawyer. Have I made myself clear?"

The hills of Kentucky were awash in a golden glow as the sun slid below the horizon. Quill's fingertips barely touched the steering wheel of his car as he guided the vehicle onto the concrete driveway of his home. With the benefit in three days, he could've easily continued staying at the temp house in Pennsylvania. The rented trailer would have kept him near the current job site for Schlabach Home Builders and within two hours of the café. But he was drained, desperate for a night in his own bed, an evening to recharge. Part of what recharged him was long drives, so he never minded the seven-hour trip between Summer Grove and home. It gave him time to think and listen to the radio.

He pressed the button on the garage door opener. After he pulled in, he turned off his car, and then he heard Lexi barking. He'd told Dan he was coming home for the night, so he must've brought her by. Did Quill smell food? He almost had the house key in the lock when the door swung open.

"Hey." Frieda smiled.

Quill suppressed a sigh. "Hi." Lexi wriggled excitedly, knocking into Quill as he patted her. He didn't need to ask Frieda how she got here. She either walked or one of his brothers or sisters-in-law drove her. "I was looking forward to downtime . . . without anyone visiting." Quill didn't sugarcoat how he felt. In reality they were distant cousins, but they were as close and as comfortable with each other as brother and sister. Unfortunately for both of them, she often needed companionship when he needed to be alone.

"I know, but I cooked to make up for wanting some time." She shrugged, a small smile lifting her lips. "Dan said you were coming in, and I . . . I just needed to tell you something in person before you headed out again." She stepped back.

He closed the front door. This remodeled rental home was about fifty years old, and once inside he could see the entire two-bedroom home — all nine hundred square feet of it. The fenced backyard for Lexi was twice this size.

Quill moved to the refrigerator and pulled out a can of Sprite. "Can't it wait?"

"I only need fifteen minutes."

Quill popped the tab on his drink and moved to his recliner. Dealing with the emotional upheaval surrounding Lovina, Isaac, and Brandi was draining. Knowing what was ahead for Ariana and Skylar was digging holes inside him. Watching her and Rudy interact as a couple falling in love was no picnic, but at least Rudy seemed to be a great guy. The part that had Quill wiped out was being around Ariana and having to act as if he knew nothing about what was ahead for her, and all the while her trust in him grew.

He pressed a button on the side of the electronic recliner and waited for the footrest and headrest to move into position. "If it's heavy or something you need help with, don't tell me." He didn't want to belabor a point, but he simply couldn't take on anything else right now.

She scratched Lexi's head. "It's neither of those . . . and I made one of your favorite dishes."

The food did smell great. "Sure. Go ahead."

"I should've gone to your Mamm's hospital room that day. You gave up years of your life to help me, and I couldn't even do as you asked and go with you into that hospital to see Berta? What kind of friend is that?"

"You're making progress. A year ago you wouldn't have crossed the state line to reenter Pennsylvania, let alone gone to the hospital." After a year of being in and out of the hospital and more than four years of seeing a psychologist, Frieda seemed to be doing particularly well these days.

"And Eli — what would he think about now?"

Quill's Daed had been complex in his thinking, and yet he lived a simple life. Even his name, Eli, had several meanings: "high," "ascended," and "my God." But Quill had thought of him only as a dad until he saw him stand up for Frieda. That's when Quill saw him as Eli, a man who understood that defending the victim was worth angering

413

every church leader. "My Daed would say you're a survivor and cut yourself some slack."

A timer on the stove went off. "That does sound like what Eli would say. But there's more on my mind. What I just said isn't even the main topic." She held up an index finger. "Let me get the turkey pie out of the oven and turn the pretzels over. I'll be right back."

"Turkey pie and homemade pretzels? Mmm."

While she went to the kitchen, he let his mind rewind back in time.

The Englisch called what Frieda's dad had done to her "medical child abuse." Some called it "Munchausen syndrome by proxy." Her dad had poisoned her, deliberately causing her illness so he could get sympathy and attention.

She was one of seven children, and she lived with her family in Ohio until she was fifteen. That's where the poisoning had taken place. When Eli learned what was happening, he went to Ohio to confront the church leaders face to face. Those men said it was God's will that they keep the matter quiet. Eli called them hypocrites, saying the only thing they wanted to protect was the status of the Amish. He said they weren't willing to face the shame of what Frieda's dad had done, because they didn't want it splattered across the news, nor did they want the Englisch investigating their lives and ways.

While trying to go through the proper Amish channels to get justice for Frieda, Eli brought her to Pennsylvania to live with them. Although the ministers in Pennsylvania tried to get to the truth and do right by Frieda, she lived in fear that they would unite with the leaders in Ohio and would force her to return home to live. Her fears had merit. Her church leaders reached out to the church leaders in Quill's district, beseeching their help in controlling Eli. But Eli continued to stand his ground on Frieda's behalf. Her church leaders had wanted to rehabilitate Frieda's dad and do so in the Amish way — by a time-fixed shunning and by having him go to a rehabilitation house for the Amish and run by the Amish. That wasn't acceptable to Eli. He feared for the other children in Frieda's family, and what Frieda's dad had done was punishable by Englisch law. Eli believed church matters should belong to the church — living by faith, obeying the Ordnung, adultery, drinking, and such. But if the matter fell under the laws of society, he believed the civil authorities should be made aware. When Eli couldn't get satisfaction through the Amish channels, he took the matter to the police. Many Amish considered that an act of betrayal. And Frieda's Daed disappeared.

Frieda was desperate to get away. Too fragile to go alone, she'd needed someone she trusted to take her. Someone who would see to it that she was hidden from the Amish and that she got the needed medical help. Eli had planned to take her away and get really good medical treatment for her, but he died from the stress of the situation.

Lexi tried to push her nose into his hand, and he shook free of his thoughts. Frieda had returned from the kitchen, and she stood near him, wringing her hands.

He lowered his recliner. "What's the subject, Frieda?" He gestured to the chair beside him.

"Ariana." She sat.

"You have my attention."

"Imagine that." She chuckled. "You've been gone a lot lately, and when you didn't say much about why, I pestered Dan about it. He said you're sticking close to Ariana for more reasons than helping her get the café. Is she okay?"

How was he supposed to answer that —

yeah, for now? Instead, he took a sip of his drink.

Frieda glanced at the clock, perhaps timing the pretzels or the fifteen minutes he'd given her. "Whatever is going on, I want to help."

"I appreciate that, but —"

"You're probably asking yourself what I could possibly do, but I've been thinking and praying a lot since I realized something's up with Ariana, and I'm ready to find my backbone and face her, to tell her the whole gut-wrenching, health-stealing, embarrassing mess that caused us to leave so suddenly five years ago." She waited for his response.

This was surprising. She meant her words, and he was pleased to see she was taking another step in the right direction. Whether she could follow through was another matter. Her dad poisoning her while pretending to care about her health mortified Frieda beyond her ability to cope. Quill didn't understand that part, but he didn't have to. It was enough simply to accept her limits in dealing with the aftermath.

"I think it's great you're strong enough to want to share that with her." He interlaced his fingers and leaned forward. "Maybe one day there will be the right time, but some very difficult things are waiting on the horizon for her, and if she knew that anyone Amish or any dad was capable of what your dad did, it might be too much for her."

Lovina kept saying that Ariana's faith would carry her through. But Ariana's worldview came from inside a bubble. And faith wouldn't stop the tsunami of reality that was heading for her.

TWENTY-SEVEN

Abram drove the wagon toward the Yoder house. He was making rounds today, gathering donated items. Susie had called each family earlier in the week, and she gave him the list of places. This stop had him more nervous than all the rest combined.

After spending the last two weeks watching Quill give up comfort and sleep as he patiently helped Ariana reach her dream, Abram was encouraged to be patient concerning Barbie. After all, whatever Barbie had against him couldn't compare to what Ariana had held against Quill. And Quill's actions had made a significant positive difference for Ariana. With Salome staying and Ariana on the verge of getting her café, his twin was happy, confident, and peaceful. Who would've thought that Quill could make that kind of difference in any Amish person's life?

He drove the rig to the hitching post.

While he was looping the reins over the post, Barbie came out of the house, carrying a pot.

She glanced up, and surprise filled her face. "Hi."

"Hello."

She looked back at the house, as if checking to see if anyone else knew he was there. "What are you doing here?"

"I came to pick up goods for tomorrow's benefit."

"Oh, ya, that's right. It slipped my mind."

Irritation worked its way through him, and he wasn't sure what to say. Did that mean no one in her household had prepared anything? Tomorrow was really important for Ariana. For him too, because he'd invested years in helping his sister save money, and if tomorrow went well, all of those years of work would accomplish their goal.

"I'm not sure why I forgot. At our last church meeting, the preachers asked us to donate items and attend the function." Barbie walked past him and toward the overgrown garden patch.

He followed her. "Should I check with anyone inside about donations or just head out?"

"Mamm and Cilla have been sewing for a

420

week. I'm sure some of it is for the cause."
Barbie dumped the scraps of food onto
what looked to be a composting pile. "Just
knock on the door."

Despite being a fairly mellow guy, Abram
was offended by her lack of interest. Was
she rude, or was he too sensitive about his
sister's big day?

"Thanks." Abram left the garden area and
climbed the porch steps. Through the screen
door he saw Barbie's Mamm, Emma, at the
kitchen sink. Cilla's wheelchair sat empty,
and he hoped that meant she was still feeling well. Sometimes she went months
without needing it. He tapped on the door.

Emma shut off the faucet, grabbed a
towel, and turned. "Hi, Abram." She
motioned. "Kumm." She angled her head
toward an open doorway. "Cilla, Abram's
here."

A moment later Cilla walked into the
room, carrying a large box. "Perfect timing."

Abram closed the distance between them
and took the box from her. "Is this for the
benefit?"

"It is."

He set the box on the table. "Can I take a
look?"

"Cilla made everything in that box

herself." Emma grinned at her daughter.

"Even so," Cilla said, "you won't be impressed."

He opened the box. It was filled with various kinds of cloth dolls, each one Amish — boys and girls — in perfect Amish attire. "Authentic clothes handsewn by an authentic Amish girl. These will fetch a great price, Cilla. Denki."

Cilla walked to the corner of the room and picked up a much smaller box. "Are you telling me you like dolls, Abram?"

He laughed. "In this case, ya, I am."

She handed him the smaller box. "Mamm sewed five small quilted wall hangings. I wish we'd had more time to make things."

Emma moved closer to her daughter. "She had a couple of bad days, or you'd have a lot more."

Barbie forgot about Ariana needing donations and didn't seem to care, yet Cilla had clearly sacrificed several days to make items. "Ariana and I really appreciate this."

Cilla beamed. "Oh, and Daed and my brothers made two beautiful birdhouses on stands. That's the really good stuff. They're in the barn, just inside the doorway to your right. Is there anything we can do to help tomorrow?"

"If you're up to it, that would be great.

The café will be in full swing, serving people, and Ariana needs to divide her time between helping at the café and making appearances at the auction block."

That's what Quill said needed to happen. The auctioneers they'd hired verified the plan, saying that people would respond better if they saw Ariana and if she interacted with them, because this wasn't just about them purchasing items. It was a charity of sorts, and people were more apt to buy when they had a face to go with the cause. Abram stacked the two boxes. "I wish I had time to visit, but I need to go. Denki, again. I'll see you tomorrow?"

Cilla looked at her Mamm, and she nodded. Cilla bit her bottom lip, smiling. "We'll be there."

Emma followed Abram onto the front porch. "Barbie, show Abram where the bird —"

As Abram went down the steps, a young man in a courting buggy drove up. A moment later Abram saw it was Saul Kurtz. Girls flocked to him. If Abram had realized Saul was his competition, he never would've asked Barbie out. Then again, she'd said yes, so maybe Saul asked after Abram had.

"Mamm," Barbie whispered, elongating the word, "I can't right now. I told you earlier I needed to stop the chores and freshen up." She glanced at Abram, looking a bit sheepish. "I hope the benefit is a huge success." She went up the stairs and into the house.

Emma sighed. "Kumm. That girl's got other things on her mind." She glanced back at Saul. "Arriving for a courting visit during the middle of a workday. I guess that's how it is for those with money."

Abram slid the boxes into the wagon. Was his family's lack of money the one thing Barbie didn't like about him? He followed Emma into the barn. She pointed out the birdhouses, and he loaded them into the wagon. "Denki for everything, Emma."

"You're very welcome. See you tomorrow."

As Abram pulled out of the driveway, he decided to prove to Barbie that he could make good money too. Once Ariana went to closing, he would be part owner of the café, and he would put every effort into getting promotions at his construction job.

Saul Kurtz wasn't winning Barbie without a fight.

Then another thought came to him. Abram had felt encouraged to be patient about Barbie because of how Quill had been so accommodating of Ariana. But if asked,

Quill could quickly list a hundred reasons why Ariana was worth his effort. Even when Ariana felt the most betrayed by Quill, she continued to look out for his best interest, protecting him by destroying the letter and diligently helping his Mamm.

But Barbie broke off their date, could not care any less about tomorrow's auction, and had plans with Saul, so was a relationship with her even worth fighting for?

Quill meandered on the outer edge of the green space, watching the people, Englisch and Amish, as they bid on items on the auction block. Shafts of sunlight peered through thin, broken clouds. A light breeze stirred the air, carrying the aromas of coffee and fresh baked goods. It was barely past noon, and Summer Grove buzzed with relaxed, happy people shopping on the square and participating in the benefit.

The hired Englisch auctioneer stood on the stage, microphone in hand, auctioning off one of the last pieces. He had been an auctioneer at other Amish events, and he was doing a great job of engaging the audience. Right now he was taking bids on another item Rudy had made. Clearly, Rudy was a skilled craftsman, and his pieces had sold for high prices.

Quill's Mamm was the guardian of the donation jar, which meant all the money went through her — whether people were paying for what they'd bought or were making a true donation. Quill had emptied his accounts and sold everything he could. He'd placed the cash in envelopes for his Mamm to sporadically add to the money till. If collections went as usual and Ariana remained her unsuspecting self, she would never realize how they'd managed to make so much money from the sales through the auction and the café.

Abram stood on the lawn next to Cilla in her wheelchair. She had been here since early morning, and she'd spent most of the time on her feet. Quill could only assume she was now too tired or maybe struggling to breathe. Cystic fibrosis was a difficult disease, but from what he understood of it, Cilla seemed to do well with it. So where was Barbie? Quill hadn't seen her all day. Abram moved beside the wheelchair and crouched, seemingly in a conversation with Cilla.

Ariana was on the platform next to the auctioneer, as she had been off and on throughout the morning. She talked to the crowd at times, making jokes and laughing with people. Quill hadn't realized she could be so comfortable with a microphone in her hand.

Suddenly a surprised look covered her face, and she hurried off the platform. He wondered what she had forgotten. While hurrying down the steps, she tripped, and Rudy, who was rarely far from her side, caught her. He looked serious as he checked to see if she was okay, but she laughed. Quill could only imagine what she was saying as she grinned at him and grasped his arm with one hand and slid the other into his. They strode toward the lively café. She had spent the largest part of her time there, baking and serving. But her sisters took over for her whenever she was needed on the platform.

Whatever would happen with Ariana over the upcoming weeks and months, she was thrilled with the support she was receiving today. When the money was counted, and she realized she could close on the café, she would have that to buoy her, no matter what else happened. But the fruit of today wasn't the only thing she had going for her. Rudy also made her happy. He was good for her, no doubt. He had her on a pedestal as if she were royalty, but they interacted like old, trustworthy friends, and the two had that certain spark couples needed. He'd caught glimpses of their interactions when they didn't realize he was around, and they played as well as they worked together. As crazy as it seemed, on a good day Quill found some comfort in seeing Ariana with what felt like his replacement.

The deacon's wife walked across the lawn, carrying a basket of baked goods. She eyed him, clearly trying to figure out who he was. Hoping to avoid a scene, he lowered his cap and turned. He'd been spotted a few times today, but the others had turned away, avoiding him as much as he avoided them.

She paused. "You're one of the Schlabach boys, right?" Her voice wavered in that elderly woman way.

He turned, offering a smile as he nodded. "Yes. I'm Quill. Beautiful day, isn't it?"

There were more people here than even Ariana had prayed for. Her Daed said it had taken three visits with the church leaders to convince them to let her have this benefit. Isaac had humbly held his ground, and he'd won. Since Isaac had shared that news with Quill, he'd caught himself thanking God throughout the days that followed.

She studied him. "I . . . I pray for you. I don't know much about what went on. It was a secretive scandal, but I believe things that weren't your fault came against you, and I've grieved over the whole distasteful mess."

He tried to thank her, but he couldn't manage to say a word. The deacon's wife hadn't condemned him? The deacon's job was to carry out the letter of the law — the Bible and the Ordnung. If the bishop came for a *correcting* visit, that was bad news. If the deacon came, it was much worse.

If she felt this way, were there others like her?

"Martha?"

She turned to see her husband coming toward them. "I best go."

"Denki for your prayers."

She smiled and started to walk off, but one leg seemed to buckle, and Quill caught her before she fell. Her husband ran toward her. "Martha, bischt du allrecht?"

She shooed him with her hand. "Ya. *Ich bin gut.*"

Within minutes a crowd of Amish had gathered, and she was still clutching Quill's hand.

"I'm fine." She finally released his hand, dusted off her dress, and pulled the basket close again. "I'm just glad Quill Schlabach was here to catch me."

So much for staying incognito.

As if realizing what she had said, she

429

gasped and looked at him apologetically. All eyes moved to him. Some of the faces quickly hardened with disapproval. That didn't surprise him any. But some seemed to indicate interest and hints of forgiveness. Considering the way he and Frieda had departed, he couldn't believe the less-than-hostile reactions.

"Geh." She shooed the people away. "Geh."

The elderly woman knew her power as the deacon's wife, and clearly she didn't mind using it. Slowly the group dispersed, many glancing back at Quill. The deacon stood firm, as did a few others. She squeezed Quill's hand before letting go. *"Nachsicht."*

Forbearance? Why would she whisper that word?

"When I pray for you, that word comes again and again. I looked it up. It means patient self-control, restraint, and tolerance, but I have no idea why it continues to come to mind concerning you."

He didn't either. Wasn't he decent at forbearing? His Daed used to say that forbearance was being patient with those who thought they were right. Maybe others needed forbearance for him, because he definitely thought he was right a lot.

"Kumm." Her husband took the basket

from her and put his hand under her elbow.

Only one person remained — Mark, a former close friend and Ariana's brother.

With steely eyes casting judgment, Mark walked toward him. "Does she know you're here?"

The *she* was Ariana, and Quill nodded.

Concern entered Mark's eyes. "Why are you back?"

The phone in Quill's pocket vibrated, the one that few had the number for, reserved for emergencies . . . and Ariana. He had bought her a cell phone, and she called when she needed something.

How was Quill supposed to answer Mark? Questions like his were part of why he avoided being seen. He glanced at the screen. It wasn't a number he recognized, so it had to be a wrong number, telemarketer, or Brandi. "I . . . need to take this call." Quill gave a brief, friendly wave as he walked away. He slid his finger across the screen. "Hello."

He could hear muffled voices, one of which was a man's. "How is it possible you never told me that my daughter was born in an Amish clinic?"

"Hello?" Quill called out. "Brandi?"

The call ended. Quill debated whether to call back, but it sounded as if he'd been called by accident. When he looked up, he realized Mark had followed him.

"Mark." Quill nodded.

"I asked why you're back."

"Business." Mostly to do with Ariana and the café, but he wasn't going to add that part. Quill's phone rang again. "I need to go, but it was good to see you."

"Ya, maybe. I suppose that depends on all that's going on that you're *not* telling me, doesn't it?" Mark walked off.

That kind of reaction was expected, but it wasn't much fun. Definitely not encouraging. Still, even former best friends had good reasons to perceive him as the enemy.

Quill swiped his finger across the phone again. "Hello."

"Quill?"

"Yes. What can I do for you?"

"It's Brandi. We're . . . we're here."

"Here?"

"On the square in front of Boscos Brewery."

He headed in that direction, walking as fast as he could. "And by *we* you mean who?"

"Skylar's dad and me. We . . . we needed to come, to ride and talk while trying to process the shock . . . you know?"

As Quill went up the sidewalk on one side

of the street, he saw Ariana and Rudy on the other side, leaving the café and heading toward the green space. She spotted Quill and smiled — a grateful, excited grin. At least he'd finally accomplished one truly good thing on her behalf.

He wasn't sure he had managed even a small response to Ariana as he hurried toward the brewery. "You both know that Ariana has not yet been told anything, right?"

"We know," the man responded. It sounded as if Brandi had pressed the button for the speaker. "I . . . need to talk to someone close to the situation."

The man didn't sound pleased, but he did seem in control. Quill continued toward the brewery. He wasn't sure he fit the category of *close,* but he was fairly well informed, and he was willing to run interference so Ariana could finish her day without incident. "I'm the only one available today."

"Then we need to meet," the man said.

When Brandi saw Quill, she got out of the vehicle.

Despite her bloodshot, swollen eyes, Brandi's blank face and softer tone seemed to indicate she was much more in control of herself than when Quill saw her four days ago. She barely nodded. "Hi."

The man got out of the car, hanging back. "You're Amish?"

A few steps ahead of the man, Brandi rolled her eyes and shook her head. "He's confused about the whole situation. But it's my fault. He didn't know I'd had her at an Amish birthing center until I told him after you left my home. I'm sorry that we just showed up like this."

"Nicholas Jenkins." The man held out his hand.

"Quill Schlabach." They shook hands. "I'm former Amish, and I've been helping Ariana's parents navigate this . . . possible incident."

"It's not a possible incident anymore." Nicholas rubbed one eyebrow with the knuckle of his thumb, looking confused and angry.

Quill glanced from Nicholas to Brandi. "You have the DNA results already?"

"Yeah." Brandi released a long stream of air, her eyes filling with tears.

Nicholas pulled a paper from his pocket. "I have friends at the lab, and I asked them to rush it. We got the results in today's mail." He thumped the paper. "I hate what's happening. Saying I'm angry doesn't touch it." He shoved the paper back in his pocket.

Quill shouldn't feel as if this was shocking

434

news, but his head spun and his pulse raced. He'd known what the results were likely to be, but apparently he'd been holding on to far more hope than he'd realized. "And?" Why did he even need to ask?

Brandi broke into fresh tears. "Skylar carries no DNA from either of us."

Quill had to rest against something. He moved to the bumper of their vehicle, propped his feet on the curb, and lowered his head, trying to stop the world from swaying.

He'd had few doubts what the results would show since the day he talked to Skylar at the mall and verified her birth date. Everything after that was a matter of going through the necessary checklist, but he'd known the truth. Nevertheless, the power of the disappointment pressing in on him was as if he had never suspected anything. "Have you told Skylar?"

"No. We talked to her about . . . The tests revealed" — Brandi squeezed her eyes shut, taking deep breaths — "other issues."

Other issues? "Is she sick?" He really didn't have the right to ask that, but that hadn't stopped him.

Brandi's shoulders slumped, and her face showed tremendous stress. "No." She glanced at Nicholas. "And I guess we could be grateful that she's not."

Nicholas drew a deep breath. "Don't play Little Miss Sunshine. There is *nothing* in this mess to be grateful for."

The man's phone rang, and he pulled it from his pocket and turned it off. "I know almost nothing about the Amish, although I spent hours Googling them yesterday. Can you help me understand how our daughter has been raised, tell me about her parents?"

Quill willed himself to stand upright and be a man about this. It seemed wise to be as courteous and friendly as possible. "Sure, I can try."

He could see how this calm, reasonable man with an undercurrent of overwhelming emotion could be Ariana's dad. Quill told him a lot and then answered dozens of questions.

Nicholas had the same long, steady gaze as Ariana, seeming inquisitive, trusting, and skeptical at the same time. "You haven't mentioned this so-called midwife. She clearly knew there was a chance the girls had been switched, and yet she's still practicing?" The anger in his tone was undeniable.

Quill had a feeling this man would be willing to file charges against Rachel. "She does still practice."

"And?"

"I can't tell you more."

"Can't or won't?"

"I probably know less than you do about what happened that night. I haven't spoken to Rachel. My only concern in all this has been Ariana."

"That's not my only concern, but it's half of it. I feel as if I" — he turned to Brandi — "*we* have two daughters to look out for in this situation."

Quill took a cleansing breath. Maybe this situation wouldn't be nearly as bad as he'd braced himself for. "Lovina and Isaac feel the same way. If we work together —"

"Yes, together. As it turns out, I think this situation may benefit both girls."

"Nicholas," Brandi scolded, "not now."

"I think now is the perfect time. Quill is clearly the go-between, a man who understands the Amish as well as people like us. What was the word Skylar used?"

"English," Brandi said.

"Yeah, she said we're called English. Apparently your forte is knowing both Amish and English, so you can tell the Brennemans my intentions. Break it to them gently, and get their feedback. If you'd rather not, I'll send my lawyer to speak with them."

"What is it you want me to tell them?"

"Skylar's drug test came back positive for a cocktail of drugs. Her supplier is her boyfriend, and I threatened to bring charges against him unless he disappears from her life completely and permanently. Let Lovina and Isaac know of the situation, and if they wish to spend time with her immediately, then we'll give Skylar a choice of rehab or time here. Either way, she'll have to do weekly drug testing. But where she lives during the next three to six months will be up to her. As much as I detest religion, I can't stop her from eventually having contact with them. They are her family, and a little Plain life might help her get her head on straight. But if she chooses rehab, Lovina and Isaac will be free to contact her afterward and free to lure her here to get to know them if she will come."

"That seems fair."

"Unfortunately, the next part won't sound fair. Ariana needs to get away from this backwoods way of life. I'm appalled at what I've learned about the Amish over the last couple of days. Religious services that last three hours? Stopping education at the eighth grade? No music? No television or movies? No freedom concerning dress or hair? My God, what do they allow?"

"Ariana loves the Amish way —"

"Of course she does. She has absolutely nothing to compare it with, and from what I read on the Internet, what precious little she has been taught clearly centers on a long list of 'thou shalt nots.' I have only one 'thou shalt not' I live by, and it's 'thou shalt not keep my child from experiencing the real world.' Now, trust me, I know how that sounds since Skylar has had that opportunity and has clearly abused it. That's something we'll spend the needed time and effort to get her past, but at least she's had every opportunity to find her talent, to explore the possibilities of where her dreams can take her."

"Ariana is an adult. In less than a week, she'll own a café that she's named Brennemans' Perks. That's her surname, Brenneman, and it's a name shared by people she adores, people she believes to be her family. She has a boyfriend, siblings, a life." Could they hear Quill's plea?

"I won't take any of that away from her. I'm only asking her to hit the Pause button. Give us and the life she was meant to have an honest chance."

"Then you're saying it's her choice whether to leave her home and people or not, right?"

"Eventually. But she needs to live with us

for a while — at least a year, I think — dividing time between her mom's home and mine."

"And if she doesn't want to go?"

"I'm hoping it doesn't come to that, but I want time with her, and I want her to get a real education and discover her hidden talents and dreams. That's what life is made of."

"For her, life is God and family."

"From what I read yesterday, her dream is probably getting married and having all the children God gives her. I won't try to strip her of that, but I want a year with her with no contact from those who want to keep her tied to her Amish roots. If she chooses to return after that year, I'll bring her here myself."

"And if she says no?"

"Let's keep it positive. If she says yes, I can open the world up to her, and I won't cause trouble for anyone in the Amish community. We keep this whole matter out of the news. My understanding is Lovina spent twenty years knowing she had the wrong blanket, and she did nothing with that information."

"Nicholas, no!" Brandi whispered loudly. "You intend to endear your daughter to us by threatening to humiliate and sue the people she loves as her parents?"

"I'm making sure this young man understands that we are far from powerless in this situation."

"You want power?" Brandi raised her eyebrows, defiance written on her face. "Then go see the midwife and threaten her, but think first, for Pete's sake. Lovina and Isaac not only have your daughter's heart, but they could win Skylar's as well. I don't like your plan of pushing Skylar to come here as punishment for her using —"

"It's not a punishment, Brandi. I've said that two dozen times. It's a way for Skylar to see all of life differently, to connect with people who may be able to turn around her destructive behavior."

"Skylar is not going to see it that way."

Quill remained quiet as the couple argued. He wanted to absorb all he could in order to help the Brennemans, but at the same time he was speechless.

"She needs help." Nicholas stared at Brandi as if dumbfounded by her argument. "And there's no room for doubt that our methods have failed. Either she gets a grip, or she becomes a junkie!"

"I get that, and I've agreed with what you want to help keep the peace for everyone involved. But you said you wouldn't threaten Lovina and Isaac with a lawsuit. I'm telling you for the thousandth time that we need to be on good terms with these people!"

"Okay." Nicholas briefly held up both hands in a gesture of surrender. "I'll save all threats for that midwife. I'll talk to that Rachel woman face to face before the sun sets tomorrow. She had to have reasons to suspect the girls may have been switched, and she chose to keep it to herself." He pointed a finger at Quill. "She needs to know she could do jail time. But I'll drop all mention of that if . . ."

Quill knew the rest. If Ariana left everyone behind and entered Nicholas's Englisch world for a year, then and only then would the man agree never to file charges or take the incident public.

Ariana isolated from her family, community, café, and Rudy for a year?

TWENTY-EIGHT

Ariana pried open her eyes, stretching as joy bounced inside her chest unlike anything she'd experienced before. Daylight had arrived but just barely. Birds sang outside the open window, and the aroma of late September was delicious. Two oak trees with their leaves turning red and gold swayed and danced outside her window.

Had she paid any attention to how beautiful this fall was? Perhaps a more important question — she giggled — what was she doing awake this early? She pulled the blankets over her head, grinning. She knew the answer. Sleep had been nearly impossible the last two nights. After the benefit on Saturday she had stayed up until the wee hours of the morning with her parents, half of her siblings, and Rudy — talking, reminiscing about the day, and playing board games. They had celebrated until exhaustion took over. None of the excitement wore off throughout all of Sunday. She'd slept about four hours last night and now was up again. Who could've possibly known that getting the money to buy the café would be *this* thrilling?

Quill, she imagined. Surprisingly, he seemed to understand her more than she did.

He'd also known how to pull off such an unusual benefit. Somehow, by methods that defied all reason, she had earned enough money to close, purchase two months of supplies for the café, and pay the mortgage for several months. She couldn't figure out how they'd done that well, but did it really matter?

The only disappointment was she hadn't seen Quill to properly thank him. There had been too many people thronging around her on Saturday. When she went by his Mamm's home on Sunday, his car was gone, and he'd left her a one-word note: Congratulations!

As much as she'd wanted to talk to him, she couldn't make herself call him on a Sunday. Unnecessary phone calls on a Sunday were frowned upon, but she would call him this morning. Too antsy to stay in bed, she quietly grabbed a clean dress and apron, careful not to wake Susie or Martha, and tiptoed into the bathroom. After getting a shower, she dressed and returned to her bedroom, peering into various bedrooms as she went. Mark's and Abram's beds were empty, but John was still asleep.

She went to her dresser and pulled out the cell phone Quill had given her. She wouldn't use it in the house. That was frowned on even more than making a call on a Sunday. Besides, it would be disrespectful of the Old Ways, but she could walk outside. He called it a TracFone, an inexpensive pay-as-you-go phone. He said it would serve her purposes, and she wouldn't have a monthly bill. All she needed to do was purchase minutes when it ran out. Having the phone during the last two weeks had been incredibly helpful. It made perfect sense why some men had cell phones for business and then turned them off and put them away before entering their homes.

With the phone in hand, she went downstairs. Where was everyone? The men — her Daed, Mark, Abram, and Emanuel — might have already gone to work, but why was biscuit dough rolled out on the counter and only half of it cut and lying on a baking pan? "Mamm?" She walked into the living room. "Salome?"

A note on yellow paper was on the message board: "Something came up. Be back soon. Please get John ready for school, do the household chores, and finish making breakfast."

She knew the Monday household-chores list quite well, and it would take her at least three very busy hours before she would have the laundry on the line and get a break . . . unless she took a break first. She squeezed the phone and went outside.

It would be best if her youngest siblings didn't wake and see her using a cell phone, so she went to the far side of the barn and turned on the phone. Leaning against the barn wall, she waited for the phone to get a signal.

Her niece squealed, "Kittens!"

"Sh," someone replied.

Ariana smiled and tried to peer through two boards of the barn wall. Esther was on the floor, three kittens in her lap.

"He's a difficult man at best."

Was that Rachel's voice? Maybe the midwife had stopped by to check on Salome. Ariana looked farther into the barn and saw the outline of several women and a pant leg of a man. The group seemed to be in a circle, talking. Her gut clenched, and she wanted to do what she always did, the good girl thing: leave and mind her own business. But she couldn't do that, not where Salome was concerned. She stayed glued in place. Had her sister already changed her mind again about leaving?

"He's demanding she leave the Amish for a year, no calls, no visits, no letters?" Salome sounded desperate. "He can't insist on that, can he?"

"You're right. He can't," Rachel said.

"But he thinks he can. Why?" Daed asked.

"It doesn't matter. I'm not here to ask favors from any of you. I'll pay my own price. I only came to warn you because when he learns that he's not going to get his way, he will go to the police, lawyers, and newspapers. I didn't want you caught off guard."

"What will happen to you?" Mamm asked.

"I went to a neighbor's house after Nicholas left my place yesterday afternoon. She's a lawyer, and . . ." Rachel broke into sobs. "I'm sorry. That's not what I came here about."

"Oh my gosh!" Salome stepped back, shock written all over her face. "The lawyer thinks you'll go to prison!"

"I knew too much and stayed quiet too long. But none of that is the point. We can't ask this of Ariana, and I will not let Nicholas intimidate us with threats."

Ariana was too confused to have even a

clue as to what they were talking about. She went to the barn door, tapped on it, and shoved it open just enough to squeeze inside.

Her parents, Salome, Emanuel, and Rachel froze, staring at her. "I . . . went to the far side of the barn for some privacy." She held up the phone, silently confessing ownership. "And I overheard . . . What *did* I overhear?"

All three women started crying.

Her Daed came to her. "We were going to talk to you this afternoon and tell you everything."

"You're scaring me."

Daed took her by the hand. "Maybe you should sit." He led her to a bale of hay and crouched in front of her. "Ariana, we love you so much. You are our little girl, and you always will be." He held her hand, his face mirroring emotions she didn't recognize. "You remember the stories about the day you were born, right?"

She nodded, still clueless what could possibly have everyone so upset.

"See . . . there was a part of that story that neither your Mamm nor I remembered. We've been going over everything in our mind again and again, but we don't recall that . . . that . . . you and the other girl born that day were put in the same bassinet while we got you to safety."

Had her heart ever beaten this hard or fast? But her mind seemed to be slogging through mud. "What are you saying?"

He stroked her hand, heartache twisting his face, but over the next few minutes he shared about the pink blanket without its embroidery and how someone had spotted the young woman who looks so much like Salome, the one they now knew to be Skylar Nash.

Ariana couldn't believe what she was hearing. There was no way it was true. "What does this man you spoke of want?"

"He's your biological dad, and he wants you to live with him for a year."

A year? She peered around her dad and looked at Rachel. The poor woman had given her life to birthing babies. She had no husband. No children. And a man threatened her with prison if Ariana didn't do as he wanted?

Ariana's body shook from deep within. "What he thinks happened the night I was born, the swapping of babies . . . He has to be mistaken."

"I thought the same thing, Ari." Salome knelt in front of her. "But Quill's investigation was very thorough."

Quill is involved in this?

"What does that mean?"

Salome held her hand. "Not much in my book. You're still our Ariana. You always will be. But you're not a biological child of Mamm and Daed."

Dozens of thoughts collided in her mind while her emotions raged like the fire through the birthing center. Her parents were trembling, and tears fell from even her Daed's eyes.

She choked back her desperate need to cry and rose to her feet. "It's okay. I'm okay." Tears welled and her voice was hoarse and wobbly. She hugged her mom, whispering reassurance that everything was going to be fine. She did the same with her Daed and Salome. "It's going to be fine. I promise." She could hardly see for the tears swimming in her eyes. "Do the others know?"

Mamm shook her head. "Nee. None of your siblings know yet, except Salome, of course."

"Okay." Ariana wiped her apron across her eyes, doing all she could to remain calm and encouraging. "I . . . I can't be here when you tell . . . them."

Her Mamm didn't even brush the flow of water from her cheek. "I understand."

Ariana needed to scream and cry and think, and she needed to do so alone. Completely alone. "I'm going for a really long walk. Okay?"

Her Daed hugged her. "You sure?"

She nodded. "Abram doesn't need me to be here when he finds out. He'll take it the hardest." She turned to Salome. "You make sure Mark is here before you tell Abram. Promise?"

"I promise."

"Gut. I'll be home before dark." The barn seemed to shift off its foundation, and when she walked outside, the sky spun while the ground rolled like waves beneath her feet. Her legs wobbled, and she did her best to hurry out of sight as quickly as possible. When she was sure no one could see her, she took off running — to where, she didn't know. But there had to be a place where she could escape this awful truth.

Because if such a place did not exist, neither would she.

TWENTY-NINE

Skylar stared into the barista's eyes, her hands shaking. The food court at the mall buzzed with activity. A tall, thin woman stood twenty feet away, watching Skylar's every move. Despite the woman's slender build, she carried herself like an intimidating tyrant. Her dad had hired her, saying she was a bodyguard of sorts.

Yeah, one to protect Skylar from herself. She didn't need a bodyguard. She needed drugs.

"What kind of coffee?" The kid drummed his fingers against the side of the cash register and glanced at the line behind her, impatient with Skylar's lack of response.

If her mind would clear for even a second, she would give him an answer. It'd been three days since her last dose of Ritalin, and her body knew it, had known it within eight hours of popping the last dose.

"How about regular coffee, a large?" He

raised his eyebrows, looking hopeful.

She nodded at his suggestion, and he flew into action. He seemed able to move at warp speed, while her whole world dragged along in slow motion. Was the sick feeling in the pit of her stomach from the news? It had hit so fast — like the flu — fine one hour, down for the count the next. Her whole life had changed in the few seconds it took her mom to stammer and cry her way through saying, "Honey, you're not our biological daughter."

Part of her wished they hadn't told her. It would be easier just to keep coping with the hand she'd been dealt — the only daughter of a dysfunctional couple. That had to be better than being the child of religious extremists. What could they offer her — repression and oppression? No thanks. She'd rather stick to becoming the best performer possible. Lots of performers used. It wasn't a big deal!

The young guy behind the counter slid the coffee to her, and she passed him a five-dollar bill before walking off.

"Wait. Your change?" He pressed the buttons on the cash register.

Ignoring him, she continued toward a table near the entrance. The woman who watched her every move stepped up and took the change. She was part of the ultimatums her dad had laid down.

Hypocrite. Nicholas Jenkins had spent years doing whatever he wanted, including seducing a teenage girl when he was thirty-five! And he dared to judge her?

She pulled out her phone. Why wasn't he here yet? They'd said five thirty, and it was five thirty-five.

All of time moved slower without her drugs. Minutes felt like hours, or they felt as if they didn't exist at all. Maybe the drugs had played a trick on her and she'd imagined her mom saying that awful thing to her.

She scooted a chair away from a small, round table and sat, watching for Quill. When her mom had told her the news, Skylar had screamed words of disbelief. Then her mom had dropped Quill's name. Skylar had halted all other rivers of conversation and focused on that one tributary. Her mom said she could call him if that would help her to believe or come to grips with her new reality.

New reality. "Great, as if my old reality wasn't insufferable enough," she mumbled.

The thin, tough-looking woman narrowed her eyes and took a few steps toward her. Skylar held up her hand and shook her head. She wasn't losing it. Not yet at least. She was just talking to herself, which clearly was cause for concern when sitting by oneself at a table in public.

Her mom said Quill knew the Amish family really well, and then she gave Skylar his phone number. So where was he?

Her feet and legs jiggled and bounced without her consent.

Dad had run Cody off, and she hadn't heard a peep from him. Her dad then ransacked her bedroom and her car, confiscating every stash she had — maybe. She might have some hidden in the outlet behind the head of her bed. But how could she find out since he had someone watching her every second of the day? She couldn't search for any hidden drugs. Not now, anyway. Did she really want them? To ravage her mind until she was unsure what was real and what wasn't?

Probably . . . if given the chance.

She gulped down the coffee, hoping it would ease the effects of not having Ritalin. The clock on her phone said it was five forty-eight.

A man wearing a ball cap hurried toward the mall entry she and Quill had used nearly three weeks ago. She couldn't see his face under the bill. Once inside, he paused, searching the food court. Quill. He didn't have that easy-going expression he'd had the day they met, but he didn't appear unpleasant either, just uncomfortable. He spotted her, walked to her table, and sat down, a weak, comforting smile on his face. She could tell it was forced.

"Hey, sorry about being a few minutes late." His voice was pleasant, as if it hadn't been inconvenient to drive from a job site to meet her here.

Skylar couldn't manage to form any words. How could so many things be going through her mind and yet she couldn't express any of them? The questions were jumbled, like a twenty-car pileup on the highway — mangled metal and lost lives.

Quill shifted in his chair. "How are you?"

His question carried weight. He actually cared. Why?

She shrugged, in no mood to answer any more questions. Her dad had asked a gazillion too many. "What happens now?"

Quill drew a deep breath. "Since you're not a minor, some of that is up to you."

Skylar rolled her eyes. She couldn't even go pee by herself since her dad had read the lab results on Saturday morning. Miss Tall-and-Thin was proof of that. A hired gun without the actual gun. Skylar didn't know what she'd expected to happen after having the drug test. She'd hoped to get to the mailbox before her mom and discard the lab results. If that didn't happen, she'd hoped the envelope would get tossed in the mail basket at home and be forgotten. Maybe her drama teacher was right. Maybe she based her life on the delusion of dreaming.

"I doubt I get any say. This new-daughter thing is my dad's excuse to trade up. Maybe even get a daughter he likes. He hates religion, but he's willing to send me to live Amish?" She scoffed. "That doesn't even make sense . . . except it's his chance to dump me. How very convenient for him."

"He thinks about things a bit oddly. I won't argue with that."

"You've met him?"

"Saturday afternoon."

"I need to pull up my grade in psychology, not quit school!"

Quill leaned forward, more engaged than ever before. "Would you be allowed to go to school if you enter rehab?"

"You know about that too?"

He leaned back, nodding. "Maybe you should consider your options and try to think in terms of what's best for you over the long haul — rehab or getting to know a family you didn't realize existed until yesterday." His voice remained calm, but his eyes showed unease.

She couldn't keep the life she had now. Both choices — entering rehab or living with an Amish family — would see to that. At least rehab had modern conveniences — electricity, some television privileges, occasional use of a landline phone, and other people her age who could identify with drug use. But she hated the idea. Becoming involved with a different family, especially an Amish one, didn't sound appealing either.

"You know," — Quill picked up her coffee and took a sip — "you aren't losing anything by getting to know the Brennemans."

Somehow his willingness to drink after her, to treat her as if they had a true closeness, did an odd thing inside her, and she craved more. "Is that their" — or should she say *my* — "surname?"

"Yeah. I know it feels awkward and scary, but this news doesn't change who you call mom and dad unless you want it to. And you've gained a wonderful family, one who would be pleased to meet you."

"They want to or they feel obligated to?"

"Definitely and positively want to. When they learned the swap was a possibility, they contacted me to uncover the truth, and they've been steadfast in their desire to spend time with you."

"Yeah, that's all great and wonderful until they get to know me."

His eyes held a depth of understanding she found eerie. "You're twenty. I doubt even you know the real you yet."

Oh, she knew herself incredibly well. "It all feels like something from a movie."

A faint smile lifted his lips. "Well, if it is, I haven't seen it."

"Yeah, but you haven't seen many movies, right?"

"True. I've been living Englisch five years. That's sixty months, and I've seen about thirty movies. I've given your lifestyle a chance, and I like it . . . most days. Why not give living Amish a chance? How many people can say they were born Amish, raised Englisch, and then, as an adult, lived Amish for a while?"

Skylar sipped her coffee, thinking. Quill had eased her mind a little. "What are they like — my birth parents?"

He looked pleased with her question. "Well, your mom and dad are hardworking, kind people who pull together daily —"

"Wait." Skylar couldn't help but interrupt. "They're still married?"

He seemed confused, and then a hint of sympathy crossed his face. "Yes. Definitely. They like each other to boot, and you have four sisters and five brothers."

"Geez! Who has that many kids?"

He chuckled. "Yeah, it's a lot, but the Amish have big families."

"And you're sure they want to meet me?"

"I promise. I was there when they first saw you . . . at the play."

She couldn't pull her eyes from his face. "Oh." Him buying tickets was a cover. He'd peppered her with questions to learn when she'd been born, and when her answer lined up, he took the Brennemans to see her in the play.

He reached across the table, tapping it gently. "Look . . ."

When he didn't finish his sentence, Skylar decided to prod him. "Well?"

He rubbed his face, looking stressed and thoughtful. "There's one more thing . . ."

"Could you possibly drag it out a little longer?"

"Wow." He paused, staring at her. "Sometimes you sound just like Susie, your eighteen-year-old sister."

She couldn't make herself acknowledge having a sister. In her life she was the one and only child of Brandi Nash and Nicholas Jenkins and the center of the universe for her mom. "That's what you were going to tell me?"

"No. But my news isn't bad, just surprising. One of your siblings is a twin brother."

"You're kidding me."

"I'm not. His name is Abram."

"A twin . . ." How weird was that. "I'm going from no siblings to nine siblings, and one is a twin. I can't wrap my mind around it."

"I'm sure." He tapped his index finger against the tabletop, looking grieved.

It dawned on her that the Brenneman girl who was really a Nash was losing a lot. "What about the other girl?"

"Other girl? You mean Susie?"

"No, the one who was swapped with me. How's she doing?"

Quill stared at the tabletop. "As far as I know, they plan to tell her late this afternoon — once everyone is home from work or school. It'll hit hard. But she'll come around."

"I bet she will hate me."

"Nah. She won't even be angry with you."

"How do you know?"

"Because I know her, and she wouldn't blame you for this mess any more than she would blame herself or Abram. You were all innocent newborns. She has great reasoning skills when it comes to difficult situations."

"You know her well enough to know how she thinks?"

"Yeah, I do."

"Is she the one you were telling me about?"

He nodded. "That's her. But don't tell anyone that, okay?"

"I won't. I swear. What's her name?"

"Ariana."

"If they weren't religious enthusiasts, I might not mind the idea of getting to know them."

"All you have is a clichéd view of who they are."

"What if they don't like me?" As soon as she voiced it, she wished she'd kept that thought in her head. What a silly thing to ask someone.

Quill gave a friendly smile. "You would be surprised how welcoming they are. Liking you won't be a problem. In fact after you meet them, and they're having family gatherings all the time — playing, talking, hugging — you might want them to like you a little less."

Skylar relaxed. Maybe she could use this situation to her advantage. Avoid rehab, stay in an Amish home for a few weeks, and leave. Maybe head for New York. "If they're so great, why'd you leave the Amish?"

"That's complicated, and I'm not free to talk about it, but I didn't want to leave. My dream was to stay and build a life with Ariana . . . when she was old enough."

"My dad is pushing me to commit to stay there for six months to a year."

He shrugged. "I've heard of worse plans — like anything that connects you and Cody."

"My drug habit is *not* his fault. He's kind and gentle and faithful."

"So that makes him a very likable, maybe lovable, enabler. And staying with him or running off with him causes you to empower the enabler."

Whoever Quill was, he was sharper than most.

They sat in silence, letting the conversation sink in. The anxiety and withdrawal symptoms didn't feel as hyperreal now. The news would be shocking for months to come. And stressful. But it didn't feel nearly as bad as it had an hour ago. Quill had a reassuring way about him, a tone that said everything would be okay.

"You know," — Quill looked across the food court — "I remember the first time I came to a mall." He shook his head, smiling. "I mean, lots of Amish kids go to the mall really young, but not me, not even on my *rumschpringe.* I didn't step into one until after I left the Amish. I walked into the food court, and everyone was passing out free samples of food I had never eaten. I gave Chinese food a try, and I nearly threw up right there."

Skylar laughed.

"I had a wild streak when it came to being daring on the farm or at school, but I hadn't really experienced your Englisch lifestyle. Other Amish had, but my Mamm liked tradition. My Daed not so much, but he detested shopping, so we never went to a mall. When I went into the mall stores that first time, I was shocked by the pictures of the almost-naked women in the underwear stores."

Skylar picked up the cup and set it down hard on the table for effect. "You hadn't ever seen a picture of a woman in her underwear?"

Quill laughed hard. "Of course I had. I was Amish, not a saint. And I had four older brothers, and at least one of them hid certain magazines under a loose floorboard in the bathroom linen closet. But for those images to be out for everyone to see was shocking. People with children just walked by it, paying little attention. I wasn't sure I could stand your world."

"Because of a woman in her underwear?"

"No, because I didn't know if I could adjust. I didn't know if these people would accept me. I was uncomfortable, and I didn't like the food, and I missed my family, friends, and the old lifestyle."

She stopped fidgeting. "So what happened?"

"I put on my big-boy pants and adjusted. I learned a lot. I figured out that if you look just at the outside of someone's culture, it seems scary and foreign. It seems less important than your own. But if you can actually experience and accept it, it starts to feel comfortable, and eventually it feels like home. You know what I mean?"

"Yeah, you're saying I have to buy different pants."

They both laughed, and Skylar's fears continued to shrink. "If I go, will I have to dress like them?"

"I doubt they would *make* you abide by their dress code, but modest clothing would be very appreciated. That's all."

She sipped her coffee again. "I've messed up before this, you know. Not gigantic or anything but big enough."

"Yeah, humans do that sometimes."

"I don't know what it is, but pills give me comfort."

Quill didn't flinch at her statement.

Skylar shrugged. "At times I just need something that takes the edge off the pain."

He seemed to understand what she meant. "Your family would like to help you with that. Their way of life is simple, but they live and love in a way that can be very healing. It's at least worth trying."

"Maybe." It would keep her out of rehab, and it would cause her dad to get rid of her bodyguard. Then she could disappear into the night.

Thirty

Around ten thirty in the morning, a driver arrived at Abram's job site, saying everyone in the family was safe but he needed to go home. Apparently the driver had spent most of the morning gathering Brenneman family members. Even though the man had said the whole family was safe, the process of being rounded up and brought home made fear nip at Abram.

This was worse than anything he'd imagined.

Daed sat on the coffee table, explaining the situation. The living room held all of Abram's siblings . . . except Ariana. The grimness on their faces reminded him of a gathering at a wake. His heart was beating as if it were trying to escape his chest, and a cold sweat broke out over his body. Mark was next to him on the couch, quietly helping Abram take in Daed's words, helping him absorb the shock that Ariana wasn't his twin.

Disbelief, tears, anger, and questions spilled out from all of them as they tried to process the news. Now, an hour later, they sat in silence, grieved and not knowing what else to ask . . . or think.

How could she not be his twin? They interacted as two people who had shared the same womb at the same time. What was she going through?

He rose. "Ariana shouldn't be out there on her own while we huddle up as if we're family and she's not."

"She wants to be alone." Mamm held Katie Ann, rocking her. "I think that's the least we can do for her."

Abram grabbed his straw hat. "I'm going to find her."

"Ya." Mark stood. "He's right."

Before Abram was out the door, his four brothers and two brothers-in-law were right behind him. He paused. "Let's spread out. John, you stick with Emanuel. We'll meet back here in three hours." It was the only way they'd know if she'd returned or if one of them had brought her back home.

He went to the barn. After putting a bridle on the horse, he swung onto her back and rode without a saddle. He scoured the area, riding down Ariana's favorite paths. He went by the community phone and dialed the number to her cell. She didn't answer, and she didn't have the mailbox set up. If he couldn't find her, he would return here and try again.

Continuing on and trying to sort through his feelings, he saw the Yoder home, and he realized he'd spent the last couple of hours slowly making his way here. He needed to talk, and since he couldn't do that with Ariana, he needed to spend time with someone who would understand.

He knocked on the door, and Mrs. Yoder answered. "Abram, kumm in." Her brows narrowed as she pointed to a chair. "You should sit. You look as if a breeze could knock you over. Is everything okay?"

Cilla rolled her wheelchair into the room. Her hazel eyes connected with his.

"You're the color of salt." Mrs. Yoder looked him over. "And your hands are trembling."

"I need to talk . . ." What was he doing? From the moment he saw the Yoder home, he realized he needed to talk to Cilla. Barbie didn't understand him, nor did she want to. But when he looked in Cilla's eyes, he saw someone who understood life in ways he could only hope to. Odd as it seemed, he hadn't realized that until now.

"Sure, to one of us? No one's here except me and Cilla."

"I . . . I came here hoping to talk with Cilla . . . if you don't mind."

Cilla rolled herself toward him. "She doesn't mind." She motioned toward the back of the house. "The porch?"

Despite having spent most of his life around Cilla, he'd barely known anything about her until recently. He'd learned a lot since then. She understood pain and disappointment like few others, and she was tender yet strong. He wasn't sure he had ever looked into kinder eyes in his life. He needed that right now.

They went to the back porch, and Cilla pulled her wheelchair near the beat-up wicker chair where he sat. "What's going on?"

He told her everything, knowing she would tell no one, not even Barbie. How did he know that? He wasn't sure, but he did.

She angled her head, looking fully sympathetic. "One of the hardest parts about life is trusting that you have the strength to face reality."

"I'm not that strong, Cilla. I know that sounds . . . awful and wimpy, but it's true. And I'm scared for Ari. Just sick about it."

"I used to think I wasn't strong enough to face my future. It terrified me. But eventually I learned that I only have to face today, and that's where our loving God, faithful family, and good friends come in. Each brings something to the day that strengthens us — just enough, but who needs more than *just enough*?" She put her hand over his. "Look inside you. Do you have enough strength for today?"

He closed his eyes, searching his heart. All he could see was a frightened little boy searching for his twin. Maybe he wasn't a man at all but merely a boy in a man's body.

Cilla squeezed his hand. "What I heard you say is that, in your own way, you know she needs her family around her, and you rallied the men to search. When she is found, you intend to look her in the eyes and tell her that you don't care about the DNA connection, that she's your twin and you are hers."

Cilla's view of him and the situation helped him breathe a bit easier. "Denki." He put his hand over hers. "I needed to hear that."

"Gut." She held his hand. "You can do this, maybe not without pain or leaning on God every minute, but you can do it."

"Ya, I . . . I agree. But I should go."

"Sure. Get. You're welcome anytime, Abram. I mean that."

"I believe you. Bye, Cilla." He went down the porch stairs and got back on his horse. When he reached the community phone, he called Ariana's cell again, but she still didn't answer. As he was leaving the shanty, an idea came to him. Numerous times over the last couple of weeks, he'd seen Quill's number on Ariana's phone, so Abram returned to the phone and called him. Daed had said she had been near the barn trying to call Quill when she had overheard Rachel talking with the family. Maybe she was with Quill, or at the least maybe he'd heard from her.

"Hello?"

"Have you heard from Ariana?"

"No. Why?"

"If you hear from her, ask her to please return home."

"How long has she been gone?"

"Since around seven this morning."

"I thought . . ."

Abram knew what he thought. Quill had been told they wouldn't explain the situation to her until after the whole family shared dinner. "She overheard my parents talking about her with the midwife early this morning. You know Ari. She faced them and asked questions. Once they told her the truth, she went for one of her long walks."

"Ten hours is a heck of a long walk, but I'm sure she's just clearing her head. Does Rudy know?"

"No. Only family for now."

"If you and your brothers are out looking for her, Rudy's going to catch wind of it. Perhaps you should consider getting to him first and telling him what's going on. You may even find that Ariana is with him."

Abram hadn't thought about Rudy. "Ya. I guess you're right."

"I should be there in about twenty minutes."

"After all I learned today, I can't say I'm all that thrilled with you helping to look for her."

"Abram, this isn't my doing."

"True enough. You're just the one who goes out of his way to get her to trust him while you're holding back secrets that will devastate her. Would you want you for a friend?" Abram hung up the phone.

Maybe he was being unfair, or maybe Quill deserved far, far more. All Abram knew was that his sister might have to leave home, and Quill had pumped her full of hope about the café for absolutely no reason.

No matter how backward or shy Abram was, Ariana helped him overcome it or cope with it. As sisters went, she was a really good one. How was he supposed to survive with her gone?

A new thought hit. How had he missed it until now? He had a twin he'd never met. Warring emotions twisted in him. She was innocent in this mess, and yet he resented that she was supposed to move into the house while Ariana was supposed to leave.

Where was God's justice?

THIRTY-ONE

Quill pulled into the Brenneman driveway and parked his car. It was too late to try to hide his involvement in the Brennemans' lives. The whole community would know plenty within a few days. He had met with Lovina and Isaac near the barn last night after everyone else had gone to bed and had filled them in on what he knew.

Lovina came outside, peering through his windows as if hopeful Ariana was with him. He lowered the window. "She hasn't returned yet?"

Lovina shook her head. "It's such a mess. Nicholas went to see the midwife yesterday, and he was breathing threats, spreading fear. Rachel was willing to go to jail rather than ask Ariana to leave, but Ari wouldn't have any part of that. Now I'm really worried. She was so upset. What if she hasn't come back yet because she fell into the creek or stumbled into a ravine or —"

"Nothing like that has happened to her, Lovina."

"She's never been gone this long."

"She's never had to sort through this kind of pain." Quill had an idea that she'd meandered through back trails, going from one favorite spot to another. If she had, that could explain how Abram had missed seeing her.

Lovina searched the horizon. "I couldn't believe how gracious and kind she was. Not one word of accusation against Rachel, her Daed, or me. She hugged us and assured us she was fine, but I've never seen her look like that." Lovina broke into tears.

"She's out gaining perspective and self-control so that when she walks back into the house, she can continue being calm and gracious. I doubt she will return before she's able to do that."

"I . . . I needed to hear that. Denki." Lovina drew a shaky breath. "How's Skylar?"

"I saw her a few hours ago. She's pretty good. Maybe more practiced with upheavals in life. Maybe hiding how she really feels. It's hard to tell. I assured her you were good and welcoming people."

"Why is he pushing Ariana to give him a year with no contact with us?"

"He feels you've had twenty years to indoctrinate her. He wants one uninterrupted year." Quill wouldn't add that Nicholas hoped to open Ariana's mind and heart to a life she would never want to leave. "But he learned the news last week. Given a little time, he may relax his demands. Like I told you when we met last night, he's given Skylar a choice of going to rehab or coming here. When I saw her today, I told her you guys want her to choose you."

"Even though you explained things to us yesterday, I could hardly hear you. I'm a little confused. I thought I understood what rehab was, but then I realized my ideas don't match up with the situation. I thought it was a place injured people go to regain their strength, but that's not right, is it?"

"That's one kind, but the type Nicholas was talking about is one that tries to get someone clean — off drugs and alcohol."

She gasped, eyes wide, seeming unable to breathe. Finally she jerked air into her lungs. "My daughter . . ." Tears rolled down her cheeks again. "I want to help her in any way we can, but we're not equipped to deal with that."

"It won't be easy. But life on this farm with the Brenneman family may be what she needs. You don't have to do this on your own. There are counselors who can help you navigate the issues. It's pretty clear to me that Nicholas would be willing to pay for anything that would help her."

"If he's willing to nudge Skylar toward us, the religious fanatics, he's desperate for answers for her."

"That sums it up pretty well. But if you and Isaac are second-guessing your decision to welcome her, and you think Nicholas needs to make rehab her only choice, we can call him. Maybe she would agree to come after a stint in rehab."

"I won't back out. It would be like saying, 'We only *thought* we wanted you.' " Wiping her cheeks, Lovina stood straight. "You can find Ariana, can't you?"

"I think so."

"Please try."

"Sure." He put the car in Reverse and backed out of the driveway.

He had an idea where she was likely to be, and he drove in that direction. When the road came to an end, he parked his vehicle and got out. As he began to walk, he called her cell phone, hoping to hear it ring. Nothing. He continued on, making his way toward what used to be their flat rock on Summer Creek. He dialed her phone again and heard it buzzing. He grabbed it and put both in his pocket. As he walked the path between the two largest rocks, he whistled, giving her warning before he broke through the opening near the creek.

There she was, sitting on the top part of a boulder. This is where they'd spent so much time talking after his Daed died. Apparently the murmur of the creek had kept her from hearing him or her phone. He whistled again, and she turned.

Her eyes were dull and her expression blank, surely from an exhausting day of trauma and tears. Without a word she turned back to face the creek.

He moved to a smaller boulder a couple of feet from her and rested against it. He waited, hoping she would find the words to talk to him . . . or yell. She needed to spill hurt on someone, rid herself of some of its poison.

When she remained silent for more than twenty minutes, he had to say something. "Your family is worried about you."

Still nothing. Finally she spoke. "Is . . . is this mess what I saw in your eyes at the café — the reluctance to my excitement?"

"Yeah."

She pulled her knees to her chin and wrapped her arms around her legs. "What are the chances that I am a Brenneman?"

He stood straight and faced her. "I'm sorry, Ari." He swallowed hard. "Skylar's already had a DNA test, and her makeup doesn't match either of her parents."

Her eyes filled with tears while staying focused on the creek, and her breathing was short and choppy. The water that had been in front of her when she'd asked her question was probably two miles downstream before she spoke again. "The test could be wrong, couldn't it?"

He heard desperation. She needed her Amish lineage to be true, and her pain cut him so deeply his chest physically hurt from the heartache. "That's not likely, and there are other factors that confirm who you are, including that you favor Brandi . . . your mom. When she saw a picture of you, she was surprised by how much you look like her mom, your grandmother."

Ariana closed her eyes, unfathomable pain etched on her face. A few minutes later she took a deep breath. "So now what?"

"I'm not sure. The goal will be to buy you time to adjust to the news without provoking Nicholas to file a lawsuit."

"I heard his name earlier today, but who is he?"

What had her parents told her? "Your . . . dad."

The water ambled by as the inescapable truth began to take shape. She finally took a breath and focused on him. "What kind of man threatens to sue someone like Rachel?"

"An upset one. For what it's worth, I think he's trying to handle this right, but he's not particularly religious, so he doesn't view suing people as wrong. To him Rachel was negligent."

She angled her head, narrowing her eyes at him. "And?"

Was she reading his body language, his tone? He took a deep breath, willing himself to tell her the truth. "He wants you away from the Amish. In his opinion they are too rigid and religious, and he's antsy to get you out as quickly as possible."

She propped her hands behind her, staring at the creek. "There's a word for how twisted this situation is, isn't there?"

"I'm not following."

"Me being forced to leave the Amish. You in the thick of it. Isn't there a word for that?"

"Many of them. Ranging from *ridiculous* to *outrageous,* but the one you're looking for is probably *ironic.*"

"That's it. Ironic." Her eyes moved heavenward, and she was quiet again for several minutes. "He's hoping that I'll change, that I'll renounce my faith and live

Englisch?"

"I think it's safe to assume that, yeah."

"You're the one always in other people's skin, knowing things about them they barely know. What do you think I'll do?"

He wanted to pump her full of encouragement, say what she needed to hear, but she could read him now, and he had no choice but to be painfully honest. "Struggle to cope for a while. Endure months of heartache and confusion. Find people you can help, like you do here. Adjust. Make a difference while biding your time to return to Summer Grove. Then you'll live out your days as a faithful Amish woman."

"Rudy wants me to marry him. He started talking about it a couple of weeks ago."

"I'm guessing you're in favor of it."

'Her serene smile said it all. "Definitely." Her brows pinched. "How am I going to tell him that my family heritage isn't what he thinks and, worse, that I have to go away and live a lifestyle neither of us agrees with?"

"Rudy has you. Biological parents aren't all that important."

"No? They must be fairly significant. Everyone in existence has a set of biological parents, and something as tiny as a drop of blood carries proof of the match."

"The proof of who you are is in the decisions you make."

"I hope you're right."

"Since you plan to marry Rudy, maybe if you two married now, Nicholas would have no reason to try to undo your Amishness. Being Amish would then be set in stone to him. The preachers would be agreeable to help you and Rudy do that. When they learn what's happening, they will do anything within reason to keep you from having to leave. You could be the first Amish person I know of to be allowed to join the faith and marry before taking instruction classes."

"No. I won't marry under duress. It would feel as if I cornered him into it, rushed to wed as if I were pregnant. There's discontent in couples who feel they had no choice but to rush into marriage. We marry on our timetable, on God's timetable, not Nicholas . . . What's his last name?"

"Jenkins." Should he tell her that Brandi didn't share that same surname?

"Does that mean my last name is now Jenkins?"

"I don't know the legalities. But for now you and Skylar keep your names."

"What am I going to do about the café?" She rubbed the center of her forehead. "Why help me get the money for it when you knew I might not be here to run it?"

"You need that café. If you don't go to closing this Thursday, someone else will buy it. Let the café be your rock during the adjustment of the news, and it'll wait for you."

"Seriously? You think I should go to closing and take on a mortgage when I won't be here to run it?"

He liked that there was some energy returning to her voice. "Susie's learned a lot the last few weeks. Martha's a little young to be a lot of help, but a motivated fifteen-year-old girl can learn quickly and be excited to be a part. Maybe Salome and your Mamm could take turns helping some too. The café won't run nearly as smoothly or successfully without you, but with the money from the benefit and them turning a decent profit, it'll remain afloat until you get back."

"They don't know enough to do the cooking and managing, not yet."

"Then you teach them between now and when you leave."

"You said something about buying time. How?"

"Insist on having a DNA test run and do so through the Amish clinic. I think you can at least get three weeks before he'll lose his patience and start proceedings against Rachel."

"Three weeks before I leave is nothing and staying away for a year feels like a lifetime."

"I know, but you can do this, Ari. You'll grow and learn from the Englisch world, maybe take some culinary classes, and then return home with a deeper understanding of what it means to be human on this spinning ball."

Anger flashed through her eyes, and she sat up. "Is that what you think?" She scooted down the rock until her feet were on the ground. "That I need to learn to get off my high horse? That I need to be broken, and then maybe I'll get why you lure Amish away from the Old Ways?"

"Okay, anger is good. Necessary, I think." He didn't like anyone responding like a sedated, confused lamb. "But that's not at all what I meant. I was just —"

"Wait." She held up her hand, her eyes narrowing. "How did Brandi see a picture of me? Even I don't own one, nor anyone in my family."

His pulse quickened. What had he done? "I snapped it with my phone."

She closed her eyes. "I'm so gullible, and you take advantage of it."

"The picture was wrong, a bad idea I

shouldn't have acted on. It was a careless, thoughtless move on my part."

"A move?" she scoffed. "A deliberate action to accomplish your goal, and once again it just went right over my head. Do you realize that you pulled me into trusting you again?"

"I've been a messenger. That's all. I didn't want this news about the night you were born to be true any more than you or your family."

"I'll keep my word about you and your brothers being able to give gifts to your Mamm and let people assume I'm buying them. You have until I leave to follow through and again after I return, but other than that —"

"Ariana, don't do this."

She was going to shut him out. Should he tell her that no one on this planet meant more to him than she did? No. For a thousand reasons he shouldn't. She wouldn't believe him, and the only thing worse than her misdirected, well-controlled wrath would be her avoidance of him because of her loyalty to Rudy.

"I appreciate all your help with the café. I really do. I couldn't have done it without you. I'll go to closing this Thursday because of you. But when you're in my life, I end up trusting you, and you end up being at the center of the worst pain imaginable."

"I get how you feel." He searched for the right words, hoping to come up with something that would change her mind. "I crossed some lines, and you have a right to be angry about the picture, but I didn't have a choice in how this played out."

"I believe you." She shrugged. "I even believe that you hate the roles you play. But you reel me in, knowing me fully, while you keep your secrets that you know will kill me. Have you been spending time with the other girl? Were you talking with her, making friends with her while helping me with the café?"

The damage was done. Her mind was made up. She wouldn't call him an enemy or traitor, but he wasn't considered a friend. "Skylar feels as lost and angry as you do. She's a music and drama student in college, and she knows even less about the Amish world than you do the Englisch one."

"Could you do me a favor? Just stay out of my life from here on. Please?"

"Ari, I can be there for you as you adjust to Englisch life. I've been there — separated from all that's familiar." If she closed him out, she would enter the Englisch world without contact from anyone familiar to her.

It would help her to have someone who knew her and understood her while she was in the Englisch world. Since he wasn't Amish, Nicholas wouldn't balk at Quill having contact, at least via the phone.

"Your motives toward me are good. I know that, and I appreciate it. But the reality of what happens between us doesn't match your goals."

His whole body ached from the sting of her words. Was this pain similar to how she felt when he blindsided her with his secrets?

"Okay. But there's a movie that will help you a lot if you'll watch it. It's called *The Village.* Some discount it, thinking it's a horror film, but it's not. It has some scenes that will make you jump, but the story is about people who've built a safe haven, living the way our forefathers did, the way the Amish do. In many ways it's a good metaphor that will help you get some perspective and adjust to your new world. The leaders of the village purposefully teach the younger generation to fear what's outside their borders. In the end love wins . . . but so do the founders of the village. Watching it will help you get a grip on understanding what's happening inside you."

"I can't imagine gaining strength through

488

a movie, but I'll think about watching it." She folded her arms, holding on tight as if she were cold. "I can't keep doing this, Quill — never knowing what secrets you're keeping or the damage they'll do. You believe in fighting for people's right to choose the life they want, and I choose for you to stay out of my life, okay?"

If he remained patient, would she change her mind? Should he even want her to? "Yeah, if that's what you want. But if you change your mind, call me." He pulled her phone out of his pocket. "You dropped it on the path not too far from here."

She took it, inspecting it while turning it over several times. "Keep it." She passed it back. "Or give it to someone else. I only needed it to reach you, and I don't need it for that anymore."

He'd known when Lovina and Isaac asked for his help that Ariana and he could end this way. Even so, words failed to describe how much this hurt. He slid the phone into his pocket. "Your family is worried. At least let me give you a lift home."

"I told them I would be home by dark, and I will."

"Apparently they don't recall you said that."

"And apparently you are on great terms

with Salome, Emanuel, and my parents, so if you wish to relieve them of any concern, find a way to get a message to them."

"Okay, I deserve that." He stifled a sigh. "If you change your mind, tonight or six months from now, I'm available anytime, day or night."

"Denki. But I won't."

"Ariana!" Rudy's voice echoed.

She glanced at Quill, giving a sad smile that said she appreciated him but was equally wary of him. "Bye."

"Bye, Ari."

She hurried down the path. "Here, Rudy. I'm here." The two rushed into each other's arms.

Quill had once again destroyed her trust. There was a biblical truth he'd witnessed many times in his life: people reaped what they'd sowed.

He was a keeper of painful secrets sowed in the dark, and he reaped darkness.

THIRTY-TWO

Skylar sat on the curb, waiting for Quill to arrive. Miss Tall-and-Thin hired gun was inside the house, having been instructed to leave her alone unless Cody showed up. Skylar and her parents had talked earlier, saying what needed to be said, but nothing made this easier.

Two huge, overstuffed suitcases were beside her. She would be a nervous wreck about now, except she'd sneaked out last night and met Cody. He'd given her a concoction of pills in a Ziploc sandwich bag. Two high-potency Xanax pills had taken the edge off. She looked in her purse, checking for the umpteenth time that the baggie was still there.

A lot had changed in the three weeks since she'd met Quill in the food court and was reeling from the news that she wasn't her parents' biological child. She'd overheard whispering and had begun to piece together why her dad was so passionate about dumping her somewhere and bringing Ariana into his life. He hadn't said it directly, but Skylar knew he hoped Ariana would be the daughter he'd never had. She probably would be, and Skylar wasn't going to remain in the state to find out.

Without any doubt her dad also hoped Ariana had the musical gifts that he and his mother had. Skylar was good, but her dad wanted great — like his side of the family. She was seething now, plotting how she would ditch the Brennemans, people who were nothing to her, and head to New York with Cody. That's where an aspiring actress ought to be — there or L.A.

She would've run off with Cody last night, but he said it wasn't a good time for him to leave town. He had business to attend to.

Whatever.

She patted the pocket of her jeans, making sure she had her phone too. Last night Cody had given her cash and a burner phone. If her parents — either set, her mom and dad or the Brennemans — thought she was trading in one kind of mandatory rehab for another, they were wrong.

Oh, and the *modest* clothes Quill suggested? That wasn't happening either.

Quill pulled into the driveway and got out. "Hi."

"Hey." She stood.

His brows knit, and he angled his head, staring at her eyes. "Your pupils are dilated. You clean?"

"I needed something to get through today, okay? It's a prescription." Not her prescription but somebody's.

He didn't look convinced, but he nodded. "Okay."

"You have no idea how hard this is! This is a dream come true for my parents, a new and better daughter. And now I'm supposed to slip a hundred years back in time and fit in. Why? So my Amish family can compare me to Ariana and decide I don't add up for them either?"

Quill picked up her bags and put them in the trunk of his car. "You have a lot of fears tormenting you, and rightfully so, but your view of the situation is lopsided. Ariana is unbending about the Old Ways, and how thrilled do you think your parents will be when she hides the controls to the television and refuses to go to the movies?" He smiled. "She's human, just like you, with strengths and weaknesses, but one man's strength is another man's annoyance."

Her anger didn't let up even a little.

"When I think of her, I see her like Kate Middleton, Duchess of Cambridge, easily able to work the crowds."

"Yeah, me too." He chuckled and opened the door for her. "But in the privacy of your mom's or dad's home, she won't be addressing any crowds. She'll have strong opinions. Your dad is pretty set in what he wants, and I think he's met his match. He just doesn't know it yet."

She climbed in. "Think she'll give him a hard time?"

"Yeah, I do. That and a lot of other things scare me for Ariana." He closed the door and went to the other side.

While Quill went around the car, Skylar opened her purse and quickly tugged on the baggie of pills, lifting it just enough to reassure herself she had plenty until Cody could get her more.

Quill opened the car door. She dropped the bag and shut her purse before he got behind the wheel of the car, but he eyed her purse.

She fastened her seat belt. "Can she sing?"

He put the key in the ignition and turned it. "Amish only sing as a group, no solos, and they do so during church service, weddings, or at what's called a singing, where singles meet, so it's not as if she's ever picked up a mic."

Tucking her purse between her legs and the seat, she could feel the lump of meds. That alone reassured her that she could cope with the next few days. "I'm still waiting for an answer."

He lifted his fingers from the steering wheel as part of an odd shrug. Clearly he didn't wish to respond. "She sang while helping out at my Mamm's and when she thought no one could hear her. You know, while tending the garden or hanging laundry on the line, and yeah, she can sing. But it holds no interest for her. Talent-wise, baking and running her café are the only things that matter."

"I guess I can be thankful for that."

Quill stopped at a red light. "You're focusing on the wrong things. Rather than pondering Ariana's future, ask yourself about your future. This is a chance at a new beginning for you, an opportunity to discover the real you without using. The Brennemans are good folk, so" — he held out his hand — "all of it. Now."

"I have no idea what you're talking about."

"May I have your purse?"

"What? No. That's an invasion of privacy."

"Choose, Skylar. Give me the pills or your purse."

"I liked you a lot better when we met at the mall that first time."

"Yeah, I liked me better then too." He bounced his hand, palm up, in front of her face. "But drugs and wallowing in self-pity help no one."

She pulled the baggie from her purse. "Who made you the police?"

"You did. Just now." He held it up, looking at the contents. "Is this all you have?"

"Yeah."

"Do you know how much trouble we could get in if the police stopped us and we had these?" He shoved the stash between the cushions of the seat. "I'll dispose of them when we stop at a gas station." He held the lower part of the steering wheel by his thumbs. "Is this your plan — to bring trouble into the Amish community and prove to them and yourself that you don't fit there?"

"I don't, so why not prove it?"

"Because you should give them a chance to like the real you — not the drug-using, rebellious girl. Is it possible you want to make them hate you? Is that easier than trying to bond? Maybe you're sure that will fail?" He waved his hand. "I'm not looking for a real answer, just sharing some thoughts. And while I'm at it, a year with your Amish family could help you become a better actress."

"Because I'll have to act as if I'm a good girl?"

"No. Because it's life experience, and I read that good actors and actresses draw from different real-life experiences. Plus the Amish are stoic, often skilled in not saying what they actually feel. So if you're smart, you'll learn to read the nuances on their faces, and then you'll learn to mimic those."

"Sometimes you remind me of a sales-man, a good one. So why'd you leave?"

He studied her before an entirely-too-good-looking smile formed on his lips. "Very few know the full reason. I can't tell all of it, but what I can say should be of interest. If I agree to tell you what I can, will you promise to call me when you're scared and *not* use drugs?"

"Extracting a promise from a user is like asking Mother Nature not to change the weather."

"But when it comes to yourself, you're just as powerful as Mother Nature."

Did he honestly believe that? "The story?"

"Complete confidentiality is required on your part."

"I can't figure it out. Are we friends?"

"We're not enemies . . . unless you bring

trouble and heartache to Summer Grove. People I care about live there, including my Mamm."

"Well, what do you know? We have something in common. My Mamm lives there too." She rolled her eyes. Maybe she shouldn't *try* to do any damage. Maybe she should be nice for a few days and then call Cody to pick her up when no one is looking.

Behind locked doors the café buzzed with the voices of Lovina and Isaac's children, the spouses of the married ones, and their grandchildren. It had been three weeks since Ariana had overheard them talking in the barn. Ariana's DNA test was conclusive. She was Brandi's daughter.

Ariana laughed, and Lovina peered into the kitchen. Ari was at the stove, standing beside Abram as she tried to teach him how to make her famous oatmeal. She'd been upbeat and kind during the day, quick to laugh and assure all of them she was fine, but Lovina had heard her sobbing into her pillow in the wee hours of the morning.

What had Lovina done? Ariana would leave soon because of a question Lovina wasn't sure she should have pursued. One thing was certain. Lovina's heart couldn't take much more. Yesterday the community had gathered, lavishing Ariana with love, speaking encouraging words, assuring her they would pray for her as they awaited her return.

This morning when Lovina had eased open the door to Ariana's bedroom, she found all her children there. Most were spread out on the floor. Some of Ariana's sisters were on the bed with her. Abram had been on a pallet beside the bed, and Ariana's hand was dangling over the side of the bed, holding his as they slept. They'd spent the first several years of life sleeping hand in hand.

Ariana set a fresh cup of coffee in front of her before wrapping her arms around Lovina and kissing her forehead. "It's going to be fine, Mamm. It'll be an adventure I'll tell my children and grandchildren, my very Amish offspring, ya?"

Lovina nodded, choking back tears.

Isaac peered out the door of the café. "Nicholas and Brandi just pulled up."

Despite the strength Ariana had shown, she'd asked that Nicholas and Brandi not be allowed to come to her home to remove her. So they'd agreed to meet here, and she would step onto the sidewalk and get into their car.

"Okay." Ariana nodded, offering a weak

smile. "Tell them I'll be out shortly."

Isaac grabbed her bags and went outside. Ariana hugged every sibling, saying something to each one. It had been her wish that they stay inside until she was in the car. It scared Lovina that Ariana had started micromanaging life in order to cope.

Rudy hung back, waiting. He would return to Indiana for the year. His Daed needed his help, and since, as part of Nicholas's agreement not to sue Rachel, he'd put restrictions on all relationships between Ariana and anyone Amish, it made sense for Rudy to go home. Maybe Nicholas would relent in a few weeks or months and at least allow letters.

What restrictions would they need to put on Skylar in order to keep the Englisch world out of their home? Would this time prove beneficial to Skylar, or had Lovina begun something that would only do harm to all involved?

Ariana moved to Lovina. "You show Skylar what it means to love the way the Brennemans do."

Quill would bring Skylar to the house in a couple of hours and drop her off. It was Skylar's request that Quill drive her.

Lovina held on to her daughter, wishing she didn't have to release her in order to have time with Skylar. "Lieb du."

"Ya, I love you too. Forever and always." Ariana motioned for Salome, and Salome put her arm around Lovina as Ariana took Rudy by the hand.

Once at the door of the café, Ariana turned. She looked different. Her hair and clothes were the same, but something was different. Lovina couldn't imagine what it was. Had becoming the owner of the café made her more confident? Maybe Lovina was seeing her as an adult leaving home. She'd never had a daughter leave home unless she was getting married.

Who would Ariana be when she returned in a year?

A horrible thought hit Lovina so hard her legs buckled. Isaac put his arms around her, steadying her.

When the year was up, what if Ariana no longer wanted to be Amish?

THIRTY-THREE

Ariana stepped out of the café, holding tightly to Rudy's hand. How could this be happening? She was an adult with a boyfriend she intended to marry and a new business — and she'd been reduced to feeling like a lost child.

The seconds ticked by in slow motion, feeling surreal. Whose life was this?

Her Daed put her bags in the trunk of the car. He closed it and stood there, watching her as if afraid to do or say the wrong thing.

Things like losing one's entire family were for people who chose to spit in the face of all that God had given them and walk away. During a rare treacherous event, some lost their family through an accident. More rare, some lost them through violence.

She fit inside none of the scenarios that made sense, and after spending a lifetime of feeling blessed by God, she felt cursed. She had thought she understood God on the topic of family. The peace of understanding His will had lived inside her for as far back as she could remember. His joy had carried her forward since she was little. Her days had a beautiful, buoyant value to them no matter how difficult the times, whether fighting lack or accepting exhaustion from hard work. But now . . . He'd revealed the truth. Her days weren't hers at all. Her joy could be stolen for all time. Confusion and grief had overtaken all her familiar emotions, all the ones that made her feel like herself and understand what she needed to do.

Her Daed grimaced, but it was the best he could do for a smile. She released Rudy's hand, and Daed engulfed her in a hug. He held her tight, trembling, but he said nothing. She longed for magic words that would comfort him, but she had none, not today.

A door on each side of the car opened, and her Daed stepped back and returned to the doorway of the café.

Ariana had put off the inevitable for as long as she could — meeting Nicholas Jenkins and Brandi Nash. They didn't feel like parents. They felt like thieves.

The man walked toward the back of the car. He stared at her. Was he swimming in that same pool of disbelief and dislike as she and her family were? He was about her Daed's age, inches shorter and not nearly as robust. Unlike her Daed's thin, silky blond hair, his hair was dark and thick and edged with silver. He lifted his hand halfway to her, as if to offer it for her to shake, but he lowered it and gave a nod. "Hi."

Ariana pursed her lips, hoping the tears stayed at bay. She nodded but not a single syllable would leave her mouth.

A woman came around the other side of the vehicle. She didn't look much older than Ariana's eldest sister. She had white-blond hair like Ariana, and she was thin. Her white pants followed the shape of her body, but they stopped just below the knee, and she had on sparkly pink sandals that matched her lacy, beaded shirt and the nail polish on her toes and fingers. She gave Ariana the once-over, her eyes moving up and down her. Clearly she didn't want this *new truth* to be real any more than Ariana did.

She gestured to the man. "This is Nicholas, your dad, and I'm Brandi, your . . . well, you know." Brandi held out her hand, and the gold charms on her wrist jingled.

Ariana tried to respond, but her hands dangled at her side, unwilling to move. Brandi reached out and lifted Ariana's hand and held it, looking at it with an obscure expression. She turned her hand palm up. "You're used to hard work."

What made Brandi say that? But Ariana nodded. Brandi smiled, and Ariana realized how very weary she was of seeing forced smiles. And of giving them.

Brandi squeezed her hand before releasing it. "You ready?"

No. Never. Not if she had a lifetime to prepare. But Ariana held her tongue and nodded. She turned to Rudy. This was it. He would go home to Indiana to work for his Daed. He would live with his family and save every penny. It was his way of coping — to halfway convince himself that his girl was no farther away than the Brenneman home while he was busy working twelve-hour days to earn money for their future.

She cupped his face. "I'm yours, Rudy, for now and forever."

He leaned in until her lips were on his. He kissed her as if he never wanted to let go of her. She would remember the warmth of his kiss, the gentle strength of his arms around her. Every sense of propriety she'd been taught about public displays of affection seemed to fade into nothingness. What did *that* matter? They were going to be separated for a year. He released his embrace and took her by the hand again.

He gestured at the sidewalk and the café, his eyes boring into hers. "I'll be right here . . . when you return." But before he finished the sentence, he lowered his eyes, and her heart skipped and ached in protest. Was he unsure of being here for her?

Maybe he feared that the café would be lost, fold up in failure, between now and then. But their time was up. She had to go, and all conversations would have to wait . . . a year.

Brandi held open the front passenger's door. "Would you like to ride up front?"

Ariana shook her head. "Nee, denki." Embarrassment burned through her. She hadn't meant to use her first language, but she let it rest and climbed into the car. Her family stood at the storefront windows of the café, watching and staying inside as she'd asked. She waved, forcing another detestable smile. Her eyes brimmed with tears.

Nicholas started the car, and shrill beeps assaulted her nerves. The beeps ended, and music, with unfamiliar sounds and pulses, sprang up from nowhere.

Abram came out of the café, and the others followed. He waved, holding one thumb up, assuring her she could do this. Her family stood on the sidewalk, waving, looking as lost and confused as she felt. She waved until their sweet faces disappeared.

Willing the tears to stop, she wiped her face. A teardrop crystal prism hung from the rearview mirror as did peacock feathers on a circular thing with threads woven inside it. Cigarettes were on the dashboard. The lyrics coming through the radio spoke of guys drinking at bars and going home with a pretty girl. It only added to her nausea.

Nicholas looked at her in his rearview mirror. He turned off the radio. "I know this is hard, although I can't really imagine what it must feel like."

She drew a deep breath. "I'm fine. Denki . . . thank you."

"You speak a different language than Englisch? I may have read about that, but it didn't click."

Didn't click? What did that mean?

She fought to find her voice. "Ya, two actually — Pennsylvania Dutch and High German."

"Can you read and write in them?"

Was this what life would be now — useless, empty conversations with people she didn't know? "Some." She was used to talks with people she'd known her whole life, people related to people who'd known her relatives for hundreds of years . . . except that wasn't true, was it? None of the people for generations back knew her family as she'd thought.

God, help. I feel as if this heartache should kill me, but I'm still here. What should I do?

Brandi turned to face her. "Maybe you could teach me . . . us some of your language."

Teach them, Ari.

The quiet voice inside her was undeniable. But what did she know? They were the overeducated ones. She knew of farms, baking, and babies. Then as if God was illuminating her mind for a moment, she knew she had a new mission. Quill told her she would find someone to help.

This situation was more important than a lone Amish girl having her life interrupted. It was eternal.

She knew God. His peace and joy. His ways, which were on the narrow path not the wide one. Nicholas and Brandi might not want her any more than she wanted them, but maybe they needed her. Ariana knew High German because it was spoken at every church meeting, and it was the language of the Bible tucked away in her suitcase. Brandi wanted to learn some of the language. The ache inside Ariana eased a bit, and she smiled to herself — a real smile, finally a real smile.

This inside-out life had a purpose. Nicholas wanted it to be about scrubbing the Amish off Ariana. Maybe Brandi hoped for that too.

But God had different plans. That's all she knew right now, all she needed to know.

Ariana relaxed against the car seat. She was safe, and she was with family.

What God needed of her next would unfold, and she would be ready.

GLOSSARY

ach — oh

Aenti — aunt

Bischt du allrecht? — Are you all right?

Daed — father or dad

denki — thank you

Englisch — non-Plain person, a term used by the Amish and Plain Mennonites

Es iss allrecht. — It is all right.

Frau — wife

Friede dezwische du Zwee. — Peace between you two.

geh — go

Gern gschehne. — You're welcome.

Grossmammi — grandmother

Guder Marye. — Good morning.

gut — good

hallo — hello

Ich bin gut. — I am good.

Ich kannscht. Bobbeli iss glei do. — I can't. The baby is almost here.

Iss mei Bobbeli allrecht? — Is my baby all right?

Kann Ich helfe? — Can I help?

Kapp — prayer cap or covering

Kumm! Mach's schnell! — Come! Make it quick!

Lieb du. — Love you.

Mamm — mom or mother

Nachsicht — forbearance

nee — no

Ordnung — order, set of rules

rumschpringe — running around

schtarkeppich — stubborn

So denk ich aa. — I think so too.

ya — yes

Ya. Ich lieb sell. —Yes. I would love that.

ABOUT THE AUTHOR

Cindy Woodsmall is a *New York Times* and CBA best-selling author of numerous works of fiction and one work of nonfiction whose connection with the Amish community has been featured widely in national media and throughout Christian news outlets. She lives outside Atlanta with her family.

If you'd like to learn more about the Amish, snag some delicious Amish recipes, or participate in giveaways, be sure to visit Cindy's website: www.cindywoodsmall.com.